SOLSTIC

MW00329612

A computer-app designer. An encrypted relic. Can she decipher the dangerous code before extremists trigger a high-tech apocalypse?

Software expert Maddy Marshall isn't sure she's ready for a hazardous role in black ops. But when an armed Russian thief makes off with a rare ancient star chart, the aikido black belt has no choice but to join her VanOps boyfriend and twin brother in the pursuit. If her royal Spanish family legends are true, the chart leads to a superconductive treasure trove capable of powering a quantum computer used as the ultimate instrument of global destruction.

Setting off on a mad dash to uncover the secrets of a Mexican archeoastronomy site, she and the VanOps team unearth a clue dating back to biblical times. But as they race across the globe to the Sahara, Turkey, and Egypt, they find themselves only a half-step ahead of sinister assassins.

Before millions die at the hands of an anti-American Russian government, can Maddy crack the secret code?

SOLSTICE SHADOWS is the second book in the fast-paced, multi-award-winning VanOps thriller series. If you like international suspense by James Rollins, Dan Brown, Steve Berry, or Clive Cussler, you'll stay up late turning the pages of Avanti Centrae's high-stakes novel.

Critical Praise for *Solstice Shadows*

Global Thriller Genre Grand-Prize Winner — 2019 Chanticleer International Book Awards

Adventure Bronze Medal Winner — 2020 Readers' Favorite Awards

"A tantalizing new series." —James Rollins, the #1 *New York Times* bestselling author of *The Last Odyssey*

"Unputdownable. Avanti Centrae packs a thriller parachute with endless suspense and a rip-cord ending. *Solstice Shadows* is meticulously researched, the history, science, and locales offering a rare 'you-are-there' authenticity. Brew a large pot of java, as you will read through the night. Brilliant." —K.J. Howe, international bestselling author of *Skyjack*

"Has that unputdownable X factor!" —Ernest Dempsey, the *USA Today* bestselling author of the Sean Wyatt adventure series

"Fast-paced action adventure with an ancient mystery at its heart — fans of Dan Brown and Steve Berry will love the VanOps thrillers." —J.F. Penn, *USA Today* bestselling author of the ARKANE thrillers

"Fans of complex and highly detailed espionage and action thrillers are certain to dive right into this mixture between Indiana Jones and Dan Brown." —Reader's Favorite, Five Stars

"Fascinating research, non-stop action, exotic settings, and a sixth sense for human nature in the battle between good and evil. It's a must-read!" —Saralyn Richard, award-winning author of *Murder in the One Percent* and *A Palette for Love and Murder*

"With non-stop action and exciting global adventure to exotic cities, I couldn't put this modern-day *Raiders of The Lost Ark* down." —Tracey Phillips, author of *Best Kept Secrets*

"Strong, skillful female warriors headline this rousing sequel." —*Kirkus Reviews*

SOLSTICE SHADOWS

A ∇ANΩPS THRILLER

AVANTI CENTRAE

THUNDER
CREEK
PRESS

GENRE: THRILLER/SUSPENSE

This is a work of fiction. Names, places, characters and incidents are either the product of the author's imagination or are used fictitiously, and any resemblance to any actual persons, living or dead, businesses, organizations, events or locales is entirely coincidental. All trademarks, service marks, registered trademarks, and registered service marks are the property of their respective owners and are used herein for identification purposes only. The publisher does not have any control over or assume any responsibility for author or third-party websites or their contents.

For Michelle

"... the Lord descended on it in fire."
—Exodus 19:18

"... a brilliant disk much larger than the full moon, a marvel never before known since the foundation of this land [Egypt]."
—Tulli Papyrus (Vatican Library)

"As above, so below, as within, so without, as the universe, so the soul . . ."
—Hermes Trismegistus

PROLOGUE

The golden forks of lightning that raged over the bruised sea reminded Ravi of a thunder-imbued romp with his Russian mistress on her four-poster bed. After their lovemaking, they'd thrown wide the bedroom's snowy-white French doors and watched the electric skies as they cooled off.

Lost in the recollection, the hard kick to his thigh came as a shock. He toppled sideways onto the cold sand, the memory forgotten.

"Ambassador Singh. Sit up and put your hands behind your back."

Guttural and accented, it was the voice of a stranger. Ravi had thought he was alone in the aquamarine cove, guarded by his expensive travel guide and the towering walls of seaweed-encrusted rock.

He pushed himself to a sitting position on his beach towel and crossed his legs, suddenly feeling cold in his swimsuit. He glanced around. Dark thunderclouds obscured the sun, violent wind whipped his short black hair, and the surf angrily pounded the beach. The guide who brought him to this remote island was lying facedown, fifty meters away, unmoving. Ravi bit his lower lip.

A man wearing a black executioner's hood moved from behind Ravi and stood between him and the tortured sea, hands on hips.

1

Rough, white rope was coiled in the man's left hand, and a length of flexible wire was attached to two wooden handles in the man's right. Ravi recognized the wire device as a garrote, traditionally used for assassinations. Ravi's stomach clenched—hard. Bile rose in his throat.

Ravi swallowed the bitter acid. "What do you want?"

The man whipped the wire of the garrote around the back of Ravi's shoulders. It stung like the bites of a million fire ants. Ravi screamed.

"Shut up. We're alone here. Put your hands behind your back. Do it now."

If he complied, Ravi knew he was doomed. He tried to get upright and lunge at the man, but his beach towel and the soft, wet sand pulled at his legs, telegraphing his intention. The man laughed and kicked Ravi in the side of his chest. Something snapped—a rib?—and he landed on his back. For a moment, his world was a starred kaleidoscope of suffering.

"This can be quick, or extremely slow and painful. Your choice. My recommendation is to roll over and put your hands behind your back."

Defeated, Ravi complied, earning him another searing jolt from his rib. A distant part of him wondered where the man was from. Not India, not with that accent.

A cold, light rain began to fall.

The man kneeled on Ravi's back and wrapped the rope tight around his wrists, binding them together like one of the creatures he'd come here to aid. A few years ago, he'd spent time with a local conservation organization helping endangered turtles recover from getting entangled in ghost fishing gear, and had so enjoyed the trip that he'd planned another while he was here in the Maldives on business anyway. It wasn't working out as imagined.

"Bend your knees."

Ravi did as he was told and the attacker jerked him upright, forcing Ravi's buttocks onto his heels. The man walked around

2

Ravi and stood in front of him again, legs wide. Ravi studied the man's hood to take his mind off the pain. There were only endless black holes at the eyes, and no mouth cutout.

Unfortunately, the distraction didn't work to reduce the agony parading across his rib and shoulders. Tears fell down Ravi's cheeks, obscured by the rain.

"Good. Now we talk. I know you're having an affair with the Russian ambassador, Zola Argones. Tell me what she has told you about Maddy Marshall and the star chart."

That's what the man wanted to know? He and Zola had mostly talked about their common goal of a lightning-fast quantum computer, with only a tangential mention of the star chart. Apparently, though, the information was deadly.

"I know little, the information is useless," Ravi rasped.

"I'll be the judge of that. Tell me now!"

Another golden bolt of lightning sizzled across the eggplant-colored sky, and a gull shrieked a plaintive cry. Suspecting he was about to die, Ravi visualized the kind eyes of his now-gray-haired wife, the broad smiles of his three children, his two beautiful and accomplished nieces, and regretted the infidelity with the Russian. When the thunder boomed again, his heart fractured into a thousand shards of remorse.

In futility, Ravi screamed a second time, and the tattooed man struck anew with the metal whip.

The man growled, "Talk to me. What did she tell you?"

But before he told the man everything, Ravi sent up a mental prayer flag to Shiva. He asked for either a miracle of deliverance, or a quick and merciful death.

CHAPTER 1

Maddy cracked her loft's front door, peered through it, and felt the hair on the back of her neck stand at attention like rows of tiny soldiers about to do battle.

There's someone in there. She pulled the entry door almost closed and put a finger to her lips to silence AJ and Vincent, who lingered behind her in the complex's dim, soundless hallway. AJ's ten-year-old eyes grew wide and her ex raised a brown eyebrow, but they both went still. Heart pounding strong and steady, every sense alert, she willed her breath to deepen so she would be ready for whatever came next.

She inched the door back open. Caution had become her friend in the last year and a half. The pencil-thin beam of light she'd seen two heartbeats ago flickered off in her bedroom and pitch-black darkness descended. Although she had closed the living room patio door when she'd left to teach at the aikido dojo, it was ajar, and damp air filled the loft. The city's skyline glittered through the windows, showing off the San Francisco Giants' baseball stadium, lit like a gargantuan ornament in festive reds and greens. The air smelled of the frigid rain that drowned the night. Her roommate had texted an hour ago that he was working late, so who was in there?

4

What did they want?

There. What was that sound?

Something like the scrape of a boot on her hardwood floor.

She listened and squinted into the gloom.

For the briefest moment, crimson light from the stadium's Christmas decorations glinted off a metal object in the bedroom doorway. A gun.

That was all the warning she needed. Maddy yanked the door shut just as the bullet splintered the jamb where her knee had been.

"Run!"

With both arms, she pushed AJ and Vincent away from the exploding shrapnel, sending all three of them sprinting down the shadowed hallway, and careening around the corner. Vincent threw his umbrella behind them and it clattered on the tile. Ten feet ahead, the red EXIT sign heralded the stairwell. A shot hit the wall just behind Maddy, knocking a chunk off a glossy Golden Gate wall mural. She cringed. She liked that mural.

Vincent pulled up short and she nearly ran into his tall frame. He strained to pull a gun from his left armpit holster, turned back, and shot once around the corner.

Frowning, Maddy put her hand on the top of gun. "Put that away," she whispered. "It'll make things worse."

Vincent answered in the cultured voice she used to find sexy. "Head downstairs."

The index finger of her left hand twitched, and she balled both hands into fists. "No, I'll wait inside the stairwell to disarm him."

"No. Go. I'll join you in a minute."

Angry at him for not trusting her aikido skills and escalating the situation, Maddy pressed AJ toward the stairwell, all the while thinking that more assailants could arrive from downstairs. She bent over and whispered, "Run upstairs to the roof and hide."

His freckled face, framed by big jug ears and perpetually messy red hair, looked up at her. He used to be a foster child from the dojo, but she thought of him as hers now, and wanted the adoption paperwork to be official—yesterday. What if she died today? Love for him poured through her heart as he nodded, fear and determination in his eyes.

As the sound of Vincent's next shot echoed down the hallway, she reached around AJ, opened the metal stairwell door and ushered him toward the wet and muddy linoleum landing. His small feet made no sound as he padded up the stairs.

Guessing that what she'd hidden in her loft had placed him in danger, her heart overflowed with guilt. But who knew it was there? She reached for her phone and dialed the police.

CHAPTER 2

3:54 P.M.

Rounding the corner of the stairwell, AJ paused to look back. Through a rectangular glass pane in the door, Maddy looked at him with wide, green eyes full of love. In the black jacket, cabbie hat, and blue jeans she typically wore after changing out of her gi, she looked fierce, as though she'd personally block anyone from hurting him. With a phone to her ear, she pointed up the stairs and mouthed "Go!"

Another gunshot boomed through the hall and AJ used it like a sprinter's starting gun, panting as he raced up the four flights of stairs to the rooftop patio. *Hide.* But where? Two metal patio tables with four chairs stood to his right, wet from the falling rain. In front of him was the city's bright skyscape. To his left, the top landing of the wrought-iron fire escape looked like prison bars.

Shivering from the cold, he moved around the back of the tall structure that enclosed the door. The area was dark and scary, but it might be a spot to hide if he could overcome his fear of the dark and make himself explore it. He hated the dark. But as his eyes adjusted and the shaking subsided, he realized there was no good hiding place back there, only large metal boxes that he guessed housed some sort of heating equipment. Afraid to make a sound, he tiptoed around the entire rooftop, avoiding shiny black puddles as best he could.

A loud sound blasted through the chill night air. Another gunshot? What if Maddy was shot? She was always kind to him, ever since he started taking classes at her dojo. His foster parents were nice, but they had five other kids at the house. He didn't get a lot of their attention. But Maddy had wanted to take him to ride roller coasters on his birthday and was trying to adopt him. She was as good a teacher as the *sensei* who owned the dojo and she often came to his rescue during his nightmares.

He walked back to the fire escape and looked down. A couple of flights below, there was a two-person patio table perched on the landing. It blocked the exit down, but at the moment he didn't care. The table was draped with a waterproof tablecloth, which meant it'd provide better cover than the larger ones up here.

The fire-escape gate creaked as he opened it and scurried down the stairs. Reaching the table, he ducked beneath it. At least it wasn't dark.

With his back to the railing, he pulled his soggy knees to his chest and tried to quiet his breathing. He quivered with fear for Maddy. For himself. Could he do anything to help her? What would he do if Maddy were killed? He lived for the dojo and nights like tonight, when they were supposed to eat popcorn and watch a movie while cuddled up on the couch in her loft. Yes, that was a better thought. Popcorn, with his big dog, Damien, curled up at their feet, chewing on a bone while they laughed at the TV. Maddy's broad-shouldered boyfriend, Bear, would be there, too, one strong hand on Maddy's arm, protecting them both.

Eyes closed, fantasy playing through his mind, he could almost shut out the sound of gunfire and distant sirens.

He'd be safe here from eyes above, but as his fingers caressed the grate beneath him, he realized he was still vulnerable from below.

CHAPTER 3

3:56 P.M.

Back to crouching behind Vincent in the dark hallway, Maddy hoped AJ had found a good place to hide, out of the rain. How long would it take the police to arrive?

What did the intruder want? The apartment held two priceless items, hidden in separate places.

Vincent held a black semi-automatic in both hands and looked around the corner, ready to shoot. She'd long ago figured out the weapon was purchased to impress her, and despite her objections, had even gone to the warehouse range with him twice for target practice. After getting over the gun's rough kickback, she'd become a decent shot, but he didn't understand that her life was about nonviolence. Guilty nightmares about the men she'd killed sixteen months ago still plagued her. Perhaps she and Vincent were no longer together because he just didn't get her.

As he took another shot at the attacker, Maddy tensed in frustration. If the invader would just get close enough, she'd disarm him with aikido. Or should they run for it? No, that could mean disaster.

She tugged Vincent's arm. "Come back to the stairs."

He glanced at her, his light brown eyes hard to read. "Okay, we only have three rounds left. Go. Be ready for me."

Gunshots ricocheted down the hallway as she ran back to the stairwell, making her ears ring and taking out a wall sconce. The area, already dim in the winter evening light, darkened to a tomb-like gloom.

"Now!" Vincent yelled, and then tore down the hall, rushing with remarkable speed through the door she was holding open. But when his front foot hit the wet landing, he slipped, fell hard on his ankle and, like a log in rapids, rolled down the stairs to the next landing, where his head hit the wall with a loud *thwack* and his eyes closed. The pistol dropped from his hand. A break in his lower leg was obvious through the blue jeans. Maddy winced in commiseration at his pain.

With Vincent now vulnerable, Maddy's plan to lure the attacker into the stairwell was no longer a good option. Time for a new approach. But only two bullets left.

In one leap, Maddy jumped down all six stairs. She grabbed the pistol and took the stairs back up, three at a time. She didn't dare look back at Vincent, but sent a hurried wish that he was alive.

Motionless, she crouched next to the metal stairwell door. She listened. After thirty seconds of no sound, she opened it just enough to peek into the hallway with one eye. *Empty. He must have stopped at the corner.* The mild tremor that had developed of late in her left index finger distracted her with its rhythmic movement. To stop it, she modified her grip on the gun to a two-hand hold and shouldered the door open wide enough to get the barrel through the gap.

The wall mural held no moving shadows. She waited. All her training was about redirecting an opponent's energy to neutralize an attack without harming anyone. It was difficult when the assailant carried a firearm, but not impossible if you could entice the attacker to close range. The modern weapon made her feel uncomfortable. But since Vincent had prevented a close-range scuffle, she was going to have to use the dreaded thing in her hands.

Sirens sounded in the distance. *Not close enough yet.*

If she had to fight, there was another weapon she'd rather have that didn't rely on bullets. Sixteen months ago, she'd found two ancient, seven-inch obelisks that she learned to use in self-defense. Only a three-inch sliver remained, hidden inside a running shoe in her closet. Untested and tiny as that ruby-colored shard was, she wanted it, and squeezed the pistol in frustration.

She thought back to her training with the Order of the Invisible Flame, and the technique she'd learned to put her in a state of enhanced awareness. Edith, one of the Guardians, had told her the skill was taught to United States military combatants, and later she'd discovered it was a specific brain wave pattern that was also used by high-performing individuals like athletes and CEOs. It gave her an advantage in a fight.

It was generally called meditation, only she did it with her eyes open. If she really concentrated on the sounds around her, everything slowed down. That's why she referred to it as *listening*. She silenced her mental chatter to mirror that brain pattern. Her senses heightened. Time seemed to stretch. She was aware of her breath, sirens. Lights grew brighter, and she felt full of life.

A moment later, shadows danced low on the shiny Golden Gate mural, revealing the shape of her attacker's weapon. A shot exploded down the hallway and grazed her hairline. Gritting her teeth against the sudden flare of pain, she fired at the corner, toward the gun, to scare him off. Over the ringing in her ears, she heard an exclamation, and a semi-automatic pistol skated across the tile. She imagined she'd hit his hand.

Footsteps echoed away from her. She hesitated for an instant, and then ran after the assailant, kicking his gun back toward the stairwell. Although that cost her only a second, by the time she reached her loft, he'd escaped via the patio. A blast of icy air hit her in the face. With unusual clarity, she could see individual drops of sleet pelting the braided rug in front of the patio door. Boots clanged on the iron fire escape.

Maddy sprang to the balcony and leaned over the edge, gun first, but the frozen rain became heavy snowflakes, obscuring her vision. Two stories down, she caught a glimpse of a man wearing an army-green balaclava slipping over the railing with something in his blood-ied hand. She swore. It was the yellow folder that contained her star chart. Had he found the shard, too?

The assailant glanced up, but not at her. The man had one eye dark as sin. The other with an iris white as the falling snow.

Maddy followed his gaze.

AJ was just two flights up, cowering under a metal patio table. The gunman reached toward his jacket and pulled out a snub-nosed pistol. Maddy fired. The thief ducked, and her shot pinged off the metal railing.

The man with the mysterious eyes dropped to the street, and disappeared around a corner.

Maddy dropped the gun and flew up the fire escape toward AJ, who trembled underneath the table. As she stepped onto the land-ing, he slid out from under the cloth and jumped into her arms. She held him like that, in the falling snow, for a long time while he sobbed.

Eventually, he pulled away and wiped his eyes. "That man . . ." His voice broke and he sucked in a breath. "He was one of my kidnappers."

CHAPTER 4

Bear's feet hit the ground with a reassuring thud and he ran three quick steps, noticing with pleasure that he was hardly limping at all from his old Afghanistan-acquired leg wound. He'd just started to collapse the small parachute when his encrypted work phone rang.

He swore. It was either Maddy or Director Bowman calling, and though he was happy to talk with either, now was a bad time. Still, it must be important because they both knew he was in training tonight. While he cut himself free of his parachute, took off his helmet, and fished around in his pocket for the phone, he counted rings. He had six until voicemail. On five he answered around the gum in his mouth, a little out of breath.

"Bear here."

"Hey."

The sound of Maddy's distinctive feminine voice sent a warm tingle up his spine. Almost a year and a half into their relationship and the effect she had on him was stronger than ever. He was still amazed she was finally dating him. All through high school, while he wanted her from afar, she'd only dated tall guys. On one of the rare occasions when she was single, he'd seen her after a football

13

game at the west shore pizza joint and couldn't find the balls to ask her out.

They'd finally gotten together sixteen months ago, and he'd been thankful every day since. With her parents dead, she spent holidays with him and his family at Lake Tahoe and they'd enjoyed some long, passionate weekends together, but sometimes he worried she'd fall for somebody else. Somebody tall. For some reason his winning ticket to the love lottery felt tenuous, like it was a coded message that would self-destruct in a blaze of smoke.

Bear struggled to control his breathing. "How's it goin', baby?"

"Not so great. The star chart was stolen tonight."

That was Maddy, always getting right to the point.

"What? Stolen?"

"Yeah, somebody broke into my loft, trashed it, and got away with the star chart."

Frowning, Bear took off his night-vision goggles. "Are you okay?"

"Yes, I'm fine." She hesitated. "Mostly. A bullet grazed my forehead."

Bear's throat constricted. "Oh my god!"

"Well, could've been worse. Funny how two inches can make a world of difference when it comes to bullets."

He took a deep breath. "True. Sounds like you got lucky."

"I did. Anyway, the cops are there now checking things out. AJ is all right, he's in the corner reading Harry Potter. My roommate wasn't home, the cat is her usual ornery self, but Vincent has a concussion and compound leg fracture and is in the hospital. I'm calling you from there."

Vincent. Her ex-fiancé. Bear's heart constricted. *Why had they been together?* He tried hard to sound neutral by playing up his southern drawl. "Wow. Sounds nasty. Will he be all right?"

"They don't know yet."

A pause. He'd heard bits and pieces about their long engagement and brutal breakup, enough to know that Maddy still hadn't

14

completely healed from the relationship. As he knew from when Amy betrayed him years ago, those things took time. Vincent, that tall bastard, was probably trying to win her back.

Bear decided the safest approach was to get more information. "Why don't you tell me what happened from the get-go?"

Maddy sighed. "You remember that tonight was the night AJ was coming over for a movie and popcorn, right?"

"Sure." He didn't, but it wasn't the time to disagree.

"I decided to let my aikido class out a little early because of the rain. The city is getting hammered—we even got snow for about an hour, which never happens. Anyway, a lot of parents were at the dojo already, so I let everyone go home."

Now that the adrenaline from the jump was wearing off, the night's bitter cold began to seep into Bear's bones like an incoming Atlantic tide. "Good idea." He paced, a quiet distance from the training tent.

"When AJ and I walked outside, Vincent was there with an umbrella and offered to walk us home. I didn't want to make a scene in front of AJ, so we all headed to my loft."

Bear released a breath he hadn't realized he was holding. She hadn't been cheating on him. "Then what happened?"

"We arrived upstairs at the loft, but when I opened the door, I saw a flicker of light inside. I was trying to see what was going on when a bullet came flying toward the door. I slammed the door just in time. We ran down the hallway and Vincent started shooting back."

Bear's jaw tightened. Wasn't the guy a stockbroker or something? "Vincent has a gun?" he asked.

Maddy hesitated. "He bought one a few weeks ago."

Bear tried to joke, but it ended up sounding like a growl. "Tryin' to protect you?"

"Who knows? But speaking of other people, why were you panting when you answered the phone?"

"We're doing a training exercise. Remember?"

"Sorry. Can you remind me?"

He wished he could tell her all about the paramilitary training. It had been months of weapons training, learning to resist interrogation, and practicing with the latest technology, like latex masks and body armor. Tonight was the last night, and it had been intense. "It's designed to be after dark. I got to wear night-vision goggles. Fun, but bone-chillin' cold out here. I can't tell you much more than that."

"Sounds dangerous, Mr. Thorenson. You be careful."

A gust of wind blew, and the scent of dead leaves filled his nose. "I will. Then how did Vincent get injured?"

"I sent AJ to hide on the roof and wanted to lure the attacker into the stairwell so I could disarm him. Vincent followed me at a run, slipped, and fell down a flight of stairs."

Bear's hand twitched as he resisted the urge to pump his fist. "I see. Then what?"

"I grabbed his gun, against all my better aikido judgment."

"I'm glad you did. And you shot the thief?"

"Did. Must have hit the guy's hand or wrist because he dropped his weapon."

"That's great! I didn't know you even knew how to fire a pistol." Even so, he could imagine her tall, lithe form peering around the corner of her loft's hallway, her sexy green eyes appraising the situation. Her arms would have been outstretched in a two-handed Weaver stance, black cabbie cap on her head. He loved how strong and powerful she was. It made him feel more a man to be with a woman like her.

But then again . . . when had she learned to shoot? Had Vincent taught her to use the gun, too? Bear didn't like the sound of that at all. And she'd been in danger.

Jaw clenched, Bear glanced up to see Jags, his trainer, formerly of the NSA, fly down the small highland, her special dark BASE-jumping parachute blocking the stars above her. She looked like a flying squirrel.

"When did the attacker hit you?" he asked tightly.

"He got me while we were exchanging shots in the hallway. I chased him but he bolted over the fire escape with the star chart."

"That could be bad. You're sure he got it?"

"Yeah. He had the folder in his hand. And as soon as he was gone, I checked the filing cabinet and it was missing."

"What about that sliver of lorandite?" Bear wished there was more of the powerful material, but what was once a set of seven-inch ruby obelisks had been reduced to a tiny, worthless shard. He had also wanted Maddy to let the US government test it instead of sending it to her friend Elena, who had connections in Germany.

"He didn't get the sliver," Maddy replied, and then she paused. "Bear, the man had one dark eye and one white one. Eerie. AJ saw him, too."

"The eyes sound strange, and let's come back to it and the AJ bit—"

Maddy interrupted. "No, wait. He recognized the thief from when he was kidnapped. Said he's a dark-haired man named Pyotr who speaks Russian."

Bear raised his eyebrows. "Oh. I remember AJ telling us about the two men who kidnapped him. We never saw Pyotr, and I don't think he's surfaced since."

"Do you think the Russians could know about the star chart somehow? They were involved before."

Bear stopped pacing, lost in thought. He stood still for a moment and blew a small bubble with his gum. "It's certainly possible."

"Yeah, it's a good working hypothesis." She paused. "Unless . . . Pyotr could be a Spaniard who speaks Russian. The only other person who even knows the star chart exists is Prince Carlos in Spain. Correction—King Carlos."

"That's right. The wise old monarch passed away two weeks ago."

"I'm sure his daughter didn't tell him anything, given she stole the chart and gave it to me in the first place. But the king would have filled creepy Carlos in on the missing chart before his death. Duty and all."

"That means the power behind our thief is either the new Spanish king or the Russians." Bear began to pace again. "I'm not sure which is worse."

Her voice rose a notch. "I know, they're both evil."

"Let's go back to the chart. Your family thought it would lead to a source of superconductive material, right?"

"Right. Like some sort of weird sky map."

"Lots of folks might want that material." Bear shivered in the cold. "It's extremely dangerous."

"We learned that the hard way. I had hoped the rumor that the chart led to more material was just gossip, but should know better after all we went through to get those obelisks."

"That was crazy."

Sixteen months ago, they'd barely evaded the Russians in a deadly race to find the obelisks. They'd been chased from Spain to Jerusalem, and farther around the world. Along with AJ's kidnapping, the death of Maddy's father and Will's wife had illustrated the personal costs, and they'd learned later the Russians had much larger plans that would have affected the entire United States. He stomped his feet a little harder as he paced. Saving the world from these kinds of threats was why he was proud to be a new member of the VanOps team.

Jags landed next to Bear and gave him a huge grin before she tore off her helmet and walked away, leaving a lingering scent of sweat and perfume. Her shaggy black hair was tossed by the wind as she headed toward the makeshift tent, looking every inch the L.A. model she'd been before college and the NSA.

"You have pictures of the star chart as backup?" he asked.

Maddy's tone turned defensive. "Of course, I have backup. One paper copy at the loft, and multiple secure cloud locations for the digital copies. I am a computer geek as well as an aikido trainer."

"I'm glad your computer skills come in handy. However, if the star chart does lead to a source of superconductive material, or even other obelisks, that's a national security risk. A huge one."

As a boy, Bear had dreamed of serving his country as a CIA officer, and even dressed up as a spy every Halloween. Now that he was an adult, he deeply loved his country and wanted to protect it, in addition to enjoying the adventure and risk. He was thrilled to be a career trainee, and truly appreciated the overarching VanOps mission to keep the country safe from obscure and extreme dangers. His biggest dream was to someday be awarded the Intelligence Star, the CIA's equivalent of the Medal of Honor. Maybe Bowman would assign him to track down this chart.

Echoing his thoughts, Maddy said, "Bear, I hate to admit it, but I think we have to figure out where that star chart leads before the Russians or King Carlos do."

"What about the city police?"

"This will be just another burglary to them. They won't care." She took a deep breath. "I'm also worried about Will. He was with us when I got the chart."

"Argones is a big boy and has been through his initial training. I only wish you were here working on the VanOps payroll, too."

"I suppose." She paused and continued with characteristic bluntness. "I just can't get used to you calling him 'Argones.' And I doubt he's suddenly become Superman."

Bear noticed she still avoided the VanOps job question. And he agreed with her assessment.

"True," Bear said. "Despite his penchant for knives, he's still a lousy shot."

"I'll call him as soon as we get off the phone."

"Good idea." Bear's tone softened. "I just hope the attacker doesn't come after you and AJ. Why don't you come on out here to DC? I'll talk to the director, see if he'll at least let me run those mismatched eyes and the name through the databases."

Based on a prior conversation with Bowman, Bear had a sense

the director would indeed be interested. The man remained obsessed with the sat feeds from that night sixteen months ago, and even though Maddy strongly wished to keep everything hush-hush, the director had figured out that *something* unusual had generated the strange-and-curious ball lightning.

"I suppose we can get his help. The main thing I pledged to keep secret was destroyed."

Bear felt pleased she was still working to keep the obelisks secret. She'd be a good operative. "Yeah, and if you want Argones and me to lend you a hand, the director is the boss."

She hesitated and he could almost see her weighing the options on a balanced set of scales. Finally, she said, "Okay, let's ask Director Bowman. I'll text you a pic of the star chart. If the Guardians are okay with it, I want to take AJ to Jerusalem tomorrow."

"Is the foster mom cool with that?"

"She is. I couched it as a Christmas vacation for him and she liked the idea of one less kid around the house."

"That's lame."

"I know, huh?"

"Are you thinkin' Elena?"

"I am. She and her new boyfriend leave for the Philippines in two days, and I want to hand-deliver AJ to her. It's a long flight to Israel, but I want to make certain he's safe and out of the way. I'll call her later to confirm."

Since their meeting at the Jerusalem Testing Society, which was now the headquarters of the Order of the Invisible Flame, Elena had become a good friend to Maddy. Bear still couldn't believe an ancient sect of royal spies existed, much less a school to test and train them. But he'd seen the place. They were modern European royalty, descendants of Isabella and Ferdinand, and, he had to admit, perfectly placed to gather intel in their roles as statesmen.

"Good idea, since he's a star witness. And you'll come to DC after?"

"Sure, I'll be in and out of Jerusalem. And we can go from

there." Her tone became softer. "But only if that heavy breathing was from training."

Bear stopped pacing again. "Maddy. I'm not the one hangin' out with my ex." With jealousy tightening his throat, the words came out stronger than he intended.

Her tone developed an edge. "We weren't hanging out."

Bear kicked himself for bringing it up. "Okay, let's table that discussion. I'll talk to the director immediately."

"Thanks. And I'll call Will. Bear?"

"Yes?"

The timbre of her voice shifted. "Do be careful with your VanOps training."

"I will. If you promise not to go around and get yourself shot. Or shot again, I should say."

"Deal. Good night, Bear."

"'Night, Maddy."

As he hung up the phone, Bear felt torn between his new job and his desire to protect Maddy and AJ. Would she ever move to the East Coast? If she was part of the team, Bear would no longer need to keep secrets from her and could do a much better job of keeping them safe. He knew from recent briefings that the Russians would stop at nothing to achieve their goals.

From the tent, Jags sprinted over to him, blue eyes blazing, phone in hand. "The Indian ambassador to Russia was just found dead on an isolated beach in the Maldives. Killed with a garrote. The director wants us back at HQS pronto."

CHAPTER 5

SÃO PAULO, BRAZIL

DECEMBER 18, 11:15 P.M. BRASILIA SUMMER TIME

Will Argones felt his boat shift and prepared to draw his knives. *Did someone just step on the back of my boat?* This was São Paulo's most secure marina, but Maddy's call had put him on edge.

Ana Therese looked at him with concern. It was a rare December evening without rain, and they were sitting on the front deck of his boat, eating, drinking, and reminiscing.

"That sounded like a scary conversation with your sister," she said in Portuguese, her tone light and quick.

He was good with languages, but his Portuguese bore the traces of his California upbringing. "Yes, someone broke into her loft tonight."

"Holy mother of god! Is she safe?"

Distracted, Will nodded. "For now. Although she's worried I may not be."

"Really? Why?"

Will drummed his fingers on the table, considering his security clearance and the oath he'd taken to safeguard national secrets. How to fill her in? And how much to tell her?

"Well, we both miss Maria horribly, don't we?"

"Yes! She was my best friend! That's why I'm glad we finally got together tonight. To remember. To grieve." Her gentle, caramel-colored eyes threatened to fill again with tears. "Looking at all the old pictures with you was good. And made me sad all over again."

The pictures were spread on the table near an almost empty bottle of good red. He'd come down here to arrange for the boat to be shipped up to a marina located in the shadow of the Washington Monument, walking distance to everything DC, but he would miss this harbor. He'd spent four good years here.

Could it have been someone on the boat?

A fishing boat chugged in the distance, and the neighbor two slips down was talking to his rat terrier, like he always did before bed. The water lapped against the starboard side and Will wondered again why he had felt the vessel shift. Not normal. He always paid attention to odd details, but now VanOps had trained him, and was paying him well, to exploit his suspicions. He'd joined the Red Team and, when he wasn't in the field, his mission was to poke holes in other teams' strategies and tactics.

A strangled meow cut through the night, followed by a splash. Will stood up, searching the dark water. There. Ripples. Will vaulted over the railing, onto the worn dock, and sprinted toward a spluttering cat close to drowning near the pier. He reached down, grabbed it by the nape of the neck, hauled it out of the water, and placed it on the wood planks. It shook water from its fur, arched its back, and hissed at him.

Will hissed back before he walked back to his boat and rejoined Ana Therese.

"That was exciting!" she said.

Will went into the galley and washed his hands. Drying them on a towel, he sat back down at the table. "Darn cat. Got my heart rate up."

The cat jumped onto the boat and walked over to him, rubbing itself on his legs. Even wet, he could see it was a thin tabby, with a pronounced M on its forehead.

She laughed. "I think it likes you."

Will took the towel and dried the purring beast. "Haven't seen it around."

"Maybe it's a sign. You should take it with you as a souvenir."

"I'll think about it."

The cat moved to a corner of the deck, laid down, and began cleaning itself. Will took a sip of wine. He hadn't cared for a pet in years. Maybe it was time.

Ana Therese picked up a picture and showed it to him. "Take a look at this one."

It was a beach snapshot of him and Maria, arm in arm as they stood next to Ana Therese and her husband, Tomás. Will's heart still ached for Maria. When he wasn't looking, he could almost hear her bustling about the boat. Even in DC, he rolled over in the mornings expecting to see her. The supreme guilt he felt for sleeping with the woman in Jerusalem so soon after Maria's murder resurfaced. He tried to tell himself that his behavior was the result of terror from being chased halfway around the world, but he still berated himself for his actions. It hadn't been respectful. He'd been in a sad daze for months, a two-pointed anchor of grief and guilt weighing down his heart.

He scratched his beard, remembering life before his loss. "Those were good times. Really good times."

As he put the snapshot down, he noticed that Ana Therese had changed since the picture was taken. Although her impish smile was the same, her face was rounder and her dark hair longer. She looked less a girl and more a woman.

She looked out over the harbor, her eyes lost in the past. "They were good times. I wish Tomás was able to be sad with us tonight, too. Sorry he is visiting his mother. He also misses Maria."

Will pulled a harmonica out of his tooled leather holder and blew a few test notes. A mournful melody filled the harbor. He stopped playing and palmed it. Silver, it was shaped like a small harp and had a gold-plated mouthpiece. "Please tell him hello when he gets back."

"I will. When did you start playing that?"

He set it on the table next to his wine glass. "I picked it up after Maria died."

He'd developed a sudden urge to play after lightning had struck him. When the desire lingered, even after the branching redness had faded from his left leg, he'd given in to it and purchased a high-end Suzuki SCT-128 professional 16-hole Tremolo Chromatic, and found it fairly easy to play the melancholy music haunting his head. Finding the talent strange, he'd done some online research and discovered a surgeon who'd left that career for classical music after being struck by lightning in New York. Will enjoyed it as a hobby.

"You're talented." She took a sip of wine. "But you're avoiding the question of why your twin feels you are not safe."

This question was about his sister and not VanOps, which meant he could share a little information. "Maddy is concerned that whoever broke into her place may come after me."

She put a hand to her mouth. "Oh, this is not good! What do you think?"

His most honest thoughts came out in a rush. "If they killed me, I could be with Maria again."

She grabbed the wine bottle and poured what was left over the side of the boat and into the water. "Enough wine for you." Then she sat back down and swatted his hand. "Stop that negative talk. She wouldn't like it."

He drained the last of the wine in his glass. It was a decent cab from a Napa Valley vineyard back home. But maybe there had been too much of it lately. "She would give me a good whack over the head, probably with that bottle."

Ana Therese said, "That's right. She would want you safe and happy." The look she gave him reminded him of one his mother might have given: half concern and half get-your-shit-together.

He was trying to get his act together. But what he couldn't tell her was that he was a newly minted junior intelligence analyst with VanOps. After Maria's death and his return to Brazil, he had been fired from his engineering job for missing too much work. The termination troubled him, but Director Bowman was true to his word. Will was interviewed, and hired after a series of psychological tests and a polygraph. Now, with more than a year of training under his belt, he was gaining confidence in his innate ability to perceive threats, and sort true hazard from imagined danger. He'd recently been added to the VanOps Red Team to act as a devil's advocate during planning sessions, tasked with evaluating the risks of proposed operations. His main role was to identify and analyze unusual threats to the US as well as opportunities to disrupt those threats.

With the help of the training staff, he'd found both his talents and his "growth opportunity areas." VanOps was exploiting his natural gift for languages, and he was also good with the never-ending fact-sorting drills and the writing of the intel reports and cables. Memorization was no problem, even when it concerned things outside his engineering purview, like models of foreign weapons. However, he sucked at using his body in the interest of self-protection. Even after weeks and months of crawling under barbed wire, mock shootouts in vacant buildings, parkour climbing instruction, high-speed driving and crashing, and shooting, he still had much work to do. They weren't prepping him for commando assaults, but even as an analyst, he would eventually need to perform intelligence-gathering missions in hostile environments. The team was too small to keep him behind a desk all the time.

The only thing that felt natural to him was knife work. He fingered the Strider SMF in his pocket, a gift from Bear. Bear and his fellow marines knew their knives. Striders were born in the War on Terror, and Will appreciated their compact size and light, titanium frame.

He cast his eyes down, trying to look contrite. "You're right. She would want me safe and happy."

After a last look at the snapshot, she stood. "It's late. Thank you for helping me remember my friend."

He stood and put the silver and gold harmonica back in its case. As she hugged him, she sobbed once, and he felt a tear leave the corner of his eye and roll down his cheek.

"I'll walk you to your car," he said, voice thick.

Five minutes later, when he stepped back onto his boat, senses alert for danger, the marine alarm sounded. His boat was taking on water.

He ran aft, threw open the hatch, and rushed downstairs. A freshwater hose had leaked into the bilge, raising the water level until it triggered the overflow sensor. He took a deep breath and looked around.

Was it an accident, or something more sinister?

CHAPTER 6

From the back seat of the old-fashioned taxi, Maddy looked out the side window. It was well after dark, but the heart of San Francisco still hummed with vigor, even in the wet hangover from the brief snow.

A well-dressed woman in heels and a knee-length fur coat marched down the street with a large Macy's bag. A uniformed delivery man double-parked and ran up to an apartment door with a double-decker set of pizza boxes in his arms. A tired-looking African American woman in nursing scrubs waited at a bus stop. Sixteen months ago, Maddy had been an ordinary member of the city, too, working at the dojo, hoping for a windfall if her software company did an initial public offering, and starting to plan her wedding with Vincent.

Now she was dating Bear, had at last moved up a black belt level to second *dan*, or *nidan*, was a member of a thousand-year-old clandestine organization, and was considering working for VanOps.

The changes from then to now made her head spin, and tonight, especially, it felt like they had come at a steep price. Not only was Vincent her *ex*-fiancé, but also he was in the hospital, severely wounded. Was his injury her fault? Perhaps. Perhaps not.

What was her fault, or at least her responsibility, was the death of those men a year ago using the superconductive obelisks. She had killed, and now she was living with the ramifications—which was why she hadn't jumped at the chance to join VanOps like Will had.

Ever since that night, she'd had nightmares. Though technically it was the same nightmare, one where she blasted the men into tiny pieces that dispersed into the night like multicolored fireflies. Only the men's eyes remained, staring at her like the Cheshire cat's disembodied smile, blaming her for snuffing out their lives. At least they weren't "real" dreams, like the one she'd had when her mom died, or the nightmare about Will's wife's death. Those dreams happened rarely, provided few specifics, and left her with a gut-wrenching feeling that something horrible was about to happen. She shuddered. Even if they weren't prophetic, the nightmares were just as disturbing.

She tried to remind herself that she had no choice. That AJ, Bear, and Will would have died that stormy night if she hadn't acted. But somehow her arguments came up empty and most mornings she woke with a heart full of shame.

Now, an important document that was given to her for safekeeping had been stolen, and the thief had left her with a bullet wound to the forehead. Her life was certainly no longer pedestrian.

The taxi stopped at a red light and a tall man with dark hair crossed the intersection in front of the cab. Dark hair. AJ had told her that the thief had black hair with those mismatched eyes. Was the man who stole the star chart working for the Russians or the Spaniards? Probably the Russians, but she thought Carlos capable and would bet he'd love to get that chart back. But what did either want with a cache of superconductive material? If a supply was out there at all. God, she wished she knew.

The light turned green and the taxi pulled forward. Without warning, a loud *pop* sounded outside the car. The taxi driver swore. The car slowed and jolted up and down. Had a tire blown? Or had it been shot?

Maddy immediately sorted through the sounds she'd heard in the last few seconds. Even suppressors left a sound signature, and there had been a distant noise. But was it gunfire? Or could she be channeling Will's penchant for paranoia?

"Flat tire?" she asked.

The cabbie's English was laced with a heavy East Indian accent. "Yes, ma'am. My apologies. I'll have it fixed in no time."

Deftly, he pulled the car into a grocery parking lot and jumped out to survey the damage. Moments later, he sat back in the front seat. "Very strange. It does look flat. Probably a nail. If you wish to wait here, it will be no problem to fix."

Maddy considered. They were just three blocks from her loft, and there was no hail of bullets raining down on them. "No worries, I'll walk the rest of the way. What do I owe you?"

He looked at the meter and eyed her carefully. "The neighborhood is . . . risky. If you are sure you want to walk, just call it an even ten dollars."

Slightly miffed at the insult to her neighborhood, Maddy fished thirteen out of her purse, told him to keep the change and headed home on foot, eyes searching the darkness. The bitter air from the bay was whipping around buildings, and gone was the snow from a few hours earlier, replaced by a freezing drizzle. She pulled her black jacket tight and was glad for the cabbie hat.

Soon she was away from the well-lit grocery parking lot and on a dark, mixed-use street. Commercial buildings, closed for the night, sat cheek-by-jowl with apartment buildings. Shared walls were common in this neighborhood, street lights intermittent. Usually there were more foot-travelers, but tonight Maddy walked alone.

One block passed, then another.

Five doors from her loft, she passed the shadowed doorway of the local mom-and-pop hardware store. A homeless man lay under a pile of cardboard and newspaper. He shifted as she walked by.

From behind, a cold, thin wire was flung over her neck.

Maddy immediately stepped backward into the attacker, acting on years of training. As she twisted, turned, and ducked, she elbowed his diaphragm, gratified to hear the air escape his lungs in a rush. Still, the wire scraped over her ear and scalp, pulling off her earring, burning her ear, and tearing the cap off her head.

Quickly, Maddy spun away on the ball of her left foot.

In the gleam of the streetlight, the attacker was bent at the waist, but his head was up. His eyes, framed by a face covered in an exotic pattern of tattoos, held an intent, hungry look. Both eyes were dark.

Whipping the wire in the air, he lashed it at her calf. Unable to dodge in time, she grimaced at the sting and swore under her breath. He lunged at her. Maddy stepped aside and, with her arm, pushed him along his original trajectory, right into the side of a parked Volkswagen Jetta. His face hit the car with such force that the car alarm engaged, piercing the night with its high-pitched demand.

"Stop now and I won't hurt you," Maddy said.

Undeterred, the man turned. Blood gushed from his nose, and it looked crooked. Broken. And yet, after only a moment, the attacker pushed off the car and came at her again, like a bull aiming for an elusive red cape.

Swiftly, she moved to the right and he rushed past. Before he could turn and regroup, a nearby screen door banged open and a male voice shouted, "Hey! What's going on out here?"

Lights came on in several apartments. A glass door slid open and a bright flashlight beam interrupted the altercation.

The attacker swung the wire in a last circle before he ran off and disappeared down the night street.

CHAPTER 7

Director Alfred Bowman looked at Bear Thorenson over the remains of his coffee. An active-duty marine for years, Thorenson still looked the part of a quintessential covert operations warrior. Stocky, almost beefy, the combat veteran had shoulders broad enough to carry the weight of the world, buzz-cut hair, arctic-blue eyes, and chiseled features. His Scandinavian background was obvious in the pale skin tone and blond hair. Since there was no dress code at VanOps, he wore his personal uniform of jeans and white T-shirt with black boots. Lightning scars ran up both of his forearms, looking like the ghosts of dead trees.

This evening, the man's eyes looked strained. There were dark circles under them, and a worried look shadowed his face. It made him look more like his father, two-star general Alan Thorenson, whom the director had known during the Iraqi war and still missed.

"Thanks for coming quickly, Thorenson."

"Thanks for arrangin' the helo so I could get here pronto," Thorenson drawled, but squirmed in his seat.

Bowman would've liked a drawl, but his words always tumbled out of his mouth quickly. "What's up, soldier? Don't like to fly anymore?"

Thorenson took a deep breath. "No. I mean, I do have a request, sir, but do you want to talk first?"

It was true—the director had called the urgent meeting and should speak first. However, the normally stoic man was making him curious. "Spit it out, son, it's late. What's on your mind?"

"Well, sir, earlier this evening a chart was stolen from Maddy's apartment in San Francisco."

Ah, Maddy Marshall. Inside, she had a mind as analytical as the computers she worked with on her day job. On the outside, she was tall, long-legged, and black-haired, with full lips and eyes as green as new spring leaves.

He also recalled the trouble she, Thorenson, and her brother, Will Argones, had gotten themselves into a year and a half ago. At least the director had been able to hire Thorenson and Argones, both of whom were working out nicely. But he didn't recall anything about a chart. She'd held that bit close. His respect for her ticked up a notch.

He gave Thorenson a glare. "I don't recall you or Argones mentioning it during that mission debrief."

Thorenson flushed. "I found out about it later, sir."

The director paused to remind Thorenson who signed his checks. "What type of chart?"

"It's a celestial chart. Basically, an ancient picture of a bunch of stars. Her family thinks it leads to a source of high-temperature superconductive material."

Why would her family think that? Could Marshall have used some type of superconductive material that night with all the lightning? To hide his interest, the director slowly sipped his decaf. Lately, there was a rush of national security attention on high-temp superconductors because it was thought they could fuel the next generation of computers, what the experts were calling quantum computing. He knew from a recent brief that India and Russia were working on a quantum computer. A highly paid team at NSA was chipping away at the problem, and China was the horse in the lead on this race and keeping progress silent as usual. The prize would be a computer so fast that it could break all encryption, basically the holy grail of spydom.

"I'm listening."

"That's all we know, except that we think it's at least two thousand years old. And that Maddy thinks a Russian or Spaniard took it."

This was proving an interesting way to end his day. "Why Russian or Spanish?"

"Well, sir, you remember that boy she's trying to adopt and that he was kidnapped?"

"Yes."

"AJ was on the fire escape and recognized the man's unique eyes. The thief was one of his kidnappers and spoke Russian while AJ was held captive."

"That supports your Russian theory. Where do the Spaniards come in?"

"The chart was torn from an ancient codex. I saw the tear while visiting Maddy's extended royal family in Spain. That King Carlos was a creepy bastard."

The director raised both eyebrows.

"Sorry, sir. But my bad guy radar went off every time I interacted with him."

The director put up a hand. "No need to apologize. It's important to trust your instincts, but equally important to dig up facts. Do you have any other relevant evidence?"

"No, sir."

This "sir" business was a little tiresome, but the man had grown up in the military. The director had already asked him to stop several times and hoped the habit would eventually drop away like a leaf from a tree.

"Let's think for a minute. What possible alliances could this Russian-speaking man have?"

Bear ticked off the options on his fingers. "He could simply be Russian. Perhaps he's a double agent and works for the Russians and the Spaniards. He could have defected from Russia. Or perhaps Spain was more involved than we knew before. I suppose he could even have an allegiance to another power."

"Nice work. What exactly is your request?" Bowman asked.

Thorenson looked at the director, squared his shoulders, and took a breath. "I know it's unusual, sir, but I'd like you to assign me to find out who stole the chart. With Maddy's help. I think it's a significant national security risk."

The director wanted a minute to think. "Will you go get me another cup of coffee?"

"Yes, sir."

"Decaf. It's late."

Thorenson jumped out of his seat and raised his arm, jerkily stopping himself from saluting at the last minute. Then he turned on his heel and walked stiffly out the door. The man had the slightest of limps. His combat file had indicated a bad scene atop an Afghan mountaintop.

While he mulled over the night's events, the director looked around his office, which had once been the glass-walled conservatory of the Revolution-era brick mansion. When he had taken the helm, he'd chosen this building as the new VanOps headquarters. The DC world knew the building as a drug and alcohol clinic, thus providing privacy by keeping the uninitiated at bay.

The conservatory's windows, which earlier in the day had showcased a bare winter's day, were what had led him to choose this room as his private domain. A switch underneath the top of his desk quickly changed the thick layers of ballistic glass-clad polycarbonate from clear to opaque. The entire building was encased in a steel Faraday-type radio-frequency shield to deter eavesdropping, and audio surveillance covered the grounds, sensitive enough to hear a tomcat on the prowl. There were also new underground tunnels that provided secret access from a nearby parking garage. He was pleased with the office security.

For ambience, he'd had a number of plants brought in to

complement his dark wood desk, burnished oak flooring, and built-in bookshelves. He liked the new office and wanted to keep it.

He'd held the office sixteen months. After being appointed by the D/CIA, the director had hired a clean slate of staff he knew he could trust, several from his former team at the counterterrorism center. One of his first tasks had been to closely study the cloud-penetrating radar satellite images from the evening Thorenson, Argones, and Maddy Marshall had nearly caused an international incident.

Although the woman was more tight-lipped than the men, the director had come to a few conclusions. First, Marshall had wielded a powerful weapon that had caused some sort of lightning. Two, she was a smart, bad-ass woman with a unique skill set and he wanted her on his team. Third, the Russians were intent on getting that weapon, and anything they wanted he wanted. And worse. Which meant he was profoundly intrigued by Thorenson's story.

Also, there was the potential funding issue. His organization was ultra-black and worked under the dark financial umbrella of the CIA's hidden DET (Directorate of Extreme Threats). His missions were autonomous. They worked as needed with the five public directorates, high-level intelligence sharing. Tasked with gathering intelligence and executing necessary covert action, they partnered with the Navy SEALs from time to time if things got dicey. A new president was elected a few weeks ago and the director worried that VanOps, perhaps even the entire DET, might not be funded under the new administration. Certainly not if the Russians got out of hand on his watch.

Another issue was the recently murdered Indian ambassador to Russia, Ravi Singh. Singh's death was why he'd called Thorenson and Jags back to the office. Before Singh's murder, Ravi had been sleeping with the Russian ambassador to India, also known as the second wife of Maddy's grandfather. Because that marriage had taken place in Russia, the director strongly doubted Marshall had ever known her step-grandmother, but any way you sliced it, Singh's connection was worrisome.

There was also the "Top Secret" encryption stamped on a part of Singh's internal file, protected by a need-to-know-only password that the director was going to have to haul in some favors to get. It all smelled of the Clandestine Service. And now Ravi Singh was dead. The director wanted to know who. And why. He planned to assign Jags, Thorenson, and Argones to track that thread.

With a glance at his computer, the director remembered recent NSA electronic intelligence. There was a single mention of Russian chatter about constellations in the intercepts. The director scratched the ten o'clock shadow on his chin; a hunch was forming, and if it was correct, the missing star chart posed a massive national security risk. And could put his organization on the new administration's chopping block if he misplayed his next move.

Thorenson walked back into the office, carrying a steaming cup of coffee. The director welcomed the mug and warmed his hands on it. The windows let in a lot of sun during the day, but at night, the cold seeped through them as if they were made of cellophane.

"Thorenson, you've done well as a trainee. It's time to take the desk chains off and make you a junior officer."

Thorenson sat up straight and smiled for just an instant.

The director continued. "I want you to find out who killed Ravi Singh. And why." The quantum information was too sensitive to share without corroborating the data, so he kept his report limited to what he knew of Singh.

Thorenson squinted, probably wondering about the chart. "Yes, sir."

"I think that objective may overlap with the star chart angle. Start with the chart."

Thorenson relaxed, nodding.

"Jags, as senior member, will lead the team." The director sipped at his coffee while making his decisions. "Under her leadership, you and Argones are to work with Marshall as a subject matter expert, or SME, to see where the star chart leads. Find out if it's a map, and, if so, find the superconductive asset and bring it back. I'll call Argones to assign him to the effort and will discuss with Jags shortly. You have my full support."

"Thank you, sir."

"And keep Marshall safe. This could turn out to be a dangerous mission, and even though she's skilled with aikido, she is a civilian."

Thorenson straightened his spine. "I understand. I will."

"Do you have a picture of the night-sky chart?"

Thorenson pulled his phone from his pocket, thumbed through some images, and turned the display toward the director. "Maddy just sent it to me. It's from a few months back."

The director shook his head. The woman needed to get on board with VanOps before she caused a problem by using insecure consumer technology. "Get her a secure phone as soon as possible and have her call me about an NDA. She's privy to this op alone, understood?"

"Yes, sir."

It was an unusual move to include Ms. Marshall on the team as an SME, but he'd been looking for a chance to recruit her as a cyber operations officer. He knew she was a sleeper member of the Order of the Invisible Flame, the EU's ancient spy agency. The Order reminded him of the Princes' School in Riyadh, Saudi Arabia, established by a king for royals and the children of important Saudis. There were long-standing information-sharing agreements between the Order and VanOps, and there had even been a few joint missions run by his predecessors and Master Mohan, the genius who ran the secret sect. Since the organizations were tight allies, the director saw no issue with having Maddy play both hands, especially since he'd done a full security clearance on her at the same time he vetted her brother. Other than some wild times in college, she was squeaky clean. He could almost see a reflection in her file.

Not that she was perfect. No, he'd learned that she could be stubborn and blunt, maybe too idealistic, and her tendency to be a perfectionist could get her in trouble. He could live with those traits, though. Maybe this mission would finally convince her to join VanOps.

He pulled the handset closer and studied the image. It looked like a cluster of stars in the middle of a timeworn piece of vellum. A small hieroglyph sat in the corner. A dual band of stars bordered the document. Although no constellation was apparent to his layman's eye, one star stood out brightly.

"After you check those strange eyes in the perp database, I suggest you research constellations."

"Thank you, sir. Yes, sir."

"Remember, if you get stuck, don't be afraid to ask an expert."

CHAPTER 8

After slicing through the crime scene tape and opening the front door, Maddy looked around her loft with the mixed emotions of relief and dismay. On the one hand, she was grateful for the haven of home after dealing with the tattooed attacker, even if it was just an illusion of safety. On the other, the place was a wreck, mirroring her life of late.

The attacker had spent most of his time in her bedroom, which, typical in converted loft spaces, was roomy enough to double as an office. The sheets were ripped off the bed and lay in a crumpled heap. Her desk area was in shambles, papers strewn across the floor. It looked like a trash bag had fallen off the back of a recycling truck on a nearby freeway and its rubbish had blown all about the room.

She walked to her closet and grabbed the white running shoe from the shelf. Removing the insole, she felt a moment of gratitude that he hadn't found the red shard of obelisk. Sometimes low-tech security worked just fine.

The skinny shard was a material called lorandite, and had probably come from a meteorite as it wasn't a substance found naturally on earth. That's what Elena's Germans had told them, at least. For a moment, she closed her fingers around it. Within seconds, it began to beat in time with her pulse. With the small size, she doubted she could channel much energy through it, and hadn't had time to really try, but she would bring it anyway. After wrapping it in a small silk handkerchief, she put it in her pocket and walked back into the common area.

In some ways, the living room was worse because, in addition to thrown couch cushions and dislodged paintings, the robber had left a trail of blood, dried now, across the formerly pristine hardwood floors. Maddy touched the bandage on her forehead. It was also possible that some of that spilled blood was her own.

Maddy was a meticulous housekeeper, as was her roommate, Robert. She hoped to get the place cleaned up before he came home from his shift at the high-end restaurant where he was the chef. He'd be mortified at the scene.

She shook her head. This was just one straw too many. In addition to her aching head and leg, tonight would be a big emotional setback for AJ. True, she'd gotten permission from his foster parents to take him somewhere safe, but who knew what effect that would have on him? Should she even pursue the adoption since danger stalked her like a jilted lover? Not to mention Bear was so transparently jealous of Vincent it made her eyes roll. And there was that pit of guilt in her gut. Add an angry software client at work and an envious friend at the dojo, and her life was a mess on multiple fronts.

She needed to clean up, regroup, and make some flight arrangements ASAP.

The doorbell rang. Maddy checked the peephole and was surprised to see her sister, Bella, who looked as much put together as Maddy felt out of sorts. Her sister's makeup was perfect, her short bob looked like she'd just been to the stylist, and her expensive jeans and blouse showed off her compact cheerleader's frame to good advantage. The shirt was maybe even ironed. How did she do all that with three kids? Sans makeup and with messy hair under her salvaged-but-dirty cabbie cap, Maddy felt like a slob.

Bella's five-year-old daughter, Izzy, was next to her, blond pig-tails bouncing as she tried to wave into the peephole. The effort made her purple skirt fly up and down, reminding Maddy of a jellyfish she'd seen once at the Monterey Aquarium.

Maddy slipped out into the hallway and shut the front door behind her.

Bella reached up to hug Maddy. "What's up with the caution tape? Did you get my text? We were in the neighborhood." She pointed at the bandage on Maddy's forehead. "What happened to you?"

Maddy hugged back. "Sorry, I haven't had a chance to check my phone—it's been quite the night."

"Oh?"

Maddy dropped to a knee and gave Izzy a hug. "How would you like to play with Michael while your mom and I visit?"

"Yeah!"

Maddy looked at Bella, who nodded. Maddy walked two doors to the left and knocked. Michael's mom answered the door, dressed in a power suit from her day at the office.

"Would Michael enjoy a playmate for a little while?" she asked.

"Sure. We've wrapped up dinner. It'll keep him off the video games for a while."

Maddy ushered Izzy into Michael's home and heard him squeal with delight.

"Okay, now. What happened?" Bella asked once they were back in the hallway. Her soprano voice was an octave higher than Maddy's.

Maddy opened the door to her loft. "I got robbed. And then almost mugged on the way home."

Bella walked in and looked around. "Wow, the burglar sure did a number on your place. You poor thing."

"Thanks."

Bella turned and hugged Maddy, who held back tears. It had been a tough night.

"Want help cleaning?" Bella asked.

"That would be great."

Heading to the kitchen, Maddy grabbed some mineral water from the slate-colored refrigerator and gave Bella a root beer. They opened the beverages, got the housework supplies from under the sink, and started by wiping up the dried trail of blood. As they worked, Maddy told Bella more about what had happened that afternoon, but was careful to downplay potential Russian or Spanish involvement—for her safety, Maddy and Will had chosen to spare Bella details of the last time they were up against the Russians.

As they cleaned, Maddy noticed her heart still raced at the retelling of the intrusion, and it felt good to work off some of that energy cleaning up her home.

Bella straightened a picture on the wall. "Do you think the break-in and the mugging were related?"

"I thought about that, but don't think so."

"Why not?"

"Different guys, for one thing. The mugger didn't seem to want anything other than to strangle me. And the attack seemed unplanned; he ran off as soon as neighbors responded to the car alarm."

"I see. A random act of city violence then?"

Maybe he wanted my purse, or to get me unconscious to rape me. But what are the odds of two unrelated attacks in one day? For Bella's benefit, Maddy said, "That's my theory."

The conversation turned to Izzy and Bella's boys. Maddy always enjoyed hearing what her nephews and niece were up to. Cub Scouts, homework, and after-school sports were all things she hoped one day to experience with AJ.

An hour later, the loft had reclaimed much of its former appeal, although the bullet hole near the doorway required attention from a carpenter and Maddy would have to spend more time at her desk putting papers in their files. But the granite countertops shone, the hardwood floors gleamed with her favorite lemon-scented polish, and the furniture and art were all back in their places. It looked like home again.

Maddy heaved a sigh of gratitude. "Thanks for the help. I appreciate it."

"No problem. I was in town getting my hair done with Izzy anyway. Happy we could stop by."

Knowing that Bella's hair had just gotten cut made Maddy feel a little better. She had embraced the hat look ever since having to shave her head. Normally, she wore her dark hair long, and she couldn't wait for it to grow again. The short style just wasn't her.

They sat down at the black kitchen table. Robert's cat ventured down the stairs and slowly came over and circled Maddy's chair, seeking a pet.

"Shy, isn't she?" Bella remarked.

Maddy reached down and stroked the calico's fur. "Yes, but that may have saved one of her lives tonight."

"Dad's golden retriever is doing well at our house, but it would be great if you could eventually take him. We already have two other dogs."

"That gives you a dog for each kid," Maddy said playfully.

"And another mouth to feed. The kids aren't old enough to take care of pets yet, which makes it all on me. You know AJ wants a dog."

The cat jumped into Maddy's lap. Her left index finger twitched. She scratched the cat's chin with the finger, eliciting a purr. "He does, but the foster paperwork is a thorny knot of trouble. Even the agency seems lost with the process half the time."

"I'm sorry it's been such a headache. But once it's resolved, think you'll want Squirrel?"

Maddy smiled. "AJ calls him Damien."

"Whatever you call him, he's a solid dog, but needs a forever home. It's not our house is what I'm saying. If it's not you, I need to find other options."

Maddy reached behind her hat and twirled a short strand of hair. "We don't have a good place. This loft is lovely, but very urban."

"That brings me to my next point. Dad's estate."

Maddy got a lump in her throat. His death, which had started them on the quest to find the obelisks, was still too fresh. "Can we deal with this later? Long day."

"Yes, but the attorney is going to need an answer soon about what we want to do with the house and vineyard. Marty and I can't afford to buy you and Will out. Will has some insurance money now. Maybe he could buy it? Or you could get a mortgage? That way we could keep the vineyard in the family. We'd love to visit on weekends."

The concept held some appeal. Maybe she and AJ could live at the vineyard and she could start a new dojo in downtown Napa or in the picturesque town of Calistoga. There might be some income from the grapes, and it would be a better place to raise AJ than in the city. She could telework and attend the occasional city meeting to keep the computer money flowing, and who knows, maybe Bear would even move in one day.

But then she told herself to slow down. It was a fine home, but unless an IPO happened at the company, she doubted she could afford it. And what if she chose to work for VanOps in Washington DC? She didn't have the energy now even to think about it.

"Maybe. I'll look into it later. I'm going to leave town for a while."

"Where are you headed?"

Maddy couldn't tell Bella that she wanted to take AJ to Jerusalem so Elena could keep him safe. The Order, which Will jokingly called a "Secret Sect of Stately Spies" because all members were royal, was off limits to the uninitiated. Perhaps AJ would be okay to visit since he was a child. She wanted to tell Bella all of it, but was bound by promises. And the less her sister knew, the safer she was in the long run.

As if expressing her disapproval, the cat twitched her tail, swatted half-heartedly at Maddy, then suddenly jumped to the floor and headed back to her cat-tree in Robert's room.

"Going to visit Bear," Maddy said. At least it was partially true.

"How's his new job working out?"

And now they were right back into another secret. Because Bear's new job involved top secret security clearance and a role with a clandestine organization, they hadn't told Bella the details. Actually, they'd been forced to obscure the truth. "Good, he likes it."

"What is he doing again?" Bella probed.

Maddy's mind raced. She hated lying. It never felt right and she couldn't remember the story half the time. After her eventful evening, this was one of those times. She'd make a lousy spy for VanOps. She racked her brain. They had gone back and forth with a cover story, before Bear had settled on one with VanOps. Which one was it?

"He's still in the marines," she explained. "Just no longer in the field."

"I thought you told me he was working as a defense contractor."

Shit! That was the other story. Maddy scrambled. "He works with a lot of defense contractors in his new job."

Bella didn't buy it. "You lied to me!"

"Bella, I—"

Bella got up, her chair making a grating sound as it scraped the floor. "Maddy, no. I don't know what's going on, but you clearly don't trust me."

As Bella pushed toward the door, Maddy followed in her wake. "Not true, I do."

"Don't talk to me about truth. I've always been able to tell when you're lying. Ever since Dad died you and Will have both been keeping secrets from me and I'm done."

"Bella!"

Bella flung open the door and walked through, angrily thrusting aside the tattered remnants of the yellow police tape. "No, Maddy. If you can't trust your only sister, who can you trust? Call me when you're ready to be honest."

Bella slammed the door.

Maddy turned and collapsed into a heap against the still-vibrating wood, her stomach a knot. Everything was going wrong. She dropped her head into her hands, defeated.

CHAPTER 9

The tapping of the baron's cane in the concrete hallway outside her cell sent a chill, cold as a Siberian winter, up Zola's spine. He was coming.

Desperate for an escape, she looked around her dirty cell again, hoping to see something she'd missed the many times before. Nothing. Just the chains attached to the ceiling and floor, meant for hands stretched up and feet spread wide, and a chipped drain in the middle of the room that she presumed was for blood and other bodily fluids. No window. The only light came from a small pane of glass in the door, and from a caged fixture, high overhead. The slab on which she sat held only a thin red blanket, which she wrapped around herself tightly to control the trembling. There was not even a seat on the toilet.

She never imagined she'd be in one of these holding cells. After all, she was the ambassador to India. At least she was until they came for her in the night. When was that? Two days ago? Three? She didn't know. Couldn't tell time in this warren of fear and stench.

Tap, tap, tap. The cane came closer.

She tried to maintain an appearance of dignity by sitting up straighter. The electronic bolt slid back with a soft thump, and Baron Sokolov walked in. Behind him, a young man in military dress obsequiously deposited a chair and then stepped smartly out of the cell.

She and the baron knew each other from years of diplomatic dinners. He always cut an imposing figure, and today was no exception. Like the young man, the baron wore a uniform, but his was so heavily decorated it had to make it hard to move when he wore it. The finely cut white hair was in perfect form, and his beard was trimmed to a point as sharp as that of the gold-plated Steller's sea eagle beak on the head of his cane.

The baron sat and leaned toward her slightly. Behind wire-rimmed glasses, his blue eyes were dark in the dim prison light. They almost looked black. In Russian he asked, "Zola, my dear, why are we here?"

Zola heard disapproval in his voice.

She nodded to him in respect. He liked respect.

"Baron Sokolov," she said, also in Russian, as dread gnawed at her insides. This situation was bad. Was there a way she could negotiate her freedom by trading on their past acquaintance? "I'm unsure why I'm here, but I'm happy to help in any way I can."

"Of course. Let's see, how to help? Did you hear that Ravi Singh was murdered five days ago?"

Zola had heard. Heard and regretted her indiscretions with him. Her breathing became shallower as her fear increased. Who would want to kill sweet Ravi? His murder had surprised her. Ravi had been killed by garrote, a weapon infamously utilized by the Hungarian secret police, the Államvédelmi Osztály, or AVO. But the AVO had been officially abolished in 1956, and even if a secret agency lingered on, she couldn't imagine what they would want with Ravi. And why did the baron care?

She chose a neutral response. "Yes, I was sad to hear Mr. Singh was killed. And with a garrote, too."

The baron looked at her keenly, and she wondered if he'd recently had plastic surgery on his eyelids. For his age, the eyes had minimal droop and his insightful gaze disarmed her.

"Mr. Singh," he said slowly. "Is that what you called him when you were in bed together?"

Zola swore to herself. How much did he know? How much was he fishing? She decided to lie. "Ravi and I were friends, yes, but I never slept with him."

The cane hit her left arm with such force she gasped.

"Save us both some time, Zola. We know you and Ravi had an affair. You'd been sleeping together for two years."

Cradling her bruised arm, she tried to think through the pain. It was that Christmas party two years ago and he'd cut a dashing figure when he'd asked her to dance with a twinkle in his eye. She'd better change course and lie as little as possible. "Yes. I'm sorry. We were sleeping together. My husband was twenty-two years my senior and, his, um—appetites, had declined with age."

The baron tapped his cane on the concrete floor. It was an ugly, impatient sound.

"What did you tell Ravi of the star chart?"

Ah, that's what he wants. The pulsing in her arm reminded her to tread carefully here or Pyotr, her son, could be in serious danger. After dinner one night, she had overheard Pyotr talking about going to the States to get that chart after the Intelligence Service had eavesdropped on the twins and found out they had it. If the baron knew her steadfast Pyotr was careless enough to be overheard . . .

"The chart my late husband talked about?" she said. "The one from his Spanish family?"

"That very one. What do you know of it?"

To protect Pyotr, she needed to sprinkle a lot of truth sugar into a coffee of lies. Although she had mentioned the chart to Ravi recently, the baron would have already killed her if he knew everything. The affair would have been easy for them to track, but in this, he was hunting for the truth.

"All I know is that my husband believed it led to a source of superconductive material," she said. "It drove him crazy, trying to figure out where it was."

Indeed, her late husband was obsessed with finding the obelisks and star chart, to the point that she wasn't sorry when he'd died. When she had overheard Pyotr talking about a mission to get the chart, she wanted to give Ravi some hope. When he'd given her an update on the quantum computer that Russia and India were working on together, a computer that required superconductive material, she saw no harm in letting him know Pyotr and her people were close to getting what they all needed. Now, she saw clearly, that thinking was a mistake. The baron was as obsessed as her husband.

His steely blue eyes bore into hers. "That's all you know? Did you tell Ravi about the star chart?"

She stopped rubbing her left arm and shook her head, controlling every move to be more convincing. "No."

He sat back in his chair and rubbed the eagle on his cane absentmindedly, rather like how her friend from the Durak card club rubbed the head of her lap dog. "What about how we plan to use the quantum computer once we get that superconductive material?"

She was able to deny this truthfully. "I'm aware of our joint research project with India, but what's the plan?"

Baron Sokolov looked hard at her, and then she noted a small, satisfied smile flash across his face.

"I can't tell you," he said simply.

She was not surprised, but she was heartened—he would not hesitate to tell her if he planned to kill her. Perhaps this questioning would end without her death after all. A small ray of hope lit the dim cell.

The baron looked at the glass window in the door, nodded to the young man outside, stood, and turned to leave. "I know you told Ravi about the star chart. You've lied to me and I can't tolerate that. But, because Pyotr is proving useful to me, I'm just going to have your tongue ripped out. At least for now."

Shocked, Zola fell to the floor at his knees and begged, her voice rapid and high-pitched. "No, I swear—"

"Watch yourself or I'll have you shipped off to friends of mine who run a sex-trafficking ring." The eagle-headed cane flew toward her head and Zola ducked ineffectually. She toppled over in agony, and the baron whisked out of the room.

As the young man pulled her off the cement floor, she wasn't sure which was worse: the searing pain that blossomed on her left ear, the dizziness that made her immediately throw up, or the knowledge that she would never speak again.

CHAPTER 10

Maddy sat on the floor with her back to her loft door, aching head in her hands. Bella and Izzy's shoes clacked on the hallway tile, clicking away toward the elevator, accusing her with their clipped sound. *Liar, liar, liar.*

Truth was, she hated deceit, especially with her sister. But the alternative of making her sister a target was far worse.

Feelings of isolation, guilt, and confusion buoyed to the surface on a wave of thoughts.

Do I have a choice about trying to figure out the star chart's secrets? No. It was my responsibility to keep it safe. My fault.

Should I go work for VanOps? I'd be with Bear, doing important work, but then I'd never be able to tell Bella the whole truth. I've always wanted to make the world a better place. At the dojo, I impact a few lives at a time. With VanOps, I could potentially save millions.

But what about relocating AJ? I'd thought that last adventure a one-off, but here we go again. Should I reconsider the adoption to keep him safe?

Then there's Vincent. We had such a great relationship for so long. Am I ready to move away from him? He wants me back. Is it over between us?

At this last, she sprang up from the floor, disturbed. Acutely aware that she needed to deal with her troubled emotions, she chose to put the processing off. She knew she needed to sit with them, to feel them, and they'd eventually dissolve, but at the moment all she wanted was a hot shower.

Fifteen minutes later, clean, warm, dry, and with a fresh bandage on her forehead, she called Elena, who "absolutely" agreed to take AJ on vacation. Right after, she called Edith and Samuel to ask permission to bring AJ. It amused Maddy to think of the ancient school with a cell phone, but why not?

Edith's already high voice rose another octave with excitement. "Do come, dear child. And bring that boy!" Edith added that they'd limit his access to sleeping quarters to prevent any secrets from filling the child's head.

She figured a note to the roommate would suffice on the home front. To explain her upcoming absence to her coworkers, she made a few phone calls to the dojo and to her computer partner. The only good news of the day was that the recent rumors of an IPO at the company had been validated with an announcement that an underwriter had been chosen to start the process. She crossed her fingers that the stock she'd been hoarding would be worth something if an offering happened.

Next, Maddy pulled out her laptop and found a flight to Israel that left in six hours. Bear and Will, as VanOps employees, could travel under assumed names, but her false passport had been confiscated. She'd have to see if Bear could get her a new one. Finally, she texted the foster mom that she'd need to pick AJ up in a few hours.

Tasks completed, she fell exhausted into bed. It would be a short night's sleep, more like a dog-tired catnap. Although she was excited to get moving and find where the star chart might lead, she felt deeply disturbed at the level of responsibility on her shoulders.

When she closed her eyes, disturbing images of the thief's strange white iris danced over the mugger's uniquely tattooed face. Tired as she was, sleep was slow in coming. Her mind chewed over a dozen questions, but three she returned to again and again. Were the night's dual attacks related? Who was behind the theft of the chart? And why did they want the superconductive material?

CHAPTER 11

In the heart of VanOps headquarters, Bear sat at his desk, working on a laptop and drinking iced tea, his morning beverage of choice. While newly remodeled, the HQS space was still a government office, meaning his desk was buried inside a cube farm, which he hated. Offices made him feel trapped. Bear was grateful that most of this mission would be in the field, but he supposed computer research was a necessary evil.

Bear got a whiff of Jags's perfume a moment before she walked into his cube.

"The director asked me to lead the Singh and star chart mission last night. Find anything online?" she asked in her throaty voice. It had a rasp to it, like that of a lifelong smoker, but Bear had never smelled smoke on her.

Bear swiveled his chair to face her. Lounging against the cube wall, she sipped at her morning java, looking refreshed and ready to tackle the day in a thin black blouse and matching sleek black pants. She wasn't a traditional beauty, especially with that choppy haircut, but Bear could see how she'd been a successful model. There was something feminine and feline about the way she moved. Attractive for sure, but not his kind of sexy. Maddy, who had texted him this morning on her way to Jerusalem with AJ, was his kind of kitten.

Bear answered her question with another. "Just to be sure we're on the same page, what did he tell you?"

"Ravi Singh, the Indian ambassador to Russia, was murdered in the Maldives, and someone, maybe Russians or Spaniards, stole a star chart that might lead to a cache of dangerous superconductive material. We're to find the cache before the 'someones' do."

"Yep, and figure out who killed Singh and why they did it. Did the director call Argones?"

"Yes, he's leaving that precious boat of his and making travel arrangements." She tried to get a peek at his computer screen. "Was hoping we could tell him where to meet."

"That would be nice, but I'm comin' up short."

"Oh yeah? What's this infamous celestial chart look like?"

Bear pulled up the image on his computer and they studied it together. Like he'd told the director, the original had been torn out of an ancient codex that he'd seen in Spain. He zoomed in, then out again, recalling the vellum of the other pages in the codex, how old the pages felt. This image, with its pointed spheres scattered about the page, was clearly designed to illustrate a set of stars. But which ones?

Jags leaned in over his shoulder. "Yep, looks like a bunch of stars. Does it match a constellation?"

"No, I checked several databases."

"That's a bummer."

"Yes."

Jags pushed some confidential Defense Advanced Research Projects Agency (DARPA) paperwork aside, put her coffee cup on his desk, and sat down. She cupped her chin in her hand.

"How old is this chart?"

Could he tell her about the obelisks and the German radiometric dating? They'd have to at some point, but he wanted to clear it with Maddy first as they'd all stuck to a story that left them out. "Don't know. But at least a thousand years old, maybe two or three times that."

"Wow, that's pretty old."

He knew that the obelisks were from about 1350 BC. It felt weird obscuring the truth from a coworker, but then again, they really didn't know the exact age of the chart. "Yes. Could very well be older than Alexander the Great."

"Yikes." She crossed her legs and began to casually swing them. "What else do you know about it?"

Bear shrugged his shoulders. "Family rumor is the chart leads to a special sort of superconductive meteor."

Jags got a faraway look in her eyes. "Hmm. That's not helpful. I caught a History's Mysteries episode last week. Didn't some old buildings point to stars somehow?"

"You mean like the pyramids?"

"Yeah."

Bear chewed a tea-flavored ice cube, relieved the conversation had turned to safer ground. "Well, the pyramids at Giza do have shafts in them. Some say those vents pointed to Orion's belt back in the day."

Jags smiled. "Exactly."

A lightbulb went off in his head. "Ah, like Chichén Itzá. Solstice markers and such. You think maybe this celestial chart might have something to do with a building?"

"Perhaps, since it's not a constellation and people couldn't fly to the moon back then. Have any better ideas?"

"Nope." Bear turned back to his computer. "Let's do some more research along those lines." He searched for ancient ruins that align with stars.

"Watching you type is boring. I'll go work the Singh angle and be back in a few."

Fifty minutes later, she returned with a single sheet of paper. "What did you find?"

Bear pointed at the screen. "Turns out there's an entire field of study called archeoastronomy—basically the anthropology of astronomy."

"Human achievements related to stars. Sounds promising."

Bear turned his chair to face her. "Yes, but no easy database where we can just upload a picture and have a system spit out an answer."

"That's unfortunate."

Bear tucked another ice cube from his cup inside his right cheek. "That it is."

"We need to find an expert."

"Bowman suggested that last night." Bear referenced a yellow sticky note he'd tacked to the side of his keyboard. "Found several. World-renowned."

"Let's see the list." Jags moved her finger down the four names and stopped on one. "Anu Kumar?"

"Yeah, she's working in Mexico right now."

Jags crossed her arms over her chest. "Really?"

"Yes, why?"

Jags extended the paper summarizing her research. "She's Singh's niece."

Bear took the information and sat back in his chair. He read it quickly. "Well, isn't that interesting."

Jags nodded. "It sure is. What do you say we start there?"

"Sure, I spoke with her boss. Called all four."

"You work fast. She have cell service?"

"Tried and no. We'll have to go in person. According to her manager, she's at Chichén Itzá, a few hours west of Cancun, deep in the Yucatán jungle."

"Good work, Junior. You'll get to practice your newfound agent-recruiting skills on her." Half Jags's mouth smiled. It was more like a smirk.

Bear's heart rate ticked up a notch at the thought of recruiting an agent to gather intel. Too bad their meet and greet would be a group effort. It wasn't quite the one-on-one in a sleazy bar he'd imagined.

Jags added, "I guess Cancun is where Argones and Maddy should meet us."

"My thinking, too."

"You going to hook Maddy up with some papers?"

Bear winced. Why hadn't he thought of that? It would be best if she traveled under another name, but she was already in the air. God, he wished she'd join VanOps. He wouldn't have to keep operational secrets from her. They could live together, or at least in the same town. Get her away from Vincent. Everything would be simpler.

"Great idea, yes," he said.

"Why is her last name Marshall and not Argones, like her brother? She's never been married, right?"

"She took her mom's maiden name. Their mom died when they were kids."

"Ah. I see. How are you communicating? Does she have a secure phone?"

Bear's temple throbbed, still embarrassed about the papers, but at least he'd thought this one through. "Not yet. Since we all need to head to Mexico, I'm thinkin' to text her and have her call me from a burner phone. I can fill her in and have her meet us down there. Bring a secure phone for her."

"I suppose that's the best you can do."

"Yeah. Now let's see if we can find the perp who took the chart. Maddy said he had mismatched eyes. One white iris, one dark brown. Speaks Russian and has a call sign of Pyotr."

Bear turned his attention to the screen, chewing on more ice. A few weeks ago, he'd sat through a boring three-hour-long training on how to use the CIA's International Persons of Interest Database, or IPID. Since he managed to stay awake through the entire training, he used what he learned to search on the mismatched eyes as a distinguishing characteristic.

Nothing.

Bear searched for Russians with Pyotr as a known alias. There were 1,342 results, sorted in alphabetical order.

Chewing his ice more roughly than usual, Bear began to scroll through the list. A last name caught his attention. He clicked on the file.

Behind him, Jags inhaled sharply. On his screen, the intense, angry look in the mismatched eyes of Pyotr Argones caused Bear to spit out his ice and swear.

CHAPTER 12

"**Y**ou can drop us here," Maddy instructed the Israeli taxi driver. It was late and hadn't been a long trip from the airport. Still, the moonless streets were darker than she expected, and quiet. A dead calm.

The man pulled the vehicle over at the curb of a high-end hotel. After paying the driver with cash she'd acquired at the airport, she and AJ headed through the lobby and out the back door into an alley, where she turned to see if they had a tail.

"Is this like a Harry Potter adventure?" AJ whispered.

"Yes," she whispered back. "We want to make sure we aren't being followed. We're going to a place to keep you safe."

The boy's eyes grew wide in the dim light. "Okay."

On the plane, after a long nap, she'd purchased Wi-Fi and researched a map of Jerusalem to find the perfect route to the warehouse. Now, taking AJ's hand, she walked them to the end of the alley and turned right onto a narrow street of shops. She wished she'd had her mom's hand to hold when she was his age. She remembered not fitting in at school. One time, she'd been playing hopscotch at recess between two of the brick buildings when two cheerleaders had approached her and made fun of her lips, which were fuller than most girls'. Even though this was a common occurrence, that day Maddy had crumpled to the ground and cried her eyes out, missing her mom. Mom had full lips, too.

Maddy looked at AJ's mop of red hair and squeezed his hand, glad she could be here for him.

Two blocks down, past a butcher, a tailor, and a bakery, they turned left and the neighborhood became more industrial. Maddy glanced around for company, but sensed they were still alone on the dark street.

AJ yawned. "Are we almost there?" It had been a long day for both of them.

She pointed to a nondescript gray warehouse in the middle of the block. "We are. It's that building up there."

All the buildings on the street had tall rollup doors in addition to a man-door. The road was extra wide, Maddy assumed, so semi-trailers could back up to unload wares.

At their destination, which was marked "J6," Maddy entered a four-letter passcode on a keypad and the door clicked open. She remembered the night they first found their way here through tunnels, using clues, and smiled to herself at the contrast.

She used a flashlight to walk to the back of the building, where she found three more doors. At the middle door, a different combination, the reverse of the first, gave them access to a plain metal stairwell. Here she found a switch and turned on the lights, and they descended three flights of stairs.

"This is fun!" AJ whispered.

Not wanting to scare him, she played along. "It is." And it was true she felt safer now that they were off the street.

She ushered the boy down a long stone hallway lit by the occasional electric sconce. The floor began as tile but soon turned to crushed rock. The yellow-tinged walls looked carved from bedrock. A thousand or more years ago, someone had exploited a natural cave system to develop this hidden, underground complex that was the center of the Jerusalem Testing Society and now the headquarters of the Order of the Invisible Flame. The red scar on her shoulder verified her membership in the Order. She was proud of that mark.

He reached up to hold her hand again. "What is this place?"

"I have friends who live here."

She wanted to tell him it was a school, but figured that was best left unsaid. Still, she couldn't help but think back to all she'd learned within these stone walls. Although difficult at times, the lessons had served her well. And made her a member of the Order.

After about five minutes, the run of wall sconces ended. She turned on her flashlight and switched off the lights behind them.

"This is a little scary," AJ whispered.

"I won't let anything bad happen to you." She hoped it was a promise she could keep.

Soon they turned a corner and came to a massive wooden door. This one had no keypad, just a black iron knocker with an elephant's head.

"Can I do it?"

She lifted him up by his waist. "Sure."

AJ pulled the knocker back and let it fall.

"Louder," she said.

He pounded the knocker with gusto. The sound reverberated down the hallway.

"That should do it," she said, and then put him down to wait.

Within twenty seconds the door flung open and Edith stood there, arms spread wide. Maddy rushed to the smaller woman, bending down for a warm hug. Maddy had become quite fond of Edith in the time that they'd known each other, and suspected Edith also cared for her in a sort of motherly way. When they pulled apart, Edith's smile split her face from ear to ear.

Edith reached out and traced the bandage on Maddy's forehead, tsking and shaking her head. "Maddy, Maddy, it's good to see you."

Edith hadn't changed. Her voice was still a high twitter, like Maddy imagined a bird would sound if it spoke, and her brown eyes remained lively behind silver-rimmed glasses. With her silver-gray hair in a bun, Edith wore a uniform that consisted of white pants, a white smock, and tiny white shoes. Maddy had noticed that Edith and Samuel, the Guardians, always wore white, too, as did Master Mohan.

"It's a pleasure to see you, too, Edith."

Edith cocked her head and looked at AJ. "And who is this little man?"

AJ put his hand out to shake. "I'm AJ."

"AJ," she said, taking it slowly. "I like that. AJ. Welcome. You'll get to stay with the master. We have a full house tonight. Come in, come in." She motioned for them to cross the threshold.

They entered into a room that was clearly a pantry, lined with shelves of canned goods and dry goods. The dim light came from an oil lantern near the door to the kitchen. Edith walked through the food prep area and into the dining room, where she stopped. "Are you hungry? You've both been traveling all the day. Such a long time."

"Could I have some toast?" AJ asked.

"Of course you can. Come with me."

Edith walked back into the kitchen and pulled a round loaf out of a cupboard. With a serrated knife she cut a slice and placed it in a toaster.

"A toaster?" Maddy asked. "How do you get power down here?"

"Used to be a big problem, yes. We had to cook in the warehouse. But a few years back, we put a large solar array on top of that building, with an amazing battery, to stay low-key. And brought wires down here into the kitchen and for the computers."

"I see."

"Are you hungry, too, dear Maddy?"

"No, I'm good."

After asking him whether he preferred butter or peanut butter—he went for the nutty version—Edith handed AJ the toast and then ushered them toward one end of a long dining room table, Maddy taking a seat at the head.

"Your hair has grown a little," Edith said. "I like the hat."

Maddy pulled her cap off and twirled it in the air before catching it and putting it back on. "Thanks."

"It's good you're learning to be more practical. Idealism only goes so far."

"You can tell that from my hat?"

"No, no. I can see it in your eyes."

Uncomfortable with both the praise and the implied criticism, Maddy recalled something Edith had said. "You have a full house?"

"Yes, these things go in cycles when the royal ones pass away. Cycles. We even have a couple of your distant cousins."

"Maybe I'll have time to meet them. But I do need to catch a plane back tomorrow morning."

"So soon, so soon."

"Yes, thank you for keeping an eye on AJ until Elena arrives."

"No problem. No issue at all. Nice to have some young blood here."

Maddy had worried about that, as the place didn't strike her as one for children. But she didn't have much choice. "How is Samuel? And the master?"

"We're all getting old, Maddy." She nodded, studying AJ as he finished his toast and rubbed his eyes. "Yes, life has been good to me."

Maddy yawned. "Why do you say 'has been'?"

Edith looked at Maddy. "I feel change in my bones." Her head bobbed again. "Never mind about that, never mind. Let's go get you both settled."

CHAPTER 13

I n a quiet bedroom inside the underground Jerusalem Testing Society, Maddy tried to sleep.

Her eyes remained open in the pitch-blackness.

Was she a bad wannabe mom for dragging AJ halfway around the world? Her left index finger, a rebel, tapped the sheet once every two seconds. The tremor had begun two weeks ago, and she'd been too busy to get to the doctor. She hoped it wasn't Parkinson's disease. Her initial online research indicated it was probably a "rest tremor." Being a lightning strike survivor, she was at risk for minor neurological damage. Perhaps another reason to reconsider the adoption.

Maddy finally dozed.

The whispered sound of a blade exiting its sheath woke her from a shallow sleep. It was the only warning she had.

Immediately, Maddy twisted to hug the wall on her left, feeling the whoosh of the knife as it sliced the back of her nightshirt before landing with a soft thud in the mattress. With no time to spare, or time to fear, Maddy pushed off the wall and brought her right elbow down on her attacker's knife arm, ignoring the pain as she rolled onto the embedded knife hilt. A startled *whoosh* escaped the attacker's lips. It seemed a female sound and the subtle scent of jasmine added to the theory that the attacker was a woman.

Maddy had to keep the aggressor away from the knife. She rolled until she felt the edge of the bed, and then sprang sideways, guessing at her attacker's location. Without any light in the room, Maddy was grateful when her flailing arms wrapped around the woman's waist. The two of them tumbled to the floor in a spaghetti tangle of arms and legs.

As they rolled back and forth across the ground, the woman landed a blow across Maddy's forehead wound, knocking the bandage into one eye and reopening the wound. It stung, but Maddy ignored the seeping blood and continued to fight. Blind, she snatched at the woman's arms, frustrated again and again at her ability to squirm away.

Maddy ground her teeth and told herself to stay focused. She was going to have to improvise. Swiftly, she shoved her opponent away and then moved backward. The next time the attacker grabbed at her wrist, Maddy twisted her own hand and used the woman's momentum to push the outstretched hand away. Maddy grabbed the wrist in a familiar motion, and then with her free hand, grasped the woman's arm above the elbow and forced the arm straight. Praying that her finger's strange behavior wouldn't interfere, Maddy stood and executed a move to lead the attacker in a tight circle downward until the foe was on the floor, facedown.

With speed born from countless dojo practice sessions, Maddy implemented a *sankyo* pin. First, she kept the attacker's arm at a ninety-degree angle from her body to prevent the other woman from spinning around. Then Maddy placed one knee on her opponent's wrist and grabbed the arm above and below the elbow joint, which immobilized the attacker's entire body. As a last step, Maddy distributed her weight to her toes, which enabled quick movement if necessary.

Satisfied that the woman was going nowhere, Maddy took a deep breath. "Help! I've been attacked."

Who was this woman? Now that she had a minute to reflect, she felt like she was sinking into an ocean of fear. They had come here for a safe handoff to Elena only to be attacked in a place she thought of as her sanctuary. The cool underground air brushed her bare back where her nightshirt was ripped by the knife, and she was thankful that at least Will's frequent knife practice had sensitized her to the unique sound that had awakened her. She willed her heart rate to slow.

"Who are you?" Maddy growled in the woman's ear.

The woman chuckled, which chilled Maddy's blood further.

In a moment, footsteps padded in the hall, reminding Maddy that AJ was down the hall. She involuntarily took a sharp breath with the realization that he might also have been attacked.

The door to her room was opened by Samuel, whose skeletal frame was clad in white. The oil lamp in his hand illuminated his short silvery hair and black-rimmed glasses. He held it high to dispel the deep shadows of the bedroom, blinding Maddy for an instant.

"Is this Edith's killer?" Samuel's deep voice boomed.

As her eyes adjusted, Maddy's mouth dropped open. Outside her doorway, a white-clad figure was sprawled on the stone floor, head askew, frail neck broken.

Edith had died trying to protect her.

CHAPTER 14

AJ woke from a nightmare to the sound of Maddy yelling.

After a moment of disorientation, he opened his eyes. The old man they called Master sat on the edge of a bed, a few feet away. A lit candle in front of a floor altar threw scary shadows across the stone wall, reminding him of Batman's Batcave. Maddy had told him the rooms might have been carved from underground caves several thousand years ago. Maybe there was treasure buried in a wall. Batman would love it here.

But had Maddy really yelled? She was always calm.

AJ threw the covers off and started toward the door, wanting to help. Ever since he'd seen Pyotr on the fire escape, Maddy had seemed guarded somehow. He hoped she still wanted to adopt him. He wanted to live with her and the big yellow dog from the vineyard he called Damien. Before he got close to the door, however, the master said something in a language AJ didn't understand. Although the words were foreign, the commanding tone was not.

AJ knew the man wouldn't understand him, but he felt the urgent need to go to Maddy and help her if he could. He pointed, repeatedly. "But she shouted!"

The master stood to put on his robe, and then walked to AJ. Kneeling down, the man gave AJ a hug and spoke quiet, mysterious words in his ear. AJ closed his eyes and held on, scared. He loved Maddy. She even stopped that man from shooting at him outside her apartment building. AJ shivered in the old man's arms at the memory. He didn't like guns. Guns had killed his parents when they went to the store.

Footsteps pounded in the hall, bringing him back to the present. He caught murmured voices, a few high-pitched comments, and then the group seemed to move away. The tone of their voices suggested a lot of excitement, maybe something wrong, but nothing urgent. Did that mean Maddy was all right?

The man pointed back to the bed AJ was sleeping in a few minutes ago and motioned for him to get in. With no other option, AJ stretched out on the mattress and let the man tuck him back under the covers. Nestled in soft sheets, he took a deep breath.

The old man gave AJ a final squeeze and pulled away, looking him in the eye while raising one eyebrow, as if to ask whether he was okay now. AJ nodded. But he remained concerned. Having a real family again depended on her. And she wouldn't have yelled like that without a good reason.

CHAPTER 15

5:30 A.M.

Two hours after the attack, Maddy was still waiting for the master to join her in a private chamber. When she'd checked in on AJ, the master had told her to wait here. She pulled off the black cabbie hat and stared at it in her hands. The color was appropriate. Edith was dead, and it was her fault.

Just like the killings that happened sixteen months ago.

A tear slid down her cheek. She missed Edith already. The tiny woman had taught her much. "Perception is all, dear child, perception is all."

Maddy grimaced. Sometimes changing your perception wasn't easy.

To distract herself, Maddy looked around the unfamiliar room. Although she'd spent a week in the compound, she'd never seen this stone-walled space. It was the size of a large dining room, perhaps twelve by fourteen feet, and the floor was covered in thick, colorful carpets, the dominant color of which was red. She sat on the rugs, buoyed by cushions, as there were no chairs. A polished wooden side table held a rose-colored vase displaying a single sunflower. The chief feature of the room, however, was the modest altar featuring ruby-framed pictures of Jesus, Buddha, and a number of other holy men and women she didn't recognize. The small candles atop it provided the only light in the space.

On the way here, she'd seen a room filled with monitors, computer equipment, and the bustle of techies. No wonder they didn't have power left over for lights! She supposed if the Order was an international espionage hub, it would need connectivity.

The master walked into the room, Nanda, his translator, trailing in his wake. She studied them as they sat across from her. Apart from his white turban and new gray beard, the master looked much as he had several months ago, although his normally mischievous eyes were shadowed. Nanda was his normal elfin self, the more-pointed-than-usual tips of his ears peeking out from under his turban.

The master performed his ritual greeting. He put his palms together in a prayer position, inclined his head, and pressed his fingers to the tip of his nose. Maddy mimicked the gestures and noted his strong presence. She felt warm and safe with him.

"Greetings, Maddy. Were you hurt in the attack?"

After he spoke through Nanda, who had a Burmese accent, the master reached out to touch her forehead, eyes lit with concern. Edith had made the same motion last night. And now she was gone. Maddy struggled to maintain her composure.

Even though she was sad, she cherished the master's interest. "I'm well. The knife only scratched my shoulder and Samuel dressed the small wound."

The master continued to speak through his translator. "I'm pleased that you reacted quickly."

"Me too, or I'd be dead."

He smiled and then his expression turned somber. "This is dangerous business. We shall mourn Edith and cherish her memory."

Maddy dropped her head. "I'm sorry."

"For what?"

"For my role in her death."

"Do not be quick to judge yourself. You were not the one who broke Edith's neck. Your personality lends itself to being judgmental, yet you did nothing wrong."

"But if I hadn't been here . . ."

He frowned. "You must learn to choose your thoughts more carefully than that."

Maddy could only close her eyes and nod. She'd consider that advice later when she was less upset.

"I asked your attacker some questions to see what she had to say," the master said.

"How did you get her to tell the truth?"

He tilted his head slightly. "Well, truth is a liquid thing."

Maddy squinted, puzzled. "What do you mean?"

His eyes locked on hers. "This will be hard for you to hear because you also like to be right."

Embarrassed, she ground her teeth. He knew her too well. Even her faults. "Go on."

"Every person knows only what they believe to be true."

She pondered that for a minute. "For example?"

"If you grew up in one of those remote Amazon tribes that never had outside contact with the world, you might not know the earth was round. You wouldn't have seen an image of the globe from space. You might think it flat, believe it flat, and call it truth."

She nodded in understanding. Perception was all. As she thought of Edith, the coal in her gut burned. "I see. What did you learn from the attacker?"

"After some negotiation and discussion, she revealed that she is your distant cousin, sent here to kill you."

"From Pri—I mean, King Carlos?"

"Yes. He thinks you have the star chart, and he feels you are a threat."

She wondered how he knew she had the chart. She and Bear had talked about it once or twice on the phone. Had her phone been tapped?

"What about Will?" she asked.

"Her orders were to kill him as well, if she could. But you were her priority."

The master's eyes grew hooded while she digested this news. She knew Carlos was a slimy bastard, but sending someone to kill her? She felt a momentary chill in the dim room and shivered.

Not knowing what else to say, she changed the subject. "I called yesterday and spoke with Edith. Did she tell you the original chart was stolen?"

He nodded.

"I feel it's important to find where the chart leads," she continued. "Do you agree?"

"I do." His eyes shifted to the altar. "But you must learn to choose."

She shook her head in confusion. "I don't understand. Choose what? As a member of the Order, do I not take direction from you?"

"Yes and no."

She closed her eyes for a moment and took a deep breath. The altercation with the intruder, last night's fight in the street, worrying about AJ, deep sadness about Edith's death, and wondering where the stolen star chart would lead all weighed on her.

With an effort she opened her eyes and tried to wrap her mind around what he was saying. "Could you please explain?"

He gave her a wry smile. "In addition to protecting the world, my job is to awaken your inner wisdom, give you a taste of infinity. There are rare times on that path where obedience is necessary but also many times when you must listen to your intuition. Make your own choices about what to believe. And what to do."

It seemed he was talking in riddles. She took another deep breath to control her frustration. "And how will I know?"

"Listen to your inner voice. Learning to move your energy through your hands was a good thing. However, you have more to learn. Much more. We all see the world through the lens of our perspective, but we choose our beliefs."

She nodded, too tired and sad to fully understand.

"You must keep doing that exercise. I will show you another exercise to activate your inner eye, your intuition. You must do them both every day."

Maddy cringed—she had not been at all consistent with the first exercise he had shown her. "Okay."

He had her sit cross-legged and instructed her to imagine a beam of light streaming into the top of her skull and out the center of her brow. Then, to some finger movements, they sang a chant together that Nanda said meant infinity, life, death, rebirth. They practiced for several minutes. The edges of the rock in her stomach started to melt.

"Continue with both kriyas every day. First, *listen and feel the Power*, then practice each for at least eleven minutes."

She wasn't sure where she would find the time, but she did feel calmer, refreshed. "Thank you."

"How else may I help?"

She thought back to her last conversation with Bear. "The VanOps director wants to hire me. Would that interfere with my duties as a member of the Order?"

"If that is your path, I'm certain we could work something out. We have worked with the agency from time to time in the past."

That made her feel better. She took a deep breath.

He looked at her closely. "Now, what else do you wish to ask me?"

How did he know these things? Her guilt bubbled to the surface. "I killed those men," she blurted. "With the obelisks."

His eyes held a solemn expression. "Yes, you did. What is your question?"

It all came out in a rush. "Was it okay? I didn't want to kill them. Killing goes against all I've learned. I've been trained to use violence against itself to bring harmony back into a situation. I haven't told my sensei. If I do, I might lose my ability to teach!"

A soft knock on the door interrupted. Nanda called for the person to enter.

A short, wiry Asian man cracked the door and peered inside. His straight black hair was tied in a knot on the top of his head. "You wished to see me, Master?"

The master waved him in, and then motioned that they should stand for introductions. "Maddy, this is an Order member named Quinn."

Maddy chose to ignore the ritual greeting and shook his hand. His grip was solid without being crushing, and he had a nice smile. "It's a pleasure."

"Why, it's a pleasure to meet you, too, Madeline," he said with a thick Irish brogue.

Maddy looked at him again, recalibrating her assessment. An Irish Asian? *I'll bet he has an interesting family history.*

"Quinn is finishing some work for me with his younger brother Doyle, and will catch up to you later. You may find him useful."

Her eyebrows rose in surprise. "Thank you. I appreciate that." Since her private question to the master had been interrupted, she decided to ask a different one. "May I ask a question about the Order?"

"Yes."

"Does each family have an artifact of power? A quest?"

The master smiled. "No."

"But then, why do royal families send sons and daughters here to pass the tests? They're dangerous."

"They are, but life-changing."

"Do they all face the duel?"

"No. Because of your family's special quest, the duel is unique to your direct branch."

She frowned. "I see."

"Did facing your fears make you a better person? A better leader?"

Maddy considered herself more a teacher than a leader, but supposed they were related. And the royal families needed fearless rulers. "Yes. I suppose so."

"And do you not find it an advantage to work with a team? And enjoy working for the greater good?"

Maddy beamed. This was easier to answer. "Yes."

"Then I think we are done here. You must catch a flight home, right?"'

"Yes, I'd best get moving." Earlier, in fact, she had gone up to the warehouse for reception and received a text from Bear asking her to call him from a disposable phone as soon as she could.

"Quinn will keep AJ safe until Elena arrives."

Maddy planned to hug AJ one more time before she left. She turned to Quinn. "Thank you."

"I'll help you disguise yourself for the trip," Quinn said.

A disguise? Like what? Maddy gave Quinn a questioning look.

All she got in return was a wicked smile.

"Lastly, be careful and learn to listen to yourself," the master said. "Your attacker was part of a team. King Carlos has charged another assassin to find and kill you and your brother."

Maddy swallowed, a wave of fear threatening to breach her emotional seawall. "Did he steal the star chart? Or is he trying to kill Will now?"

"She didn't know."

"Great." Maddy figured her sarcastic tone would transcend the language barrier.

Nanda translated, and the master looked at her with kind eyes before he replied. "Do be careful, Maddy. She also told us that this Spanish killer has a tattooed face and a penchant for the garrote. He is a formidable opponent."

CHAPTER 16

In Pushkinskaya Square, the baron sat beside Pyotr on a park bench. The day was cold but the sky shone a deep, brilliant blue. The square bustled with pedestrians, who hunched inside their wool coats, hiding from the Siberian wind that buffeted their exposed faces, plumes of frozen breath escaping their mouths and noses as they rushed to get out of the cold. Not far from their bench, at the center of the square, stood the dominating monument of Pushkin, his curly hair and sideburns dusted with the prior night's snow. Full of excitement, the vivid day reminded the baron of the promise Pushkin articulated in his poem "Winter's Morning," which the baron often enjoyed while at his estate.

In one bare hand, the baron held his eagle-headed cane. In the other, a copy of the star chart that Pyotr had stolen from Maddy Marshall's apartment in San Francisco. Although his hands were cold, gloves would have prevented him from caressing his cane. And true Russians shunned gloves, even in the coldest weather.

The baron had read the report detailing the theft, but he wanted a firsthand account. Since it was the two of them, he spoke Russian. "Thank you for retrieving this, Pyotr. You did well."

"Thank you."

"Why did you not bring the Marshall woman?"

Shifting on the bench, Pyotr tucked his bandaged right hand into a coat pocket. "She surprised me. Came home early. And she had a gun."

Although he replied in Russian, Pyotr's accent had been beaten out of him when he was a child. Only a ghost of it remained.

"You're trained to handle these things. What happened?"

"First a man shot at me, then she hit my finger with a lucky bullet. My weapon spun out of my hand and I was forced to flee. But I did obtain this chart. That was my primary objective, was it not?"

Pyotr was quite arrogant. The baron would leave it for now. He glanced at the chart. "Did anyone see you?"

Pyotr's strange eyes were hidden behind dark sunglasses, but from the way his head moved, the baron knew he was searching for hidden men. Pyotr didn't answer.

The baron leaned back on the bench. "I see."

"I was wearing a balaclava. As I said, she came home early."

"Perhaps this will work to our advantage."

"How so?"

"I predict the theft will renew Maddy Marshall's interest in the chart. She and her VanOps boyfriend will try to decipher a backup copy, especially once they figure out you stole it."

"You want me to follow her?"

"Follow her from the shadows until you can kidnap her or she leads you to the prize."

"Can't our people just figure out where it leads?"

"I have our best cryptographers working to figure out if it's some type of code or map. But we must have alternate plans. Your father was certain it points to a cache of superconductive material."

"You believe it points there, too?"

"Yes, we cleaned up after his mess and found several tiny shards. Do you still have the piece that I gave you?"

"Yes. I wish it were bigger."

"That's all we recovered. They were made from a rare type of high-temperature superconductor that is most likely from a meteor. We need to find more of it. Much more."

"Why is that so important?'

The baron hesitated, tapping his cane. He knew Pyotr, one of his most competent and lethal assets, would be more inspired if he understood the stakes, but the plan was top secret. In addition, the man had been careless once, as evidenced by the interview the baron had conducted with his mother, Zola, a few hours earlier.

They were planning the ultimate modern weapon. Once they had enough superconductive material to fuel the super-fast computer, first they would use it to hack the United States' critical infrastructure. What would those American soccer moms do if they couldn't buy groceries with their credit cards? How would truck drivers deliver food to stores with no gasoline? If dams didn't work, how would the farmers and firefighters have water to use? With no power, doctors wouldn't even be able to perform surgeries.

The baron watched a flock of pigeons pick at the scraps he'd spread on the ground earlier. He thought about the Internet of Things and all the crumbs it controlled. Things like ATM machines, gas pump chips, modern cash registers, thermostats, switches and valves that controlled rail lines and dams, locks, and smart utility meters. Small, everyday devices that ran the world.

Those everyday things had a host of easily exploitable security vulnerabilities. From weak passwords and poor network encryption to the ability to deny service and shut them off. But it would take a lot of processing power to do all that at once. And they had to be ready for the second stage, to disable the military's computers.

Americans were proud of their militias and their right to bear arms. Too proud. Many had AK47s. With no food, water, power, cash, or gasoline, there would be chaos. Armed fighting for basic survival. It would make the COVID-19 pandemic look like child's play.

And the military would be needed to keep them from killing each other.

Once the military was deployed, he and his team would launch the second wave of the cyber-attack. That special quantum computer would have enough power to break all known encryption safeguards. They would have the keys to the entire NSA kingdom. They would go after military networks, servers, and storage. They'd use the supercomputer to break US top secret encryption and disrupt their command and control structure, especially their signals intelligence and communications channels. He and the team would send fake emails and false information. And delete data on hard drives and other storage. The generals wouldn't know what was going on.

The plan was to invade both coasts at once. Staging had begun in the Far East for California, and they planned to use subs and air drops for Washington DC and New York City. Midnight on New Year's Eve was zero point. Because of the large celebrations and unusual levels of alcohol consumption, analysts had determined it was the perfect time to sow the first seeds of chaos.

They just needed more superconductive material. And soon.

The baron threw more crumbs to the birds. Pyotr took off his sunglasses, clearly frustrated at the slow response to his question.

The baron was still considering a test in the Philippines, perfect because of its size and isolation. His engineering team was rabid for a trial, saying the technology was too new, and too much was at stake. They said it could be disguised as a normal hack from a member of the ransom-hungry underground, like something the famous Iceman would do. The Kremlin was also demanding a test. The baron didn't want to show their hand, but figured he would need to give in soon.

However, he decided Pyotr didn't need any of those details. "You don't need to know why."

Pyotr scowled.

"But it's the key to Russian superiority, and you are critical to its success. And time is short."

"I understand."

The baron's tone deepened. "I'm not sure you do."

Pyotr huffed. "Why's that?"

"Because your mother overheard our conversation when I assigned you the original mission to retrieve the chart. And she told the Indian ambassador."

Pyotr's mismatched eyes narrowed. "I was unaware of that. It won't happen again."

"No, it won't, because I had her tongue ripped out."

Pyotr inhaled sharply. His hand snapped the sunglasses he'd been holding, and he threw down the pieces. He leaned his face toward the baron, enunciating every word. "You—did—what?"

"Move back. Now. I have men stationed throughout the square and if you raise a finger to me, you will be shot in the head."

Pyotr stiffened, held the pose for a moment longer, and then shifted back. But a menacing look remained in his eyes. "You cut out my mother's tongue?"

"Yes. I brought it for you."

The baron took a small glass jar from inside his coat and handed it to Pyotr.

Pyotr hesitated. His hand trembled slightly as he held it up to the morning's light. The tongue was in a yellow-tinged bath of form-aldehyde, and had lost some of its pinkish color. To the baron, it looked like a smaller version of the light-brown veal tongue found in his late mother's summer salad recipe.

Abruptly, Pyotr stood and threw the glass jar on the cobbles of the square with an exaggerated, overhead baseball-pitch swing. The sound of breaking glass rang through the square, and several pedestrians turned to look before habitual Russian privacy took hold. Two of the baron's men reached under their coats for weapons, but he shook a quick and subtle "no." This was the precise reaction he wanted. They'd been told to expect an outburst and stood down.

The baron used his cane to stand and then turned and faced Pyotr's indignation. "Don't blame me for this. It was your mistake, and hers. Worse will come her way if you fail in your mission. Or discuss the plan with anyone."

They stared at each other for a long moment. Pyotr's dark eye twitched once. He reminded the baron of a crouched tiger, ready to pounce.

Time to channel that energy. "Now go," the baron commanded. "Kidnap the Marshall woman or follow her to the material."

For a heartbeat, Pyotr stood, body tense with rage, arms held tight at his sides. Then he turned and stalked off.

Appropriately motivated, the baron thought, pleased.

CHAPTER 17

The plane bounced hard as it landed, eventually rolling to a stop. Maddy was grateful for the layover in Frankfurt, as the trip from Jerusalem to Cancun was slated to take over eighteen hours. She wanted to stretch her legs, get a decent meal, and change her disguise.

As she moved down the jet bridge toward the airport gate, she felt her phone vibrate, not once, twice, but about ten times. It had found service. Well, it would have to wait.

After a short walk, during which she remained alert to make sure she wasn't being followed, she threaded her way into a tourist shop and purchased a soft green alpine hat, a beer-themed sweatshirt, hiking shoes, and a pair of men's reading glasses.

Her next stop was the ladies' room. She found a private, handicapped space, and stepped inside. Looking at herself in the mirror, she smiled. For the trip here, Quinn had suggested a cowgirl look, and she had taken to it, even mimicking Bear's drawl at customs. Wearing a disguise was a lot like dressing up for Halloween.

Except I'll be killed if I screw up. That sobering thought wiped the smile from her face.

She took off the cowboy hat, large buckled belt, the western shirt and cowboy boots. From her brassiere, she removed the pads that had added several cup sizes to her chest. The horse-like false teeth came out next, along with the cheek pads that had changed the contours of her face. It all went in the trash bin. Thankfully, her forehead was healing. She'd nixed the bandage in Jerusalem and could rely on the hats to cover it.

She went about reassembling herself as an androgynous German tourist. Besides removing her makeup and putting on the hiking boots, she wrapped her breasts in an Ace bandage before donning the Oktoberfest sweatshirt and the alpine-green hat. She also swapped out her western turquoise jewelry for a more muted set of small hoops. According to Quinn, many airports now had such sophisticated cameras that they could spot a pinkie ring in a crowd.

The false papers that Quinn had provided had matched both disguises. She didn't figure she was on the wrong side of the German government, but who knew what allies King Carlos had nurtured over the years?

Satisfied with her new appearance, she left the restroom and discovered a chocolate shop on the way to her next gate, where she loaded up on a few bars of dark. Further down the terminal, she entered a nearby restaurant, relaxed into a secluded booth, and ordered fries and a sandwich. Meat, of course. Germans love their meat.

Finally, she pulled the phone out of her purse and scanned the screen. There was a short note from Elena saying she'd gotten AJ and they were headed to the Philippines with her new French boyfriend, Garrod. And there were three text messages from Vincent, two email messages from that irate software client, and a variety of news alerts, spam, and notifications. What did Vincent want?

She read through his texts.

"Hey, I'm awake. Can't kill me that easy. LOL."

"Was hoping you'd be here when I came to, instead it's just my mom. Aack! ☺"

The last one was sent an hour later. "Miss you bad. I was a fool. Come visit and I'll buy ya ice cream!"

Her heart beat faster. She flipped the phone face down on the table and took a drink of her German beer, a light Paulaner Munich Helles. Had he just said he wanted her back? She'd figured that's where he was going with the "let's go to the shooting range" date-not-date and the whole "walk you home from work" thing, but there it was. In black and white.

She took another sip of beer. Turned the phone over. Looked at it again.

Huh. Yeah, that's pretty much what he said.

Now what? Before meeting Bear, she'd woken up every morning hoping for a text like this. One that said he'd realized what an idiot he was for dumping her for that ravishing beauty he'd met on a work trip. At least he broke up with Maddy before sleeping with . . . her. Or did he? When he came home from that trip, he threw all his laundry in the washer and had plastered her with kisses. Guilty behavior.

She swore. He probably had slept with the beauty queen. Not that it mattered now.

Her sandwich arrived, all meat and bread. Not even the pretense of lettuce. At least it tasted good . . . until she remembered the sandwich Edith had made for AJ. The last meal she'd ever made. The food turned to ashes in her mouth.

The phone buzzed with another message from Vincent. It wouldn't hurt to let him know she was busy. She texted him. "Glad you're better. Can't visit now, on way to the pyramids near the place we vacationed last year. Hoping for some beach time. Later."

She turned to the messages from the client. And closed her eyes in frustration. This particular software customer had been a pain from the start, and every step of the way toward developing his custom application was getting more painful. He was a little bit like her twin, a Negative Nellie, but Will was learning to channel his skepticism and even offer the occasional solution. Not this client.

It was all problems. Everything. Was. A. Problem. He was driving her nuts.

She put the phone down, deciding she could come up with a super-polite reply later on the plane. Clients could be such a thorn in her side. Maybe she should consider the VanOps employment offer. Was there a signing bonus? She'd have to remember to ask Bear what it paid.

Bear. She couldn't imagine him sneaking around on her with another woman. He was a good man. A solid hunk with a heart that had been tattooed with her name since high school. On the other hand, he needed to get over this jealous thing with Vincent. Even if her ex was pulling out the flamethrower in an effort to reignite the lingering sparks.

She managed another bite of her sandwich and tipped her glass. The last swallow of beer kaput, she grabbed her purse and headed toward her next flight, alert for assassins who might see through her new disguise.

CHAPTER 18

CANCUN, MEXICO

DECEMBER 20, 9:12 P.M. EST

Hours later, Maddy stood on the beachside patio of their Cancun hotel without a disguise, and showed Bear where the knife had sliced her shoulder blade during the attack in Jerusalem.

"It's not a bad wound," she insisted.

He sweetly kissed the bandage. "No, you've had worse."

She turned to face him and put her hand to her hairline. "Wait, you forgot the forehead." Sure, it was healing, but why not get something out of it?

After kissing the top of her head, he wrapped her in a warm embrace. Finally, she let herself melt, tired from a full day in the air. She and Bear had an hour alone before she could get a solid night's sleep.

After a short reunion, her brother, Will, had already hunkered down for the night in his room down the hall. A female VanOps officer named Jags had also claimed the need for an early bedtime, although she looked the type who enjoyed a night on the town. The early good-nights must have been to give her and Bear some space, as Will had never been much for an early bedtime. Maybe VanOps was changing him. Was that a good thing? Would it change her if she joined?

Bear pulled away and looked Maddy in the eye. "You did well in that knife fight. It could've gone south in a blink."

Maddy appreciated the compliment, but was reminded of the hole in her heart. "Thanks. It did go south for Edith." She kept getting flashes of the dim hallway and the slight white form lying on the floor with a broken neck.

"Yeah. That's pretty sad."

Bear took her hand, and they each sat down on a tall patio chair, facing the ocean. The moment of mourning stretched.

After a time, Bear said, "I'm worried about the tattooed assassin your attacker mentioned. What else did you learn about him?"

"Well, the main point was that King Carlos has sent a team to kill me. And Will."

"Agreed, but what else?"

"Well, the fact that this assassin likes to use the garrote on his victims probably means he's the one who attacked me on my way home from the hospital."

Bear's eyes grew wide and he raised his voice. "Um, what attack on the way home from the hospital?"

Maddy liked that Bear worried about her. "The one I haven't had a chance to tell you about yet because we didn't want to talk too long on the . . ." She paused, trying to recall the unfamiliar term. ". . . burner phone, at the airport."

"Ah. Well, tell me about it now."

Maddy recapped the taxi's flat tire and the frightening violence that had ensued just down the street from her loft. She'd lost an earring in the scuffle but was able to recover her hat. "After hearing about the garrote, I realized that must've been what the attacker used when he tried to strangle me."

"Did you get lucky, or are you just good?"

"Given how close I came to being strangled, I count myself quite lucky." She touched her neck. "Although years of training help."

Bear reached out and traced the skin, too. After a moment, he looked at her. "Sounds like two different snakes are after the same apple. And you."

"That makes sense, as the two attackers that night had very

different eyes. Did you get a database hit on the man from the loft?"

"I did, from the information you and AJ provided. The man with the mismatched eyes is a government assassin. Wanted in Ukraine and England for killing former Soviet spies."

"Ouch."

"Yes. He's also your grandfather's son with his Russian wife. Pyotr Argones."

Maddy tensed. "Well, isn't that peachy? My uncle, the killer and thief."

"Yep. The funny thing is we were right from the get-go, but instead of King Carlos *or* the Russians, it's both."

"Think we can ask Director Bowman to look into the Spanish assassin, too?" At least VanOps was good for information discovery.

"Sure, know your enemy and all." He paused. "Thanks for telling me about the Spaniard. It gives me a clue on something else that I'm not sure if I can tell you about."

"I hate that about your job." Maddy dropped her head and closed her eyes for a second, feeling overwhelmed. "It sure would be nice to just relax here with you for a week."

"It would."

Maddy looked up and out to sea. The balmy night was filled with surf sounds. She and Bear had talked about taking a vacation together, but it kept not working out. Usually because his job got in the way.

Maddy's phone chirped, signaling an email. "It's from Elena. They're on their way to the Philippines. It's a postcard." Despite it being from across the globe, the scene looked a lot like the tropical beach in front of them.

"Reminds me," Bear said. "No more need to track down burner phones. I've got a new secure phone for you compliments of Director Bowman."

Maddy looked at him and raised an eyebrow. She wondered what the director wanted in return.

Bear kissed her cheek. "No strings attached."

"You sure?"

"Well, just some nondisclosure paperwork for you to fill out."

"Okay. Let's set the phone up in the morning before we head out."

"All right." Bear looked her in the eyes. "Hey, speaking of keeping things quiet, I think we're going to need to tell the archeoastronomer about the obelisks. Jags too."

Maddy crossed her arms. "Why's that?"

"During our mission planning, I had a hard time keeping the info from Jags."

"Ah," Maddy said.

"I know you gave your word to keep them secret, but they're an important clue. The hieroglyphs that were inscribed on them might mean something."

Maddy grimaced. "You're probably right. But let me sleep on it. The master told me to keep quiet about them."

"Okay."

"I'm thirsty. Want a beer?" Maddy asked.

"Sure, thanks."

After handing over her unsecured phone, she went to the small hotel kitchen. From the stocked mini-refrigerator she grabbed a Modelo for Bear and mineral water for herself. As she walked back to the patio, she studied him. His blond, Scandinavian features reminded her of a Norse god. He sat on the edge of the tall chair, leaning forward, which showed off his muscular back and broad shoulders. The unique lightning scars on his arms were sexy. When he sat, she wasn't aware of their height difference, which she found bothered her less as time went on.

The email, however, had irritated her.

"Think we'll ever get to go to a place like that?" she asked lightly, sitting down across the small mosaic table and handing Bear his beer.

Bear put the phone down and looked at her with a twinkle in his clear blue eyes. "Sure, maybe we'll even see a beach in Mexico."

She got serious. "It would be nice if we weren't here to keep world peace. You know, like taking a real vacation together."

"I'm a guy who loves a vacation."

She and Vincent had taken several holidays a year. They even came to Cancun once—although she decided not to mention that now. Especially since they had spent most of that week in bed, having smoking hot sex. Sex with him had always been intense. At least, before he broke up with her. Until the breakup, she had trusted Vincent. Could she have that with Bear, too?

She drank from her water bottle. "Seems you love your job, though."

"I do." He paused. "What's wrong with that? You love helpin' out at the dojo, don't you?"

"Yes, but I'm not a spy," she said sharply.

Bear ran his hand through his blond buzz cut. "Whoa! Is that what's buggin' you? You decide you want to go back to that bastard Vincent?"

"Of course not!"

"He's not a spy."

"Enough." Maddy put out a hand to stop the conversation. She looked into the darkness, staring at the whitecapped sea. At the moment, their chat was a choppy storm, but like wind during hurricane season, this conversation could escalate into a category-five argument. She didn't want that. "Just give me a second."

Maddy took a deep breath and stepped a few feet away, to the other side of the patio. She owned her own emotions, like it or not. She needed to learn to discuss them without blaming him for them.

To defuse the situation, she turned and gave him a quick kiss. "I'm sorry. I'm pretty wiped out from flying to Jerusalem and back. I'm not even sure what day it is. But yes, I'm bothered that you work for VanOps."

"Will's on the team, too."

"I'm not sleeping with Will." She rubbed her forehead. "I feel irritated. I'm working to calm myself down, but it's been bothering me for a while, and I wanted to discuss it with you."

Bear took a breath, and his shoulders relaxed, perhaps appreciating that she wasn't going to explode. "Okay, where's this feelin' coming from?"

"I sense that it comes down to trust and honor."

"Could you explain?"

"I need to know that your work is honorable."

"Example?"

"Oh, you know. Little things like water boarding, Iran/Contra, assassinations, and regime change. But it's more than that. It's a culture of secrecy."

"What else? What's really bugging you?"

She threw her hands up. "I couldn't even tell my sister what you do! We had a big fight the night of the break-in."

"Ah, I see. That's awkward."

Irritation crept into Maddy's voice again. "Awkward? She's my only sister. And I *do* trust her."

"But you want to keep her safe."

Maddy sighed. "Yes, I do."

"There's the rub."

"I'm just not liking the rub. You've kept things from me before. Will you have to again? For my safety?"

Bear pulled at the label on the beer bottle. "Spying is in my blood, Maddy. It might be in your blood, too. The director still wants to hire you."

Maddy swore under her breath. "You know that's a pretty big leap for me. Life is good here. Well, in California. Being at the dojo is a blast. I make a difference for those kids. And while I could live without the software work, it's not bad."

"As cover, perhaps you could also work at a dojo in DC."

"That's the other thing. DC isn't my kind of town. Too many stuffed shirts. I'm a California girl, one who's been wanting a little less city and a little more elbow room. AJ wants a dog. Maybe it would even be neat to live at my dad's vineyard someday! Will and I are going to have to make a decision soon."

"I know. And I'd like that too. Tell you what. Why don't you see what it's like to be on this mission before you make any big decisions?"

She made a noncommittal noise.

"I know you're into nonviolence. VanOps is not paramilitary, even though we get that kind of training for self-protection. And the covert ops we do aren't the shoot-'em-up-bang-bang kind. There's a lot of leg work. It's mostly about gathering intel. Analyzing it. A mission can avoid a lot of violence in the long run."

Maddy recalled killing those men. She'd have to set aside some time for that exercise the master had shown her. Today was already gone. She'd make time tomorrow.

"How would you feel about preventing a war?" Bear continued. "Or some other type of bloodbath?"

She looked out to sea and mulled over his question. Part of her liked the idea of being important, making a difference in the world. That's why she liked belonging to the Order. But the master had given her no assignment, other than agreeing with her that they must find where the star chart led. Which, if the Russians wanted it, might fall into the category of preventing some type of bloodbath.

She looked at him. "That would feel like a special blend of pride and accomplishment."

"It would." He took a sip of beer. "Did you know the CIA stopped a Y2K plot?"

"I remember the hysteria before it. Dad bought bags of rice and beans, and we had rolls of toilet paper falling out of the linen closet. What kind of plot?"

"The kind that was designed to kill thousands of folks, including some at religious sites in Jordan, and the spot where Jesus was baptized. Some in America, too."

"That's cool. That the plot was stopped, I mean."

"Yes. I think it is honorable work and I love keeping our country safe through the world's second-oldest profession." He grinned.

She stifled a yawn, and flirted back. "I can see you in the world's first-oldest profession. You'd make a handsome gigolo."

"Ha! Me?"

"Absolutely. Just wish I wasn't too exhausted to kick your tires."

Bear finished his beer. "Why don't we get some shut-eye? I can see you're wiped out, and we have a big day tomorrow heading out to the ruins and meeting the archeoastronomer."

She rubbed her eyes, thinking back over the tedious ride from the airport, which had taken twice as long as it should have with all the starting, stopping, and looking to see if they'd been shadowed.

He reached out and held her hand. "A vacation is in the cards at some point. I promise."

As Bear led her to the bedroom, she realized that he'd never promised to be truthful with her. And when he kissed her goodnight, an annoying part of her noted that she also hadn't been forthcoming with him about Vincent, past or present. Secrets within secrets.

Her family had founded the Order. Was spying in her blood, too?

CHAPTER 19

Will rode in the back seat of the open-top Jeep Wrangler that Bear had rented for the trip to the Chichén Itzá ruins. It was an overcast morning. The road through the dense, humid jungle was roughly paved, forcing Will to hold onto the roll bar above his head as Bear navigated around potholes. Although sweat already drenched his favorite linen shirt, Will looked forward to meeting the archeoastronomer and seeing the ancient city.

When the director had called with the assignment to find out more about the murder of Ravi Singh, Will was dealing with the ramifications of his boat's alarm. His friends at the marina jumped into action and helped him haul the boat out of the water into dry dock. The vessel was already repaired and was now on its way to DC and its new mooring, along with Paulo, the formerly feral cat. That night, he'd written the incident off as an accident due to a cracked and worn water line, but in light of the recent attacks on Maddy was again thinking about the possibility of ill intent. Either way, he was caught off guard with the director's call, and felt he was still playing catch-up.

The attractive woman next to him in the back seat was a prime example. The Jeep hit a hole and they shared a quick smile as they both bounced into the air. He'd gotten to know Jags superficially when she was an instructor at VanOps training. For example, he knew that she was most recently at NSA, where she'd captured SIGINT at rest, which he'd learned meant collecting signal-related intel from cables and databases, and that her name was (understandably) short for Jarmilla Agiashvili. Of Georgian descent, she was a slender, black-haired woman with blue eyes, a perfect smile, and a personality that emanated an intriguing mix of strength and femininity. Her messy-looking hair reminded him of one of his favorite TV actresses, and she always dressed in stylish clothing. He'd felt an instant kinship to her when he noticed she wore a Rolex, as did he.

Maria had berated him once for buying the watch. Now Will wished she was around to berate him about anything.

Will also wished he knew more about Jags. As team leader, their lives were in her hands.

Before he could think on the mission further, Will felt Bear decelerate. Ahead, a red and white crossbar announced a guard station. They were in the middle of the forested Yucatán Peninsula. No other cars in sight.

"Why's there a guard shack here?" he asked.

"Good question," Maddy said, from the passenger seat.

Bear slowed further as they approached the lowered gate. When they were fifty yards away, an armed and uniformed guard left the shack. The sentry walked to the middle of the road, put a rifle to his shoulder, and fired at them.

With a loud clap, the front windshield erupted into a spider web. Will's bicep burned as shattering glass flew onto his face and clothes. The pain increased as Bear swerved the Jeep to the left, throwing him into Jags's shoulder. The network of lines on the windshield grew, distorting visibility.

"Bear!" Maddy yelled.

"Duck!" Bear shouted, and then slammed his knuckles into the broken window. Fist-sized chunks of safety glass flew up and then pinged on the road behind them. The Jeep lurched forward as Bear pounded the gas pedal to the floor.

Unfazed, the shooter stood his ground.

Righting herself, Jags grabbed ahold of the roll bar, stood, and fired three shots at the gunman in rapid succession. The man fell to the asphalt, and rolled on his belly toward the jungle.

Bear gave the shooter a wide berth as they zoomed past. Will caught a brief glimpse of a tattooed face with a fat nose beneath the man's green military cap.

"Get down!" he yelled, looking back. The man was aiming at them again from the side of the road. He reached over and pulled Maddy and Jags into their seats. A final bullet pinged off the Jeep's metal roll bar before they raced out of range around a corner.

Jags sat up and looked back down the road. "What the hell?" Her voice sounded more gruff than usual.

Will was glad the road had curved and the shooter was now out of sight. His heart pounded a fast, staccato rhythm in his chest. "That was close. Too close."

Bear put a hand on Maddy's leg. "You okay?"

Maddy yanked the cap off her head and looked behind them. Anger and disbelief colored her tone. "I'm fine, but that was the tattooed guy that attacked me in the city. The Spanish assassin. How'd he know we'd be here?"

Will took a deep breath to slow down his heart rate. "You sure? Maybe it was a deranged guard."

"C'mon, Sir Skeptalot. Really?" Bear asked.

Will hated that high school nickname. "Could be. We have no way of knowing if we were the specific target."

Maddy's voice was heavy with derision. "Except that in the last few days my apartment has been robbed, and a man with a tattooed face tried to kill me. And that's before I went to Jerusalem and someone else attacked me."

Jags looked at Will. "She has a point."

A small tremor shook Will's hands. "Okay, then what do you think just happened?"

"Somehow he found out we were heading this way and took out

the real guard," Bear said.

Will balled his hands into fists and his mind raced. "Plausible," he had to admit. But how could the man have figured out they were on the road and in the Jeep? It was unlikely there was a leak at VanOps, although . . . had Maddy flown on her own passport? If the man had some Spanish SIGINT in his back pocket, or if he'd done a lot of legwork, he could have set the trap. "If your theory is right, what can we do about it?"

"We'll keep our eyes peeled when we get to Chichén Itzá. That's the main place this road leads. It's better to take him out there," Bear growled.

"Why not circle back now?"

"A full-frontal assault while he's shooting at us? Too dangerous," Jags replied.

"Maybe we'll get lucky and the real guard will take him out for us," Maddy said. "If he's still alive."

Bear pulled over to the side of the road. "On second thought, I agree with Argones. Why don't you leave us here and we'll ambush the bastard?"

"We may have to split up at some point, but no, not yet," Jags insisted. "I may have hit him. He rolled toward the jungle. Let's be on guard at the ruins, though."

Clearly uncomfortable with her decision, Bear slowly pulled back onto the road.

Will grumbled, "I hope we don't regret it." No one responded, so he asked, "Maddy, did you fly here under your own name?"

"No, but I did have to fly into Jerusalem with my own passport. I suppose that gunman could have been watching all departing flights for women my age."

Will still wasn't convinced. "But how would he deduce we were coming here?"

"Isn't Anu Kumar well known?"

"Yes, she's world-renowned in the archeoastronomy field," Bear replied.

"That means anyone who knew about the star chart could have figured out we were headed here!" Maddy swore and pounded her foot onto the floorboard.

Silence descended over the group. Will's upper arm started to ache and he pulled aside his linen shirt. He looked down at the thin snake of blood staining his right bicep. "That bullet grazed my arm."

Jags looked over at him and smirked. "Sure did. But you'll live. I have a first aid kit in my purse."

She reached down by her feet, rummaged through a large, orange purse and pulled out a familiar-looking kit. Although her words had been rough, she was tender when treating and bandaging his arm.

As the mission's dangers became startlingly clear to Will, he was only somewhat comforted by the weight of the VanOps-issued Sig Sauer P229 pistol under his left armpit, which Bear had called a Sig while raving about the wonderful new trigger. Will didn't care about what the trigger could or couldn't do, and felt far more comforted by the knife sheaths at his wrist and ankles.

In truth, he hadn't expected to see field action already. Bowman had told him during hiring that most VanOps analysts were not limited to desk work. Still, Will's heart continued to drum like a condemned man's as he picked tempered glass out of his clothes and wondered if he should have returned fire.

Thankfully, they soon pulled into a bustling tent-filled camp. As Bear brought the Jeep to a stop, a short man with a thin black mustache and wearing a broad-brimmed hat, tan vest, and khaki pants came up and introduced himself as Adelino.

Bear gave the man a mock salute. "Can you point me to Anu Kumar's tent?"

The man pointed. "That's her purple and gold tent at the end of the row. But we haven't seen her in over two hours, which is unusual. We were just about to go looking for her."

CHAPTER 20

Five minutes after they arrived at the Chichén Itzá camp, a warm rain began to fall from the leaden sky. Maddy followed the group to a temporary shelter so they could discuss how to find Anu while keeping an eye out for the assassin. Bear wanted to leave a lookout with the cars, but Jags overruled him, arguing that since there was only one gunman, they'd be safer together.

Just as they were about to initiate a search for Anu, Adelino exclaimed that she was coming out of the jungle. When Anu Kumar entered the sphere of the camp, she was immediately surrounded by her friends and colleagues.

Maddy turned to Bear. "Looks like bees descending on a flower."

He smirked at her. "Reminds me of flies on shit."

Maddy winced. Bear had a good sense of humor, but wasn't above juvenile remarks from time to time. That comment would have gone over better with his military buddies.

As Anu made her way over to their shelter, Maddy crossed her arms and studied her. Just over five feet tall, she seemed to be in her early thirties. Her most striking feature was a fall of straight black waist-length hair that made Maddy yearn for long hair again. The delicate jewel that hung between her eyebrows and the loose red, green, and gold blouse she wore tied above her khaki pants gave her an air of mystique. Her round face looked quick to smile, but her eyes held haunted shadows, like she had just seen a ghost.

Anu set her mouth in a firm line. "What can I do for you?"

Noticing Anu's tone and body language, Maddy doubled down on her charm with an extravagant smile. "Thank you very much for your time—we are greatly appreciative."

That, at least, earned a wan smile.

Anu took a kerchief from her pocket and dabbed at raindrops on her forehead. Her musical voice held the hint of a British accent. "My boss has asked me to help you, but I have other work as well. Today is the winter solstice."

Maddy tried flattery. "Of course, we heard you're the leading expert in this field."

Anu grimaced. "We'll see. I was taking measurements at El Castillo before I took a break in this horrid rain. I don't know why everyone was concerned about my walk around the Sacred Cenote. At any rate, why don't you all follow me back to El Castillo and we can talk on the way?"

"Thank you, ma'am. I'm a history buff and would love to see it," Bear said.

While Anu led them down a graveled path in the direction of the central ruins, the rain turned to mist. Jags took pictures with her phone and Bear and Will remained overtly on edge. All three were clearly on high alert for the assassin that was stalking them.

Maddy took advantage of the moment to study the structures around her, all dating back to a time when the Maya and Toltec ruled this world. Stone columns adorned with lifelike jaguar friezes reached up to embrace the stars, and in between them were carved statues of gods and men. In some ways, the ruins reminded her of Myanmar's Bagan, where they'd found a clue that led to the obelisks.

Since the conversation with Bear, she'd been mulling over the need to bring the obelisks into this mission. The master had told her to keep them secret, but he'd also told her to listen to her inner voice. Reluctantly, she decided Bear was right. The hieroglyphs inscribed on the obelisks could be essential to figuring out this puzzle.

After a time, Anu turned to Maddy. "How is it that I can help you? My boss mentioned a star chart. Nothing else."

While they walked, Maddy told Anu about the star chart that was recently stolen from her loft. And when they arrived in the shadow of a majestic stepped pyramid, she showed Anu images of the star chart, and the obelisks with their hieroglyphic inscriptions, using her hand to protect her new phone from the weather. Jags looked over Maddy's shoulder, having not seen the photographs before now, while Bear gave Maddy a "good-decision" wink and jumped in to tell Anu about the age of the vellum. Seeing the obelisk secret was out of the bag, Will added that the obelisk shards had been carbon-dated to about a thousand-to-fifteen-hundred years before Alexander the Great. Maddy left out how she had channeled energy through the obelisks and killed two men in the process.

Jags gave Bear a pointed stare, probably giving him hell for leaving her out of the loop until now.

"Can you decipher the chart for us?" Maddy asked.

Anu ran the beads of her bracelet between her fingers. "I need more information. What else can you tell me?"

Bear hesitated, before saying, "We suspect the star chart leads to a cache of the same type of material that was used to make the obelisks. Perhaps a meteor."

A light sparked in Anu's eyes. "What makes you think that?"

Will moved to stand next to Maddy. Smartly dressed as ever, he looked leaner and stronger than the last time she'd seen him, and she found his well-trimmed beard not only hid the childhood scar on his chin but also seemed to make him look more serious and intelligent. At least until he leaned over to whisper in Maddy's ear. "Hope you don't need to throw lightning from a huge meteorite. Might kill us all."

Maddy swatted him away. His eyes danced with delight and he gave her his boyish, lopsided grin. So much for serious.

"The obelisks are made from lorandite, which doesn't occur on earth," Bear was telling Anu. "And it's important due to its potential scientific utilization as a superconductive material."

Anu stiffened. "What type of utilization? That's not my field."

Will ran a hand through his wavy black hair. "Well, those high-speed trains in Japan use superconductors. There's also a lot of interest in crazy-fast quantum computing, as well as possible uses in communications and medicine, like MRI machines."

Still mindful that the gunman may have followed them, Maddy listened to the forest and watched the path for any sign that he'd found them.

"Interesting. I had no idea." Anu idly rubbed her upper arm. "Who created the star chart that may or may not point to this stellar superconductive material?"

"Stellar? Good one." Will smiled and flicked a bug from his expensive white linen shirt. "Perhaps the Egyptians."

Anu's posture remained rigid. "Most ancient civilizations studied the stars, including the Chinese, the Babylonians, the Irish, the Scottish, the English, the Maya, Aztec, and Inca, as well as Native Americans. It would help to narrow down the search."

"The twins' Iberian ancestor, Ramiro, hid the obelisks." Bear said, nodding to Maddy and Will. "But we suspect they were Egyptian because of the hieroglyphic writing on them and the choice of form. That said, we never had a chance to carbon-date the chart and have no idea who created it."

"That complicates things. Let me think this over while we look at El Castillo. Also, when we return to camp, let's have Adelino take a look at the hieroglyphics. He's our Egyptian expert," Anu said.

Bear's eyes wandered toward the pyramid. He was clearly dying to learn more about it. "What research brings you here to Chichén Itzá?"

"Where do I start? There's El Caracol, or The Observatory, down the road. Different windows align to different celestial events, everything from summer solstice sunrise and the northernmost place Venus sets to the winter solstice sunset." Anu looked up at the sky. "I'm hoping for a break in the weather. Like I said, I'd love to discover something new here. My career could use a big break."

Bear nodded. "Bummer about the rain."

Anu continued, waving her hand at the stone monument in front of them. "This is the most iconic structure in Mexico: a twenty-five-meter-high step pyramid called El Castillo. In English it's The Pyramid of Kukulkán, also known as *The Castle*." Bear opened his mouth to ask a question, but she pushed on. "And there's much to learn throughout the entire city. Maya watched the skies, had sacred stars, tallied the days, and performed rituals with their temples."

"What about the Russian doll pyramid effect?" Bear asked.

Maddy smiled to herself; Bear had studied up on the place.

"What's that?" Will asked.

Anu gestured with her hands. "A few years ago, using a type of penetrating radar, archeologists discovered a smaller third pyramid inside the one we already knew rested beneath this larger outer pyramid."

Will's green eyes lit up. "A pyramid within a pyramid within a pyramid?"

"Yes, that's why my friends are here. I'm here to look at the winter solstice and to study what the Maya and Itzá peoples knew about the stars. Ancient civilizations can teach us many things. For instance, last year mathematicians took a closer look at a Babylonian trigonometry tablet and realized their mathematical methods were more advanced than our own."

Will nodded his head several times. "I read about that."

"What does this pyramid have to do with the stars?" Maddy asked.

"Nearly everything! The whole pyramid is a sacred calendar."

"Can you elaborate?" Jags asked.

"Yes. As an example, there are four flights of stairs, one on each face of the pyramid. Each flight has exactly ninety-one steps. When you add the top platform, you get 365 days in a year."

Jags tilted her head. "That's fascinating."

"It is. Another example. There are eighteen terraces on each side of the stairways, equating to the number of months in the Maya religious calendar."

Bear swatted a mosquito. "That's neat, but isn't the real spectacle here at the spring and fall equinox?"

Anu favored him with the first genuine smile Maddy had seen from the woman. "Yes. Thousands gathered then and now. The Maya aligned the pyramid to make a special optical illusion during those times. As the sun sets, the terrace corners cast diamond-patterned shadows, representing the body of their feathered serpent god, Kukulkán."

Maddy pointed to the bottom of the stairs. "Do those huge carved snake heads help the illusion?"

"That they do."

"What about winter solstice?" Maddy persisted.

"Similar thing, smaller scale. This pyramid has two sides bathed in light, two in darkness." Anu pointed southwest, along a path. "But see the smaller pyramid over there, the Ossario?"

They all nodded.

"Late in the afternoon of winter solstice—today if the weather clears—a serpentine shadow can be seen wriggling its way down the face of the structure on one of those balustrades."

Maddy could imagine the cheering crowd and the magic as the sun moved lower and created a magnificent snake god. "Too bad we won't be able to see it." From the pained look on Bear's face, she could tell he agreed.

Anu shook her head. "It is. The effect will last for another day or two. No more. That pyramid has only been reconstructed in the last twenty years. I'm here to study the phenomenon, along with the fascinating observatory I mentioned earlier. The design of El Caracol is unique in the world. There is much for me to study here." Anu opened her notebook. "Now, if you'll excuse me."

She collected a few dimensions from the ancient stone pyramid with a yellow tape measure, jotted them down, and then led them back toward camp.

While they walked back along the gravel path, Anu again rubbed her upper arm. Now the spot looked red and a little swollen.

"Is your arm okay?" Maddy asked. "I have some salve in my purse."

Anu looked at her arm, frowning. "No, I'm fine. Just a nasty mosquito bite. You get them out here," she said with a hint of patronization.

Maddy already had a few bites herself, so she changed the subject. "Bear, you mentioned the star chart doesn't relate to any known constellation. Is that right?"

Bear looked at Anu. "Yes, that's why we thought you might be able to help."

Anu looked down at her dirty khakis. "I'm sorry. I've never seen anything like it. I'm sure you could find someone more qualified."

"What if your assistance could lead us to your uncle Ravi's killer?" Jags asked.

Anu froze, and looked at Jags with wide, shocked eyes.

CHAPTER 21

The recruitment was not going well.

Bear felt Anu's surprise like the waves of a small explosion. The woman, who smelled oddly of fear, stopped walking and turned to look at Jags. Like ducklings following their mother's lead, Maddy and Argones also stopped. Bear had not told Maddy about the connection Anu had with Ravi Singh for security reasons, assuming Maddy was read into only the star chart part of the mission and not the Singh part. With Jags throwing it out there, clearly his assumption was wrong. He berated himself and wondered if he and Maddy would fight about it later.

At last, Anu composed herself enough to speak. "What does my uncle Ravi's death have to do with the star chart?"

Exactly what they were sent here to find out. But to do that, they needed to stay alive. As he had been doing for the last hour, Bear scanned the area for the Spanish assassin. He had a better than average sense of smell, which had saved his bacon a time or two when he was in the marines, so he flared his nostrils and took a deep breath, seeking any sort of strange scent. Nothing.

Having stirred the ant's nest with her question about Ravi, Jags now dissembled. "We believe he may have been killed because of information he'd been given about it."

"Given to him by whom?" Anu pressed.

"I'm not at liberty to say."

"Oh, come on, this is my uncle's death we're talking about!" Anu's voice quavered.

"I understand and I'm sorry. What I can say is that your assistance with the star chart might lead us to his killer."

Radiating pure disgust, Anu marched off for the cluster of archeologist tents. The rest of them followed in her angry wake.

As they walked, Bear wished they could take time to explore this ancient city. He'd read one of the largest ball courts in Mesoamerica was here. Its acoustics were amazing. You could hear a conversation happening at one end of the court while standing almost a hundred feet away at the other end of the field. Some archeologists believed losers of the games also lost their heads. Fascinating culture. If you were a winner.

There was a crash in the forest to their right. A gunshot? Broken branch? He pulled his weapon and swiveled his head to search the dense underbrush, but saw nothing unusual. From his right, Argones threw a knife into the forest. Bear's heart rate went into overdrive as the blade whooshed through the humid air. Bear felt the tension of battle.

Without warning, Argones jumped off the trail.

Maddy raised her voice. "Will, where—?"

Her twin put a hand out as if to say, "Wait there," and disappeared into the jungle. Bear didn't obey, following close on his heels.

Thirty seconds later, Argones found his knife, embedded in an iguana. Bear breathed a sigh of relief and holstered his weapon, but his heart still raced; the assassin was out there. He could feel it.

"Did you have to kill it?" Jags asked when they returned with Will's skewered kill.

Argones looked at her sideways. "I heard something. Thought it was dangerous."

Jags put her hands on her hips and bit back the sarcastic comment Bear could see forming on her lips.

Argones winced and seemed to withdraw into himself at the criticism. As far as Bear was concerned, he was just glad the man's aim had improved enough to take out an iguana in a rain forest. Bear patted him on the back. "'Better safe than dead' is a fine motto, bro."

When they arrived back in camp five minutes later, Anu's mouth was still set in an angry line. She motioned for them to have a seat at a lopsided picnic table. The camp was silent and still. Bear wondered if all the archeologists had gone back into the field. But something felt off. It was too quiet.

Anu pointed to a bright blue cooler atop a scarred plank. "I'll find Adelino to have him look at the hieroglyphs."

Bear filled up four water glasses from the cooler and distributed them to the team, wishing for an icy cold glass of sweet tea. He sat down next to Maddy, rubbing her back for a second, but alert for trouble.

Argones still seemed quiet, perhaps still stinging from Jags's comment about the dead lizard. Bear turned to her. "Do you have a thing about iguanas?"

Jags took a deep breath, but before she could respond, Anu burst out of a far tent.

"Adelino's dead!"

CHAPTER 22

Will turned around in time to see Anu rush away from the camouflage-colored tent, yelling again that Adelino had been killed.

He jumped to his feet and she ran into him. Unsure what to do, he folded her in his arms as she dropped her head to his chest and wailed.

Jags was right behind him. With gun drawn, she parted the tent's curtained flap, peered inside, and grimaced. "Looks like an execution-style killing. Let's check the rest of the camp." She looked at Bear, whose pistol was drawn as well. "Bear, take that side. I've got this. Argones, draw your weapon and stay here with Maddy and Anu."

Will gently extracted Anu from his embrace so Maddy could usher the distraught woman over to the picnic table. As Anu continued to sob, Will reached into his shoulder harness, drew his pistol, and caressed the knife he held in his left hand. He'd had a bad feeling ever since they'd walked back into camp. The place was unnaturally quiet. There weren't even birds singing.

Although he was unnerved, he was shocked that he didn't feel scared. Maybe that would come later, but in the moment, he felt an

111

exhilarating rush of awareness as he evaluated every sound, every movement. People teased him about his suspicious nature, but he was learning that it prepared him well for when true danger struck. He was seldom caught off guard.

Bear and Jags completed their sweep of the camp and jogged back toward the table with jaws set and eyes dark.

"What did you find?" Maddy asked.

Bear's drawl was more pronounced than usual. "Nothin' good. Four more bodies, up around the last tent. Looked like they were talkin' in a group when they were ambushed. All shot in the head."

"Must've used a suppressor or we'd have heard the shots. We weren't that far away," Jags added.

Will wondered if that's what he'd heard in the distance, prompting the sacrifice of the iguana.

Anu slammed her fists onto the wood table. "No! No!"

The woman needed to be quiet. The killer was still out there.

Reading his expression, Maddy whispered something in her ear. Anu nodded once before crossing her arms on the table and dropping her head into them to cry like a child.

Maddy looked up. "Those were her friends. All of them. On top of the death of her uncle."

Will tapped his leg. "We need to get out of here. Now!"

Maddy put her arm on Anu's back and whispered something else, and the sobbing slowed.

Bear's eyes lit up. "I think it's time now to split up. We'll be safer and more efficient. Argones, Jags, why don't the two of you take the Jeep and focus on the obelisks? Try to find someone who can decipher the inscriptions. Maddy, Anu, and I will take a car from camp and concentrate on the star chart."

Jags nodded her approval.

Will started moving, mentally urging the rest of the group to do the same. "Neither group should head back to Cancun. If we've been made, we need to throw off our pursuers."

Maddy talked with Anu ⏹for a moment, and then reported in a

fast voice, "She says there are two towns within a few hours' drive. Merida, closer and to the northwest, and Chetumal, south, on the Belize border. Both have small airports. She has other friends at a dig outside Chetumal and thinks we can be safe there tonight. It's a fairly random location."

Bear touched Anu's arm, but she pushed his hand away. "That's fine. But we need to hurry—let's go."

Red eyes still overflowing with tears, Anu looked at Will and Jags. "On the pictures of the obelisks, there was writing about winter solstice, but most of it I couldn't read. The hieroglyphs were coded somehow. The priests often used new glyphs to create specialized puns or codes. You need to go to the Valley of the Kings in Egypt. Gerald Crookbottom is there. If anyone can figure out what they say, he can."

Jags and Maddy nodded their assent. Bear's eyes scanned the jungle, while his hands were on Maddy, trying to push her toward the parking lot.

Winter solstice was today. It would take an entire day to get to Egypt. If there was something to be learned about that date, they'd best make haste. For many reasons. Will bounced up and down on his toes, wanting to run for the cars. *At least I'll get to travel with Jags.*

Bear threw Will the Jeep keys. "Jags, I assume you'll clear tactics with the director. Now let's get out of here."

CHAPTER 23

Maddy, Bear, and Anu ran for the parking lot outside the archeological camp at a dead sprint. Fortunately, it wasn't far, but Maddy's heart was thudding. A handful of cars, trucks, and SUVs were parked ahead.

Anu headed for a white Range Rover. "Over here." She jumped into the passenger seat and turned to Bear, her voice shaky. "I'm upset. Will you drive?"

As Bear got into the driver's side, Maddy went for the back seat. After Anu tossed Bear the keys, he fired up the vehicle and sped out of the lot, kicking up gravel and dust in their wake.

Anu pointed right. "That way."

They pulled onto a paved road, and a sign appeared for Chetumal.

Maddy turned around and checked for a tail. She breathed a little easier when there was no sign of pursuit. "Nobody back there."

"Good," Bear replied.

As her heart rate slowed, Maddy kicked herself that they'd not dealt with the attacker back in the woods. Had he killed all the archeologists? Or was someone else behind the crime? Was it a message? Had they meant to kill Anu too? What did the murders have to do with the star chart, if anything? If Anu was right about the short winter solstice timeline, were they already too late?

The Range Rover thundered away, while Maddy's head filled with questions. But there were no easy answers.

CHAPTER 24

Will watched Bear, Maddy, and Anu peel down the gravel road in their Range Rover. A large cloud of dust followed them. If anyone was watching, they had just announced their departure to the world.

He figured the gunman from the guard shack for the massacre of the archeologists at the camp, but at the moment was more concerned about getting out of Mexico alive.

Will fired up the Jeep's engine, shifted into gear, and took off, trying not to raise another cloud of dust.

"I'll check our escape route," Jags said.

"Okay, but can you see if there's some sort of paper in the glove box first?"

Jags rummaged around and handed the rental contract to Will. Most of the windshield was gone. He used the paper to protect his hand as he punched out the remaining glass. He heard it shattering on the road behind them.

Where were they going? He had a general idea that they needed to head northwest but needed specifics. They hit the first intersection. He sensed a left turn.

Confirming, Jags looked at her sat phone. "Go left."

"This road takes us into that small town, right?"

"Yes, then we can either cut up and hit the highway, or continue on this road, which leads to Merida."

"I like the backroad option—you?"

"That suits me."

With his breathing finally slowing, Will found himself appreciating Jags as a travel companion. Not only did she still look the part of the model he'd heard she once was, he liked her steady, no-nonsense attitude, laced with a bite of smart-ass. And there was something different about her, something that intrigued him, but he couldn't tell yet what it was.

Will checked his mirrors. *Perhaps we haven't been followed.*

In a blink they were through the small town of Piste. The place had a lichen-covered church, a motel called the Piramide Inn, and a water tower, which stood as a proud sentinel over the whitewashed homes.

"See the motorbike behind us?" Jags asked. "It's coming up fast."

He looked back. "Yep, see it now."

Even with the Jeep's accelerator to the floor, the motorbike could easily catch them, if that was its intention. The Jeep was no nimble race car.

Jags pointed. "Side road up ahead. Take it!"

Will liked that idea. Not only could they use it to see if the bike had nefarious intentions, they'd have better luck evading any shots if they could dart into the trees. He slowed as much as he dared and jammed the Jeep down the narrow, dirt track.

In California, he'd have thought it a logging road—here he wasn't sure. Perhaps it led to another tiny town, or a plot of land for farming? He was glad to see that it curved.

Jags turned around to watch the road as Will kept his eyes on the rearview window.

"He followed us," Jags said. Then, "Shit, he has a gun."

Will swore. This was a bad situation. He thought about telling her to get her weapon ready, but she was his supervisor.

Jags was a step ahead of him anyway. Her weapon was already in her hand as she searched for an opening between the trees and dust.

Just in time, too. A bullet pinged off the back of the Jeep. Will waited for Jags to get off a few shots before he twisted the wheel back and forth. Even with the recent rain, Will was glad to see the movement kicked up a fair amount of earth. They needed every advantage as the motorbike gained on them.

Jags put a hand on his arm. "Steady it for a sec."

As instructed, Will straightened out to allow Jags time to shoot. He watched his mirror. A tiny spark flew from the front of the bike.

Ping! Another of their pursuer's shots hit the Jeep. Will returned to jerking the Jeep's wheel back and forth.

"That hit the wheel well. He's aiming at the tires," Jags said.

"Return the favor!"

"I can't! Visibility is horrible."

"Shoot low."

"Okay. Drive straight again for just a minute."

Will slowed his aggressive driving tactics, allowing Jags to release an angry volley of shots.

The strategy worked. The rider flipped over the handlebars and landed in the dirt, unmoving.

"Ha!" Jags announced, triumphant.

They exchanged a high five.

He steadied the wheel and accelerated. "Let's hope that buys us time to get to Egypt."

"It better."

He took a deep breath. "I wonder if that was the killer from the camp."

"That's what I'm thinking. And from the guard shack." She reached for her phone. "I'm calling the local police. They need to know about those murders, and maybe they can catch this guy."

"Good idea. We need to keep moving." Will drummed his fingers on his leg. "Or do we? Maybe we should go nab him while he's passed out. We could question him, see what he knows. Otherwise he may continue to be a thorn."

Jags frowned and looked back. "Hmm, that's dangerous, but I think you're right."

They turned the Jeep around, located the motorbike, and searched the deep jungle. But there was no sign of the rider.

CHAPTER 25

As Bear accelerated through the jungle toward Chetumal, his mind raced. Why hadn't there been a firefight once they'd returned to the tents? The killer must've gone back into the jungle to search for them, although he probably was on their trail now. God knows they all made enough noise to wake an alligator when they left.

So far, Bear saw no sign that they were being followed, but he hoped like hell that didn't mean the killer was following Argones and Jags instead. He spared a glance in the rearview mirror at Maddy. Her green blouse looked disheveled, and her lovely face sagged with worry and exhaustion. Maybe it hadn't been such a great idea to bring her along.

Anu had been quiet during the drive, staring out the passenger side window of the Range Rover. He supposed he'd be quiet, too, if all his friends had just been killed. "I'm sorry about what happened back there," he tried.

Maddy leaned forward and put a hand on Anu's shoulder. "Me too. I'm sorry for your loss."

Anu shrugged off the touch. "First my uncle Ravi and now this . . . this massacre. Do you think these deaths have anything to do with the star chart?"

In the rearview mirror, Bear exchanged a quick look with Maddy. How much to tell Anu? Maddy nodded, agreeing that it was time to put more cards on the table if they had any hope of getting her to fully cooperate. In class, Bear and Will learned an acronym shortcut about how to recruit potential agents. MICE: money, ideology, compromise, ego. He figured Anu would respond to stroking her ego. Granted, no one had really taught him how to recruit a potential agent who'd just had so much of her life torn away.

Still, he had to try. "We could really use your expertise. We didn't have a chance to tell you when we met, but Maddy has been attacked several times, including the night the chart was stolen."

Anu closed her eyes, bowed her head, and rubbed the bridge of her nose with her right hand. "Besides my friends, I'm going to miss the rest of solstice week at Chichén Itzá."

Bear patted her arm with caution, treating her like the angry, wounded cat he once saved. He still had the scars from its claws. "I know. But it's a good idea to stick with us for a while. We'll do our best to keep you safe."

Anu clenched and unclenched her fists several times before surreptitiously wiping a tear from her cheek. She took a deep breath. "Who is it that is after this special chart?" A note of anger crept into her voice. "This chart that's so extraordinary that everyone needs to die for it." Anu slipped a beaded bracelet off her wrist and began to move the orange beads through her fingers with rhythmic, practiced gestures.

"We're not sure exactly," he admitted, "but both the Russians and the Spaniards appear to be involved in the hunt."

"We're pretty certain there's an international security risk, as anything the Russians want is something they shouldn't have," Maddy added. "Especially something they're willing to kill for."

Anu looked sideways at Bear. "But all you have to go on is a copy of the chart and a report from Germany about the age and composition of destroyed obelisks?"

"You're catchin' on."

Anu's breath exploded from her lungs. "It's a needle in a haystack!"

Maddy sat forward in her seat. "Well, we also have the inscriptions on the obelisks. Thank you for the tip on the Egyptian cryptographer."

Anu sighed. "Can I look at a picture of the chart again?"

Maddy handed Anu her new phone. They'd transferred all her data to it this morning. "Here you go."

Bear watched Anu out of the corner of his eye as he drove. Would she thaw? She'd had one hell of a day.

She brought the image close to her face, increased the resolution, and gazed out the car window again. "It still doesn't look familiar. You said back there that it didn't match any constellations. I assume you mean the eighty-eight official sets of stars. How about asterisms?"

"What are they?"

"Familiar groupings of stars. The Big Dipper, for instance, is part of Ursa Major."

"I see."

"Did you check the pattern against a database?"

"A few," Bear replied.

"Which ones?"

"NASA, Yale, and an open-source planetarium."

"Those should be fairly complete. We have one other that we could check. It's more historical, less scientific."

"That sounds good. We have an office in Belize City," Bear said.

Anu stiffened. "No! We said we were going to Chetumal first."

Maddy interjected, "I don't think we should go to Chetumal. We could have been overheard as we left camp."

"But I have friends at that dig!" Anu cried. "I'd feel safer there."

Bear's tone was colder than he intended. "Would you prefer they all die like your friends at Chichén Itzá?"

At that, Anu slammed her small fist against the closed window and refused to say another word the remainder of the trip.

CHAPTER 26

When they arrived in Belize City, Maddy was starving. "Can we eat before we head to a hotel for the night?"

Bear met her eyes in the rearview mirror. "Good idea. I'm hungry too. Find anyplace worth checking out?"

Maddy had looked online with her phone. "I did. Looks like the best food in town is on a pier. Anu, are you okay with that?"

Anu's demeanor remained quiet and frosty.

When she didn't answer, he said quietly to Maddy, "Let's go."

Maddy gave Bear the address and he navigated to the destination.

The restaurant had a traditional thatched roof and a big wooden deck over the water. It reminded Maddy of Fisherman's Wharf, minus the fog. They had missed sunset, and dark skies blanketed the harbor.

They asked for a discreet booth in the back. An attractive waitress with shoulder-length black hair, wide eyes, and a wider smile sat them and brought the menu.

As they looked at food choices, Maddy reflected on Anu's odd behavior, how she only seemed to want to help them in fits and starts. True, the woman had a lot to grieve. Was that all it was? *My own grief is still fresh*, she thought. Or was there something else going on with her? Even before they found all her friends dead, her demeanor had seemed suspicious. Then there was the anger in the car, but that could be written off as not being able to be with her friends or finish her work back at the dig. Maddy didn't like dealing with her own irritability, much less other people's rage. However, there was something about Anu that just felt off.

Bear tried to break the ice. "Menu looks good. What are y'all going to have?"

Anu ignored the question and stared out to sea.

Maddy put her menu down. "I think I'll try the stew. Fish, cassava, plantains, and yams . . . all boiled together with coconut milk. What's not to like?"

Bear laughed. "Have at it. I'm going to have lobster, conch fritters, and key lime pie."

Maddy smiled at his obvious love of good food. If she ignored Anu and their circumstances, maybe she could pretend it was the vacation she'd been wanting.

The waitress took their order. At least Anu spoke up to order her own food.

The topic of her relationship with Bear reminded Maddy of Vincent, and she hoped he and AJ were both faring well. If she joined VanOps, the door would close on Vincent, which Maddy, in this moment, was okay with. Times like now she felt she was better off without him. He was always a little too happy-go-lucky, especially when it came to flirting with other women, like their good-looking waitress. Maddy appreciated that Bear only had eyes for her, even if they still had some trust issues to work out.

Continuing that mental thread, Maddy wondered what it would be like to live in the same place as Bear. But how would she keep AJ safe if she joined VanOps? She wasn't even a member, and AJ's life was already at risk again. In a town full of spies, would there be some type of secure schooling? Would VanOps training give her skills to keep him safer?

The meals arrived, interrupting her reverie, and they all dug in to food that certainly earned its reputation. Forty-five minutes later, Bear excused himself to the restroom, and Maddy wondered if Anu was ready to speak yet.

"How was your dinner, Anu? Mine was spicier than I expected."

"I was hungrier than I thought I'd be," Anu admitted.

"Your grilled fish looked pretty good."

"It was." Anu hesitated. "I'm sorry about earlier. It's been a tough day."

"It has."

"I've realized you were right to not put my friends in danger. Thank you."

"You're welcome. It's hard to think clearly when you're upset."

"Yes. I was in shock. I've decided I want to help."

Maddy's heart beat a little faster at this surprising announcement. "That's wonderful." She hoped Anu would stop flip-flopping for good.

"Perhaps, as Jags said, my assistance might lead to Uncle Ravi's killer. Or perhaps it will keep that superconductive material out of dangerous hands. Either way, please forgive my rude behavior and allow me to provide support."

"Certainly."

The waitress checked in to see if Bear still wanted the key lime pie, and Maddy said he did. She decided on mousse for dessert. She was a sucker for chocolate. Anu passed on anything sweet.

When Bear returned, Maddy reported that Anu had offered her formal assistance on the mission.

Bear looked at Anu. Maddy thought she detected a gleam of pride in his eyes. "That's fantastic. Welcome to the team."

"Thank you. I've been thinking that it would help if we knew more about who created the chart. The Egyptians are certainly possible, given the obelisks, but even if we narrow it to Egypt, their influence was felt for a thousand miles in several directions, and over the course of millennia."

The waitress brought Bear's pie and Maddy's chocolate mousse. Maddy looked at Anu. "That doesn't narrow it down as much as

I'd hoped. Can you tell us a little more about the ancient sites?"

"Yes, it's been my focus of study for the last decade. Ancient civilizations combined their use of the stars with architecture and everyday life in a number of interesting ways. First, they observed them, like the Inca sky walkers at Machu Picchu."

Bear took a bite of pie. "I've always wanted to go to Machu Picchu. What's your favorite there?"

"Tough question. There's a building called the Torreon. The northeast window is centered on the June solstice sunrise, while the tail of Scorpius can be seen rising through the southeast stone opening."

"That's pretty cool. What else?"

"Ancient peoples used the skies for worship. Historical sites are full of divine planets and sacred stars. Humans had gods of rain, fertility, and storm to honor the connection between sky and earth."

"Like the Roman gods who governed the days of the week?" Bear asked.

The last of Anu's icy demeanor melted, and she beamed at him. "Yes. Saturn's Day to 'Saturday,' Moon and 'Monday', are pretty obvious, but most people don't know that Wednesday is from the Latin 'Dies Mercurii', or the day of Mercury. The other days of the midweek are similarly named. Nice job."

"Thanks. I like history. Tell us more please."

"We've planned entire cities around the stars, as at Beijing and Teotihuacan," Anu said.

That amazed Maddy. "Beijing? Really?"

"Oh, yes! Beijing's primary axis is north-south and is laid out on a sacred cosmological plan. The Monument to the People's Heroes, the flagpole in Tiananmen Square, and Mao's Mausoleum are all on the main axis between the two great gates of old Imperial Beijing."

Bear's tone held surprise as well. "Didn't know that."

"Many of their architectural names read like an astronomy litany, too. Sun Gate, Gate of Heavenly Peace, Earthly Tranquility, etc."

"Fascinating. What else?"

"We've tallied days using stone rings—"

Maddy interrupted, saying, "Stonehenge!"

Anu smiled. "Yes, among others. There are rings all over the British Isles and even some in Africa."

"At least I knew one," Maddy said.

Anu continued. "Humans have kept vigils with sun priests, buried our dead in pyramids and tombs aligned with the stars, and created temples that are physically and symbolically united, such as the solar sanctuaries of Egypt's New Kingdom. I could go on for hours."

"I've studied some of the places, but didn't know the depth and breadth of the astronomy of those lost civilizations. I'm impressed," Bear said.

"Don't be impressed by me. Be awestruck by those earlier peoples and how much they knew about the ancient skies. Astronomy was a common theme across most prehistoric cultures."

Maddy felt overwhelmed. "No wonder you called it a needle-in-a-haystack search."

Bear frowned. "At least we have some good clues on the obelisks, and perhaps our search tomorrow will turn up something in your database. Let's find a hotel and get a good night's sleep."

The restaurant took Mexican *pesos*. They paid the bill with cash and headed to the restaurant exit. With Anu on board, and a plan of attack, Maddy felt lighter. Until Bear insisted on checking under the car for explosives.

CHAPTER 27

MERIDA, MEXICO

DECEMBER 21, 8 P.M. CST

Under the watchful eyes of the cathedral's twin towers, Will and Jags strode through Merida's shadowed town square, the Plaza Grande, searching for a place to eat while keeping an eye out for their attacker. When they hadn't been able to get a flight out until the next day, they'd decided to act as bait.

Although well after dark, the square was vibrantly alive. Street vendors hawked panama hats, hammocks, beautiful jewelry, and savory meat pies. Others offered to paint a handsome portrait of the two of them in ten minutes flat. After hearing the horses *clop-clop-clop* through the streets, Jags had wanted to tour the town in a blue-and-white carriage, but Will vetoed the suggestion. He was hungry and feeling antsy that they hadn't found the man on the motorbike yet.

The sights and sounds reminded Will of the many times that he and Maria had wandered the evening streets of São Paulo. He wondered how the new cat was doing in DC at the boarding facility.

The church's hourly bells began to peal, and he turned to view the open archways and unique Spanish architecture on the bone-colored towers. The steeples stood like matching sentinels, ones that had guarded the town for generations.

Abruptly, Jags took off running after a barefoot girl who looked to be around ten. "Hey! Come back here!"

Although the girl had home court advantage, Jags had longer legs. She and the young girl ran through the square, around merchants, palm trees, and flag poles. Within a minute, Jags was marching the girl back toward Will as vendors shook their heads with pinched mouths and sour eyes.

Will got a better look at the child as they approached. Her face had a slash of dirt across the forehead and her mismatched clothing was at least one size too small. Dust covered her bare feet and legs. Yet through all the grime, there was a bright, if belligerent, gaze. The girl dragged her feet until she stood in front of him.

Jags looked at the child. "Give it back and apologize."

"*No hablo inglés.*"

From his time in Brazil, Will had learned Portuguese and Spanish. He understood the girl to say she didn't speak English. In her tongue, he said, "I speak Spanish. Give what back?"

The girl flashed hot eyes up at Jags. "Tell her to let me go."

"She'll let you go, but first, what do you have?"

The girl pouted and shut her mouth, pursing her lips together as if to keep any sound from escaping.

Will looked at Jags. "What does she have?"

Jags grimaced. "Your wallet."

Probing his right pocket, he realized it was indeed missing his wallet. The child had a light touch, he'd grant her that. He reached his hand toward the girl, palm up. "Hand it over."

With an offended frown, the girl reached into her clothes and produced his wallet. "I didn't think she'd catch me. She's fast."

This time he placed the billfold in his front pants pocket, where it would be safer. "She is. And thank you."

The girl rolled her eyes.

Jags held out a twenty-dollar bill she'd slipped from her pocketbook, and then released the pickpocket. The child snatched the money and scampered off.

Will looked at Jags. "You're rewarding bad behavior?"

"Not exactly." Jags crossed her arms in front of her chest.

Noticing the defensive body language, he changed the subject. "You've got some killer powers of observation."

Jags looked away. "I suppose I do. Long story."

"Want to tell me over food?"

"Sure."

Deciding on an outdoor café, they ordered dinner and a Malbec blend from Argentina as the crowd in the plaza began to thin. Every time Will tried to make eye contact with Jags, she made a point of watching the other café patrons, the square—anything but him.

"Do you want to talk about it?" he asked softly.

"Not in detail."

"Okay. I'm all ears, though, if you want to share."

Jags grimaced and glanced at him. "Let's just say that I had a troubled youth myself, so I know what to look for. The kid nabbed your wallet when you turned to look at the church."

The wine arrived and Will tasted it. *Not bad.* "I see."

"Well, you don't, but that's okay. I felt sorry for her, and gave her a few bucks. She's going to have a tough life here, begging and stealing."

Will had grown up in Lake Tahoe and its largely upper-middle-class world. Chagrined, he realized she was right. He didn't see. He couldn't imagine life on the streets, in the States or here. "I'm sorry."

"No reason to apologize. At least I learned some useful skills from that time."

Will was fascinated, imagining everything from picking locks to hot-wiring cars. "Like what?"

"Never mind." Jags's mouth was set in a solid line so he didn't push. "Let's talk about other things," she said abruptly.

"Okay. Pick a topic."

"I heard you lost your wife. I'm sorry to hear that."

Will hadn't expected the conversation to take this turn. "Thanks. It's only been a year and a half, but sometimes feels like decades."

"A lot has changed for you."

He took a sip of wine. "It has. I got fired from my old engineering job as soon as I got back to Brazil, and was glad to get the job with VanOps."

"Fired? Ouch. That's a double whammy."

"It was." A woman who looked a little bit like Maria walked by. Will debated telling Jags about his dirty secret. She had opened up a little. Maybe he should, too. "I've also been dealing with a lot of guilt."

Jags leaned forward. "About what?"

Will looked away. "When we were on the run, I met a beautiful girl who came on to me, but Maria had just been gone a week."

"What happened?"

Will frowned, sensing the familiar anchor weighing down his heart. "I slept with her."

Jags put her hand on the table. "Wait. You feel guilty for sleeping with a woman after your wife died?"

Her challenging tone surprised Will. "Yes."

"Why?"

He sipped his wine. "It felt . . . unfaithful."

"But—she was dead."

"Yes, but—"

"No buts. Isn't marriage until 'death do us part'?"

He hadn't thought about it that way. "Uh, that was our vow."

Jags leaned back. "Well, then. Get over it, Pope Pious."

Will sat up straighter. She had a point. Maria was dead. His marriage vow, unbroken.

The anchor in his heart began to tug free of the sand. It never ceased to fascinate him how a different idea could change how he felt about something. "I'll still miss her."

"Of course you will. But no need to carry that millstone of guilt around your neck."

He smiled. "I suppose not."

They ate for a time in companionable silence.

As Jags finished her food, she asked, "Do you think Thorenson and your sister will be able to learn anything from Anu?"

"You mean about her uncle?"

"Yeah. She's the only lead we have to his murder."

"She didn't seem very forthcoming." Will recalled their meeting. "She acted more put out than anything."

Jags nodded. "We'll check in with them later. Meanwhile, where do you think the shooter on the motorcycle went?"

"I'm guessing he ran off into the forest when he heard us coming back. That's what I'd have done. We're lucky he didn't shoot at us from the trees."

"True. Maybe he ran out of ammo or lost his gun. He did go ass over teakettle across the handlebars."

"Or maybe he was hurt."

"Could be. If it *is* the same guy I shot back at the guard shack, which is my theory for now." Jags sipped her wine. "While we have time, tell me more about this star chart and the obelisks. Someone seems to have left out a mention of said obelisks during an earlier debrief."

She glared at him, but he felt no heat in her stare.

Will spent the coffee and dessert part of the meal telling Jags the story of how they found the obelisks, and how Maddy was given the star chart. To respect Maddy's privacy, he left out the Order of the Invisible Flame. And the men she killed.

When finished, he circled back to the thought of the motorbike attacker on their trail. "I think we still need to be on the lookout for that killer." He glanced outside, certain the man was on their trail. "On the upside, it seems like he followed us instead of the others."

"True. And we can handle him."

Will was glad Jags had confidence. He still felt out of his league. With a deep, mournful tone, the church bells tolled the ten o'clock hour. He hoped they weren't ringing the sound of his demise.

CHAPTER 28

From the motel bed in Belize City, Bear watched as Maddy did some sort of floor exercise that she'd learned from the master. She sat cross-legged, with her stomach pulled in, her chest out, and her chin slightly tucked. Her hands were on her knees, her forefinger and thumb touching as she chanted, in a sing-song voice, "Sa ta na ma." As each syllable was sung, she pressed her thumb to the tip of a different finger, from index to pinky.

The exercise looked strange, but Bear trusted the master. Not to mention she'd said Alzheimer's doctors were advocating the action as a preventive tool, which was cool. And truth be told, weird exercise or no, Maddy looked downright sexy. For once, her hat was off and her short, messy hair framed her face. Her sensual lips were inviting, perhaps because she looked relaxed. He wished she would come to bed for a little love.

He was also jealous that she had a good way to relax. Bear tried to release the tension from the day by leaning back into the pillows and stretching his neck and shoulders, but it didn't help. They were up against some sick bastards—that was certain. After checking in to the motel, Bear called Argones and Jags and learned that they were chased through the jungle but not wounded. At least Elena had texted to say that she and AJ had arrived in the Philippines and were well.

Maddy took a last, deep breath and opened her eyes.

"Feel better?" he asked.

She stretched her back. "I do. I'm still processing through some bits and pieces."

"Want to talk about it?"

"Maybe. In your time with the marines, did you have to kill people?"

Ah, she was still feeling guilty. "I did."

She unfolded her long legs from the floor and moved up to sit cross-legged on the bed. "What was it like for you? After?"

He took a slow breath. Guys never talked about this kind of crappy stuff. You did what you had to do. Nobody liked it, but you made yourself forget about it. Still, he would try.

"The first time, I puked," he said.

"Really?"

"Yeah." He smiled. "I didn't like it any more than you did."

"What about the macho marine thing?"

"Well, I didn't let anyone see me throw up. And maybe my situation was different. We were trained to kill, and were in battles with enemies who had come to kill or be killed."

She nodded slowly.

He went on. "Listen, you've been trained in aikido. Nonviolent aikido. It's no wonder you feel—well, how do you feel?"

She paused. "I guess I feel guilty."

Her emerald-green eyes held depths he couldn't read, so he took her hands in his. "That's understandable." He paused, and then went out on a limb. "But you have some talents that could really help the world. You need to get over it."

"I'm not sure I can. What if I have to kill again?"

"Then you do. It's not like you're doin' it for fun."

"I don't know if I want that responsibility."

"What if . . ." He tried to think of the right scenario. "Okay, what if we had a time machine and you could go back to 1935 and kill Hitler before he had a chance to send all those Jews to the gas chamber? Do you do it?"

She pulled her hands from his and climbed under the sheets. "The famous Hitler argument." She yawned. "Yeah. Save millions. But I wouldn't like it."

He scooted down and put his arm around her. Before she'd flown into Cancun last night, it had been awhile since they'd seen each other, and he was ready to connect with her. She smelled good. "Exactly. That's what makes us the good guys."

Her response was mumbled. "I suppose."

Bear began to reply but realized she was already asleep.

He snuggled down next to her and hoped like hell she'd get her conscience lined up with the work they had to do. Maybe she shouldn't join VanOps. It would be a bad day for them all if they found themselves in a sticky situation and she choked.

CHAPTER 29

Maddy saw Adelino's khaki-covered corpse lying atop a sky-high mountain of bodies, blank eyes staring at clouds of buzzing flies that swarmed and reformed like a flock of starlings. Then, she was on top of Mount Everest, throwing balls of lightning toward one enemy with red flames for eyes, and another with a large nose like Pinocchio. One of the men shot and killed her, Bear, Will, and AJ. As she floated toward the sky as a spirit, she looked down on their bodies. The gunman blew smoke off the tip of his pistol, like a villain in a classic Western who had just exterminated the white-hat-wearing hero.

In a shift, Maddy watched as an attacker with a tattooed face wrapped Will's neck in a deadly embrace with a boa constrictor, and cut off his air supply. A moment later, Will's entire head floated away while the man sang, "Momma had a baby and its head popped off."

She woke, off-kilter from the nightmares. Out of context, that last part would have made her giggle. But this one wasn't funny in the least. Bile moved into her throat and for a moment she wondered if she would vomit.

Bear slept beside her in the humid, predawn darkness. She'd been so tired last night she'd fallen asleep before even kissing him good night. They'd had a good chat, though, about—what was it? Ah yes, killing Hitler in a time machine. That recycled example made her smile. But she felt some progress had been made in tearing down the wall of guilty self-condemnation that was plastered over her heart.

But the dream! God, she hoped it wasn't one of her prescient dreams. Her most recent "real" dream had occurred well over a year ago when she'd seen Will's wife die in a dream the night before it had actually happened. She could still see blood splattered everywhere. Her belly lurched, thinking back.

Bear rolled over toward her and his breathing changed. He spooned her. "Mornin', beautiful."

She tried to relax into his embrace. "Hi, handsome."

"What's wrong?"

Wow, he'd seen right through her. Vincent never did that. "How'd you know?"

Maddy rolled over to look at Bear and he opened his eyes. "You're tense."

"I had a bad dream."

"You mentioned that you get a kind of real dream once in a while. Was it one of those?"

"I'm not sure."

He shifted onto an elbow to look at her. "Tell me about it."

"Will was killed, murdered. By that maniac tattooed guy who tried to strangle me back home. He cut off Will's head! While singing a childhood rhyme that we used to chant while flipping the heads off dandelions." She could still hear the refrain in her head.

"That's strange." Bear asked, "How do we know if it's a real dream or not?"

"It's not exactly a science."

Bear stroked her short hair. "I know, but what've been the characteristics of the real ones?"

"There's a certain feeling that I wake up with."

"What kind of feelin'?"

She scrunched up her nose in distaste. "A sort of certainty. A dread."

"Did you have that?"

"No, but . . ."

"But what?"

"What if I just woke up too soon?"

"Wait. You want your brother to be decapitated?" he teased.

She poked him under the arm. "Of course not!"

Bear kissed her ear. "How about hopin' for the best and plannin' for the worst?"

She appreciated his distraction and ideas. "Like how?"

"Like telling him to be careful. Protect his neck."

"Oh, hell no."

"Why not?"

"Do you know my brother at all yet? Mr. Paranoid? He'll freak out."

"He might, but then he'll take precautions."

Rain began to lash the motel room window. Maddy turned onto her back and stared at the ceiling, thinking. The master had told her to listen to her intuition, but was this an intuitive hit or not? She was glad she had done those exercises last night.

"But if I'm wrong," she said slowly, "I've concerned him for nothing."

"Perhaps." Bear hugged her close. "What if it was you?"

She felt a pang. Would she want to know? What would she do with her life if she knew her days were numbered?

"I'll think about it," Maddy replied.

"Fair enough."

She kissed him on the forehead and headed for the shower. "In the meantime, don't we have a star chart to track down?"

The shower's hot water ran cold after only a minute. While dressing, Maddy continued to hear the singsong refrain from the nightmare. "Momma had a baby and its head popped off."

Disturbing. *Was it a real dream or not?*

CHAPTER 30

AJ sat on the floor of the outdoor balcony as evening fell, playing with the Lego pieces that Elena and her French boyfriend, Garrod, had bought at the airport. It was a fancier set than the one at his foster parents' house. That set didn't have this awesome dinosaur skeleton.

Absorbed in his play, he blocked out the adults' conversation. Garrod reminded AJ of the scarecrow in *The Wizard of Oz*, all skinny, floppy limbs, and tall goofiness. But AJ thought Elena was pretty, with her golden red hair and round hazel eyes. While they always spoke to him nicely, AJ was pretty sure they didn't want him around, as they were doing a lot of kissy face while they drank their wine.

He missed Maddy and worried she was going to back out on the adoption since it had been so much trouble for her to get him to safety. Kids from the foster home said the older you got, the harder it was to find a forever home. If Maddy didn't want him, he'd end up in the foster system forever. He hoped Pyotr didn't hurt her.

The Lego set had come with a special male figurine that AJ imagined was Pyotr. The dinosaur stalked the Russian and his mismatched eyes around the coffee table jungle. Pyotr was fast and nimble as he ran through the rainforest, taunting the dinosaur. The beast thundered through the trees, using its strength to knock large palms down as he closed in on Pyotr.

When the dinosaur came around a large rock outcropping, Pyotr jumped from the boulder onto the dinosaur's back and slashed at its neck. The big animal reared up, trying to remove the man, but Pyotr held tight. Tail lashing, it rubbed its neck against the rock, and Pyotr fell off. The dinosaur stomped on Pyotr, and with a high-pitched scream, the man expired on the jungle floor.

AJ glanced up, seeking inspiration from the skyline for his next Lego creation, the building that the dinosaur would destroy next. The view from the balcony was impressive, in a city kind of way. Elena said they'd be here for just tonight and would head to the beach tomorrow. AJ liked beaches. Sandcastles. Swimming. But the urban lights below looked like home, San Francisco. There was a mixture of buildings, some tall like the building they were in now, some short. They were all lit up, which reminded AJ that it was almost Christmas. He hadn't seen many decorations on the way here from the airport.

AJ wondered if he'd get to spend the holiday with Maddy. When she had whispered goodbye to him in Jerusalem, she told him to think of a present Santa could bring him. He'd learned years ago that Santa wasn't real, but grownups seemed to enjoy the game. AJ didn't let on. Maybe he'd ask for another box of Legos, one with a cool black helicopter. He just hoped he'd get to see her soon.

As he tried to match several Lego pieces to form an imposing Jurassic jaw structure, the lights, all of them, out in the city and inside the hotel, went dark. AJ's heart fluttered wildly in his chest, and a strangled cry escaped his lips.

CHAPTER 31

Through the pouring rain, Bear squinted up at the building that was supposedly the Belize City field office.

Anu crossed her arms and huddled under the hooded cloak and umbrella Bear had managed to get from a *mercado*. After much debate, he had eventually decided it was safe to bring Ravi's niece along. Blindfolded. She hadn't been happy about the arrangements.

Maddy looked up and down the street. "Are you sure this is the right place?"

He was certain he had the correct address. As part of their VanOps training, they had to memorize safe houses and field offices in various countries. It was 1492 Columbine, which he'd remembered thanks to Columbus and the horrible Columbine shooting. "Yeah, I'm sure."

As certain as he was, he understood their hesitation. They'd taken a planned surveillance detection route, stopping for *agua* here and a *caramelo* there, and the closer they'd gotten to their destination, the more dangerous the neighborhood looked. He glanced up and down the street before he rang the doorbell. Three-story houses without yards crowded next to one another, their multicolored shades of paint, now peeling, heralding more prosperous times. Laundry hung from balconies. Barefooted children rushed by on bicycles, heedless of the downpour, which fell in thick waves. The unresponsive door in front of him had once been painted blue. Bear just hoped there was good internet inside so Anu could help them with the star chart mission. And maybe she knew something about her uncle's death.

He raised his fist and rapped again on the entrance.

After a long minute, the faded door creaked open a few inches. A brown eye peered out and asked something in Spanish. To Bear's surprise, Anu stepped forward and answered. She must have picked up some of the language from working in the region. Bear couldn't understand the exchange.

Anu asked. "Is there some secret passcode? He says he can't help us."

Bear searched his memory, hoping like hell he *was* correct about the address, as showing up in the wrong place with a blindfolded woman would mean trouble. "Tell him, 'The full moon's eclipse hides the honor of the sun.'"

Anu complied and the door opened all the way to reveal a tall man with short black hair and a strikingly long neck.

This time, the man spoke in English. "The dark of the moon shows the way."

Aha. He did speak English. That matched the response Bear expected.

Stepping out of the rain and into the house gave Bear a chance to study their new friend. The man's neck reminded him of the National Geographic photographs of African tribes, but his face had the wide look of a Central American native. Perhaps he was even Mayan. The man introduced himself as José. Bear doubted it was his real name.

José took the umbrella from Anu, and Maddy gently removed the blindfold from Anu's eyes, careful not to disturb the jeweled bindi. Anu blinked several times.

Afterwards, José led them to a sparse room containing a dining room table atop a shabby rug. Although the room had a picture window, the light was murky thanks to tightly closed blinds. Bear peeked through and saw a dirty canal full of dilapidated fishing boats. On the side wall, a battered hutch was the only other piece of furniture in the room.

Maddy got to the point. "Is there a place we can use a secure computer?"

José looked at Bear, a question in his eyes, and Bear motioned to proceed.

José reached into a drawer of the hutch and pulled out a small black box. He walked over to Bear and pantomimed putting the box up to his eye. Realizing it was a retina scanner, Bear let José hold the device up to his left eye. When it blinked green twice, José smiled broadly and gave a thumbs-up.

Next, José had them help him move the dining room table and rug. Underneath was a trap door, which revealed a staircase. Bear felt a keen sense of excitement at entering a hidden room as part of a field mission.

Anu gasped as soon as they reached the bottom. The basement room held a suite of computer monitors that would rival the Cape Canaveral command center before a rocket launch.

Several workstations were occupied. A young oval-faced woman wearing a white blouse and black skirt stood, walked over, and held out her hand to Bear.

"Officer Thorenson, you may call me Katrina." She exuded a calm, professional manner and had stylish black hair, tinted with red, and tied back in a bun. Her handshake was firm. Her Spanish accent, slight.

"Nice to meet you, ma'am." He glanced around the bank of displays. Most held visual feeds of rioting in urban Asian streets, although two featured light streaking by the dark moon. "Y'all have an impressive setup here."

She led them to the screen where she'd been sitting. "This is breaking news—take a look."

Unbranded video footage of scene after chaotic scene played out on the monitor. There were unlit gas stations surrounded by lines of vehicles snaking into the night. People paced around the cars in futility. Crowds pooled through the black streets, rushed into storefronts, broke windows, and mouthed unheard chants. High-rises and office towers loomed in the background, stark against the dim sky.

"Where is this? What's going on?" Maddy asked.

"The Philippines," Katrina replied.

Maddy clutched at the back of Katrina's empty chair. The air left Bear's lungs with the realization that AJ was there.

Katrina nodded to the monitors. "Incoming reports indicate that the country is experiencing pandemonium. A few hours ago, around nine thirty p.m. local time, power went out and gas pumps across the country could no longer dispense gasoline."

Maddy's voice raised an octave. "None of them work? And there's no electricity?"

"Correct. Only places with generators have power, like some cell towers."

"What's with the rioting?" Anu asked.

"No gasoline means no transportation, as well as the inability to move food and goods. Lack of power has caused panic. Social media updates have caused considerable fear."

Maddy frowned, her knuckles white.

"Look here," Katrina pointed to another screen. "There's also a single large petrochemical estate. It's on fire. There have been several explosions."

The screen zoomed in on a large industrial plant complex. Multiple fires burned throughout the area. Bear's stomach was in knots, thinking about AJ being anywhere near all that chaos. He wanted to parachute in there, like Rambo on a mission, and snatch the little guy out. Bear put a hand on Maddy's back, suspecting she felt five times more anxious than he did.

"Does the director know?" Bear asked.

"Yes. And he wants to speak with you."

CHAPTER 32

Giraffe-necked José led Maddy and Bear out of the computer room, down a long hallway, and into a small, windowless room that held a messy conference table and office chairs. Anu was to be given access to the archeologist's star database while they spoke with the director.

As soon as José shut the door and left them alone, Maddy grabbed the coffee cups, napkins, and paper plates from the table and threw them into the trash can. She needed to blow off some steam.

Sitting down, Maddy felt her blood pressure rise further as she contemplated the mess in the Philippines. She remembered AJ's vulnerable smile when she'd pulled him from under the patio table and swept him up into her arms. He reminded her of a wet, wide-eyed kitten. She loved him with all her heart, and yet here he was, in danger again. Maddy yanked the cap off her head and squeezed it between her hands, resisting the urge to throw it against the wall.

It pained her that the only thing she could do about it was to have a conversation with the director. Her traitorous index finger moved up and down and she shoved that hand under the table, not wanting Bear to see it. Atop the conference room table were a number of white goggles, like those she wore snow skiing, next

145

to matching bracelets. A square device was mounted in the ceiling. Doing her best to push the riots from her mind, Maddy picked up a set of goggles and turned to Bear. "Are these virtual-reality devices?"

"Yep. Oculus Rift virtual-reality headsets. A military advance in meeting technology. Can't tell you more."

She'd been in many virtual meetings, but none with VR gear. Bear donned the eyewear and snapped the thick plastic bracelets on his wrists. Maddy followed suit.

All of a sudden, she was in a botanical garden that sprawled atop a seaside cliff. Colorful flowers grew everywhere while the surf crashed below. A lifelike Bear sat next to her on a park bench, wearing the same jeans and black T-shirt he'd put on this morning. A handsome African American man, clean-shaven, mid-fifties, with sharp eyes and short graying hair, sat on a bench across from them.

"Would you prefer a quieter beach?" the man asked, motioning with his arm. His tone was deep but his words were machine-gun fast.

Before she had a chance to respond, they were in a private café bordered by white sand. Bear had his arm around her shoulders, while the gray-haired gentleman, the man she assumed was the director, occupied the chair across the table.

The director looked at her and smiled. "Perhaps a museum?"

Maddy blinked and the three of them were in a brightly lit hall. Naked Greek sculptures atop pedestals stood all around. The technology was impressive, but—

She slammed her hand down on the table with enough force to make her point. "Enough already. It's a neat toy, but don't we have more important things to talk about?"

The director nodded. "I like that you keep your eye on the prize. Yes, let's get down to business. We need to discuss the Philippines, but let's take things in chronological order. Argones and Jags called the local authorities to handle the killings at the ruins."

"Have the police learned anything?" Bear asked.

"Nothing noteworthy, but we did pick up some SIGINT chatter about Singh. It is looking like he was killed for information about the star chart. And it's possible his killer was at the ruins."

Maddy reminded herself that in this context SIGINT meant signals intelligence. To her, it was a UNIX computer command to interrupt a signal and stop a process.

Bear filled the director in on what they had learned about the tat-tooed assassin and Maddy's odd-eyed relative, and that *both* Russia and Spain seemed to be involved. He added that Singh's niece was helping them work the star chart angle.

"Good work, Thorenson. I think we both suspected Russian involvement after the incident last year."

Maddy cringed inwardly. Even though she'd told Jags and Anu about the obelisks, she felt annoyed that he knew anything about that evening.

"Thank you, sir."

The director narrowed his eyes. "This has become a DEFCON 3 situation."

Maddy tugged at her cap. That sounded bad.

Bear sat up straighter. "Why's that, sir? Do you have new data?"

"Yes, but what we discuss today cannot leave this room. Highly classified, but Argones and Jags are cleared. As for Madeline, until I can talk her into joining VanOps, I have an NDA for her to sign." He looked at Maddy. "Work for you?"

"Fine." When he gave her the secured phone, Bear had given her advanced notice about the paperwork and she saw no harm in keeping their secrets. It might even give her leverage if she needed to remind them to keep hers.

"Good. Here's the deal: Ravi Singh was an agent working for the CIA, keeping us in the loop on Indian/Russian plans to build a quantum computer."

Bear's word came out in a rush. "An agent? That complicates things."

"Yes, it does."

The guy was on the agency payroll. Maddy wondered if Anu knew about that. Or could Anu also be a spy, perhaps even for the Russians or Spaniards? It would explain her odd behavior.

"What's a quantum computer?" Bear asked.

Maddy turned to his avatar. "One that's super-fast. The prototypes are already a hundred million times faster than laptops."

The director continued. "Yes. And the quantum computer India and Russia have been building relies on superconductive material for its cooling mechanism. That's why they want the material for their project, code-named *Firepit*. If that chart leads to the material we think it does, and if the chaos in the Philippines is any indication of what they can do, we're in deep, deep trouble."

CHAPTER 33

Through the VR goggles, the director watched as Maddy Marshall easily connected the dots. She was the full package, all right: smart, discreet, and able to handle herself in a fight. He wanted her on the team but could sense her resistance. He'd have to play the long game with her. Maybe he'd put the request through Master Mohan; that might build some trust.

Officer Thorenson tilted his head. "This computer is ultrafast, so what? I'm not seeing the national security risk."

"Good question, Thorenson. A quantum computer is the holy grail of encryption breaking. Imagine you've got all your money stored in your house, locked up tight in case a burglar comes a-calling."

"Okay."

"Now imagine someone just gave them all the keys."

Thorenson frowned. "Oh."

"A quantum computer can give our enemies the keys to the house, garage, car, and the safety deposit box. NSA, military, and corporate keys, too. Secure encryption we've had for decades would be irrelevant. And what's more, we have reason to believe the Russians are behind the power and gas station hack in the Philippines. Perhaps testing out their quantum computer."

Marshall stiffened.

The director continued. "We think it was a test run of what they're planning for the United States."

Marshall scowled. "That wouldn't be good."

"It would be even worse if they found a way to hack other things at the same time. Like ATM machines. Or water treatment plants."

Marshall nodded. "One of my coworkers has been trying to educate our software clients about vulnerabilities in their IoT infrastructure. Most have invested their security dollars in ring-fencing their data centers and aren't interested in the edge."

"Translate for a layman, please," Thorenson drawled.

Marshall looked at the director but he waved her on. "IoT stands for the Internet of Things. Automation is great, but brings risks. Nowadays, everything from self-driving cars to gas stations and ATMs use hardware and software. If not properly secured, hackers can access the software and change it. Get the keys to the locks, like the director mentioned."

"Sounds bad."

"It is. Most companies think they only need to protect where their servers live and don't want to spend more money securing all the little mini-processors, or 'things' that feed information back to the data center."

Thorenson stretched his hands. "I see."

"If a foreign power wanted to wreak havoc on civilization, they'd only need to disrupt the automation that we use in our everyday lives. Transportation. Water. Power. Think of what social isolation during a pandemic would be like without a shower or the internet."

"Now imagine those scenes from the Philippines playing out across America," the director added. "Chaos. Rioting. Civil unrest. And when we're confused and fighting amongst ourselves . . ."

"They crack our military codes and attack," Bear said grimly. "If that's what the Russians are planning, sir, forgive me for sayin', but we're up shit creek."

"Yes, Thorenson. And the four of you are our only paddles."

CHAPTER 34

Maddy shifted in her seat, uncomfortable with what the director was saying. A quantum computer in the hands of the Russians was sure to spell disaster. But was it her job to stop them? She had signed up to track down the family star chart, not save the world from a Russian plot.

Maddy crossed her arms. "I get the risks. But why us? Don't you have another team who's better suited?"

The director shrugged. "Another directorate, the Clandestine Service, has been working on Firepit for some time, but as you can imagine, the computer itself is extremely well guarded. We don't know where it is."

Maddy realized the problem was thornier than she had first thought. "Ouch." They didn't even know from where the Philippines hack was originating.

"That's why Ravi was such a powerful asset for us," he said. "He was about to meet with one of our officers in the Maldives and tell us its location. We need to find who was behind his death to see if we can track down the leak."

"Okay, but you still haven't answered my question. Why us?"

"This is the type of mission for which Jags, Thorenson, and your

151

brother have trained. They all have unique skill sets useful for stopping extraordinary threats, as do you. Small, nimble teams often have the best chance of success, and can avoid the painful casualties of all-out war. We help keep the peace."

That made sense. Nobody wanted another world war, especially a nuclear one. Maybe small acts of self-defense-type violence were worth saving millions. Maddy's shoulders relaxed a notch.

The director pressed his advantage. "I hate to tell you, but it gets worse. Recent satellite passes have caught images of Russian military buildup above Japan, in eastern Russia, and to the west near Ukraine. We suspect that if they are able to power their quantum computer, they'll use their military to invade." He paused for effect. "And we believe they will invade both coasts simultaneously."

Maddy visualized the major cities along both seaboards. San Francisco, LA, San Diego, Seattle, New York, Charleston, and undoubtedly the nation's capital. Millions of lives. And her family. A northern California invasion would put Bella and the kids in jeopardy. Maddy remembered the joy on Izzy's face when the child had jumped up and down in front of Maddy's loft door. She felt ill. That delight would be gone forever.

Maddy wanted to keep that innocence alive.

"Thorenson, this mission has morphed into something far larger than Ravi Singh's murder. I need you all to track down the star chart and bring back any superconductive material you find at the end of that rainbow." Bowman paused. "It's the key asset. Do whatever it takes. And quickly. Miss Marshall, it could be dangerous, but I need your skills. Are you in?"

Maddy ground her teeth—she didn't like the idea of all that lorandite in government hands, not to mention this mission had spun far beyond what she'd initially considered. But she could also feel her heart beating faster, excited. Millions of lives were on the line. She could make a difference here, a big difference. Maybe even help get AJ out of the Philippines faster.

Maddy looked at the director. "I'm in."

"Great. I'll get the new employee paperwork—"

Maddy interrupted. "No, not in as an employee. Not yet. Can I help as a private citizen?"

Director Bowman seemed surprised for a moment, but quickly recovered. "Okay, we'll talk about a permanent role when the mission is complete. Yes, I'll get the NDA and will make it happen. You'll be a cyber subject matter expert."

"All right. Sounds good."

The director looked at Bear. "Do you have everything you need? Sat phones, weapons, ammunition, papers, cash?"

"A few gaps, sir."

"Work with Katrina and José on logistics. They'll get you what you need."

"Yes, sir." Bear paused. "Sir, what if it's a large meteorite? The Willamette Meteorite is ten feet tall and weighs sixteen tons."

"Just find the bloody thing first. If we have to, we'll bring in a strike team."

The director must have cut the virtual-reality conference because everything went black. Maddy removed her goggles and bracelets while Bear did the same.

Maddy looked Bear in the eye. "Against my better judgment, you're stuck with me for a while. Let's keep that material out of the hands of the Russians."

He gave her a quick hug. "I'm glad you're sticking it out."

"Where do we start?"

Bear stretched his shoulders. "I have an idea about that."

She just prayed she wouldn't have to kill anyone else along the way.

CHAPTER 35

MOSCOW, RUSSIA

DECEMBER 22, 11:28 P.M. MOSCOW STANDARD TIME

O n a quiet side street near Taganka Square, the baron exited his car, heard the cry of an owl, and smiled. It was a good omen.

He limped toward the plain neoclassical building in front of him called Bunker 42. The rest of the world knew the place as a museum and entertainment complex, catering to those who wanted a unique spot to hold a child's birthday party or tour the glorious past. An impressive bit of secretive engineering, the former Cold War bunker was buried sixty-five meters under the ground and featured arched rooms barely tall enough to fit an R-17 Scud missile on its side. To him, the place felt like a claustrophobic submarine.

What the rest of the world didn't know, however, was that another fifteen meters below the museum there was a laboratory he and his peers used to help ferret out sensitive information. It was the perfect location: near the Kremlin, yet hidden.

The sense of privilege put lightness in the baron's step as he used his key card in the side elevator to access the hidden floor.

After a short walk down a sterile, well-lit hallway lined by bulletproof metal doors with opaque glass windows, he arrived at a door that carried the name and credentials of Iosif Levenfish, Egyptologist.

Iosif's head was down when the baron entered, so focused on his work that he hadn't heard the door open. Or he'd ignored it. The baron tapped his cane with more force than usual as he walked over to the bald scientist. "Levenfish."

The man looked up with blank eyes, blinking behind his round John Lennon frames. "Baron Sokolov," he said in Russian. "Why are you here?" The scientist's voice was high enough to belong to a woman.

"You called me this morning."

The man had a reputation as an idiot savant, and the baron often thought it was more idiot than savant. He grasped the head of his cane fiercely, visualizing pounding the man's head into a bloody pulp. Unfortunately, he needed the information this fool had.

"Right. I did. Exciting stuff." Levenfish turned his attention back to the table. The Argones family star chart was magnified and displayed on a large color monitor.

"Show me what you've found."

The man's pasty face was as white as his lab smock. "Oh my, there's so much. First, this document was produced around 1350 BC, give or take a decade," he reported.

"So?"

"There was a massive—like *six thousand nuclear warheads* massive—volcanic eruption on what is now known as the Greek island of Santorini."

"And?"

This time when Levenfish looked up, excitement sparked in his eyes. "Recent ice core research places the eruption about twenty years before this chart was made."

The baron ground his teeth. He loved the black sandy beaches of Santorini, but where was the man going with this nonsense? He repeated his question, drawing out the syllable. "And?"

"Well, it explains the Exodus of Moses from Egypt."

In frustration, the baron squeezed his eyes shut for a second. Levenfish was Jewish—had his religion colored his research?

"How so?" he said coolly.

"The column of fire they followed. Could have been the volcanic plume. The parting of the Red Sea. Could have been Lake Manzala, and a tsunami over the narrow causeway."

The baron pounded his cane onto the floor. "I don't care about Moses," he hissed. "I care about where that chart leads."

The man's brown eyes grew wide behind his wire-rim glasses. "Well. But. You do care."

The baron shouted. "Why?!"

"You're looking for a meteorite, right?"

"I think so."

"What if that's what caused the famous burning bush?"

The baron fumed. *This man is ridiculous. Religion has addled his brain.* "What about the rest of the chart?" He also had the state's best astronomers working on it, but he'd wanted another opinion.

Iosif removed his glasses and stared at the baron without expression. "I don't know."

"What?" The baron pointed to the corner of the document. "Even that little hieroglyph?"

Two spots of color highlighted the man's pale cheeks. "I'm sorry. I have no idea. There's no correlation to anything we have on record."

The baron swallowed his pride. They needed a clue. "Come on. A theory. Anything?"

The crazy bastard hesitated. "I think if you find Mount Sinai and the burning bush, you'll find the meteorite you're looking for."

"I thought no one could agree on where Mount Sinai is located."

The scientist's face fell. "Well. Yes. That's true."

The baron turned on his heel and stalked to the lab door, slamming it on his way out.

CHAPTER 36

MERIDA AIRPORT, MEXICO

DECEMBER 22, 8:35 A.M. CST

Will inhaled the humid Yucatán air as he and Jags stepped from the taxi onto the sidewalk outside the tiny Merida airport, having ditched the Jeep the night before. Along the street, palm trees swayed in the breeze, waving them goodbye. He was a little sad to leave—the warm ≈Latin culture had reminded him of home and Maria—but they needed to get moving to decipher the hieroglyphs on the obelisks.

Jags's secure satellite phone rang. She turned to Will. "It's Thorenson. Let's sit on a bench and take the call."

Will looked around the airport drop-off zone. After confirming there was no one close enough to eavesdrop, he agreed they might as well enjoy a last minute of sunshine. According to the taxi driver, rain was on the way. "Okay."

They stood their bags on end and both sat on a concrete bench. Will guessed it was the smoking section, given the ashtrays that bookended the seat. He was glad he'd given up the habit.

"Jags here." She listened for a moment, and then turned to Will. "Your sister is with him on speaker. They're in the Belize City field office."

She motioned for Will to put an earbud in his ear. He reached in his pocket and put in the tiny earpiece.

"Ginsu is listening as well. We're outside the airport, but on a private bench," Jags said.

Bear's voice was rough. "Ginsu? Never mind. This is highly classified intel."

"What's up?"

"We just met with Director Bowman. Things are worse than we thought. We're at DEFCON 3, and the Philippine islands are in chaos."

DEFCON 3? Shit! "Why three?"

"The short answer is we're in deep trouble. If we don't find this superconductive material before the Russians do, it could lead to a US invasion. Both coasts," Bear replied.

Will's memory rewound black-and-white newsreels from his youth. He could hear tanks rumbling and bombs dropping. "An invasion? Tanks? Bombs?"

"Yes, there's military buildup in eastern Russia, above Japan. And near Ukraine, too."

Will grimaced at Jags. "How's that tie into the Philippines?"

"We suspect the Russians are testing a fast computer there that they'd use to soften us up for an invasion."

Maddy jumped in. "A quantum computer. One that can break civilian and military encryption as easily as you can log into your bank account."

"What did they do to the Philippines with this test?" Jags asked.

"All the power and gas stations in the country have been hacked. The entire archipelago is rioting. Elena and her boyfriend are vacationing there now with AJ. I hope they can get out. I haven't had a chance to call her yet," Maddy replied.

Will's mind raced with implications. A shadow fell, cooling the area. Gray clouds were rolling in, one already blotting out the sun. "That's horrible."

Jags looked at Will with concern in her eyes. "With COVID-19, people went crazy over toilet paper. I can just see what would happen in the States without power and gas. Every man, woman, and child who has a gun would be killing strangers for groceries."

"And the National Guard would be spread out, tryin' to keep the peace. Military, too. It would make us ripe for an attack," Bear said.

"And it might not be just power and gas. If their encryption-breaking technology is good, it could disrupt water processing facilities, the manufacturing supply chain, ATMs, cars, airplanes. You name it. No power means no internet. And that's just on the civilian side," Maddy said.

"I've been thinking about military implications, too. They could send false emails, obtain access to all our maps and plans, listen in on all our communication. Everything we do is electronic," Bear added.

Will groaned. "You're just full of happy news."

"It gets better. I also dreamed you were strangled," Maddy said.

Will glared at the phone. "Oh, for Pete's sake. Seriously?"

Maddy's voice caught. "Yes, I didn't want to tell you. I don't think it was a real dream, but you need to be careful. Remember, we've got two sets of bad guys after us. And one is a Spaniard fond of that garrote."

Will took a deep breath and shook his head to clear it. "What kind of bastard uses a weapon like that instead of a knife or gun?"

"I honestly don't know," Maddy said. "Maybe somebody sick in the head who likes to see blood on his hands?"

"Great. An up-close-and-personal psychopath." Will decided he would have to deal with that threat later. "Any other fantastic news? We're about to catch a flight to Egypt."

Movement in the crowd near the airport entrance caught Will's eye and he stiffened. He elbowed Jags and pointed.

"Nah, y'all go for it. The director wants us to get on the ball, hunt down the superconductive material, and bring it home at any cost," Bear said.

Jags jumped in, her eyes on the crowd. "Okay, we're on it. Headquarters has confirmed Crookbottom, the Egyptian cryptographer, is working in the Valley of the Kings. We'll head there as soon as we land."

"Great. We have an idea we're lookin' into on our end."

"Get close to Anu, Maddy. Learn what you can from her," Jags added.

Last night's pickpocket appeared out of the throng and ran toward them. Will's heart sank.

"Gotta go," Jags said. She disconnected the call and put the phone in her pocket.

How had the girl found them? And what did she want? It couldn't be good.

CHAPTER 37

In the conference room of the field office, Bear signed off the call with Jags and stood up.

"Will sounded worried and I'm still not sure it was a good idea to tell him about that dream," Maddy said as they headed back to the computer room. "What if we worried him for nothing?"

Bear gave her a quick kiss. "This way he'll be ready if the worst happens."

Maddy, wearing jeans and a white blouse, scowled before kissing Bear back.

As she pulled back, José motioned for them to follow him into another windowless conference room, smaller than the last. Anu sat at a computer, her brightly colored blouse the only decoration in the room. José handed Bear a file and left.

Bear looked inside the file and pulled out a photograph of a man he recognized right away.

"What'd he give you?" Maddy asked, as Anu turned to listen to their conversation.

Bear showed her the eight-by-ten image of a dark-eyed man, clean-shaven, his face covered in a complex pattern of tattoos. "Look familiar?"

"He's the man who attacked me on the street outside the loft," Maddy replied. "Looks like the man who shot at us at the guard shack." Her voice deepened as she turned to look at Anu. "And probably the man who killed your friends."

Bear grabbed one of the few sheets of paper in the folder. "The file on him is pretty thin. He's a Spaniard. Not been in trouble with the law in the past. Name is Lex Argones."

"Argones? Another cousin of mine?"

"Must be."

Maddy shook her head. "Fantastic. I just love my family."

Bear felt bad for Maddy but didn't know what to say. "Lucky you. Why would someone tattoo their face like that?"

"No clue."

Bear riffled through the folder. There was a last page. He pulled it out and scanned it. "Here's an update on Pyotr about his mother, the ambassador to India. She's missing."

"Missing?" Maddy took the sheet and studied it. "This VanOps analyst suspects she was having an affair with Ravi Singh."

Anu gasped. "He wouldn't."

Maddy handed the sheet to Anu. "There's a few pics on the back. They look pretty cozy."

Anu's hand trembled as she reviewed the document. "It can't be true. He loved my aunt."

With nothing to gain by Anu's agitation, Bear pointed to the monitor. "Find anything?"

Anu threw the page down on the desk. "No. No constellations or asterisms we've mapped from ancient sites match the image either."

Bear walked over to Anu's chair and sat down. "Let me search for a minute."

He pulled up his favorite internet search site and typed in a phrase as the women argued about Singh's alleged affair. It was as he suspected.

"We're going to Ephesus," he announced, stopping their argument flat. "I'll tell you about it on the plane. Let's go."

CHAPTER 38

MERIDA AIRPORT, MEXICO

DECEMBER 22, 8:44 A.M. CST

The pickpocket ran up to Will and Jags. "You have to go. Now!"

"Why? What's going on?" Will asked.

"There is a man after you. He's been asking around town. He has a fat nose, and everyone is scared of him."

Will translated for Jags and the two of them exchanged a concerned look.

Remembering Maddy's dream about the tattooed guy that strangled him, Will felt fear, his old friend, grab hold of his chest. "Any tattoos on his face?" he asked the girl.

"No."

That was strange. Could the guy be a disguise artist? Or was this someone else? "How did you find out?"

"After you caught me, everyone laughed at me." She looked down and blushed. "They said I should let him find you, but I thought you were nice."

Will touched her shoulder. "Thank you."

"But you have to hurry. He's headed here in a taxi." She smiled with pride. "I had a friend bring me on a motorcycle that skipped through the cars."

163

Will reached into his pocket and handed her a twenty. "You did well. Here."

The girl refused it, but Will pushed it into her palm. She grabbed it and ran off as fast as the wind.

Will turned to Jags and raised an eyebrow. They had been planning to go through Paris to Cairo, but that flight didn't leave for an hour, and they needed to leave now.

Her eyes darted around the airport. "This place is too public," she said. "No time to pack our weapons. Let's dump them and our bags. Ideas on evasion tactics?"

They dropped their weapons into the nearby waste can and abandoned their bags to the bench.

Will ran toward the automatic double-wide airport doors. "Let's get the next flight going anywhere. We'll at least be able to get some distance between us and him."

"I like distance. The last thing we want is an airport shootout."

They hustled inside, sprinting toward the first departure monitor to scan it for the next flight out.

"Looks like Morocco on Mexicana. If we can get a seat, it leaves in fifteen," Jags said.

"I've never been to Morocco," he replied as they raced toward the airline desk twenty meters away. Thankfully, there was no line.

"Me neither." Jags took a long breath and handed the airline attendant a credit card and her passport. "Two tickets to Marrakech, please."

At this point, Will didn't care if they were going to Timbuctoo. He also provided his passport and vainly tried to stop his foot from tapping.

The attendant ran the card and handed them their tickets. "Gate 3B. Hurry. I'll tell them to hold the door."

Outside, down the departures lane, a white taxi screamed to a halt.

Jags grabbed the tickets and they tore down the row of airline check-ins toward the central aisle that opened to the gates. Only two people stood in front of them in the security line. Will's heart raced and his entire body broke out in a sweat. Through the plate glass, Will got a glimpse of a man with blond hair and a swollen nose stepping out of a taxi. Jags went through the tall metal scanner. Will walked in and raised his hands above his head.

"Step over here, sir."

The security guard pulled Will over and waved a wand over him. Will held his breath.

Jags looked over her shoulder and Will followed her gaze. The blond man wasted precious seconds searching the crowd outside the airport.

"You're free to go," the guard said.

They rushed away from security. The gates were just ahead of them.

Panting, they stopped at gate 3B and handed their tickets to the airline employee. He ushered them onto the plane. The door shut behind them with a whoosh. They found their seats just as the distended clouds overhead broke and drops poured out of the leaden sky.

Will didn't relax until the plane began to taxi. He looked out the round airplane window through rain-splattered glass, squinting into the airport. The man, who had to be the assassin on their trail, strode back and forth between the gates, talking with gate attendants.

They may have dodged the killer, but he and Jags were too conspicuous. The cutthroat was sure to learn which flight they took.

Will sat back in his seat and closed his eyes. Safe, but for how long?

CHAPTER 39

The baron glanced out his office window at Pushkinskaya Square. Ever since that disastrous conversation with Levenfish, he'd been awaiting a call from Pyotr.

All was dark now, but earlier in the day, the sky had been blue for a change, as blue as the skies in Greece. Back when he'd been a pawn in the KGB's game, he had wrangled field assignments near the Mediterranean this time of year so that he could read sublime poetry in the golden rays of a seaside setting sun. He loved his country, but he also appreciated warm weather in the winter. Now that he was an older man and had progressed in his career, he was stuck behind a desk, moving the chess pieces.

He stroked the hand-carved eagle head on the top of his cane. *Other than the strange Mount Sinai theory, everything else is coming together.* Maybe he could find an excuse to take a trip to the Far East to check on the military buildup and see if he could spot an elusive Russian sea eagle.

His desk phone rang.

"Pyotr here, checking in."

"Are you on a secure line?"

"Of course."

The baron noted a pause. "But what?"

"I had to visit our Belize City office and obtain a new mobile unit."

"Why?"

"I was attacked in Chichén Itzá by a man who had tattoos all over his face. He surprised me from behind, tried to choke me with a garrote. I fought him off, but he got away with my phone."

The baron let out a disappointed breath. "Pyotr." He paused to let the depth of his annoyance seep into the line. "You let someone steal your phone?"

"It was encrypted, and I've had the tech guys here remotely wipe its data," he said. "But that brings me to another thing: I want backup on this mission."

The baron laughed. "That's funny. You mess up and want to be rewarded. Tell me another joke."

"I'm serious. In addition to the twins and Officers Thorenson and Agiashvili, there's this tattooed man who clearly has operational training as well. I'm outnumbered here."

"That man was probably Lex Argones. He's a Spaniard, disguise artist, also in on the hunt. Intelligence sources indicate the new Spanish king wants his star chart back."

"Whoever he was, he was good. You know I'm no pushover."

This at least was true. He'd been awarded the SVR Golden Scythe medal for recent wet work in Iran. "Pushover or no, it's your job to keep tabs on your equipment. For that mistake your mother loses a finger."

"No—" Pyotr bit off the rest of what he intended to say.

"Yes. I will take my time sawing it off, like I did her tongue. Maybe you need a babysitter to soothe your temper."

Pyotr took a deep breath and said in a low voice, full of gravel. "I don't need a babysitter. I need somebody who has my back."

"Are you still in Belize City?"

"Yes, the targets are flying out today. I'll follow discreetly."

"Good. Since you have a way to follow them and didn't let Lex kill you, I'll authorize one of our new high-tech vests."

"A vest? That's it?"

"Yes. A single operative is easier to hide in the shadows." The baron paused. "Well, here's a crumb. One of our researchers thinks the star chart leads to Mount Sinai."

"Which is where, exactly?"

"Scholars disagree." He paused. He'd done some quick research after the conversation under Bunker 42 and it had only confirmed his suspicions that experts argued incessantly over its location. "Could be Mount Catherine, Jebel Musa, Arabia, or even Saudi Arabia."

"That's what, a thousand square kilometers? What about the chart?"

"I have others working to decode it. But I think you, or the Americans, will figure it out."

"It's a grain of sand in the desert. You must be kidding."

"No. Once you find the cache, I'll send in an extraction team. It just better be soon! We need some prep time before zero point, New Year's Eve. Let me know once you have eyes on."

"But I—"

"No buts, or I will send you a babysitter and the price will be another of your mother's fingers."

Pyotr swore and hung up.

The baron smiled. Being chess master wasn't that bad after all.

CHAPTER 40

While Bear and Anu took restroom breaks, Maddy used her secure phone to make a call. "Elena, are you guys okay over there?"

Maddy was in the deserted lounge of the military hangar, waiting to board the Air Force jet. José had arranged the flight, and Maddy was glad they wouldn't need to fly commercial, in the interests of both security and privacy. She was a little miffed that Bear had made the arrangements without fully briefing them, but she decided to go along with his plan for now. Time was short, nobody else had any ideas, and he said he'd fill them in on the plane.

Elena's German upbringing was clear when she spoke. "We are safe for now, but I'm not sure that will last."

"What's going on?" she asked.

"It appears there is no power or gasoline in the Philippines, anywhere. I am not sure how we'll fly out, as many rumors indicate the airport is shut down, too."

"Oh, no!"

"Yes, Maddy, you should see it. Right now, we are hiding on the sixth floor of a Davao City hotel not far from the ocean, but people

169

are rioting in the dark street below. Frightening. We do not know if we are safe, even here."

Maddy bit her lip, wishing she could share what she knew about the Russians being the probable cause of the civil unrest. "How's AJ doing? He hates the dark."

"Here, speak with him."

Maddy fought the block in her throat. Now was not the time to be upset. "AJ, is that you?"

"Maddy!"

The cry in his voice made her scrunch her face and ball her non-phone hand into a fist. "Are you okay?"

"It's dark!"

She squeezed her eyes shut, feeling his fear like a terrified herd of horses pounding their hooves across her chest.

Maddy took a breath and opened her eyes. How to comfort him from half a world away? "It'll be day again soon, and you've got Elena there to keep you safe." What was that new boyfriend's name again?

"Garrod is here, too," AJ said, as if reading her thoughts.

"I'm glad. AJ—if you look close enough, you'll find light in even the blackest dark."

AJ sniffed. "Thanks, Maddy. I'll be brave."

"That's my little man."

But what kind of potential mother was she, putting him in this kind of danger? Maybe she should call off the adoption right now. She hesitated.

"Is everything okay, Maddy?"

No, she needed to think things through. "I'm just worried about you and can't wait to see your freckles. Big hug! Can I talk with Elena again?"

After a pause, Elena returned. "I'm back."

Maddy nibbled on a small piece of dark chocolate to buoy her spirits. "Do you have any other information about the situation?"

"It's intense. We still have cell signal from backup generators, and have been madly consuming all the news we can get. They are saying that it is a software issue and should be resolved soon, but I'm not sure."

"Lucky you have a signal."

"Yes, for now," Elena agreed. "We heard the hotel is trying to find generators, but for now, nothing."

"Why the riots?"

"People here don't always use cars, but their buses, boats, and motorbikes need to use the Benzin. There's much worry."

"Benzin, you mean gasoline?"

"Yes, sorry. It seems like social media is throwing fuel on the flames. Everyone is panicked that it will cause shortages of essentials like food and water."

"I can see that."

"Right. It makes me wonder. It all seems odd."

"It does." Again, Maddy searched for a way to share what she knew, but would it even be helpful? "Even if it's not a software glitch, I think at this point you need to think safety. What's your plan?"

"We've filled the bathtub with water as a start."

"Smart thinking. Is this a room service hotel?"

"Yes, why?" Elena asked.

"Maybe you should order some food that will keep for a day or so."

"Excellent idea, Maddy—we'll do that if they're able to serve."

Maddy played with a tuft of hair sticking out from under her cap. This was nerve-wracking. "Turn off one of your phones to conserve the battery."

"We were thinking about heading to an embassy, but there's too much chaos in the streets."

"Yeah, I'd also suggest you just stay put in that hotel."

"Okay. Wait, hear that?"

Maddy strained her ears. "Are those automatic weapons?"

"I think so. We've heard explosions, too. Looking down into the

171

street now. People are streaming away from one end of the street, running like rats."

"Mass panic?"

"Yes. The military is going to have to be deployed to quell the unrest."

"Oh no!" *Those poor people.* This type of disruption coming to the cities and towns of the United States sent a cold wave of fear through her. Maddy's hand began to shake. "Anything I can do to help, Elena?"

"I cannot think of anything, Maddy—just wish us well."

"That I'll do. Take care of yourselves. Stay put!"

"Okay, we'll call or text when things calm down."

"Yes, please stay in touch."

But how long would their batteries last?

Elena hung up. Maddy stared out the window at the large airplane. They had to keep that type of disaster from the States. Had to. Or it would become a bloodbath.

CHAPTER 41

"**A**ccording to legend, Ephesus was founded by the Amazons," Bear said.

They were all on the plane that José had acquired for the express purpose of getting the three of them to Turkey. They'd been in the air for about an hour, and all he could see out the window was an ocean of deep blue. The Atlantic.

Maddy had filled him in on her upsetting conversation with Elena and AJ before they embarked. She took her cap off and ran her fingers through her hair above the small bullet scar, a sign she was riled up. He couldn't blame her. This mission would be disastrous if they failed. He also felt that pumped-up, pre-battle feeling. He wanted to find one of the Russians planning the takedown and pummel them with his fists.

She'd also told him that Vincent had texted her that he was released from the hospital. He wanted to thrash Vincent, too. Not that Bear would *really* beat the guy up, but why had the ex been sniffing around that night in the first place? The weasel had gone cheating around on her, broke up with her, and now probably wanted her back. The guy was a true-blue scumbag.

To calm all three of them down, he'd decided to relay background on why they were headed to Ephesus. Across from them, Anu had been staring out the window ever since takeoff, having reverted to silence since their trip to the Belize office, but she turned her gaze on him now. "Amazons?"

"What do they have to do with the star chart?" Maddy asked.

"Y'all remember that the lorandite obelisks were most likely from a meteorite, don't you?" Bear replied.

Both women nodded, but Anu still seemed unanimated.

"Why not look for historical records of meteorites, especially ones that inspired local religions?"

"Sure," Maddy agreed.

"While we were in the field office, I remembered that I'd read somewhere about legends surroundin' Ephesus. They believe a deity descended from the sky."

Maddy sat up a little straighter. "I like it. But isn't it a ways from Egypt?"

Anu answered, saying, "History tells us the Egyptians were often at war with the Hittites, which was true during the chart's time period. There were many chariot battles fought in Syria, and their influence may have extended up to the Anatolian plateau in Turkey."

"That's pretty clever then, Bear," Maddy said.

Bear looked at Anu. "You seem to know a lot about Ephesus. What else can you tell us about it?"

Anu glanced out the airplane window for a long moment before answering. Her orange beads moved through her fingers like water. "To begin, it's believed that the Temple of Artemis was founded when the Amazon goddess fell from heaven."

"Aha. A true warrior goddess?" Maddy put her cap back on.

Bear told her he liked her short hair but secretly preferred it long.

"Yes," Anu said. "Several burial digs in that region point to the possibility that females may have participated in battle. Some of the entombed women were dressed as men and carried bows."

"I always thought Amazons were a myth. Anyway, is the city old enough to align with our pre–Alexander the Great timeline?" Maddy asked.

"Oh yes," Anu replied. "The town was first inhabited at the end of the Bronze Age. The location changed a few times due to flooding, and of course each ruler had a whim. An Ionian migration began around 1200 BCE, which means the city is known as an Ionian Greek city, even though Carians and Lelegians were there first."

"Okay, sounds like the right time period. Know anything about the meteorite?"

Anu smiled faintly at Bear. "This is where Bear's idea gets bonus points. Meteorite falls have inspired cultish worship around the world. There is some thought amongst my peers that the Temple of Artemis cult may have stemmed from the observation of a meteorite that they imagined fell from Jupiter."

"Really?" Maddy asked, then promptly leaned over and kissed his clean-shaven cheek. The kiss warmed Bear in a way that he'd like to get used to. Vincent could go to hell.

Anu nodded. "Yes, there are even reports that a sacred stone was once enshrined at the temple."

Bear remembered an image from his search. "That temple was one of the Seven Wonders of the Ancient World."

"Indeed, it was. Perhaps you should have been an archeologist."

Bear smiled. "I thought about it for a minute. Decided I wanted something a little more exciting."

Anu smirked. "Well, it appears you've found the right line of work."

Maddy poked him with her elbow. "Maybe too exciting."

To change the subject, Bear asked Anu, "Isn't there some ground-penetrating radar that can be used to search for meteorites?"

"Yes, actually. In 2006, a scientist developed a new algorithm that combined ground-penetrating radar with 3D imaging to find meteorites more quickly." She paused. "Or you could use a gradiometer. They're useful for magnetic surveying. But I prefer the radar."

Bear liked the idea of using a tool for the job. "You're the expert. When we're done talkin', I'll put José and Katrina to work on seeing what they can find for us when we land in Istanbul. Too bad he couldn't get us a direct flight to Ephesus, but maybe we can pick up the tools on the way."

Anu shivered and crossed her arms. Her right hand massaged her left shoulder for a moment. She opened her mouth to speak.

Maddy jumped in. "Is that mosquito bite still bothering you?"

For a moment, Bear thought he read confusion in Anu's eyes.

"No, it's fine. Just itches a little." Anu put her hand in her lap. "Bear, I like your plan. See if you can also get an XRF analyzer to do some elemental analysis. I'll be right back."

Bear watched Anu walk to the front of the plane and enter the restroom. He reached over and held Maddy's hand.

"There's something not right about her," Maddy whispered in Bear's ear.

"What do you mean?" Bear whispered back.

"She keeps rubbing that left shoulder. All my mosquito bites from the jungle don't itch anymore. And she just seems off. Closed."

"She did seem thrown by your question. But maybe she's grieving. She lost a bunch of friends yesterday."

"But she was like that when we showed up. Before everybody died."

Bear chewed an ice cube from the Air Force–supplied iced tea. "Well, we did interrupt her work. And then Jags told her Uncle Ravi's death was related to our mission. And the affair. I might be upset, too."

Maddy scrunched up her mouth in a sign Bear knew meant she disagreed. "I don't know, Bear. She doesn't feel right."

The bathroom door opened. Bear pressed Maddy's hand and released it.

"Just watch her," Maddy added.

"All right."

Anu sat down, leaned her seat back, and closed her eyes.

While looking out the airplane window at the ocean below, Bear surreptitiously studied her. What did Maddy see that he didn't? His heart rate ticked up. Could Anu be a double agent?

CHAPTER 42

ISTANBUL, TURKEY

DECEMBER 23, 3:55 A.M. EASTERN EUROPEAN TIME

From the rooftop patio of the Turkish safe house, Anu looked out over the dark waters of the Bosphorus and Golden Horn. Bear and Maddy had gone to sleep shortly after they'd arrived, but Anu was too wound up. She'd come up here to clear her head with the cool night air after the flight, hoping to relax enough to sleep. Moving to the railing, she rubbed her bruised lower back.

The sight from the private roof terrace was a stunning portrait of shimmering city lights reflected on a calm sea, drops of gold against an endless blanket of black. She'd never been to Istanbul, and would normally be enthralled by the clash of history and a twenty-first-century city. Even more so, since the city sat at the intersection of continents, where Europe met Asia. But not tonight. Anu stared at the water, seeking her own equilibrium.

The last time she'd come to a body of water seeking solace, she'd been ambushed. Had it been such a short time since she'd been accosted while walking the ruins? Anu closed her eyes and again felt the man's hands tighten around her wrists as he held them roughly behind her back.

"You're hurting me," she had cried.

"Good. You must understand your life is at stake."

She'd been walking around Chichén Itzá's Sacred Cenote, a sixty-meter-wide body of water the Maya had used as a sacrificial gate to their rain god Chaac. Twenty-two-meter-tall cliffs of sheer white stone encircled the death bowl that held countless skeletons, even those of children. Bones had been dredged from the bottom, along with gold masks, turquoise, jade pendants, and other items from as far away as Colombia. These days, the threat in the well was related to venomous snakes.

Because it was private, she liked to go there when the company of her colleagues became too much. But as she walked by the old steam baths, a stranger had leaped out of hiding and twisted her arms behind her in a painful dance. He'd pushed her to the edge of the cliff; she knew that if she wasn't careful, she would end up the Cenote's latest victim.

She'd never been in a situation like this and fear ran from her throat down to her toes. Vainly, she twisted in his grip and tried to see his face. "What do you want?"

"I want you to stop moving, stay quiet, and answer my questions. You scream and I shoot you on your way into that water. Understand?"

His accent was razor thin, and she couldn't place it.

For a brief moment she'd contemplated pushing them both into the water. Would he be able to shoot her on the way down?

As if reading her mind, he had tightened his grip on her wrists. "Don't try anything brave or stupid. Do you love your nieces?"

He must have known she did. Her sister's girls were young and nothing alike, but she loved them both with her whole heart. Her sister and husband lived in an upscale apartment in Bengaluru, in the heart of India. The threat to them riled her up and fear became anger.

"What do you know of my family?"

"I know they live on H. Siddaiah Road, number seventeen, near the Botanical Gardens. And I know they will all die by my hand unless you do as I say."

In her mind, a chorus of swearwords bellowed a livid lament. She had no good choice. "What is going on and what do you want me to do?"

"You have an appointment with some Americans today, yes?"

When her boss had called, saying they needed help and people in high places would appreciate her time, she'd thought it an annoying favor only. But this man seemed to think it was more. "Yes, they will arrive soon."

"They are spies. They stole a star chart that belonged to my father. I have stolen it back from them and need to find out where it leads."

The funny thing was, she had not believed him, thinking that anyone threating her life must be lying.

"I am going to inject you with a tiny GPS unit," he said. "I will follow you as you lead them to the superconductive material at the end of their trail."

"That sounds painful."

"It won't hurt nearly as much as the bullet I will put inside your gut if you refuse or remove it from your arm. Is that what you want?"

She felt defeated. "No."

He gripped her wrists tighter. "There may come a time where I need other help. You will do what I say at that time, yes?" When she'd only nodded, he twisted her hand until she squeaked in pain. "Say it," he demanded.

"Yes, yes, whatever you need. Just leave me and my family alone."

Before she could think of any way to resist, he'd switched her wrists to one strong hand and jabbed a needle into her left shoulder, near the place where she had the polio vaccine as a child. It hurt like a nasty hornet sting. He threw the syringe into the Cenote.

"And if you tell the American liars about our little chat, your family at number seventeen will be tortured to death," he whispered.

As punctuation on their meeting, he punched her in the right kidney. "This will help you remember our bargain."

A flower of pain blossomed throughout her side and back. She swayed toward the edge of the well and fell to her hands and knees on the edge. As he slid into the jungle, she got a quick glimpse of his form. Anu gasped for air and struggled to stay conscious. Losing the battle, white dots swam in her vision and she passed out.

By the time she recovered enough to stand, she was alone with the ghosts of those who had died in the sacrificial quest for rain. As if in answer to those ancient prayers, a shower had fallen from the heavens, washing the tears from her face.

Was he the one who had killed her friends? As a warning? She had not seen his face, and had no idea if he was the Russian or the Spaniard.

After the massacre, in her Belize hotel room, a threatening note had been slipped under her door. She'd no doubt that was from him.

Now, thousands of miles away, as she stared out at the lights of Istanbul, Anu desperately tried to figure a way out of the nightmare that had become her life. If she told Maddy and Bear, her family would suffer. But if I stay quiet, he might kill me anyway once he has what he wants.

Even death began to appear an inviting escape.

CHAPTER 43

Under the shadow of the city's ancient orange-red walls made of chalk and clay, Will looked around the open market to see if anyone had followed them, as he figured the assassin was hot on their trail. However, the arcade's complexity made it almost impossible to see if they were being watched. Or tracked.

From his time in South America, he was used to the sights and sounds of a bazaar, but the connected marketplaces, or souks, in the old quarter of Marrakech took the concept to a new level. The number of kiosks was dizzying, varying from dark and mysterious hobbits' closets to sparkling Aladdin's caves. Snake charmers with defanged serpents sat next to dentists creating makeshift dentures.

Will pointed. "Do you think the dentists use the snake fangs?"

Jags laughed. "The noise is getting to you."

"Probably."

It was a din. Vendors hawked everything from timeless Berber carpets and handmade leather bags, pottery, perfumes, alligator skins, and snakes to mint, dates, cashews, and modern electronic goods.

To disguise themselves, they had already purchased a change of clothes from Souk Semmarine. Jags wore a tan full-length *jilbab*, which reminded Will of a long-tailed coat, along with an ochre hijab over her unruly black hair.

Jags twirled. "What do you think of my outfit?" She made her voice even more raspy than usual.

She looked stunning. "The part of you I can see looks marvelous. And local."

Her sense of humor matched his and he appreciated her strong intellect. Though his heart remained tender from the loss of Maria, he was beginning to have fond feelings toward Jags.

"Perfect."

On his part, he sported a long bone-colored robe tailored like a shirt, known as a *thobe*, and a pair of loose trousers. "What about me? Do I fit in?"

"Yes, Mohammad. With that headscarf and black rope band, you look like a handsome native."

His Spanish heritage helped. And the well-trimmed beard.

"Are you sure we have time for this extra shopping?" Jags asked.

"No, but I'll regret it if we don't look."

"I've heard you can find anything in these souks."

"True. But this is a rather obscure item."

Jags pulled on his sleeve. "Take a look over here."

Will turned to look around Souk Haddadine, known for its lanterns and ironware. Wires hung across stalls and stunning glass lamps dangled everywhere.

Jags pointed to a table of knives.

"Oh, that's great," he said. "Hated leaving my knives in the trash can back at Merida."

"You didn't have much choice."

Will thumbed the knives for sharpness. "No. But if we can catch a short flight to Egypt, I'll have time to check a bag. These are too nice to throw away."

Will haggled for three well-balanced throwing knives and associated wrist and ankle scabbards. Then he asked the vendor if he knew of a stall that might sell what else they sought. The man advised him to go to a different stall in the same warren, using the Moorish minaret of the twelfth-century Koutoubia Mosque as a reference point. A unique symbol of the city, Will was sure it could be seen for miles.

As they jostled their way through the crowds, the scent of spices and cooking meat filled the air. It seemed Marrakech was as much a crossroads today as it had been in the past. Will heard Italian, German, some type of Scandinavian language, and, of course, Arabic as they parted the sea of strangers.

"Still think the train to Casablanca, then a flight to Luxor?" Will asked.

"Yeah, I think it's the safest plan. As you pointed out, the assassin will have guessed what flight we took. It wasn't the world's busiest airport."

At that, Will glanced around the crowds again, but no one looked suspicious. Maddy had texted him that the name of the tattooed assassin was Lex Argones. Didn't the man feel guilty hunting his own cousins? Will didn't understand it.

When they finally reached the stall, Will was shocked that they had the article he wanted. Pleased, he didn't even haggle. He was putting the item in his pocket as his phone rang. He recognized the number.

"Argones here."

"Argones, it's Director Bowman. We tracked your papers from Mexico. Are you still in Marrakech?"

"Yes, sir. Arrived an hour ago. What's up?"

"You're being hunted by an assassin named Lex Argones."

"Maddy gave us a heads-up. Distant cousin, right?"

"Yes, why I called you and not Jags. But the point is that he's hot on your trail."

"We figured out that a disguise artist showing facial tats followed us from Chichén Itzá. Our theory is that was Lex and he's the one that killed everyone at the dig."

"SIGINT has picked up some of his comms. He guessed your flight and is well connected in Morocco."

"We're about to catch a train to Casablanca."

"Don't. He's already chatted with the station master. He has roadblocks set up north of town and is watching for you both at the airport."

Will's heart beat faster. "We're disguised."

"Won't matter. Even if you get around the roadblocks, facial recognition software has gotten pretty good. A car is your best bet. Better yet, get an SUV and head to Fes through the desert. You can get a flight to Egypt from there."

"Through the desert? What about sandstorms?"

"It's December. Not likely. It's the best way to throw him off. He's not expecting you to head that way. You have to move. Go now."

The phone went silent in Will's ear. He turned to Jags. "New plan. The director says Lex, our formerly tattooed killer, is well connected here."

"Crap."

"Yes. Our best bet is an SUV south, through the desert and mountains, then up to Fes."

"It's out of our way."

"That's the idea. And heading north won't work. Roadblocks. We need to lose him and get to Luxor without a tail."

"I suppose it is good misdirection. And can't argue with the boss."

Will hailed a taxi, cursing King Carlos and his tattooed minion under his breath. The pair of blue-uniformed police officers headed their way inspired an additional round of swearing.

CHAPTER 44

Bear clenched his jaw. "C'mon, Maddy, it's just not safe for the two of you to stay here!"

Maddy stood by the window of their small but functional studio, her back to the stunning view of the storied Golden Horn estuary. Today, dark jeans covered her long legs, and she wore a close-fitting hunter-green sweater that reminded him of the one she wore on their first real date. The day beyond her was cloudy and cold, but Bear still hoped he'd have the opportunity to explore the area; as a history junkie, this city was pure opium. It wouldn't be today, though, as Katrina had lined up the ground-penetrating radar unit in Ankara. Now if he could just convince Maddy that she and Anu needed to come with him.

"We're in a safe house. Isn't the idea that it's safe?" Maddy asked.

Although he was now a junior VanOps field officer, he wasn't sure yet who he could trust here in Turkey. "Theoretically yes, but we'll all be safer together. I'm point on this mission and you're under my protection."

"Yes, but I need to try and bond with Anu. Didn't Jags, who is team leader, ask that I get close to her?"

That was a low blow. His body tensed.

"Yes," he drawled. "Jags is in charge of the overall mission. But I'm in charge here." And she had made the request, but he didn't want to admit that.

Her eyes narrowed. "If you go throwing that bossy bullshit around, I'll walk."

He took a deep breath and tried to soften his voice and relax his shoulders. He'd seen her temper and that was the last thing he wanted. "Okay, I'm not tryin' to tell you what to do."

"Good. It's the perfect time to try to bond with her. I'm telling you, there's something not right with her."

"I'm not seeing that. It would be fun to think of her as a double agent, but I've thought about it and she's just grieving."

Maddy crossed her arms. "I don't think so."

"I do."

"We may have to agree to disagree on that point," she snipped.

"For now." When Maddy remained firmly in the defensive position, he added, "For the purposes of inquiry only, how would you try to bond with her if you did stay here?"

Maddy gestured toward the ceiling. "I'm thinking brunch on the terrace upstairs."

"It's a nasty, cold day. And what if there's a sniper watchin' the building?"

Maddy let out an exasperated breath. "Oh my god, now you sound like Will."

Bear swore under his breath. He was not paranoid like Argones, but there were dangers to consider. "Maddy, stop being stubborn. This is serious."

"It is, I agree. If Anu knows something, our lives could depend on worming it out of her. Besides, no one knows we're here, right?"

"As far as we know, we haven't been followed from Mexico," Bear admitted.

"Aren't you just going to go, grab the unit and a bite to eat, and come back here?"

Bear gritted his teeth. "That's the plan. Couldn't get one of those XRF things Anu wanted. Or a gradiometer."

"I rest my case."

Maddy was a hard woman to argue with—or perhaps he just hadn't found the right tactic. "Would be a lot more fun if you came along."

"Fun? C'mon, Vincent. Now who isn't taking things seriously?"

Her eyes widened as she realized her gaffe, but it was too late. Bear's simmering frustration ignited into full-blown anger.

He growled, "I am *not* your ex. Fine, I'm leavin'. Just. Stay. Here."

Before he said words he would regret, Bear grabbed the keys to the green SUV and left, pulling the door closed behind him with a bang. It closed louder than he intended, but he decided he didn't regret it; he was mad as hell and maybe she'd think twice about doing something dangerous if she knew it.

He stomped down the hallway. They bloody well better stay safe while he was gone.

CHAPTER 45

At first, Will wasn't sure whether the slow-moving Moroccan motorcycle police were after them or not. After all, they were deep in the belly of Souk Haddadine, which all sorts of pimps and drug-dealers called home to prey on tourists. And even if he and Jags *were* the target, would their disguises hold? He doubted it.

Turning to watch the cops from the corner of his eye, he touched Jags's arm.

"What?"

"Do *not* look over your left shoulder. Cops on bikes. We're just two people looking at this pretty brass candlestick."

Jags swore under her breath and picked up the shiny piece of metalwork from a table full of similar items while Will, tensed for action, watched the uniformed officers search the crowd. Suddenly, one of the men looked right at him, poked his friend, and gunned the motorcycle in their direction.

Will knocked the candlestick out of Jags's hands. "Run!"

Jags sprinted off, away from the police, and Will followed, pulling the table crashing down behind them to impede the policemen's progress down the cobbled street. They only had a seventy-meter head start.

Fear gave his feet wings and they flew down the lanes, turning left, right, right, left, making random choices, flying by coffee shops, rug stores, and the ever-present lanterns. The cops couldn't drive fast down the crowded lanes, but the commotion he and Jags were leaving behind was too obvious a wake. Not to mention that Will's legs ached and his lungs burned. He couldn't keep running for long.

As they turned a corner, he had an idea and pulled up short. He grabbed Jags by the forearm and pointed. She nodded, and they put their plan into action, grabbing a nearby coil of wire meant for showcasing lanterns and heading to opposite sides of the narrow street.

The growling of the motorcycles came closer, closer yet, and then the bikes drove around the corner and right into their wire trap. The police tumbled over their handlebars. Before the machines even hit the ground, Will and Jags jumped on the motorcycles, roaring away down the streets.

Will panted, not believing the plan had worked. Before he had a chance to relax, though, his ears picked up a horrible sound—other motorcycles. He checked the mirrors, and pounded his fist into his thigh. There were two more behind them. The first policemen must've called for backup.

Jags motioned with her head for him to follow her, then gunned her bike, and took off like a rocket. Will followed, threading his motorcycle between the vendors and the tourists who clogged the passageway. A siren wailed. It took Will a second to figure out that it was coming from the direction of Jags, who had found an alarm on her motorbike. It helped clear the path, but also let the police know exactly where they were headed.

Jags skidded right around a corner, and Will slowed, following her into the turn, and then she made another quick left. The streets seemed to be getting narrower as they zoomed down a long straightaway. The police were behind them—too far to shoot, but not by much.

When Jags veered right and turned down a sidewalk, people jumped out of the way, swearing and waving their fists. Will tried to knock goods off tables to make the path more of a gauntlet for the cops, but he needed to keep both hands on the handlebars most of the time.

They turned right onto a street and accelerated. All of a sudden, heart thudding, Will realized the problem: it was a dead end.

With the cops hot on their heels, they couldn't turn around.

After skidding to a stop, Jags dumped her bike, rushed the wall, and vaulted over it. Amped up, Will followed suit.

The other side of the wall held more of the same market.

"Act like a normal tourist," Jags whispered.

He sucked in some air. "I'll try."

They walked, and made a quick left, then a right.

Ahead, a stall vendor was in the process of lowering a brown metal door. Will rushed forward, pulling Jags along and making it inside just as the door shut behind them. The shopkeeper yelled and gesticulated wildly, but Will put his finger to his lips in the universal sign for quiet, pulled some bills out of his wallet, and handed them over. The man looked over the funds, squinted in suspicion, but nodded his agreement.

Will pantomimed leaving out the back and the shopkeeper waved them into the depths of the shop. It was a clothing store for locals, filled with cloth in all shapes and sizes. Jags grabbed a black *jilbab* and a red headscarf, handing the shopkeeper more bills. He seized the money before shooing them out the back door. They exited into a deserted narrow alley.

"Which way?" Will asked, his throat raw from all the running. He was still breathing heavily—he needed to work out more.

"First, we change." Jags handed Will the red cloth. "Put it on your head, Superman."

As Will swapped out his headscarf and wiped his face with the old one, she changed out of her tan disguise and put on the black *jilbab*, which made her look like most of the other local women.

Transformation complete, they threw their original disguises in the trash.

"Now let's get the hell out of here in the first taxi we can find."

CHAPTER 46

Pyotr looked around the cheap hotel room, his head still hurting from where Lex had knocked him out near that camp in Mexico. Why had the man stolen his phone and not killed him? Professional courtesy? Perhaps. But now he owed the guy, and he hated owing anyone. At least he'd been able to keep the concussion hidden from the baron.

He was sitting in an overstuffed armchair near a pane of glass that let in the gray light of a Turkish morning. It was a cold, cloudy day and the window was dirty, but the small sliver of lorandite still gleamed red in his hand.

On the desk stood his new phone with the GPS monitoring app that he'd used to follow Anu Kumar here to Istanbul. Thanks to the SVR's interception of the Marshall woman's text conversation with her ex-boyfriend, he'd been able to beat them to Chichén Itzá. Realizing it would be near impossible to isolate and kidnap Marshall, he'd chosen the archeoastronomer as a way to follow the group. The GPS gadget was from the team back in Russia, who had stocked him with a detection-proof implant—new tech that supposedly noticed if a sweeper wand was nearby and turned itself off.

At the moment, the monitoring map showed that they were several blocks down the street, probably in a CIA safe house.

He turned back to the lorandite spike in his palm. He loved technology, but also loved ancient mysteries, like this tiny piece of mysterious material. The crimson shard, about fifteen centimeters long and half a centimeter wide, was sharp at both ends. He felt the points. Quite sharp.

From his helicopter all those months ago, he'd seen the balls of lightning the baron had told him were caused by this material. Perhaps the stuff was even the source of his father's death. Pyotr knew that what they hunted was a much larger mass of it, maybe a meteorite that had fallen to earth millennia ago.

But what made it remarkable was that when he closed his fingers around it, he could feel it pulse.

Not a rapid movement. Instead it felt like holding the slow, steady rhythm of his own heartbeat in his hand. Fascinating. For years, he had trained with the ultra-dark forces of the Soviet military machine, his life given away at a young age. His father had used him as a pawn in his quest to gain standing with the military, to earn trust, and that had meant endless exercises. Esoteric yogic rituals to stay warm while immersed in ice. Attempts at remote killing while having an out-of-body experience. The last had never worked for anyone, top secret CIA Stargate program included, but he was good at most of the other dark arts. How, then, did one create ball lightning with this lorandite?

Soviet scientists who had studied the material didn't understand much about ball lightning, and even questioned its very existence. Pyotr had seen it, though, and knew it was real. In one report, the scientists had hypothesized that static electricity was responsible for generating the unusual globes, but Pyotr felt it was something else, something related to the ability to move energy in his body. The pulse called to him. Why not try that?

Pyotr closed his eyes and put his mind in a meditative state, a trance-like zone that he had been taught using secular light-and-sound methods. His breath deepened, and the thumping pulse slowed. He wrapped his awareness around the tiny spike and sent energy to it from deep in his belly.

The shard grew hot. Black energy was his favorite and he pulled it from volcanic rocks deep in the earth. Up through his feet, into his heart, and out through his hands.

A sudden, sharp bite on the tip of his fingers caused him to open his eyes. Bouncing around the room was a blue globe, about the size of a coin. It whizzed by his head, and landed in the window curtain, catching the drape on fire.

Pyotr smiled as he pulled the fabric to the floor and stomped out the flame.

With a little more practice, he'd be ready when the fools led him to the meteorite.

CHAPTER 47

little over an hour after Bear left in a huff, an embarrassed Maddy knocked on the door of Anu's apartment. Had she really called him Vincent? Arggh! She clenched her teeth. That's what she got for not controlling her anger better. After all those years with her ex, his name had just slipped out. Remembering the flash of hurt in Bear's eyes, she wondered if he would ever forgive her.

She would try to make it up to him later. After Bear left, she'd wanted to check in with the Order in Jerusalem, but there was that NDA she'd signed. Instead, she did her exercises. Now to see if she could make any headway befriending Anu. Both of their sleeping quarters were on the third floor of the Istanbul safe house. Maddy knocked again.

When Anu opened the door, she looked tired. Dark circles lined her ebony eyes, her long hair was uncombed, and no jeweled bindi adorned her forehead. Had she just woken up? But no, she was dressed, in a brightly patterned blouse and gray slacks.

"Would you like to have Turkish coffee on the patio roof while we wait for Bear to return with the radar unit? There's olives and cheese up there," Maddy said.

"How long will he be?"

"According to Katrina, the unit is in Ankara, about four hours from here. Bear should be back later this afternoon and we can head to Ephesus tonight or in the morning."

Anu put her hands on her hips. "Then I'm going out."

Maddy took a step back. "But Bear asked us to stay here."

Anu narrowed her eyes. "Do you take orders from him? Am I a prisoner?"

At these questions, Maddy could already sense where the conversation was going, yet felt powerless to stop it. She had a momentary image of a barrel headed downstream toward Niagara Falls, certain to break into pieces on the rocks below.

"No, of course not," she said.

"Then there is a museum I want to see. And I can't wear these clothes another day."

"But—"

Anu took a breath and seemed to reassess. "Why don't you come with me?"

Maddy considered. Bear would be even angrier, but it was tempting. They'd arrived late last night, but the darkness couldn't hide the city's graceful mosques, sprawling palaces, and intriguing monuments, many of which were decked out in lights for the holiday season. On their meandering "surveillance detection route" from the airport, Maddy had watched the ancient city with fascination and had wished for a chance to explore it. And it wasn't like she was going just for fun—she'd been ordered to bond with the woman. If Anu was going to be stubborn and leave the safe house, this was the best way to do it while still keeping her out of danger.

"All right. Since we've seen no sign of pursuit on our end, let's see some sights," Maddy said.

Anu opened the door and gestured for Maddy to come in. "Give me a few minutes in the bathroom to finish getting ready."

As Anu retreated into the restroom, Maddy studied the designer furnishings, which were in the same minimalist vein as those in their bedroom down the hall. Wanting to see if Anu's room also shared a fantastic view, Maddy headed to the window.

As she did, however, a single sheet of paper tucked underneath a magazine on the nightstand caught Maddy's eye. Given that Anu had fled Chichén Itzá with nothing, it seemed odd.

Maddy listened. The faucet ran in the bathroom. Slipping the paper from the magazine, Maddy unfolded it and read the bold words typed on the white page.

"I'm watching you."

Shocked, Maddy swiftly replaced the paper under the magazine and bolted to the window, the view forgotten. Her heart thumped.

While part of her mind was diverted by the brashness of her action, the other part went into high gear, trying to process this disturbing information. The note was typed. Plain paper. No way to check handwriting.

Who is watching Anu? And what did the threat mean to their mission?

CHAPTER 48

Bear stood and gazed at the ancient inscriptions on the mounted plaque near the Augusteum, the morning's argument with Maddy temporarily forgotten. Two hours into the drive, his breathing had calmed down, and he'd realized that, even though her comment about Vincent hurt worse than a slap to the face, it was an unintentional slip of the tongue, probably from years of arguing with the rat. As he loaded the lawn-mower-sized ground-penetrating radar into his SUV in Ankara, he'd decided that he wouldn't even mention it when he got back to Istanbul. Water under the bridge.

Thinking to grab a quick bite before heading back, he'd headed to the nearby park, one that the guidebook mentioned had plentiful street vendors as well as this two-thousand-year-old former temple holding the "Queen of Inscriptions." Though the cold, dark afternoon threatened rain, or even snow, he was unable to resist. He couldn't help but stop for a few moments of awe and admiration, imagining what the structure looked like in the time of Augustus. Side walls and an ornamented doorframe were all that remained now behind the hedge of waist-high protective glass, but he could see where six proud columns once stood.

"Hello, what is your name?"

Bear turned toward the speaker. She was quite attractive, in a sorority-girl way. He noted a French/Spanish accent and she smelled of honey, perhaps due to a product she used to condition her long white-blonde hair. Dressed in a thick yellow-daisy-colored jacket against the cold, her curious blue eyes swept over him in a way that made him feel like she was undressing him.

Surely, he imagined her intention. Must have been a hangover from the disagreement with Maddy.

"My name is John," he said, sticking to the secrecy of the mission. "What's yours?"

"Justine. And this is my dog Joshua." She pointed to an inquisitive black-and-tan Jack Russell terrier.

"It's nice to meet you, Justine." He bent to scratch the Jack Russell behind the ears, missing Colonel, the German Shepherd at his mom's house. "What are you two up to today?"

"We live in that apartment building over there," she added, nodding to a red-roofed structure across the street. "We come out for walks at lunchtime and sometimes visit the park nearby. Are you enjoying the Temple of Augustus?"

Bear liked her accent. Spanish with a lot of French. Maybe she'd grown up near the Pyrenees.

"I sure am. I had to run an errand here in town and couldn't resist comin' by for some lunch and a look. I love history."

She put her hand on his arm. "You've come to the right place."

That decided it. She was flirting with him. "Yeah? What do you know of it?"

"I'm getting my doctorate here in Istanbul at the university, in history. What would you like to know?"

"Did King Midas really establish the town?"

She looked at him sideways. "Most people don't know that. Yes, most historians think so. Of course, there are several kings who had the name, but most think it was the famous king Midas, the one with the golden touch, who helped the town get a foothold."

Bear smiled. "What can you tell me about the Res Gestae Divi Augusti here? I'm sure I mispronounced the Latin."

She returned the smile. "You did pretty well pronouncing the Deeds of the Divine Augustus. Drawl and all. Are you from the southern part of the United States?"

Bear bowed. "Yes, ma'am."

Justine turned back to the plaque. "I've always wanted to get to know a man from the States," she said. "I'm learning to read Latin. It's not that different from French. Anyway, the Augusteum was built between 25 and 20 BC."

"Is that the original on the wall?" Bear pointed and put his hand on the railing above the small glass partition. "Wish the barrier wasn't here."

She touched his hand. "I don't like barriers either."

He coughed and put some space between them; this was getting uncomfortable.

She continued breezily, as though it hadn't happened. "No, the original was in Rome, on two bronze columns near the Mausoleum of Augustus, but those were lost. Two other surviving inscriptions are incomplete. This is one of the best-preserved texts."

"What's it say?"

"It's an aggrandized version of his accomplishments."

"Ah, early public relations. I read there's been much disagreement over the purpose of the document."

She gave him another curious glance. "Yes, some say it was intended as an account of his stewardship, while others think it was more an epitaph. Everyone has a perspective."

Bear looked up. Icy rain had begun to fall in misty sheets from the low, pregnant clouds. "Interesting. Does he mention the assassination of his adoptive father, Julius Caesar?"

Justine shivered. "I think he left that out. Let's see."

She leaned into him as she scanned the text.

He swore. This was swiftly entering dangerous territory. All he'd wanted was a quick lunch and a look at this fascinating old wall.

He stepped away and bent down to pat the dog's head. "I need to get going."

"Wait. Have you eaten? I could make you something up at my apartment. It's much warmer than out here in the frigid rain."

In an earlier time in his life he'd have been tempted, but his heart belonged to Maddy, even if she did piss him off sometimes. Or, as he was learning about his emotions, if his thoughts about her caused him to get riled up. "It was a pleasure meeting you, but I need to complete an errand before the roads ice up." *And get back to my girlfriend.*

She stepped closer, leaning into him until her lips were close to his. "Are you sure?"

He shivered but took a step back. "I'm sure."

"That's too bad. I should have enjoyed getting to know you better. *Au revoir*, then. Enjoy your time in Turkey."

She donned a green beret against the rain and headed down the length of the glass wall, one hand sensually gliding along the top rail, while the Jack Russell terrier meandered after her on his retractable leash. Bear watched for a moment and then moved in the direction of the vendors he'd seen when he arrived.

To his dismay, the food sellers had packed up, scared off by the weather. Perhaps he'd stop in the café he spotted earlier and obtain a soup or warm sandwich. A savory, mouth-watering smell drifted from the shop in waves, even through the heavy rain shower.

As he opened the door to the shop, a high-pitched scream pierced the afternoon. Bear swiftly pivoted and looked back over his shoulder. Two men had grabbed Justine, one on each side, and were holding her by the arms while the terrier nipped at their heels.

CHAPTER 49

A cold apprehension tickled Maddy's spine as she and Anu strode past the glass-encased globe of the ancient world that marked the entrance to the drab, two-story Istanbul Museum for History of Science and Technology in Islam. The feeling had been dogging her ever since seeing the ominous note on Anu's bedside.

Three simple words, and yet, such a profound effect. "I'm watching you."

Even though she took no responsibility for Bear's outburst, he'd had a point about staying safe. Pleased she had managed to keep her own anger from flaring, she hoped he was calming down as the day wore on. And hoped her outing with Anu would continue to be uneventful, especially since Bear would never have wanted them to leave in the first place.

Rain was brewing, perhaps even a Christmas snow. A warm rush of air enveloped Maddy as they entered the museum. At the ticket kiosk, Anu insisted on paying her own way. As Maddy watched the transaction with the red-jacketed clerk, several questions swirled through her mind. Could there be any innocent explanation for such a note?

Maddy decided to assume for the moment it was a valid threat. The next question that followed was, who was the watcher? The tattooed assassin, Lex Argones? Or Pyotr, her odd-eyed uncle? Or perhaps it was a scorned lover. Not likely, but she should use this time together to probe Anu's past in order to eliminate that possibility.

Tickets in hand, they walked past the booth and into the quiet foyer. Not many museum guests today.

Maddy pointed to a room with low cushions. "Want to listen to the videotaped introduction? The man at the kiosk recommended it."

Anu glanced at her guidebook. "No, I don't think so, for me anyway. I'm just interested in the astronomy section, but feel free."

"No, that's all right."

They walked down a tiled floor path lined with glass display cases. Maddy noted one was full of sharp objects she hoped were medical instruments rather than torture devices. After a few hallway twists and turns, they arrived in the museum's astronomy section.

"Think there's anything here that can help us figure out the star chart?" Maddy asked.

"It's possible—that's why I wanted to come look at this collection of astrolabes. I woke up this morning recalling this collection was here in Istanbul."

It was odd that Anu hadn't mentioned that earlier. Or was it? This woman was so private.

"What's an astrolabe?" Maddy asked.

"It's an inclinometer."

"A what?"

"It measures inclines."

"What do inclines have to do with stars?"

Anu laughed. "I guess your background doesn't include astronomy."

Maddy felt a little put off. "That's right. Aikido and computers."

"Okay, no worries. I'm ignorant on both of those subjects."

Maddy relaxed a bit. If she wanted to gain this woman's trust and confidence, she needed to put up with a little fun at her expense. "Please teach me about inclines and astrolabes."

"Think about it this way. Angles are a great way to measure how far up in the sky a specific star appears. Astronomers and navigators used these instruments to measure the inclined position of a celestial body."

"Ah, that makes sense. What practical purpose did they serve?"

"Many. They were used to navigate the deserts and then the seas, measure local latitude, and identify stars and planets. They were even used to find the way to Mecca." Anu walked over to a device underneath a glass display case. "This is an early astrolabe that has been pulled apart to illustrate how it works. See the various layers?"

Bronze plates were held apart by fishing line, and Maddy could indeed see how it all fit together.

"There was a different sheet for each latitude. To show local sky."

It clicked for Maddy. "Oh, like a template."

"Right."

"How could the star chart we have fit in?"

"It's a long shot, but perhaps the chart may have been used to create a plate."

Maddy allowed her hopes to rise. It would be nice to have a solid lead instead of traipsing about the world looking for fallen meteors. Time to find where the star chart led was growing short.

"Interesting. How old are the oldest astrolabes?" Maddy asked.

"Let's look around. See if we can find out."

They took a minute to find the oldest device, and read the card, which also had translations in French, German, and a few other languages.

Maddy felt disappointed. "It sounds like we don't have a match. They think the astrolabe was invented just a few hundred years before Christ and we suspect the star chart is a thousand years older than that."

Anu's face looked crestfallen. "I was afraid of that. This isn't my area of expertise, which is why I wanted to come look."

Maddy snapped a few pictures with her phone. "There's a chance they're wrong about the timing of the earliest devices."

Anu smiled. "True. We scientists know all about being wrong. It's why we cloak our guesses under 'hypotheses.'"

"Well, it was worth looking. Let's keep the idea—who knows, perhaps Will and Jags will find the other parts of a device. I hope they're in Egypt by now."

"Surely." Anu surveyed the rest of the exhibition with clear longing. "We have some time before Bear is due back, right? Do you want to look around a bit more?"

Maddy hadn't had a chance to try to bond over a heart-to-heart conversation. She agreed.

They left the astronomy section and moved into the hall. A curly-haired worker wearing the museum's trademark red jacket swept dust from the floor.

They walked into a geography hall, where they were both drawn to different items. Maddy found one of the earliest known globes and studied it before her eyes were pulled to a wall map of the Middle East. It was from fifteen hundred years before Christ, which would make it the correct time period. She noted that Jericho was in the land of Canaan while Jerusalem wasn't present. In Egypt, Memphis and Thebes stood out. Farther northeast, toward where they were in Turkey, lay the ancient town of Aleppo, which was in the news a few years ago as the Syrians suffered through civil war. Ugarit was below Aleppo, near the coast.

"Hey Anu, do you think this map is the right part of the world?"

Anu circled over toward Maddy and glanced up at the early map. "Based on what we know so far, I think it represents the region I've been visualizing."

Wanting to show Bear later, Maddy shot a photo. "Some of the exhibits here would have interested my ex-boyfriend," she said, hoping self-disclosure might tempt Anu to be more open about her own life.

Anu looked at Maddy with curiosity. "Are you glad he's your ex? Or do you miss him sometimes?"

That was insightful. Maybe vulnerability would work.

"I do miss him. After being together for years, we were engaged to be married before he . . ." Maddy let her voice break. "He went off with another woman."

She looked away, realizing what she said was the painful truth. How long would it take her to get over the bastard?

"And you and Bear?" Anu asked. Concern must have flashed across Maddy's face, because Anu added, "I'm sorry. I heard you two shouting this morning."

Oh god, she'd heard them. Maddy flushed. "Sorry about that. He wanted us to stay back at the house today where we'd be safe."

"Everyone disagrees sometimes. It's how we handle those differences of perception that matter."

Maddy appreciated the understanding. "Good point, thanks. Anyway, that was our first real disagreement, and I am enjoying getting to know him. It's just . . . sometimes I still miss Vincent. Can you understand that?"

Anu patted Maddy's arm. "Yes, I understand. Your heart was broken, but is healing now with Bear. These things take time."

Seeing that Anu was more engaged in this conversation than any they'd had to date, Maddy leaned in. "The thing is . . . Vincent recently said he wanted me back."

Anu's eyes widened. "It's like a soap opera! What are you going to do?"

Maddy exaggerated. "I don't know." Now the clincher. "Have you ever been in a similar situation? Do you have any advice?"

Anu looked off down the hall of historical objects and paused for a heartbeat before answering. "No, I'm sorry. My field work isn't conducive to relationships, much to my mother's chagrin. She thinks I'm too old and wants to arrange a wedding for me."

Maddy's heart sank. It wasn't an ex following Anu then. It had to be Pyotr, or Lex with his tattooed face. A curly-haired man wearing a raincoat turned the corner and walked past them. With a start, Maddy realized it was the same man who'd been sweeping the hallway and she hadn't recognized him without his red jacket.

Maddy froze. Bear's question, "Why would someone tattoo their face like that?" drummed in her head. The answer came in an instant. As a disguise. Who would remember anything else?

CHAPTER 50

Through a thick curtain of freezing rain, Bear's heart raced as he tried to make out the details of the crime occurring at the other end of the deserted square.

Who tried to abduct someone in broad daylight? Were they going to rape Justine? Kill her? She was an innocent history student. The violation of her made him furious and rekindled the morning's angry fire.

Bear scanned the area. He was the only witness to the attack. This part of the plaza was now deserted. A small part of him considered that this might be a snare, but rage at the injustice filled him and he found himself slamming the door of the inviting café and sprinting toward the crime. He pulled his 9 mm Glock from his leather underarm holster as he ran alongside the glass barrier that kept tourists out of the rock-strewn temple area.

In seconds he closed the distance. When he was about twenty-five feet away, the man to Justine's left pushed her away, swung around, and aimed a gun at Bear, firing. The sound shocked the empty square, ricocheting through the rain before fading to silence.

Bear's combat training had taken hold the instant the man swung the weapon his way. He dove over the glass barrier and into the area of ruins below, savagely returning fire as he launched himself into the air. The shooter fell backward. Bear used a shoulder roll to soften his landing and ended up behind one of the Roman stone blocks that littered the area. It provided cover, although Bear was now five feet below ground level and at a disadvantage. As bullets pinged off the ancient stones, Bear winced at the damage.

He wormed on his stomach toward a larger block. When he was able to glance up, both the man who'd been on Justine's right and Justine were shooting at him over the glass wall. Bear growled with frustration. Justine had played him all along. It was a trap, but who knew he was here?

He'd puzzle that out later. Now he had to get out of here alive.

Ping! A chip of flying stone caught him on the chin. Bear grimaced.

Bear didn't want to shoot at Justine, but with no choice, he returned her fire, and then shot at the man. A slug skimmed across the intricate lightning scar on Bear's right forearm, but his aim was true. Glass shattered. The man fell over the partition and landed with a smack in the wet grass, while Justine's body slumped over the glass wall, the pistol hanging from her fingers like a suspended raindrop before slipping from her grasp.

A searing pain in Bear's forearm made him grind his teeth and look at the wound through his torn jacket. An oozing line of blood started near his wrist and ended near his elbow. He thanked the local gods that the slug hadn't broken a bone. This wound was painful as sin but it should heal fast with no surgery, just stitches. He'd have a new scar atop the network of old lines.

Hoping it would stop the bleeding long enough to get back to Istanbul, he ripped the bottom of his T-shirt off and used it to apply pressure.

A clattering sound made him look up. Freed from the other end of his leash, the Jack Russell terrier ran down the length of the wall in the opposite direction, the plastic end of his retractable leash dragging behind him on the sidewalk.

Otherwise, it was silent. His hit on the original shooter must've also been fatal. Swearing, Bear hit his thigh. He hated killing as much as Maddy did. But when it came to kill or be killed, he did what he had to do.

He took a deep breath and waited thirty seconds. Then, on the off chance the first shooter was still alive, Bear picked himself up from the ground and peered around the stone, senses alert as he peered through the rocks that now looked like a blood-stained Roman graveyard.

After confirming the body of the original shooter was not moving, he shuffled over and searched it, seeking a wallet or clue to how they'd found him. In a pants pocket, Bear found a grainy black-and-white picture of himself driving the green SUV. The attackers must've hacked traffic cams. They were good.

The assailants must not have had a sniper rifle, though, and Justine no combat training. Otherwise, why didn't she try to stab him up close, and why hadn't they picked him off when he headed back to the café? Curious. Maybe these were local guns for hire.

Sirens wailed in the distance. It would complicate their mission if he were found here.

He needed to disappear into the mist. And fast.

CHAPTER 51

GÜLHANE PARK, ISTANBUL

DECEMBER 23, 3:42 P.M. EASTERN EUROPEAN TIME

They were on their way through the park that housed the museum when Maddy realized they were being tailed.

For a while, she pretended not to notice, taking in the sights around her. Gülhane Park was amazing, even in the dead of winter, thanks to its wide paths and impressive fountains and statues that, unlike them, were immune to the cold wind and freezing rain. But then she wondered if telling Anu would spook the woman into sharing any information about the disturbing bedside note.

"I think we're being followed. Don't look back," she whispered.

Anu stiffened but kept walking. "What makes you think that?"

Maddy hated that Bear was right to want them to have stayed at the safe house, but there was no denying what she saw. She'd also registered the man didn't have the strange but ubiquitous head bandage that she'd read signaled a recent hair transplant, all the rage in Turkey. He wasn't here for medical reasons. "I see a dark-haired man moving in a way that looks familiar to me."

Anu flushed. "What do we do? Can we call for help?"

Interesting that Anu didn't ask for more details.

"I'm not certain." Maddy pointed with her head. "Why don't we duck into that restaurant?"

Anu agreed, and they entered an eatery on the edge of the park. Although it was late afternoon, the restaurant was busy. Maddy took her cabbie cap off and nervously ran her fingers through her short hair, while Anu's breathing remained shallow. They both snuck glances out the window.

After a short wait, they were able to get a linen-covered window table, where they reviewed the menu and ordered a token meal. Maddy's stomach was doing flip-flops. She waited to see where Anu would take the conversation. Would she confess knowledge or deny everything?

Anu leaned toward Maddy. "How can you be so calm when you think someone is following us?"

Maddy took a drink of water from the table. When her finger started to tremble, she put her left hand under the table. "Well, I've learned to wait and see if what appears to be a problem really is."

Anu scanned the room. "Who do you think it is?"

"I *think* it's Pyotr, the Russian. But I'm not sure. Russia and Spain both have agents on our heels."

"What if he tries to kidnap us? Or kill us?"

"He's at a distance, if there is even a 'he.'" Maddy tried to make light of the situation. "Plus, if we get in trouble, I'll never hear the end of it from Bear."

The conversation paused and Maddy heard the babble of four different languages at once. Then, in English, a couple at a nearby table mentioned the Philippines.

Maddy wondered if the country had gotten their power and gas stations back online yet. She'd seen a screaming headline about the riots on a newspaper as they walked into the restaurant, but print was old news nowadays and much could have changed since the paper came out. How were AJ and Elena? And what would happen to her nephews and pigtailed niece should they fail? Maddy bit her lower lip in concern before she turned her attention back to Anu.

Before she could start up conversation, a group of traveling students caught her attention. They were arguing about where to go next. One of them suggested Greece. Another Egypt.

Her ears perked up. She thought of the map she'd captured in the museum.

"What do you know of the time period when the chart was made? Specifically, what was going on near Egypt?"

The waitress brought Turkish coffee in a silver pot. Anu poured and took a sip. "When we met, Will mentioned the obelisks had been carbon-dated to about a thousand to fifteen hundred years before Alexander the Great. Do you have a more specific date?"

"1350 BC, give or take."

Anu looked away, thinking, and then returned her gaze to Maddy. "That was about fifteen hundred years after the Great Pyramid was built. Amenhotep III died around then and his successors, Akhenaten and his wife Nefertiti, abandoned traditional polytheism and established the worship of Aten, one of the first monotheistic religions. Also, biblical scholars would say that was the time of Moses."

"Curious." Maddy tried her coffee. Strong. "Think Moses was even real?"

"I doubt it. Even the tale of being pulled from the Nile is a familiar myth."

"A myth?"

"Yes. The first ruler of the Akkadian empire was set in a basket of rushes and found in the river. That was a thousand years before Moses supposedly lived."

"Didn't know that," Maddy said. "Is there any archeological evidence from the forty years in the desert, or Mount Sinai?"

Anu folded her hands and put them on the table, the orange beads between her fingers. "There's much controversy around Mount Sinai's location."

"What're some of the contenders?"

"It's not my area of expertise, but many archeologists protest it could be at Jebel Musa next to Mount Catherine. Or perhaps

Mount Helal within modern Egypt. Petra, Edom, and some volcanos in northwest Saudi Arabia have all been discussed. The Great Pyramid theory even has a few supporters."

"The Great Pyramid? That's funny," Maddy said.

Anu smiled briefly. "But speaking of pyramids, I have a question. Back at Chichén Itzá, you and Bear mentioned that you found obelisks made of this superconductive material, but that they were destroyed. Will you tell me now what happened?"

Despite the clutch of fear that came from the thought of revisiting that night, Maddy considered the request. While she still felt guilty about killing the men, it might be a good idea for Anu to know not to touch the meteorite if they found it. And perhaps her confession would make Anu feel safe enough to share what was going on with her. *Has to work eventually, right?*

Taking a deep breath, Maddy fingered the shard in her jeans pocket and shared the story of finding the obelisks. As she did, Anu's face grew more and more surprised. The distraction seemed to relax Anu, too, as she had stopped fiddling with her beads.

When Maddy finished, Anu exclaimed, "You channeled your energy into the obelisks and made ball lightning! Is this something commonly done with aikido?"

Maddy laughed, but kept watch on the pedestrians that passed on the street outside the restaurant. "No. Although it's not uncommon for very advanced martial artists to be able to direct energy in a fight. Some say the masters are able to throw opponents without touching them."

"Fascinating. My father practices a lot of yoga. When I was young and had an ache or a pain, he would put his hands on me and they would get warm. Can you make your hands warm like that?"

Normally, Maddy wouldn't try something like that in a public place, but she needed this woman as an ally, and could also use some practice moving her energy. And it wouldn't hurt to be ready if they were attacked.

"Let me see."

After doing another scan outside the window, Maddy closed her eyes and took a deep breath. She *listened*, which for her meant focusing on sounds around her and letting her mind quiet. The rain outside sounded like tiny drumbeats on the roof. Glassware tinkled, and there were several conversations in what she figured was Turkish. She recognized an Australian accent, thought of her roommate, Robert, and brought her attention back to the room. In a few moments, her mind felt quiet, and she tuned into her energy. Her navel point beat a slow, rhythmic pulse, and with visualization, she pulled the energy up to her heart. She imagined AJ, with his red hair and adorable ears that stuck out from his little head, and her heart swelled with love. She pushed that love to her hands and reached out for Anu. Anu's hands found hers and Maddy sent light into Anu's palms.

Ten seconds passed.

"Wow! You're the real deal," Anu said.

Maddy opened her eyes to find the other woman's wide with surprise.

"Your hands are three times hotter than my father's hands ever were," Anu said. "That's amazing. I meditate sometimes, and pray, but have never felt my energy, much less been able to direct it."

Maddy withdrew her hands and took another drink of water. "It took me a long time, and much practice, using techniques from my aikido sensei . . . and others." Anu didn't need to know about the master, or the Order of the Invisible Flame, she decided just as the waitress brought their food.

"Perhaps the energy you generate reacts with the superconductive material," Anu said after taking a few thoughtful bites of her meal.

Maddy found her hummus delicious but was distracted when a tall man with black hair walked by under an umbrella.

"To me, it seemed like the obelisks focused the energy and magnified it. I still had to direct it," she said, keeping her eyes trained outside. "I want to warn you. If we are able to find the material that was used to create the obelisks, don't touch it. Ball lightning seems to fly from the material regardless, and when untrained hands touch it, the power is raw, untamed, and dangerous."

Honeyed baklava arrived, for dessert. Maddy took a bite and found it too sweet. Her next bite was smaller.

Anu nodded. "I'll take your advice."

They both ate in silence for a minute.

"I'm starting to see why everyone wants this material. It can be used as many sorts of weapons," Anu said.

Maddy knew in her gut Anu was still holding something back. "It can. Have you remembered anything about conversations with your uncle that might be useful?"

Anu shook her head. "I'm sorry. No."

Maddy curled her toes in frustration and glanced out the window again. About a hundred feet away, another man with jet-black hair stood against a tree. Clean-shaven, and about the right build, he seemed immune to the freezing rain. He walked to a nearby park bench and sat down. The way he moved convinced her. It was Pyotr—she'd seen that same grace when he'd jumped away from her loft.

She put her fork down, appetite lost.

She managed to add, "The material makes a good personal weapon, and scientific applications abound."

"I'm sad my uncle Ravi was mixed up in this somehow. I hope we can figure out who killed him."

"Yes, I hope so, too." Maddy decided to go for broke. "Take a quick glance over your shoulder, out the window, and look at the man on the park bench about thirty meters away."

Anu did as Maddy asked and immediately dropped her fork. She raised a trembling hand to her mouth.

"It's Pyotr, the Russian who's after us. Have you seen him before?" Maddy asked.

Anu turned back toward Maddy, clearly panicked. "No, where would I have seen him?"

Maddy knew she was lying. "Good question. Let's pay the check and get out of here."

Irritated that Anu still wouldn't share what she knew, and dying to know how they'd been followed, Maddy strategized how to get back to the safe house without their tail. The back door seemed like their only option.

CHAPTER 52

Stranded on the side of the desert road, Will barely refrained from kicking the tire of the asinine vehicle they'd rented back in Marrakech. "I can't believe this stupid rental car broke down."

Jags stood next to him, examining the dusty Toyota Corolla. "I know. Time is ticking to get to that cryptographer in the Valley of the Kings."

"And it will be dark in a few hours."

"It looked decent enough back at the car lot. Old, but decent."

Will popped the hood and peered inside. "It did. And it seemed a good idea to rent from a smaller agency."

"Yeah, the big boys were more likely to require a credit card and have a GPS on board." She pointed toward the motor. "See anything obvious, Sherlock?"

"No, not yet. Are there any tools in the trunk?"

"Let me look."

While Jags went around to the back of the silver Corolla, Will listened to the eerie quiet surrounding them. They were in the middle of nowhere. Or, more accurately, they were on the Moroccan edge of the Sahara, not far from Errachidia. But it felt like nowhere.

Sounded like nowhere, too.

After moving through the Atlas Mountains, and turning north at the lush sandstone city of Ouarzazate, they'd traveled through several towns, all of which had a surprising amount of greenery. In their hours of travel, they'd seen everything from snow-covered mountains and plateaus to sand-covered plains, shallow basins, and several large oasis depressions. There was a lot more vegetation than he expected in this part of the world.

But now, all that stretched in front of him were vast, rolling acres of barren sand dunes, which sometimes overran the highway in a way that reminded Will of the snow in Lake Tahoe. No car had passed them for at least two hours. The dry silence crept into his bones. Even the distant wind sounded like lost spirits.

Jags shut the trunk with a thud before walking back to join him at the front of the car. They had both ditched their disguises in the car's back seat early on.

Will found even her mundane movements fascinating. With a jolt, he realized he wasn't just fond of her—he was attracted to her. He hadn't been with anyone in over a year and although his heart had felt lighter since the conversation with Jags in Merida, his interest took him by surprise.

"Find anything?" he asked.

She waved her arms at the desolation. "No. It's as empty as this desert."

Will crossed his arms and leaned back onto the hood of the car, thinking about her and their situation. Did she have any interest in him? "This could be a problem."

She gave him a dry look. "You mean because we're stranded out here?"

Will scratched at his beard. "Not much traffic on this road."

"Good thing we at least brought dinner and some extra water."

"True. I'm more worried about tonight, though. It's pleasant enough here now, but if we're stuck here through the night, we could end up like icicles."

As Jags pushed her hair out of her eyes, he couldn't help but think that maybe they could keep each other warm.

Jags turned to look under the hood again. "This engine looks pretty straightforward. I wonder what's wrong with it."

"I don't know. It just died. We have gas and it appears to have coolant."

"Strange. Do you think we were somehow sabotaged?"

"It's a possibility."

Will leaned over the engine and looked closer. "Hmm, wait a minute."

"What?"

Will dug around and held up two wires. Each terminated with a round connector. "See this?"

"Where's it go?"

Will grabbed the key-ring flashlight off his belt and the knife from his pocket. Then he shined the light around the engine. "Aha! It goes to the electric fuel pump. A screw must've come out."

"We have hit a few bumps. Just need a screw, then?"

"Yes, and I have an idea."

Will walked around to the trunk, opened it, and checked some of the connectors that held the car jack assembly together. After finding one that would work, he walked back around to the front of the car and installed it.

"Pretty clever, MacGyver," Jags said.

She graced him with a smile that made his heart jump.

Will closed the hood and noticed a shift in the sound of the wind. "Oh no. Is that what I think it is?" He pointed to the sepia half-light on the eastern horizon.

Jags looked in the direction he pointed and frowned. "Didn't you say it wasn't sandstorm season?"

He grimaced. "It's not. But they can occur any time."

Jags swore, and his stomach lurched. Sandstorms were one of Mother Nature's most violent and unpredictable phenomena. People died in them. He and Jags had been so distracted with the car that they hadn't noticed the ominous wall of death heading straight for them.

Wind whipped hair around Jags's face. "It's getting closer."

"Too fast."

Lightning danced within the clouds, like eerie shadow puppets. Here a slash of light, there a striking forked tongue. Will began to sweat with fear. They'd be swallowed up, and might be fried by the lightning.

Jags's voice trembled with horror. "What do we do?"

"There's no place for us to go!" Will yelled. "They can move at up to seventy-five miles an hour. And can be up to sixty miles wide." The width of this one took up the entire horizon.

"We can't outrun the thing?"

"No, and it's coming from the direction we need to go."

He pounded his fist on the top of the car as dust flew. The black roiling sand cloud was growing larger by the second, ready to scour away everything in its path.

CHAPTER 53

GÜLHANE PARK, ISTANBUL

DECEMBER 23, 4:15 P.M. EASTERN EUROPEAN TIME

In the dim light of the late afternoon, Pyotr sat on the stony park bench and shivered. The women were in a restaurant enjoying a fine, hot meal while, thanks to Baron Sokolov, he was forced to wait out here in the freezing rain.

Anger still churned in his gut when he thought about the stunt the baron had pulled in the square with his mother's tongue. What a bastard. And giving him no backup until he found the cache. The man was a cheap son of a bitch. How the hell was he supposed to operate under these conditions?

Still, at long last, he had an opportunity now to grab the Marshall woman. He would grab the archeoastronomer too. Shooting them would be counterproductive, given he needed the information they had regarding the chart.

The only problem was his rental vehicle was two blocks away. However, earlier he'd had an idea on how to get them from the back of the restaurant into his car.

After the women had entered the restaurant, Pyotr had scoped out the back of the place. Like many eateries, it sat up against an alley for easier deliveries and waste removal. Then he had settled across from them in plain sight on the park bench, showing himself to ensure they would go out the back door.

The women stood. It looked like they had paid the check and were heading out the back. Just as planned.

CHAPTER 54

Maddy put her hand in her pocket and wrapped her fingers around her only weapon, the pathetically small sliver of lorandite.

"This makes me nervous," Anu said as they headed toward the restaurant's back door.

"Me too."

Maddy had considered calling the local police, but who knew what connections her enemies had here in Turkey, and by then Pyotr was no longer sitting on the park bench. Maddy wondered, what would Bear do? And would he ever forgive her if they didn't get out of this tight spot?

As soon as they exited the faded-red exterior door, Maddy turned left, as the alley dead-ended to their right. Icy rain drizzled from the darkened sky, heralding the arrival of nightfall. A brisk wind made Maddy tug her coat a little tighter. On both sides of the alley, large waste bins backed up to the other commercial doorways. Otherwise, the lane was empty. Cars and trucks rushed by on the next street, 150 feet away.

Alert and breathing into the area behind her navel to steady herself, Maddy headed toward the thoroughfare, holding the small sliver of lorandite tight in her fist. Anu was a half-step behind her. They had almost made it when Maddy noticed movement behind one of the trash containers. Before she could react, a dark-haired man jumped in front of them and sprayed heavy mist from a palm-sized aerosol can toward her face. Pepper spray!

Anu jumped back. Maddy turned her head, squeezed her eyes shut, and instinctively grabbed Pyotr's outstretched hand, pulling him past her in a smooth motion as her eyes began to sting. He hadn't scored a direct hit, but it still hurt.

She ignored the agony and twisted his wrist, applying more pressure, up through his arm, until she could flip him over onto his back. Pyotr went down with a crack. His head on the pavement? But he broke her grip and she dropped the shard.

Anu screamed.

Maddy squinted through burning eyes, knowing their best chance was to build on her counter-attack. She lunged downward and clawed at his wrists, trying to get a hold, but he'd rolled to her right and stood. She sprung after him and slipped on the wet street, the world a blur as he kicked at her face. At the last moment, she reached out and grabbed his leather boot. Twisted. Pyotr howled and jerked his leg away.

Maddy blinked rapidly. "Stop this and we'll help you get your mother back."

Pyotr ignored her. He kicked again, and she was able to get a grasp on the kicking foot. She pushed the boot upward on its trajectory, this time using the strength of her entire body. Not a classic aikido move, but using his momentum against him was the same principle. He grunted, landing on his back in a puddle. Maddy attempted to pin him again, but he punched her in the diaphragm before dodging away. Air left her lungs and she collapsed on her hands and knees.

Through watering eyes, Maddy saw him reach down and pick up the small lorandite shard she'd dropped when he first attacked. She swore.

"Help me! Help me!" Anu wailed.

A nearby door slammed opened and a man rushed out, yelling in a language Maddy didn't understand. Pyotr gave Maddy a final painful kick in the ribs and ran off, his boots slapping on the wet pavement.

CHAPTER 55

Will looked out the car window at the menacing wall of sand, which loomed over them with the long, black shadow of a tidal wave. The wind moaned and cried.

Jags sat next to him. "Do you think we'll be safe in here?"

From his vantage point in the driver's seat, Will could see gritty projectiles start to ping onto the vehicle. But with the storm's arrival, they were losing light fast.

Will drummed his fingers on his leg. "I sure hope so. Sounds pretty dreadful out there. Reminds me of howling blizzards when I was a kid."

"Uh-oh, feel the car starting to sway?"

"Yeah, like my boat in rough water."

"It's scaring the pants off me, but there's nothing we can do now. Let's change the subject."

Will had to raise his voice to be heard over the whistling wind. "Okay. What do you want to talk about?"

"What's your legend?"

"You mean my cover story?"

"Yeah."

"I still tell everyone that I'm a test engineer, just for a DC software firm instead of the manufacturing outfit I was working for down in Brazil."

"Are they buying it?"

"For the most part. I think my other sister, Bella, isn't fooled. What about you? What's your legend?"

She laughed. "I tell people I'm an accountant."

Will chuckled too, relieved to be talking about something besides the sand that was blasting the paint off their rental car in a possible prelude to burying them alive. And imagining her as a bookkeeper amused him. "An accountant? I'm not seeing it. I get a visual of a conservative, suit-wearing, glasses-on-end-of-her-nose auditor."

"C'mon, Mr. Engineer. Not all accountants are stuffy."

"I suppose that's true," Will admitted. "But wouldn't it help your legend to fit into the pigeonhole just a little?"

"Hey! I did take some accounting classes in college, and can at least fake the debit/credit lingo if I run into a real accountant at a party."

"That's good. And it helps my story that I spent years as a real test engineer. It would be nice to tell my sister about it, though."

"Nice, but dangerous. The less our loved ones know, the better."

Will wondered if she had loved ones. She'd never mentioned anyone. Didn't wear a ring. It was almost dark in the car. Thinking he only lived once, and that life could end at any time, Will tried to figure out how to make a romantic play.

"Want me to turn on my flashlight?" he asked.

"Sure." She took a deep breath. "When we were back in Marrakech, I logged in for a minute while you rented the car. The chaos in the Philippines was all over my feed. Looks like the terror has spread throughout the islands and there are a lot of folks dead."

Will took a deep breath. "I saw that too. There are riots up and down all the major streets."

"And it would be worse in the States. I'm scared for our country."

"I am, too. The political left and right are polarized in a way I've never seen. Throw in a real crisis and we'd have a dangerous flashpoint."

"You don't think people would come together to help each other out?"

"Sure, some would. But without gasoline, food or cash, power or water, society would break down. We already have mass shootings on an unprecedented scale. All those AR-15s would wreak havoc on lives and community trust."

Jags took a deep breath. "That's depressing."

"Maybe it's human nature. And the Russians are counting on everyone to take care of only themselves at the cost of the whole."

"I want to change the subject again."

Will played the light from the flashlight outside the window and set it down on the dashboard. So far, there was no accumulation of sand around the car. "Okay." He wanted to set a different mood, too. "Look, it's pretty how the light catches the blowing sand."

"It is. Kind of like miniature swirling white fireworks."

They admired nature's power and dangerous beauty for a moment. Will pulled the harmonica from its case and played a slow blues song.

When he finished, Jags asked, "When did you start playing?"

"After lightning struck me in Egypt."

"That reminds me. Tell me about how Maddy was able to work her magic there."

"Ah. Well, it wasn't magic."

"That's what I'm curious about. Looked like a lot of energy moving around, even through the clouds in the sat images I looked at. What the hell happened up there?"

"Maddy will have a different version of the story if you ask her. She's more into ki, life force energy, that sort of thing. I come at it from a physics perspective."

"Okay, Mr. Physics, what happened?"

"Have you ever heard of zero-point energy?"

She smiled in the flashlight's dim light. "No, I'm an accountant, remember?"

"Oh, right! Okay, how about superconductors?"

"You've mentioned them, but fill me in."

Will took a deep breath. It was always a challenge explaining these concepts to someone without a scientific background. "Let's start with the easy stuff. Superconductivity is the ability of certain materials to conduct electrical current with nearly zero resistance."

"Like copper wire in your house?"

"Yes, but with even lower resistance."

"Why is that important?"

"Well, resistance restricts the flow of electricity and wastes energy as heat. Whereas an electrical current flowing through a loop of superconductive wire can flow indefinitely without a power source. It's highly efficient."

"Indefinitely? Wow, that's cool."

Will enjoyed showing off his knowledge to her. "Yes, very cool. What Maddy worked with were obelisks made with not just your everyday superconductive material, which needs to be super cold to be super effective, but lorandite, which has low resistance at almost everyday temperatures."

"Okay, what did she do with these amazing obelisks?" Her voice took on the tone of a TV announcer. "Were they two for the price of one? And if I buy now, do I get a set of Ginsu knives with my purchase?"

Will hooted. "Uh, no, sorry, *I* keep the knives."

"What is zero-point energy then?" she said after a beat. "You know, the thing you said at the beginning before I got the extra crash course."

"Funny, some people would call it God. It's the empty space between everything else." When she looked contemplative, he added, "Did I mention I'm kind of a geek? Physics tells us that things that appear solid really aren't. There's astonishing amounts of empty space around and within all matter, and it all contains background energy."

"I vaguely remember that from some high school class. Or maybe it was a Facebook post."

"Physicists call that background energy 'zero-point energy' or ZPE."

"And you think Maddy harnessed this somehow?"

"Yes."

"How?"

"She used her aikido skills to move it." He wanted to mention the master, and the exercises he'd given Maddy, but thought better of it.

"Metaphysics met physics?"

Will grinned. He liked this woman. "Yes."

"All right. If I buy that, how'd we get the ball lightning?"

"My hypothesis is that she was able to generate and channel enough of her own energy to trigger an as-yet-unknown reaction with the superconductive obelisks."

"Unknown, huh? So, your scientific theory ran out of gas?"

That made him laugh again. "Pretty much. Maybe there was a bunch of static electricity from all the traditional lightning crashing around."

"If you say so. Are Bear's forearm scars from that traditional lightning?"

"Yes. It was intense."

The car shook with a violent gust of wind.

Jags was quiet for a minute. "If you hadn't seen it with your own eyes, would you have believed it?"

Will was quick to answer. "Oh, hell no."

"But you expect me to believe it?"

"I can understand why you wouldn't. However, if we do find a source of that material, I advise you to use extreme caution. Don't handle it. Untrained human touch seems to cause the energy to go wild."

"Great." She shook her head. "And we're supposed to bring this stuff back home to stop the Russians from invading America?"

"Bingo."

Jags rolled her neck on her shoulders. "Good grief, Charlie Brown. It all gives me a headache."

Will reached over. "Here, let me rub your shoulders for you."

Jags stiffened, but as he kneaded her muscles, she relaxed. Was this his chance to make a move? He had such a hard time reading women.

"It's been a stressful and hectic few days," he said after a few moments.

"It has been."

Her shoulders felt knotted under his fingers. It had been awhile since he'd given a back rub. The last time had been . . . Maria. He knew she wouldn't want him to be a mourning monk forever. And Jags was a cherry-apple-red Ferrari kind of a woman. Will wondered if he could handle her. He'd sure like to give it a try.

The howling beast outside the car was showing signs of diminishing, and it appeared they wouldn't get buried alive. He might not have another chance like this.

He leaned toward her ear. "What do you think about—"

Jags elbowed him in the chest. "Absolutely not."

Not hard, but he got the point.

Will pulled his hands back into his lap. "Okay, I'm sorry. I shouldn't have."

Jags crossed her arms and laid her seat back. "The wind is dying down. Let's get a little shut-eye so we can get moving as soon as the storm passes."

Chagrined and embarrassed, Will leaned his driver's seat back. As far as he could figure, the million-to-one chance that they would find the source of the obelisks was better than the odds for him to ever understand women.

CHAPTER 56

Maddy felt shock chill her heart when Bear walked through the safe house door. With an oozing cut on his chin and a blood-soaked homemade bandage on his arm, he looked like he'd been in a war. At least his limp was no more pronounced than usual. Seeing him, she was glad Anu had gone to bed early.

Maddy leaped up from the couch and ran over. "Oh my god! Bear, what happened?"

"I think it was the Spanish." He gently touched her face. "But could ask you the same thing. Your eyes are red and puffy."

"I'm just a little bruised and have a pepper-spray hangover. Let me look at that arm. You've got blood everywhere!"

She peeled back the ruined shirt. A jagged cut stretched about six inches along his right forearm, right through the tree-like lightning scar.

He looked at it. "I think it's just a surface wound."

"It's a little more than that! But it does appear to have missed the bone and artery." She sighed with relief. "Still, you need stitches. Is there someone here who can help with that?"

"The woman who gave us the keys last night. The keeper. She should be able to help."

"I'll go get her."

An hour later, Maddy and a medicated, stitched-up Bear sat at a small table inside their studio and brought each other up to speed while sipping ice tea. After she heard Bear's story, Maddy felt annoyed that someone had attempted to lure Bear with a woman. Could their argument have been overheard this morning? Or was it just standard spy operating procedure?

When they finished their discussion, Bear stretched his right arm. "Could've been worse."

"Yes, you got lucky. Guess that arm will be out of commission for a few weeks, though."

"We'll see."

"Well, don't go breaking open the stitches."

"I'll be careful. How're your ribs?"

"Bruised but not cracked. The worst was the air getting knocked out of my lungs. I hate that."

"Me too. I'm just glad you're okay after sneaking out of here." Bear touched her arm with his good hand. "That was not a good idea."

"I know, I know. We shouldn't have left the safe house." Maddy looked down. "I'm so sorry I called you Vincent. You're not mad any longer?"

"No. I'm sorry I stormed out of here. I was just worried."

"We all get heated up from time to time. But thank you for not calling me names."

"I learned that name callin' lesson a long time ago. Can never take those things back. Figured I'd better leave before I said something stupid."

"I understand. Sometimes I have to count to ten or leave when I get pissed off, too."

Bear kissed her gently on the lips. "Do we have time to kiss and make up?"

"With your arm like that?"

"We can get creative."

"Let's see if you can stay awake with those pain pills on board. Before we head to bed, though, I want to tell you a few more things."

"Okay."

Maddy frowned. "I dropped that little sliver of lorandite in the fight."

Bear chewed an ice cube. "You brought it, huh? Did he get it?"

Maddy pursed her lips, disgusted at herself. "He did."

"It was too small to do much with, though, wasn't it?"

"I only tried once, and all it did was spark."

Bear's eyes lit with mischief. "A good fire starter, eh?"

"It could have been operator error."

"I doubt it." He gave her a small smile. "Not the end of the world. But I do wonder how Pyotr found you. We should borrow an electronic sweeper from the woman downstairs and check ourselves for tracking devices."

"Okay," Maddy said, and then considered how to broach the next topic. She lowered her voice. "About Anu . . . before we left, I found a note on her side table. It said someone was watching her."

Bear's eyes narrowed. "Watchin' her? Who?"

"Pyotr? Lex? I also wondered if Lex's tats could be a disguise."

"Oh, you mean like one of those high-tech masks?" Bear grabbed his tea and found another ice cube to chew on.

"Yeah."

"Hm. Could be."

Maddy resisted rubbing her eyes. They were still irritated. Anu had gotten lucky and missed most of the spray. "What if they're the same guy?"

Bear stretched. "Lex and Pyotr?"

"Yeah."

"Like the Spaniards and Russians working together?"

"Sure. Or maybe the Russians planted the background about Lex."

"I'll need to sleep on that." Bear tilted his head. "Maybe you are right about there being something fishy about Anu. She insisted on leaving the safe house, right?"

"Yes."

"And then you were followed. We need to keep a closer eye on her." Bear yawned. "Excellent work, Maddy. Lots of new ideas."

Maddy's heart warmed with the praise. "Thank you."

"Tell me about the museum."

"Okay, we saw old star navigation devices called astrolabes. A dead end. A perfume extraction machine that I thought your sensitive nose might like. And this." She got her phone out and showed him the picture she had taken of the ancient map of the Middle East.

The map fascinated her. It was what the world had looked like when the chart was created. Memphis stood in Cairo's stead. Tyre, Damascus, Megido, and Jericho were the main city-towns in the land of Canaan. As earlier in the afternoon, the only other places she recognized were Aleppo and Thebes. Thebes was near the Valley of the Kings, where Will and Jags were headed. She hoped they'd get there soon.

Bear took a quick look. "That's pretty cool. I got to see a wall with writing on it from Augustus."

"You mean you got to see the Roman wall for a minute before that woman tried to seduce you?" Maddy put her phone down, intending to give Bear a knock-your-socks-off kiss that would let him know it was good he had declined the offer.

But his head had fallen to the table and he was fast asleep.

CHAPTER 57

The baron cradled the high-powered hunting rifle on his shoulder and aimed.

Deep in the woods, he was enjoying morning target practice on his remote family estate outside of Moscow. He'd left his current fourteen-year-old mistress lounging naked in bed to visit this private glade. The sun peeked over the treetops, lighting up the meter of sparkling snow. Songbirds serenaded him. Out here, the demands of his job felt as far away as the hidden stars above.

Not that things were going poorly. To the contrary, the test in the Philippines was still generating riots, mobs, and civil unrest. Restless groups roamed the streets, unable to purchase food because the trucks that supplied the stores didn't have petrol. So far, seventeen people had died in the uprisings, and while the international community was working hard to provide supplies, any relief remained days away. Even better, it appeared there was no way to contain the computer hack. Every time the local experts tried, the algorithm reconfigured itself. But the very best part was that the Kremlin wanted to use it on not only the US but also their allies, to prevent NATO intervention. His superiors loved him.

The baron smiled, aimed, and fired. The head of the cardboard target sprouted a hole between its eyes.

He'd come to this clearing since he was a child. The property had been lost to the family in the Revolution of 1917, but his father used his military connections after the Second World War to reacquire the estate. Although his father and mother had summered here for a few years before he was born, there would be no opportunity for family holidays. His father was captured by the Americans while on a Cold War mission in West Germany and returned in a body bag when the baron was a year old. As a child, he played on the nearby headstone, imagining his father's gun-toting ghost shooting American bad guys.

Once he had gained enough rank in the military, the baron researched his father's file and found out the body came back bruised and battered. His early distaste for America blossomed into a virulent hatred. This discreet property, a three-hour drive from Moscow, was the only place the baron had ever known peace.

He aimed again at the target.

Occasionally he imagined that the target was his mother or step-father. After his father's death, Mother had descended into an alcoholic depression, shunning the rest of the family and keeping just her son for company. She dressed him in adult clothes and made him sleep in her bed, often invading him in ways no mother should as part of some sick attempt to replace his father. When he was six, she found an adult male, but Nicholas was too fond of vodka and the belt.

Since neither enjoyed the woods like the baron did, he often escaped to the forested land. Now he imagined his mother's leering face and fired again, skewering the right eye of the target. The smell of alcohol on his stepfather's breath haunted him. The left eye of the target exploded.

It was too bad he'd had to wait until he was an adult to kill his stepfather, but it had taken a few years and some military training for him to feel confident he could stage it as an accident. It was while cutting through his stepfather's thigh with a chainsaw, not far from this meadow, that he discovered how much he enjoyed inflicting pain on others. His high lasted for weeks, and not a tear was shed when his mother took her own life two months later.

After his stepfather's death, the baron turned his new talents to intelligence missions that involved pressuring prisoners of war into revealing their secrets. The trick was to get the truth out of them early, as too much pain would make them either pass out or agree to anything just to make the discomfort stop. He had a talent his peers envied, and his rise through the ranks was meteoric.

The only stain on his otherwise stellar career came with the acquisition of his permanent limp. It was during the Chechnya conflict, right before the beautiful day the twin towers fell in New York. On a back street in Austria, an altercation with an African American operative went bad. He managed to bash the man's head to pieces, but suffered the calf wound. Fortunately, he wasn't publicly embarrassed about the incident, but it did provide a daily fuel for his hatred toward the United States.

For his final shot of the morning, he imagined the US flag plastered over the heart of the cardboard dummy. With a quick pull of the trigger, the target blew apart. A broad smile blossomed over his face.

It was Christmas Eve morning and time to head back into Moscow and put the final pieces of his plan in play.

He felt generous. Maybe it was time to give Pyotr some help after all.

CHAPTER 58

Will still felt embarrassed about his failed romantic pass the night before. After the sandstorm had moved on, they'd found a cheap hotel near the airport in Fes, and caught an early morning flight to Luxor.

"Where do you think we'll find the cryptographer?" Jags asked him as they stood in the passport check line at the Luxor airport.

The airport was small, and the line short. No one looked out of place.

"I don't know," Will replied. "HQS was able to find out that he was working here, but not much more. He's a retired Oxford professor and an expert on hieroglyphs, especially the ones with dual meanings. Oh, and he's bald, with white and bushy sideburns. HQS did find a picture."

Will tried to keep his tone casual as they talked.

For her part, Jags also seemed to be trying hard to ignore what had or, more accurately, hadn't happened between them last night. "Okay, we're looking for a bald Englishman with funky facial hair."

Will stretched his long legs, sore from being crammed into a tiny airplane. "Yes."

"I'm hungry. It looks like there are a whopping three hotels in Luxor. Why don't we get breakfast at one of them and ask at the desks to see where he's staying?"

"Good idea. Let's also find a store. I'm ready for a change of clothes."

Two hours later, they stood at the base of sheer limestone cliffs reaching up toward a crystal-blue sky. The air was still, but felt dry and smelled crisp, reminding Will of morning ski runs. Still, he felt uneasy. While he didn't think anyone had followed them here, this site was at the end of a narrow gorge, which itself was at the terminating tip of the Valley of the Kings. The place would be a perfect spot for an ambush.

He looked at the cliff. There was a small opening, halfway up the stone face. "Do you think it's safe to go up there?"

A wooden ladder was mounted atop a small ramp. Jags started to climb. "Sure, they said he was in this tomb."

Although Will had made progress on a lifelong fear of heights, he wasn't keen on climbing if he didn't have to. He steadied the ladder while she climbed. "What if they were lying?"

Halfway up, she looked down. "Why would the hotel staff do that? They said everyone in town knows he's working on KV34. Even the guard we bribed said he works here every day."

Will swore to himself. He was going to have to crawl up the bloody thing. Stupid Egyptians, with their penchant for destroying their stone ramps after the tomb was built. That protection measure had never worked anyway.

Jags reached the top and stepped off the ladder. "That wasn't too bad. And there's a nice view of the winding canyon from up here. C'mon up, Tarzan."

She bent down and held the top of the ladder. Will tested it. The thing looked like the remains of a pick-up-sticks game, but it felt sturdy enough. And it wasn't too tall, maybe seventy-five rungs. *Don't look down. I'll be fine if I don't look down.*

Slowly, he grasped one wooden rung after another and focused on his hands as they moved. This whole visit was a bloody waste of time. Right hand. Left hand.

After the longest minute of his life, he arrived at the top, somewhat out of breath and sweating. As he swung his legs onto the platform, he gave Jags a half-triumphant, half-green smile.

She put her hands on her hips. "You're afraid of heights."

"Correction. I used to be afraid of heights."

"You look a little uncomfortable."

"Yes, but last time I tried to climb a ladder I puked. This is progress."

"Well then, congratulations. You'll have to tell me someday how you managed that. In the meantime, are you ready to go find Professor Crookbottom?"

Will was careful not to look down at the canyon. "The only way out is in. Yes, let's see if anyone is home."

They crawled through a small hole in the side of the tan cliff wall and onto the landing of a rough-cut stairwell. As soon as Will pulled out his flashlight and turned it on, they scrambled down the steps, Jags in the lead.

"Be careful," Will warned.

"I will."

Into the darkness, he yelled, "Professor Crookbottom!"

The answer was the echo of his own voice, rumbling down the narrow corridors. The place already gave Will the creeps.

The stairs gave way to an undecorated, sloping corridor, which ended in another descending staircase.

"It's pretty quiet in here," Will said. "Maybe we should just go back to King Tut's tomb and wait for him there."

Jags marched down the second staircase and continued into another corridor. "We'll find him."

"Slow down! It's dangerous in here."

Will rushed to walk next to Jags, his light shining ahead. The flashlight illuminated a large pit, with yellow stars on the ceiling above. The frescos on the surrounding walls reminded Will of candles with different colored bases. What concerned him was the pit. It looked to be five meters wide and almost as long. He shined his beam down the well and couldn't see the bottom.

"Think this was designed to keep robbers out?" Jags asked.

"Yes, but it wasn't very effective. Looks like the professor got planks in here long enough to cross, just like grave robbers did."

With his right foot, Will probed the two side-by-side boards, and eventually put weight on one of them, wishing there was a third board to make the crossing wider.

Jags jumped in front of him and danced across the boards like a tightrope walker. Once across, she turned to look back at him, grinning an ornery smile.

He scowled. "Brat!"

"Just watch the boards."

Will's throat emitted a low growl as he stepped onto the boards, took three steps with his long legs, and made the far side. Relief escaped his lungs in a rush.

"No pits in here," he said when they reached the next corridor.

"None that we can see."

"Oh, *that's* reassuring." He shined his light around the walls. "It is pretty cool in here, though. Look at those frescos."

The walls were covered in yellow and blue paint. He made out a gridded star pattern below what must have once been incense burners. In the middle of the room stood two unadorned pillars. The light revealed a staircase at the far end.

Jags tried to herald the professor. "Professor Crookbottom! Are you here?"

The eerie silence of centuries responded.

They walked to the next set of stairs and headed down. Will counted twenty-two treads. Light at the far end of the oval room revealed a man kneeling in front of a beautiful red quartzite sarcophagus. The man had a bald pate.

"Professor?" Will asked.

The man held up a hand and waved them away. Will ignored

the gesture and crossed the richly painted chamber, noting the glass panels that had been installed to protect the detailed friezes. Rows of stick figures walked, sat, traveled by boat, all against a yellow background. Like the space above, this room also held two pillars, but these were adorned with hieroglyphic paintings. The ceiling held thousands of delicate stars.

"Professor Crookbottom?" Will asked again.

The man was studying the lid of the inscribed sarcophagus with a device that looked like a handheld magnifying lens. True to his photograph, the professor had thick, white sideburns and wore rectangular glasses on the end of his nose. White gloves covered his hands.

Will touched the man on the shoulder. "Professor Crookbottom, we have to speak with you."

The professor didn't look up. "I'm occupied. Go away," he said in clipped British tones.

"Anu Kumar sent us. We're in trouble and could really use your help," Jags tried.

"I'm old and don't care."

Will and Jags exchanged a look over the man's bare head. Then, before Will could react, Jags reached down and yanked the magnifying device from the professor's hands, moving it swiftly behind her back.

The professor turned on his knees, fingers groping through the air for the lens. "Young lady, I need that to continue my work."

"And you'll have it back as soon as you answer a few questions."

He got to his feet with difficulty, reached into his suit pocket, and took a drink from a decorated metal flask. "Why on earth would I help someone so rude?"

"To get your lens back?"

The professor stared at Jags with narrowed eyes. Jags looked back calmly. Will watched them both, awestruck at Jags's behavior.

The moment stretched. The professor glanced at the sarcophagus, looked back at Jags, and rolled his eyes. "All right then. What do you want?"

From a pocket, Will produced his phone and scrolled to the images he'd stored of the obelisks. "Thank you for helping us. There's much on the line. What do these inscriptions say?"

Professor Crookbottom took the phone from Will's hand and studied the image for about a minute, using his thick fingers to zoom in and out.

He handed the mobile back to Will. "Quite odd. Coded. Where did you get these?" He shook his head. "It says the winter solstice period only lasts for four days. You'll find the precise place you seek at the end of the world, inside the Pure Mountain near Napata. Look to the side of the white crown. Now, I need to get back to my sarcophagus."

Will swore. He'd never heard of Napata or a Pure Mountain. This whole visit was a big waste of time.

"And do you know where that is?" Jags insisted.

The professor reached for his flask as he spoke. "Of course. Thutmose the third, the same pharaoh who built this tomb, established that area as the southern border of his empire around 1450 BCE. It's now known as Jebel Barkal and is located in the Sudan."

CHAPTER 59

EPHESUS, TURKEY

DECEMBER 24, 10:05 A.M. EASTERN EUROPEAN TIME

Having parked near the Ephesus ruins, Bear exited the SUV, still mulling over how someone was watching Anu. Or following her. He looked at her out of the corner of his eye. Before they'd left the Istanbul safe house, he'd borrowed an electronic sweeper and had carefully gone over every inch of the three of them. The sweeper had remained mute.

As Maddy and Anu came around the vehicle, he opened the hatch, anxious to see if he could use the ground-penetrating radar machine with his wounded arm, but was distracted by the single bone-colored Ionic column drawn against the leaden sky. *There's so much history to explore here!* He knew the hollowed-out bowl of the Temple of Artemis lay straight ahead, down a stone path and beyond the column. At least the tourist burden today was light, due to the holidays and the lousy weather.

He turned to Maddy, looking great today in jeans and a tight black jacket that showed off her form. "Hey, Maddy, did you know the Temple of Artemis was destroyed by fire the night Alexander the Great was born?"

Maddy smiled. "How auspicious. I didn't know that."

He wondered if she cared about the temple or was just humoring him. "Yep, an omen. The temple used to be one of the seven wonders of the ancient world."

Her phone buzzed, and she looked down at it, frowning.

Is Vincent still contacting her? Bear's gut sank.

She put the phone in her pocket.

His phone rang. "Bear here," he snarled.

Argones's voice was on the other end of the connection. "Hey, what's wrong? It's Will and Jags."

The area around the SUV was deserted. Bear motioned Maddy over and tried to modulate his tone. "Nothin'." He punched a button on the phone. "Maddy and Anu are here. Argones, you're on speaker."

"Good!" Argones's voice held excitement. "We solved the inscriptions on the obelisks! Well, we found Professor Crookbottom and he solved them."

Maddy's eyes lit up. "That's great. What do they say?"

"We need to go to Sudan."

Maddy frowned. "What? Why?"

"He said there's an Egyptian holy mountain there."

Anu nodded. "Not surprising. The Egyptians ranged pretty far south. There are actually three times as many pyramids in Nubia as there are in Egypt."

"Three times?" Argones asked. "Anyway, he said that the winter solstice lasts four days and that in order to find the precise place we seek, we need to go to end of the world, inside the Pure Mountain near Napata. And look to the side of the white crown."

Bear's ears perked up. He'd read about the place. "Y'all are going to Jebel Barkal! That's fantastic."

"You should have been with us, Bear. I had no idea what he was talking about." Will paused. "What do you know about it?"

"Thutmose the Third conquered that area because they thought the pinnacle on the side of the mountain was a uraeus."

"What's a uraeus?" Jags asked in her throaty voice.

"It's a rearing cobra," Bear replied. "The ancient Egyptians thought it was a symbol for the serpent goddess, Wadjet, and it became associated with the pharaohs. They all wore that symbol on their crowns, near their foreheads. So, when they saw an image of a uraeus in the pinnacle on Jebel Barkal, it meant that they had dominion over that land."

Anu interjected, "It's neat they wore it on their foreheads."

Bear turned to look at Anu. "Why?"

"The serpent is also the symbol in India for kundalini, or ki, the energy that Maddy is good at moving around. Focusing on the forehead helps it rise. Interesting connection."

"Never mind all that," Will said. "We were in the tomb of Thutmose. That's where we met the professor."

Bear ground his teeth with envy. The Valley of the Kings was high on his bucket list. That meant they'd walked right through the Red Chapel mortuary temple of Queen Hatshepsut. She had ruled the world's most advanced nation for twenty years before Thutmose the Third led a revolt. She was said to have dressed as a king, even wearing false beards. Argones and Jags had also passed King Tut's tomb, and sixty-one other burial chambers. Bear wanted to see the valley and the pyramid-shaped mountain that towered above it, whose shape may have lured the Egyptians there in the first place. Some other time.

Maddy nudged Bear. "What else do you know about Jebel Barkal?"

Bear loved how focused she could be. "It's not far from the Nile, has an imposing profile that can be seen for miles. I'm guessing the clue refers to a cave somewhere near the top of the pinnacle."

Argones's voice went up an octave. "A cave? In the cliff face?"

Bear recalled Argones wasn't a big fan of heights, but there was no way to break it to him gently. "You best take climbing gear. Jags, call Katrina and see if she can get you supplies in the nearest town."

"Okay, thanks. We also need a plane."

Surprised, Bear threw a piece of gum into his mouth. "Why?"

"Because we checked on how to get there from here and it's an eighty-nine-hour car drive," Jags said, with a tone as dry as the desert.

"No way!" Maddy said.

"Yep, there are no good roads, so you take a ferry right down the Nile."

Bear's mental image of the distance between the Valley of the Kings and Jebel Barkal hadn't seemed that far. "The director said we'd have whatever resources we need. I'm sure Katrina can hook you up."

"Sounds good," Argones said.

"I'm jealous you guys get to go there," Bear continued. "Here in Ephesus, we're getting ready to try out some ground-penetrating radar."

He turned to the SUV and gave the four-wheeled unit inside the back a push. It was lighter than many lawnmowers he'd known, and had a tablet-sized display mounted at the top.

"What do you think you'll find?" Jags asked.

"Hopin' to find the meteorite."

"Will," Maddy interrupted. "Tell me again about the solstice, and did the professor say we'll find the 'precise place' we seek?"

"Yeah, he said winter solstice only lasts four days, and the exact place would be found there. I thought that was odd, too."

"Winter solstice is our timeframe then. Today's the twenty-fourth," Maddy said. She frowned. "That makes tomorrow our deadline."

Bear swore.

"Could this be a three-part puzzle?" Maddy continued. "Time, exact place, and something else?"

"That's very possible," Anu said.

Maddy scrunched her forehead again. "Oh boy. The inscriptions show the when, but there's an exact where? Maybe the star chart leads to a general area, like a nation, or town, that's necessary for the more specific pieces of the puzzle to make sense."

Anu raised a dark eyebrow. "Like equinox, the serpent stairs, and Chichén Itzá."

Bear was awed by how Maddy's mind worked. He should have thought of that. "I'll bet you're right, Maddy."

"That's like three-part authentication."

Bear didn't follow. "Huh?"

"It shows a high degree of sophistication and means we need to figure out what the star chart says." Maddy waved her arm to encompass Ephesus. "I doubt we'll find anything here."

"Perhaps not, but we need to try."

Maddy nodded.

Into the phone, Bear said, "Gotta go." He hung up.

Bear put his hand on the radar unit. "Let's get this out of the back of the SUV and give it a shot," he said. "We have no other leads."

"Okay, but let's hurry. Time is running out."

CHAPTER 60

They were running out of time and Maddy was running out of patience.

The temple grounds were smaller than she expected, and all around were farms and orchards. With the hills in the distance, it reminded her of northern California. Only she couldn't enjoy the scenery. Bear walked back and forth, holding the ground-penetrating radar unit in front of him as he traversed the land surrounding the ruins. It was like watching the futile efforts of a beach-combing treasure hunter.

While she had checked out the old amphitheater and the façade of the ancient stone library, Bear had continued searching, even with his hurt arm. He broke for one phone call, and that was it. She offered to take a turn, but he waved her away, frowning, seemingly irritated.

It was a chilly, dreary day, and she suspected his arm ached. Her ribs did. But after that conversation with Will, she had a hunch that they weren't going to find anything here. It seemed too far north.

They needed to figure out the mystery of the star chart, to know how to fit all the puzzle pieces together.

Nearby, Anu sat on a piece of crumbled stone that was over two thousand years old, and stared pensively at Bear. Although Maddy felt closer to her after their misadventure in the alley with Pyotr, she still wasn't being fully honest with them. Of this, Maddy felt certain.

Interrupting her thoughts, a man strode toward her from the parking lot, stepping with purpose. Was he a threat? Another assassin? He moved like one. All stealthy grace. But then she realized he looked familiar. Short curly hair, dark eyes, thin lips, and no facial hair on his wide cheekbones. His build was slim, and he wore tight-fitting black jeans and a burnt-orange jacket, which he had zipped to his throat against the brisk day. Also, he waved as he approached. Most assassins didn't wave, did they?

Then she recognized him. Quinn.

The master must have decided it was time to send in help. But how had he found them?

Quinn smiled through perfect white teeth. "Hello, Maddy Marshall."

That Irish accent. So disconcerting.

"Hi, Quinn." Maddy began to relax, but she wanted to make sure he was a legitimate messenger and not a covert imposter. "Are you of the Order?"

Quinn didn't reply. Instead, he unzipped his jacket and handed it to her. Underneath, he wore a gray cashmere turtleneck, which he pulled over his head to show her the mark on his shoulder. She reached out and felt it. There could be no mistake—it matched her scar. That was all she needed. He'd been through the same tribulations she had, and he'd made it through. She handed him the harvest-themed jacket and gave him a brief hug.

"How'd you find me?"

"You're wearing a cabbie hat."

She laughed. She waited for him to tell her more, but he just shrugged his shoulders with a mischievous look on his face.

"I see," she said. "How's Samuel holding up?"

"About as you'd expect."

Maddy winced. "Any word on AJ and Elena?"

Quinn shook his head and pursed his lips. "Bad time to be in the Philippines. The place is still a mess."

"Is it? Haven't seen any news lately."

Quinn put his hands on his hips and exhaled sharply. "Yes, twenty-seven confirmed deaths, most due to street violence."

"Oh no, when was the last time you heard from them?"

"It's been at least two days."

She hadn't heard anything either. Was AJ safe? Hungry? Thirsty? Scared? Maddy hugged herself, fighting back tears. "Is there anything we can do?"

"Find out where the computer is that's driving the hack. The master is convinced the Russians are behind it. Quite an impressive job. They didn't leave many fingerprints. And plan to include NATO allies in the attack."

Maddy shook her head in wonder and dismay. How'd he know so many details about their mission? NATO allies? In any case, she'd need to make Bear aware of this new complication.

"We're in deep trouble, Quinn. Time's running out and we haven't learned anything about the hack, or made much progress on figuring out the star chart."

"May I see it?"

Maddy unlocked her phone and showed him the picture that she'd transferred to her new phone in Cancun. "Sure. We think it leads to an ancient meteorite."

He took the unit from her and studied the picture by zooming in and out of the image and turning the phone in different directions.

Maddy tilted her head. "Hmm, I hadn't thought to turn it upside down."

"Edith always said that perception is all."

Maddy remembered hearing the same thing. The words from months ago echoed in her head. *Perception is all, dear child, perception is all.* But was it? What about those men she killed? What about Edith? Dead was dead. She shoved those thoughts aside and looked again at the star chart. When it was upside down, it reminded her of something. What?

Quinn handed the phone back to her. "Sorry, no clue what it means." An idea lit his face. "But if you're looking for meteorites, in the 1970s, one was uncovered during an archeological dig in Danebury, England."

"Oh?"

"Yes, it was found deposited in an Iron Age pit from around twelve hundred years before Christ."

"It was deliberately placed there? It seems pretty far away from Egypt, but the timing is close. Let's talk with Bear. Maybe we should go check it out." She studied the image on the phone a moment longer, and then put the device in her pocket. "We have to figure it out somehow."

"The master agrees." A haunted look entered his eyes. "I'm afraid I bear other bad news."

"What's that?"

"A few hours ago, a set of tourists bribed their way into a tomb in the Valley of the Kings and found Professor Crookbottom, the cryptographer, strangled with a garrote."

Maddy's heart skipped a beat. If the man was dead, that meant Lex was hot on the trail of Will and Jags.

CHAPTER 61

DAVAO CITY, PHILIPPINES

DECEMBER 24, 5:38 P.M. PHILIPPINE TIME

AJ sat on the uncomfortable hotel sofa next to Elena, glued to the smartphone Elena held in her slender hand, watching local news.

He was hungry. They'd been stuck in this hotel room for days and now it was night again. In the chaos of the riots, the hotel staff had deserted. Garrod had raided the kitchen yesterday, and while he'd found a few things to eat that others had overlooked—cooked rice, a block of yellow cheese, oatmeal they'd made using water from the bathtub—AJ wondered what they'd eat next. It all tasted awful, but he didn't care. They also didn't have much water left.

"Oh my god, watch this!" Elena said.

AJ peered at the tiny screen. Garrod's phone was dead, and Elena's didn't have much battery life left. They usually watched without letting him see, but tonight he'd begged to be included. There was nothing else for him to do. He was tired of the Lego set.

"That's right down the street!" Garrod exclaimed.

It was a grocery store. Armed guards stood at the front of the market, but the crowd was too big now. Even though guards opened fire into the throng, people surged into the store like a tidal wave.

AJ put his hand to his mouth in horror. "How many people got shot?"

Elena stroked the hair on his head. "I don't know, little man."

"What if the crowd comes here?"

"There's no food here."

"What if they want money? What if they come knocking down our doors?"

Elena and Garrod exchanged a look that scared AJ down to his toes.

After a pause, Elena said, "We'll be safe here."

"What about when the phone dies? Or the food and water run out?"

"I've sent messages to the master. He's trying to help us, but the airport isn't working right now. I'm sure everything will be okay soon."

AJ knew she was lying. Adults always got this funny look in their eyes when they lied, and their voices changed, just a little. His foster mom lied sometimes. Usually about stupid things like if she'd had a drink or not. Maddy didn't lie. He loved her for that.

AJ chewed his fingernail. The video of the grocery was over and another one was playing. AJ caught a glimpse of explosions and fires. People were in boats, rowing out to sea. Elena turned the phone off. "Do you want some cheese?"

"Yes, please. I'm hungry again."

They got up and headed toward the small bar sink. That's when the sound of loud voices and boots thumped up the stairwell. Someone yelled in a language he didn't understand and pounded on the entrance of the room next door.

AJ began to shake and grabbed Elena's hand. The crowd was coming. His fear had come true.

CHAPTER 62

From the back of the small, noisy airplane, Will pointed to a flat-topped outcropping in the middle of the desert.

"Think that's it?" he shouted in Jags's ear.

Jags nodded. The old military plane that Katrina had dug up from god-knows-where was loud. Jags had stopped speaking shortly after they'd taken off from the Luxor airport, unable to scream above the din.

When Will had first seen the rickety old craft, he cursed Katrina.

"They just don't make 'em like they used to," Jags kidded.

They both laughed at the joke and buckled up in seats that reminded Will of canvas camp chairs. At least the machine had seats. He hated to think how uncomfortable the flight would have been without them.

He looked out the window again and checked his Rolex. Although they were still miles away, they'd arrive soon, and it was about the time the pilot had predicted. Other than the twisting, green-bordered Nile, there was nothing out here but the miles of bare sand stretching beneath them like a tan-colored ocean. Wait. Now he could see ruins at the base of the cliff and royal pyramids in the distance. A small town sat on the other side of the river.

Jebel Barkal. They were almost there.

Although the flight had given him time to catch his breath, he had time to worry, too. They'd been running between shadows for days and he was exhausted. And, if he was honest with himself, he was scared. Climbing mountains was *not* something he wanted to do.

At least the gear was fresh. He'd figured the equipment would be as old as the plane and was pleased to discover it was brand new, even though he hoped he'd never have to use it. Maybe Bear was wrong for once and there would be a path to where they needed to go.

The even bigger surprise was that he hadn't thrown up. Sixteen months ago, he'd taken Maddy's advice on dealing with his fear of heights, by feeling into the fear instead of avoiding it. After a lifetime of avoiding heights, he still didn't fully trust that the fear was gone, but at least he hadn't tossed his cookies. He was two for two on that score.

Still, he wasn't looking forward to a further test.

As they neared the peak, the pilot circled to help them get eyes on any caves that might hold the secrets they came to find. Jags was sitting in the window seat, which forced Will to lean over to see around her. He felt uncomfortable sitting close to her. She had no interest in him. He'd been a moron making a pass at her. In a sandstorm, no less. He shook his head at his stupidity.

As the plane buzzed through the air to the other side of the out-cropping, there was the infamous pinnacle, on the south side. Will studied it. If he looked at it with the type of eyes that he used to look for shapes in puffy clouds, he could discern the profile of a squatting god. The pharaoh's snake-like uraeus the Egyptians had seen in the rock must be the knob on the top of the god's head—aka the "white crown." Will could see why the Egyptians were fascinated with the pinnacle.

Will recalled Professor Crookbottom's translation. "You'll find the precise place you seek at the end of the world, inside the Pure Mountain near Napata. Look to the side of the white crown."

The white crown. Will looked at the mountain, next to the god's head. There it was. Excited, he poked Jags and pointed at the small cave a third of the way down from the top of the hulking stone, at eye level with the squatting god. Will calculated the distance from the desert floor. He'd read the pinnacle was seventy-five meters high. That meant the black opening was at sixty meters, roughly two hundred feet up from the ground. Bear was wrong, though. It looked like the back of the mountain had a sloped section that might work as a ramp.

Will swallowed. Even if they were able to boulder hop to the top, they would still have to rappel down the cliff face to get to the cavern. Good Lord!

Could he do it?

CHAPTER 63

EPHESUS, TURKEY

DECEMBER 24, 11:37 A.M. EASTERN EUROPEAN TIME

Maddy studied Quinn's distinctive face for any signs he'd been joking. "The Egyptian cryptographer's dead? The one that Will and Jags spoke with?"

"I'm sorry, but it appears so," he replied, in a thicker than usual Irish brogue.

Maddy frowned. "Give me a minute. I need to text my brother."

She sent a warning to Will on her secure phone, hoping he had reception in Sudan. According to Bear, even satellite phones weren't perfect. They required a line of sight.

She finished the text. "Let's gather the others and tell them."

As they walked toward Anu, Maddy pulled her jacket close for warmth against the cold wind. She looked toward the turreted castle in the distance, oddly inconsistent with the Greek and Roman surroundings. She shivered and wished the sun would come out from the blanket of clouds, if only for a moment. The death of Crookbottom and the dreary day were putting her on edge.

"Sounds good. Hey, the master sent along some old texts from the library. I have them in the boot of the car."

"The Order has a library?"

"Aye, it does. A room full of dusty volumes fallin' apart at the seams."

"Not your cup of tea, eh?"

"Not my thing. My brother Doyle's the smart one." He grinned like a wolf. "I am a man of action."

"Okay, man of action, we're going to leave out details about the Order when we talk to Anu here."

"All righty."

Anu, who still sat on the stump of an old stone column, turned as they approached. Her eyes narrowed when she spotted Quinn. Maddy wondered if she trusted anyone.

"Anu, this is Quinn. He's a friend of ours."

Anu stood, glaring. "What kind of friend?"

Quinn turned on the charm, reaching out to take her hand. "The kind that is here to keep you safe."

Anu tossed her head. "We'll see."

"Let's go see how Bear's doing," Maddy said, to disperse the tension.

Under the leaden sky, the three of them walked into the grassy field where Bear was still using the ground-penetrating radar on the ancient soil. Maddy watched where she placed her feet, as the ground was littered with both small and large rocks.

When they were ten feet away, Bear looked up, stopping abruptly near a tall pile of rubble with another stone column extending up from the center. He turned off the machine. "What's up?"

Maddy realized she never told Bear about Quinn. She had been unsure if the master would be able to assign Quinn to their cause, and admittedly had also been a bit preoccupied with running for her life. She slipped her arm around Bear's waist, knowing that his calm disposition was usually ruffled only when he felt threatened in some way.

"Bear, this is Quinn. He's a friend from Jerusalem."

She hoped the reference to the underground school's location would keep Bear from asking questions in front of Anu.

Bear extended his hand and the men shook.

"It's a pleasure," Quinn said. "How's your work a-goin' here then?"

Bear grimaced. "Yeah, not so hot."

"Maddy tells me you're trying to find a meteorite."

"That's right," Bear admitted. "Could be in any of these surrounding orchards."

"I know of one in England from the right time period."

Bear shook his head. "England's too far north."

"Are you sure about that?" Quinn laughed. "The Romans didn't think so."

"We need something a thousand years earlier."

Maddy interrupted. "Quinn also brought some books for us to look at."

"Old buckets of dust if you ask me," Quinn said.

"What kind of books?" Anu interjected, finally thawing a notch.

"About stars and Egypt, that kind of thing."

"Well, let's take a look." Anu began to pull away from the group. "Where are they?"

"In the boot of my car." Quinn pointed to the parking lot. "The silver sedan."

Anu and Quinn peeled off and walked slowly toward the car. Maddy squeezed Bear's waist. "Are you almost done here?"

He looked at her, eyes narrow and still smoldering. She wondered what he was upset about now. Did he feel threatened about Quinn? If so, the jealousy routine was getting old.

"I suppose so," Bear said finally. "Not findin' a thing."

"Okay, why don't you wrap up and come join us in the parking lot?"

He turned back to his radar unit, flipping the machine back on. "Fine."

Deciding it was not the time to argue, Maddy turned and walked quickly to catch up to the others. They'd almost reached the car when the rear windshield of the silver sedan exploded into a thousand shards of light.

CHAPTER 64

At first, Bear thought the sound he heard was the radar machine hitting a rock. It took him a half second to realize gunshots were flying, but as soon as he did, he dove to the ground and rolled in the direction of the nearby pile of stones. The ache in his right forearm was immediately forgotten.

Bear pulled his Glock from its harness and scanned for two things. Was Maddy safe? Where were the shots coming from? Adrenaline poured into him as he peered beyond the ancient column that rose from the center of the stone pile. Muscles tensed for the fight and his heart pounded in his chest.

Ping! He yanked his head back. There was now a chip in the stone, inches from where his nose had been a second ago. He growled. They were using suppressors, which meant he couldn't tell where the shooter or shooters were hiding. He guessed the orchard. There were too many people up near the amphitheater.

From what he'd been able to tell, Maddy, Anu, and the too-well-dressed Quinn had found cover on the other side of Quinn's vehicle. The guy reminded Bear of an asshole he'd known in the service. Why had Maddy not told him Quinn was coming? At least the director had called to give a heads-up earlier, but that raised other questions about the relationship between VanOps and the Order.

Those thoughts would have to wait. At least Maddy was taking shelter.

As bullets ricocheted off the tiny rocks around him, throwing chips and dust into the air, Bear slithered up against the column, letting loose his own volley of shots. Thank god he had a couple of spare magazines in his belt, having reloaded in the safe house after coming back from Ankara. There! He spied a muzzle flash from the trees to his right. Cautiously, he dropped down again and looked the other way. Yep, more flashes from that direction, too.

Bear ground his teeth. There were at least two shooters, maybe three, and they were just a little too far away for his weapon to be effective. They were outgunned. Or maybe not—Quinn was nestled between the car door and the vehicle, aiming a long-barreled weapon toward the orchard.

Aiming toward the first flash, Bear let off two shots and glanced toward the car. Next to Quinn's car, a red-haired tourist ducked into a small Peugeot.

Wait. Was that Maddy firing from inside the car? Had Quinn come prepared with extra firepower? Bear shook his head. Maddy shooting a gun. God, how he loved her. She'd better stay safe, though. Who were they? Spaniards? Russians? It didn't truly matter. They'd clearly come for blood.

Bear ducked back as screams sounded in the distance. Tourists had heard the chatter of gunfire. Bear hoped they'd find cover. It was his group the attackers were after.

Using his left hand, Bear peered around the column the other way and shot toward the place in the trees that had been the source of the last attack. Bear recalled that there was a Turkish military base right before the short driveway to the temple's parking area. His weapon had no suppressor, and there were reports from Quinn's rifle as well. If they could hold on, reinforcements should arrive soon.

Ping, ping. Two bullets hit the other side of the column. Crack. A rock flew up and hit him in the knee. He swore and reloaded.

As he turned and fired again, a siren cried. It sounded different than those in the States, but its intent was plain.

Bear rolled to a different place on his belly and peered out between some rocks. A black-haired figure sprinted away. Two other figures dressed in black peeled off and followed.

Bear jumped to his feet, firing at all three before sprinting after them. It looked like they were headed toward the cemetery across the road. A shot whizzed by Bear's ear. He reached the trees and kept running. Quinn and Maddy ran after them, too. Shit! The enemy combatants jumped in an old blue car and it sped down the road, heading in his direction. But the distance to the road was too great for him to get close enough for an accurate shot.

In desperation, Bear stopped running and fired toward the speeding vehicle. The front windshield shattered, and the car swerved. Was it a hit? Or just a surprise?

The vehicle righted itself and raced off. Breathing hard, Bear swore again, and started to move toward Maddy to make sure she was okay.

However, before he could reach her, a military vehicle churned into the drive, spinning up gravel as it skidded to a stop.

A command barked through a bullhorn. Even though it was in Turkish, Bear had no problem understanding it from tone alone: *Drop your weapons.*

Bear let his Glock fall to the ground and put his hands in the air. How were they going to get out of this mess?

CHAPTER 65

1:25 P.M.

Frustrated, Maddy paced the length of her dim cell in the Turkish military jail. Two steps, turn, two steps, turn.

She was alone, her party having been divided as soon as they'd arrived, handcuffed, at the military complex. The only light in the room came from a tiny barred window nestled high in the cinder-block wall. After the firefight at the temple, the military had taken control of the situation, and had discovered the weapons she and her friends had used to defend themselves. The attackers had gotten away before the military police had shown up, making it look, to the Turks anyway, like she, Bear, and Quinn were terrorists. Shuddering, she wondered what the Turkish military did to suspected extremists.

She hoped the red-haired tourist who had taken shelter in the small car next to theirs would back up their story of simply returning fire. But he'd suffered a surface wound in the melee and was rushed to the hospital. The image of bright red blood on his cheek made her grimace.

Not much English was spoken by the men who arrested them. If they were lucky, the men had sent for someone who could translate.

Meanwhile, precious time was being wasted. She needed to

figure out where to go next. According to what Crookbottom had told Will, they needed to be somewhere within four days of winter solstice. But where? As she recalled the sun's solstice snake trick at Chichén Itzá, another idea struck her. If shadows were part of the puzzle, they didn't last all day. They were different at sunrise, noon, and sunset. She scowled.

And how had Pyotr found them again? A traitor? A bug or GPS tracker? But Bear had swept them all with a wand before leaving Istanbul. She was pretty sure it was Pyotr running off through the trees. The man had a distinctive, graceful way of moving.

All the problems they faced gave her a chill. She rubbed her arms as she paced inside the lockup. There was a khaki blanket on the cot, but it looked torn and filthy. Now that the fight-or-flight hormones had worn off, her limbs felt heavy and there was an ache in her chest. True, they hadn't rested well in days, but she was starting to realize when something was bothering her. When her energy felt off.

The truth was she was berating herself for taking Quinn's extra weapon and shooting at the attackers. It wasn't the aikido way. But what choice had there been? Afraid of what she'd find, she had been putting off dealing with the guilt from killing those men over a year ago, yet here was more shame to pile on the heap. And then there was what this all meant for AJ and Elena and Bella and Izzy and . . .

Blushing from shame, she bit her lower lip. Quinn's arrival had also reminded her of the exercises from the master. She wasn't being consistent about them, either.

An idea came to her. She could be stuck here for hours. Why not? She was ready to feel better. Carefully, she folded the light-green blanket, attempting to cover the dirtiest sections inside the folds. Then she positioned it on the cot and sat on it cross-legged.

Closing her eyes and placing her hands on her knees, she took a few deep breaths to center herself. For a time, she practiced the exercise from the master, chanting and moving her fingers in rhythm. Next, she turned her radio dial of awareness to her ears. As she was taught, she *listened*, allowing all the sounds of the prison to come to her.

Soft crying came from a cell nearby. Also close, a scratching sound. Further away, a steady clanging, like someone playing drums on the frame of their cot. An unrecognizable squeaking started, squawked, and stopped. Soon, her thoughts floated away. She became aware of her breath and became one with the sounds.

At that point, she turned her attention to the weight in her chest, the iceberg that had been there since she'd woken from the surgery in Egypt and realized that she had killed those men. The place seemed to be more on the right side of her chest than the left, near where the bullet had ripped into her, just below her collarbone. Was it simply a physical ache? She didn't think so, and continued to feel into it.

It seemed to be as wide as her hand, but deep. She knew from experience to look with her mind's eye for a color, texture, or any other clue that would lead her to the source of the emotion. This one was red, marred by vivid hashing. Allowing the sensations, not stopping to analyze, she continued to dive into the center of the color. Like a dream, the crimson became blood on Will's face.

In a flash she was six years old, back in her sick bed, the day her mom and Grandma Emma had died in a car crash. To report the accident, Will had walked to a stranger's house with a deep cut on his chin and a broken arm. When he arrived home with their father later, they'd come to her room. Will's arm was in a cast, and he had stiches on his chin. As her dad told her that her mom was dead, she'd imagined the blood, just inside the cut, held back by only the thinnest of thread and healing skin. It was her fault. She should have made her mom listen. The night before, she'd had a nightmare that ended with a flash of her mom's car mangled and had woken screaming.

Her mom had hushed, soothed, and petted her as Maddy sobbed, "Your car, don't die," and eventually she fell back to sleep, but the horrible feeling had remained the next day. The bronchitis had kept her from going with Will to the birthday party. The icy road had claimed her mother and Grandma Emma shortly thereafter.

Overwhelmed, Maddy sobbed, and allowed herself to feel the loss. Why hadn't she been able to stop them? She had felt guilty for months after that incident, seeing that cut on Will's chin, and the cast on his arm, and sank into the feeling now.

The sensation started to dissipate, bringing with it the hint of a realization about her gifts and responsibilities. Comprehension glimmered, just out of sight.

Clipped boot steps sounded in the hallway. They stopped outside her cage. She tried to hold onto understanding, but it slipped back into mental fog.

"Maddy Marshall?"

Maddy brought her awareness into the present and opened her eyes to slits, annoyed at the interruption. "Yes." At least the man spoke English.

"I'm Captain Yasin. Come with me."

Maddy wiped her eyes, took a deep breath, and rose, uncertain as to whether she was being led to freedom or to torture.

CHAPTER 66

JEBEL BARKAL

DECEMBER 24, 2:03 P.M. EASTERN AFRICAN TIME

Will peeked over the edge of the cliff before rapidly jerking back. It was a long way down. Needing to feel the ground beneath him, he went back to the rocks where Jags lay prone and settled down beside her. He closed his eyes for a moment, trying to control his breathing.

"Do you see the cave?" he asked.

"No, but I'm pretty sure it's right below us."

He wiped the sweat from his eyes. It was a hot, windy desert day and the sun held dominion in a cloudless sky. It had taken a while to get up here. "How can you tell?"

With her head, she motioned right, to the rock outcropping that the Egyptians had thought resembled a pharaoh. "As we flew in, I took a mental bearing from the statue."

"Dear god. We're going to rappel down there?"

"Yes, and we're going to do it in a hurry. You saw the text from your sister."

Will sat up. "Can you believe he's dead? Crookbottom. We just talked with him."

"That's how death is, soldier."

Will recalled losing Maria. She'd been there, and then she wasn't.

271

He swallowed hard and looked down at the dry landscape and the slender Egyptian pillars far below on the desert floor.

As if sensing his discomfort, Jags softened her tone. "C'mon. Help me anchor this rope." She gestured to a tan-colored boulder set a few steps from the edge, and nearly as tall as he was.

Will looked back down the slope they'd climbed minutes before, grateful that they found a way to rock hop up the rear of the crag. In the interest of time, they had opted to land in the desert instead of at the nearby airport. The pilot had laughed his fool head off about going rogue, but Will had worried about rocks and divots until they'd come to a full stop. That's when the sweating began. It hadn't been an easy ascent, and he still felt out of breath.

Will put his shoulder into the rock that she'd pointed out and shoved. It didn't move. "Not going anywhere."

"Good." She looped the heavy climbing rope around its base and hammered an anchor into the back around the line. Next, she took the blue-and-white threaded cable and pulled it hand over hand until she reached the end. The wind whipped the hanging rope around her thin legs. "Now we knot both ends so we stop instead of drop."

Will grimaced at her bad poetry. He stepped into his belay harness and clipped it around his waist. "We're going to be pretty vulnerable if Crookbottom's killer arrives while we're down there."

"I know. That's why I want you to put this on." Jags handed him a backpack.

"You're insane."

"You took the training."

"I did, but this is way below the recommended height." The wind whistled up the crag. "And it's crazy windy today."

"Let's just hope we don't have to use them."

Will had no good response to that. He struggled into all of his equipment.

Jags caught his eye. "Before we head into the cave, any other word from your sister?"

Will reached in his pocket but fumbled as he brought the phone out. The small antennae broke as it hit the ground.

He swore and reached down to pick it up. "Oh my god. I can't believe I dropped the bloody thing."

Jags took the device from him and studied it. "Yeah, reception might be a challenge now. And no word." She handed the phone back to him. "At least yours still has some battery left. Mine's almost dead."

Will pocketed the damaged device and glanced toward the edge, gathering his courage. "I guess it's time."

"You ready?"

Sweating from every pore, he double-checked the buckles on all of his equipment and then closed his eyes, imagining hanging to the side of the cliff by only a rope, buffeted by gusts.

Jags interrupted his thoughts. "Stop that. We're going to go down together. Clip in." She grabbed the rope and clipped it into her harness.

Will repeated her movements and then pulled against the anchor, facing the rock. They were using a military-grade assisted braking device to slow their descent, and he tested that, too. "Don't look down, right?"

Jags stood two meters to his left, her short black hair even messier than usual. "Exactly. On my count, add weight and walk backward. Slow and easy."

Will nodded, heart thudding in his chest like a drum.

Jags's eyes bore into his. "One, two, three, weight."

Together, they moved backward, toward the cliff edge. At the brink, he looked over his shoulder and swayed.

"Stop it!" Jags barked. "Look at your feet."

Will took a deep breath and did as he was told.

"Put your right hand down on the rope and let's go."

Wishing for gloves, he put his hands in position. Right hand below, left hand above.

"Now!"

Will allowed the rope to move through the brake and stepped backward into nothingness. For a moment, he stopped breathing, dizzy with dismay.

"Breathe," Jags commanded.

Will took a deep breath and felt the harness around his waist take his weight. As taught, he let himself walk down the side of the uneven cliff. He focused on his shoes, watching Jags out of the corner of his left eye. Gusts of wind threatened to toss him to the hard desert rocks below. Breathing hard, every second took all of his concentration.

All of a sudden, they were at the mouth of the cave. Will pushed off and swung down and inward.

Two coiled snakes, tan, with triangular heads and a rattlesnake-like pattern, sunned themselves on the edge. As one, they opened their mouths.

He was headed right toward their venomous fangs.

CHAPTER 67

EPHESUS, TURKEY

DECEMBER 24, 2:05 P.M. EASTERN EUROPEAN TIME

Maddy strode across the military complex parking lot. "Let me guess, the director was able to pull a few strings."

Bear walked at her side. "That's right. Once Captain Yasin showed up, I was able to set him straight and had him call HQS."

"What about that tourist they took to the hospital?" Quinn asked as he touched Anu's lower back. The two of them had been trailing behind, heads bent together talking.

"Yeah, he felt well enough to corroborate our story. That helped."

Maddy spotted their green SUV, and Quinn's sedan. "They brought our cars over from the temple parking lot?"

Bear nodded. "I suspect they searched them."

They reached the vehicles and looked inside, where Bear's suspicions were confirmed. Their clothes and supplies were strewn across the seats, and the dinged-up radar unit was tilted over in the back of the SUV.

"They could've cleaned up after themselves," Maddy remarked.

Bear chuckled. "We're lucky they loaded up the radar unit. Let's get out of this neighborhood, spiffy up, and regroup."

Anu and Quinn made eye contact before murmuring their assent. Everyone seemed in a hurry to be gone from the military jail.

"One car or two?" Quinn asked. "The one I was driving seems to not have fared very well."

Maddy took a closer look at the silver sedan. The rear windshield was shot out, and bullet holes traced the doors in an almost artful pattern. Quinn had an understated sense of humor. The car was a wreck. "How about we just take the SUV?"

"Good idea," Bear agreed. "That sedan is a poster child for trouble."

"What about the books?" Anu asked.

Quinn gave her a dazzling smile. Maddy began to wonder if the flower of attraction was blooming between the two of them. "Yes, we'll want those."

Opening the trunk, Quinn handed the ancient texts to Anu, who loaded them with care into the back seat of the SUV. As Bear hopped into the driver's seat, Maddy rode next to him, and Anu and Quinn settled into the mess in the back, working together to clean and organize what they could.

Bear headed west, past the cemetery and the entrance to the Temple of Artemis. After about five minutes, he pulled the car down a dirt road, and parked near a locked gate. They were surrounded by a mature orchard.

"Time is running short." He turned to the back seat. "Y'all have any ideas about where we should head next?"

Quinn held up a black book with a labyrinthine design on the cover. "I have an old friend who owns a villa a few hours from here. I suggest we hole up there and review these."

"I hate putting anyone else in harm's way." Maddy remembered the blood on the face of the red-haired tourist. "Somehow, that Russian is still following us. And now he has friends."

Anu glanced out the window, orange beads moving between her fingers.

Maddy fixed her gaze on the woman. "Does anyone have any ideas about how he could be tailing us?"

Anu said nothing. Maddy clenched her fists in frustration.

After several beats, Quinn broke the silence. "I don't know how we're being followed, but my friend is former military and an electronics geek. His villa is in a private spot on the sea and has a nice level of security. It's in a tiny town called Oren."

Maddy and Bear exchanged a glance. It was their best choice.

"All right then," Bear said. "Give me directions."

Maddy reached for two of the tomes in the back seat. "And let's see if we can glean anything from those old books along the way."

As Bear headed to Oren on Quinn's directions, Maddy examined her two books while fighting off car sickness. One had a soft brown cover, made of a material that looked like leather. Perhaps calfskin. The other was made of two thin slabs of wood, held together at the spine by something pale, stretched tight. Sinew, she guessed. Neither had any writing on the exterior.

Using the utmost care, she opened the first. Inside was pinched handwriting in a language she didn't recognize. Maybe old Italian? The other one looked to be written in Arabic. No images were apparent as she thumbed through the pages. She turned over her shoulder to look at Quinn. "Do you know anything else about these books?"

"No." He glanced through his own book. "Only that the master said he chose them for their Egyptian content."

Anu held hers toward Maddy. "This one isn't even that old."

Maddy took it. "Want these old ones? I can't read them."

"Sure," Anu replied. "I'll take a look."

At least the book Maddy held now was more traditionally bound and typeset. She recognized a pattern of letters. The darned thing was written in French. After turning a few pages, though, some illustrations gave life to the words. One image was a map of Egypt. Another, the pyramids at Giza. A third showed a Star of David superimposed over the map of Egypt. Different points of the star corresponded to various Egyptian cities, with Cairo situated dead center.

She held the page open to Bear. "Look at this."

He glanced her way. "I'm a little busy driving."

She put the open book in front of him and grabbed the steering wheel. "I've seen you multitask." The two-lane road had little traffic, and compared to getting shot at, this seemed a small risk. In the back, Anu and Quinn leaned forward.

Bear studied it for a second. "Looks like a star."

"Star of David," Quinn added.

"How does it help us?" Bear asked.

Maddy took the book back from Bear and relinquished the wheel. "I'm not sure," she confessed. But something about it niggled at her.

"Any other interesting images in there?" Bear asked.

Maddy continued to page through the French book. "Just a few of what look like standard Egyptian constellations." Quinn and Anu returned to studying their own volumes.

After a few more minutes, Maddy began to feel nauseous and had to stop reading. She turned to Bear. "Any sign of a tail?"

He glanced in the rearview mirror. "Right now, we're in the clear."

And yet as they sped off into the dark afternoon, Maddy remained convinced Pyotr was somehow on their trail.

CHAPTER 68

With a silent scream, Will swung toward the venomous snakes.

Acting on instinct, he brought his feet into his chest like he was on a rope swing, dangling over a lake rather than two coiled serpents on the edge of the cliff. Before he realized he'd missed his chance to drop into the shadow of the cave, he was flailing out again. Toward the snakes.

Jags was a half second behind him. Since she was two meters to his left, she wasn't lined up with the cave opening, and had to push sideways off the rock wall to swing in. The snakes pivoted to the new threat. At the last moment, Will dropped his legs and kicked at both snakes, scooping them over the edge with the back of his boots.

He sailed for a moment over the precipice, looked down, and gasped just as Jags grabbed him and pulled him onto the thin ledge. A meter in, tall rocks flanked both sides of a narrow opening.

He stood for a second, trembling with fear and excitement. After he caught his breath, he broke into a smile and gave her a high five, which she returned with a loud slap.

"We did it," Will announced.

"Of course we did, Doubting Thomas." Jags unclipped the climbing line from her harness. "Give me your rope."

Will obeyed, and then reached for the monogramed key-ring flashlight from Maria on his belt. Maybe he'd still join her today, but it wouldn't be because of those snakes.

Will turned the light on, walked between the tall sentinel rocks, and lit up the cave. "Deeper than I thought."

Jags finished tying off their ropes and stood next to him. "Yes, and these rocks do a decent job of hiding it. If we hadn't known where to look . . ." Her voice trailed off.

"We'd have never found it."

Jags pushed a hand through her messy hair, trying to get it out of her eyes. Wind whipped it back out of place. "Let's hope our luck holds and there are no more snakes."

"Not my favorite."

"Nor mine. Nice move kicking them over the edge."

Will blushed at the praise, and wished his action had been more intentional. "Thank you." He moved the beam of light around. "Don't see any here."

"Let's move then."

As they inched their way forward, the howling wind began to subside. Jags pulled out a bright flashlight as well, and their twin beams illuminated a cavern about three meters wide, and the same tall. After a long fifteen meters, it took an abrupt right.

Will walked into a thick mass of spider webs. "Ack." He waved at the webs.

"Be careful. Camel spiders live in this terrain."

Will swallowed. He didn't want to meet up with one of those. They were large and hairy. "I'm careful," he squeaked. Then he lowered his voice. "Looks like the tunnel is narrowing."

"It is," Jags agreed.

All exterior light from the tunnel's entrance fled, and they walked on in a darkness lit only by flashlights. The cry of the wind ceased, replaced by the scuffle of their boots on sand.

A faint sound echoed down the passageway.

"Shhh." Will grabbed Jags's arm. "Did you hear that?"

"No. What?"

Will furrowed his brow and walked a few steps back toward the entrance, listening hard. "I thought I heard a boom. Like an explosion."

After a moment he returned to Jags's side.

"I don't hear anything else," he said tersely. He could have sworn he had heard something. And his gut told him it was bad. They needed to hurry.

"Okay, let's keep moving then."

But as they turned the next corner, they found their way blocked by a pile of large stones.

CHAPTER 69

The view from the deck of the white villa was stunning. The cloud bank that had hovered overhead all day was breaking into pieces. Rays of the setting sun speared the leaden clouds in a captivating juxtaposition of dark and light over the Mediterranean Sea.

Maddy turned to Bear. "Not a vacation, but sure is a lovely view."

He murmured agreement, putting his arm around her.

For a moment, she was content. Behind them, still seated at the table where they'd all had a slow roasted chicken-and-peppers dinner a few minutes ago, Quinn and Anu were poring over the books. As Quinn had predicted, their youthful host, Mahmoud, a nearly bald man with thick glasses, had graciously offered them his home and its high-tech security system. He had also shown them his room full of impressive electronic wizardry. Although she didn't feel exactly safe, the knot in her stomach was a bit looser, and she noted the tight, guilty feeling in her chest was almost gone.

Her phone buzzed.

She pulled it out of her pocket and looked down. It was another email from Vincent. "Hey gorgeous, recovery is coming along fine. Want to have lunch?"

"What does he want?" Bear growled.

She frowned and turned to face him. "You're spying on my phone?"

Anger sparked in his eyes. "No, it was right in front of me."

Tired of his jealousy, she could feel heat rising in her face. "Well, it's none of your business."

His voice rose. "Actually, it is my business. You're my business."

"What, I can't have friends?" she said, and started herding him away from the villa, onto the paved path that ran along the beach. Anu and Quinn didn't need to hear this and were both putting their hands over their ears to make light of the situation. Maddy didn't find it funny.

"Friends? You gotta be kiddin' me. He's your ex and wants you back."

She rolled her eyes. "But I don't want him back."

Bear pointed at the phone in her hand. "That's not what I see. Why are you still letting him email you?"

"I can't control what the guy does." She stopped walking by a concrete bench and spread her arms wide to make her point.

"No, but have you tried to put a stop to it?"

Although a small part of her was tempted by Vincent's advances, they were through and she wanted Bear to let it go. "Bear, we broke up. How can you not see that?"

"I see that he wants you back."

Her temper was a bucking horse. "So, what?"

Bear spat the next words. "You need to tell him to bugger off."

She threw her hands to the sky. "Then what?"

Bear took a deep breath. "Then we're good."

With an effort, Maddy reined in her anger. There was a grain of truth to Bear's point, but she wouldn't be with him if she really wanted Vincent back. Didn't Bear trust her? His jealousy only made her miss Vincent more. "Why aren't we good now? How can you not see that I want you, not him?"

Frustrated, she crossed her arms, turned, and faced out to sea.

The sun broke through a set of low-lying clouds and lit a previously obscured mountain behind the town. *How can you not see?*

The answer came to her in a flash. Perspective. He was coming from a different perspective.

Then, pieces of the star chart puzzle crashed together in her mind. Quinn turning it upside down. The Star of David in the French book. The old map from the museum. Perspective. *Bless you, Edith!* She turned and put a hand on Bear's chest.

"The star chart! I have an idea." She kissed him, full on the lips, and ran back to the patio.

CHAPTER 70

Stunned, Bear watched as Maddy sprinted up the steps of the whitewashed villa toward Quinn and Anu. His lips still tingled. One minute they had been arguing about that tall bastard, Vincent, the next, her eyes lit up like the Christmas lights decorating the villa's wrought-iron porch.

Curious, he followed her, but at a slow enough pace so he could cool down. With a last deep breath of the salt-tinged air, he climbed the steps.

Maddy pawed through the pile of papers on the glass-topped patio table. "Where is it?"

"What?" Quinn asked.

"The printout of the star chart."

Anu reached under a pile and pulled out the larger copy they'd made an hour earlier. Then Maddy shoved aside several books, one toppling over the side. Strange, she didn't seem to notice. In the cleared space, she put the paper down and stared at it.

She yanked her phone out of her pocket and started swiping through pictures. Soon she came to the photo of the map she'd taken back in Istanbul. She turned to Quinn. "Can we use Mahmoud's printer again?"

"I'm sure we can."

"Great. We need a printout of this map."

"Okay, I'll see what I can do." Quinn took the phone from her and disappeared into the house.

Maddy bounced on her toes, her excitement clear. While they waited, she studied the star chart, murmuring, and turning it upside down.

After several minutes, Quinn returned. He handed her the phone and the printout.

"Excellent." She superimposed the star chart on top of the printout of the map. "Who has a flashlight?"

Bear handed her one and she beamed it at the pages. She held them up and moved the flashlight, apparently trying to see the map through the page with the star chart.

She shook her head. "No, no, the map is too big. I'm sure he has a copy function on that printer. We need it—" She eyed both pages. "Try reducing fifty percent."

Quinn eyed her with skepticism, but did as she asked.

While Quinn was gone, Maddy tried placing the map on top of the chart, but stood with her hands on her hips, clearly frustrated.

"What are you trying to do?" Bear asked.

"You'll see in a minute."

Intrigued, Anu leaned over and studied them, and as she did, her eyes lit up with understanding. Bear started to feel stupid.

Quinn exited the villa's French door and waved the document with pride. "Okay, fifty percent."

"Great." She placed the reduced image of the map on top of the star chart and grabbed a pencil. "Bear, shine that light here. I need to see the chart through the paper."

Bear did as instructed. She took the pencil, aligned the two images, and began to circle cities on the map. With a sharp intake of breath, Bear understood. The star chart wasn't a chart of the stars or a constellation. It was a map of ancient cities. They'd been looking at it all wrong, from the earth up to the heavens, instead of from the sky down. Those clever men.

Maddy circled four cities on the map, each corresponding to points on the chart. "It's all perspective," she whispered.

Several other cities got small marks, while she checked and double-checked the alignment of the chart with the map. She saved the biggest star on the chart for last.

"Oh my god." With big bold strokes, she circled a blank spot on the map and threw her pencil onto the glass tabletop. "There's nothing there."

"What do you mean?" Bear asked.

"All the other points relate to ancient cities. This spot is in the middle of nowhere." Maddy placed the pages on the table, returned her hands to her hips and turned to face the sea. "I must have been wrong."

While Quinn stood stroking his chin, Anu reached out and grabbed the two pieces of paper. After a minute, she said, "Perhaps not."

They all turned to her.

"Based on the other ancient cities," Anu said, "this looks like the general area where Petra is located."

Maddy pointed to the pages. "Why isn't it on the map then?"

"If we're right about the age of the star chart, Petra was built a thousand years later," Anu answered.

"I don't get it," Quinn said.

Maddy sighed. "Yeah, that timing doesn't work at all."

Bear thought he knew the answer. "It could be like a pirate map, using other landmarks as clues. Besides that, many sites, especially religious ones, were built on top of older places that held a spiritual significance."

"That's right," Anu said, excitement mounting in her tone. "We see that behavior all the time as archeologists." She looked away. "I want to say some sort of sanctuary has been there since ancient times. If my memory serves, the Madianites were in the area as early as 1340 BC. I think Petra is even in some campaign accounts of the Egyptians."

"Folks can worship at a site for thousands of years before someone decides to build a temple there," Bear added. "The Temple of Artemis was like that."

A gleam of hope returned to Maddy's eyes. "It could be Petra then?"

Bear nodded and smiled. "It looks that way. There's nothing else out there."

Maddy hugged him, and he hugged her back. Quinn and Anu grinned at each other.

After a moment of celebration, Anu said, "I hate to spoil the party, but Petra is a large site. We still need to know the exact time to be there, and where on the site to look."

Maddy looked south as she took in this news. "Then Will and Jags had better be making progress on their half of the deal."

CHAPTER 71

JEBEL BARKAL

DECEMBER 24, 5:15 P.M. EASTERN AFRICAN TIME

Annoyed, Will threw the last of the stones behind him. "That should do it."

Jags stood and stretched her back. "I hope so—it's taken us way too long to clear the tunnel."

Will bounced on his toes. "I know. With the friendly family assassin on our tail, every minute matters."

After stumbling across the blockage, they had discussed whether it was a natural or man-made pile, and figured it to be a cave-in, rather than a trap.

"Let's hope we don't come across another blockade," Jags said.

Alert for danger, they continued to walk down the cave, which narrowed until it was wide enough for just one of them to pass at a time. When Jags took the lead, Will felt a small hit to his ingrained sense of manhood—men go first into danger—and then reminded himself that she was the senior officer here. It was smart to let her scout.

The tunnel twisted right again, and then after another twenty meters, made a sharp left that seemed to double back in the direction they'd come from. The height dropped, too, and soon Will found himself hunched over. He considered crawling, although . . .

what if there *were* booby traps? He'd seen Indiana Jones movies too many times. Would they find other natural predators besides spiders and snakes? Would their batteries last?

Without warning, Jags stopped, and Will ran into her back. "Sorry," he mumbled.

"It's okay," Jags said, excitement in her tone. "Look at this."

She stepped forward, and Will followed, at last able to stand up straight. They were in an oval cavern about the size of a small bedroom.

"I think we've hit the jackpot," he said.

"No kidding."

Will pointed to a mural that depicted a lion's head in shaded profile. "Check that out."

The sun's rays coming out the other side looked as if they would ignite the mane at any moment. The artistry was stunning, and had a subtle Egyptian feel.

Jags swung her beam to an image to the left of the lion's head. "And that. Looks like it depicts a tunnel being lit by the sun."

"Sunrise or sunset?" Will knew timing was everything.

"No idea."

Will swung his light around the cave, taking in the other images. An arrow pointed to a spot above where a stream poured out of rocks. That made sense. Look above the stream. But to the right was a series of more complicated hieroglyphs. He wished he knew what they said. He should learn to read them someday. "Maybe these explain."

"Maybe so. Let's get some pictures." Jags pulled out her phone. "Get some with your phone, too, in case my battery dies. It's in the red."

"Good idea."

With the military sat phone, Will took pictures of the lion, the sun, the stream, and the hieroglyphs. Bear and Maddy needed to see these pictures as soon as possible, and Will hoped Anu could make sense of whatever the artists had intended.

Once finished, though, he glanced at the screen. This deep in the cave, they had no service at all.

CHAPTER 72

OREN, TURKEY

DECEMBER 24, 5:22 P.M. EASTERN EUROPEAN TIME

Anu glanced around the table at her companions, all seated with beverages at the villa's glass patio table, while the last rays of the day's sun faded. As she worked the orange beads through her fingers, Anu kept her eyes on the view. Not for any picturesque reasons, but to keep an eye out for Pyotr.

Wanting to know everything about Petra, Bear and Maddy peppered her with questions. She was grateful that she had visited the ruins once on holiday. However, talk of the ancient city reminded her of Chichén Itzá and Pyotr's attack, and what she suspected was his ability to track them through what he'd shot into her upper arm. Likely a tiny GPS, although if so, she didn't understand why Bear's wand hadn't discovered it back in Istanbul. Pyotr would be able to follow them to the ends of the earth. She shuddered, chilled to the bone.

"Who built Petra?" Maddy asked.

The question brought Anu back to the present. She blinked. "The Nabateans."

"Never heard of them," Quinn said.

Anu found his unique heritage striking, and liked his sense of humor. Under other circumstances, she might have found him attractive.

"They were a little-understood Middle Eastern culture, right?" Bear asked.

Anu took a drink of water to wet her dry throat. "Right. They ruled most of present-day Jordan for about four hundred years around the time of Christ."

"Somethin' about the Silk Road."

"Yes, Petra was built at the crossroads of the Silk Road and the Incense Route from Arabia to Damascus."

"But isn't it out in the middle of the desert? Where'd they get water?" Maddy asked.

Anu looked at her. "That's a great question."

"Oh, why?"

"Not long ago, archeologists found an extensive irrigation system from a nearby spring. There were channels to funnel rainwater, an aqueduct system, and a swimming pool over forty meters long."

"Oh my god," Maddy said. "Surrounded by all that sand."

"They even had gardens with vines and date palms," Anu said.

Quinn crossed his arms. "Neat, but the place seems dry as a bone now."

"Pretty much," Anu agreed. "The city fell into decline after Christianity became the only sanctioned world religion. Then a series of earthquakes destroyed their water system."

"Do you think they drew the star chart?" Maddy asked.

"Hard to say." Anu wished they'd slow down with their questions. They were as rapid as those gunshots in Ephesus this morning. She cringed at the memory of hiding in the backseat of Quinn's car. "Perhaps the people who came before, assuming this is the right spot."

Bear stretched his shoulders. "Anu, you were able to visit it once?"

"Yes, the religious beliefs of the people there are curious. There's some thought there could be a relationship between the gods they worshiped and the Vedic deity Shiva." Brought up Hindu, Shiva was dear to Anu's heart.

Bear chewed on an ice cube. "Interesting."

"Yes, the Nabateans built a few other local cities with names like Shivta and Tel Sheva. They, along with the nation that became Yemen—which was called Sheba by the Hebrews—all point to that connection."

"Okay, but let's stay focused. What about the archeoastronomy aspects?" Maddy asked.

"That's the main reason I visited. Recently, results were published in the *Nexus Network Journal* and showed how many buildings are aligned with the equinoxes and solstices."

"Do you have an example?" Quinn asked.

"Sure, two. During winter solstice, the setting sun creates beautiful light and shadow effects around a podium inside Ad Deir, or the Monastery, where the Nabateans held religious festivities for their main god." Anu paused, remembering the other. "Also, the Urn Tomb has corners that light up at each solstice."

Bear narrowed his eyes. "How long on either side of the solstice?"

"For both, usually no more than five days before and after."

"That's bad," Bear said. "We are running out of time."

"Yes." Anu prayed that somehow, this ordeal would soon be over.

"Any Egyptian connection?" Maddy asked.

"The Egyptian influence is obvious. Obelisks and funerary tombs are found throughout the city."

Maddy and Bear exchanged a look. Maddy asked, "Any history of meteorites?"

Anu dreaded this important question. "A rare one was found a few years ago in the Srout area of Jordan, but Petra is not traditionally associated with a meteorite. No."

Maddy frowned.

"Then, it was either hidden well, or we're looking in the wrong spot," Bear said.

Maddy played with a stray lock of dark hair as she brainstormed. Anu found Maddy's habit strange for someone who wore a hat all the time.

"We've seen how powerful just two obelisks from the meteorite are," Maddy said. "If it were me, I'd hide the thing deep."

Bear attacked another ice cube. "Me, too."

Anu wasn't fond of his ice-chewing habit.

"How much of the city has been excavated?" Quinn asked.

Anu didn't want to break this bad news either. "Fifteen percent."

Quinn gave a small whistle. "Even if Petra is in the right general location, it'll be like looking for a single grain of sand in the desert."

Anu nodded. "I'm afraid so."

"Wait. Remember? According to Crookbottom, Will and Jags should be searching for the 'precise place' we seek." Maddy glanced toward her phone. "They should be checking in soon."

The device rang. Maddy looked at the screen. "Good, that's him."

Anu had heard of these types of connections between twins, but seeing it firsthand was unnerving.

As Maddy took the call from her brother, Anu scanned the sea. Nothing yet. But Pyotr was clever. In her gut, she knew he was coming.

CHAPTER 73

OREN, TURKEY

DECEMBER 24, 5:35 P.M. EASTERN EUROPEAN TIME

Maddy picked up the phone. "Hi, Will."

"Maddy, are—okay?" The reception was poor and his voice cracked in and out. Still, she thought it sounded like he was breathing hard.

She hit the speaker button. "We had a shooting incident this morning, but no wounds. You?"

"So far—good, and we found—!"

"You're breaking up. Repeat." Maddy's eyes locked with Bear's. *What have they found out there?*

"—cave."

"Will, can you hear me?"

"Broken antenna—"

Maddy closed her eyes in frustration. She listened with all her being.

"—found cave-in."

"What else?"

"—lion silhou—sun behind."

Anu's eyes lit up and she stared at the phone.

"What?" Maddy asked her.

Anu leaned forward. "Petra. There are lions, even winged lions, in several places there."

That confirmed Petra as the star chart's location. Excited, Maddy yelled into the phone, "Will. Petra. Head to Petra!"

"What?"

"Petra!"

His voice got loud, and then sounded like it was coming from a distance. "Okay, —head to Petra!"

"What else did you find?"

"Trying—photos. Jags's phone—"

God, this bad reception was annoying. She yelled, enunciating both words. "Keep trying."

"*Jags!*"

The panic in his voice made her heart jump in her chest.

As she listened in growing horror, sounds of a struggle came through the line. A thunk, and Maddy imagined the phone dropping to the ground. Grunts of pain, a slap, and with her mind's eye, Maddy saw her twin and Jags fighting off an attack. It had to be Lex.

Then all went silent.

CHAPTER 74

Will struggled as he tried to free himself from the assassin's deadly embrace. The man had some sort of wire to his throat, and Jags lay unmoving on the rock floor nearby.

Moments earlier, not wanting to waste another precious instant, they'd headed closer to the cave's entrance, seeking reception and the remaining light of day. But as soon as they'd gotten ahold of Maddy, a shadow had appeared with tornado-like force and knocked Jags to the ground. Before he could react, the sat phone crashed to the floor and Will was caught in a death grip.

Now Will flailed and kicked with his legs, scattering tiny rocks. His foot connected with something solid and it tumbled over the ledge. He feared it was his satellite phone.

As he fought, he blessed Maddy, for her strange dream had encouraged him to buy a Kevlar throat protector in Marrakech. He'd be dead now if it wasn't for her. The wire was bruising his neck, but the shield protected his air supply.

Will attempted to turn his head to the side and push the man's arms overhead, but the angle didn't work. The guy was shorter than he was, and Will couldn't get underneath his arms. Did he dare pull his hands away? Did he have another choice?

He shoved backward and pushed the attacker into the rock wall. There was a rewarding grunt, but the man held on and pulled tighter. Will thrashed in the man's grip, using his long legs in a scramble for leverage. His right ankle slipped, twisted, and a new pain shot up the side of his calf. The agony spurred a decision.

With no better choice, he dropped his right hand, pulled a knife from his wrist sheath, and plunged it backward until he felt the blade slice through flesh and grind into bone.

The assassin gasped and the wire around Will's throat grew slack. Will slammed backward again, knocking the man into the wall with all his might. The wire garrote fell to the ground.

In a flash, Jags was next to him, punching the attacker in the stomach, and then kneeing him in the chin when he fell forward, sending his head snapping backward and into a rock. As fast as it had begun, it was over. Above a swollen nose, the haunted eyes fell shut, and Lex Argones's body sank to the floor. Although the hair was a bright, dyed blond, the man's face held no tattoos.

Before Will could make sense of it all, Jags rolled Lex onto his stomach and pulled the assassin's arms behind his back. "Grab that climbing rope."

"But—"

"Shut up. Just do it."

He quit arguing and handed it to her. She pulled Lex deeper into the cave and wrapped the cord around his wrists and ankles.

Finished trussing the man like a pig for a roast, Jags ripped the knife out of Lex's hip. In the dim light, blood oozed from the wound, which meant the gash wouldn't kill him. She handed the knife to Will, who wiped the blade clean on Lex's dark pants.

"Now what?" Will demanded.

Jags moved toward the cave opening. "Now we get the hell out of here."

He pointed at Lex. "You just used the climbing rope."

"We'll have to use our backup plan."

Will's skin prickled at the thought of BASE jumping off the cliff.

"What about him?"

"We'll send reinforcements back for him. We can't carry him."

Will hated the idea, but had to ask the question. "Should we leave him alive then?"

Jags tilted her head and looked at him. "Didn't think you had it in you, Killer."

"Not my first choice."

"Nor mine. And not necessary. He's stuck here until we send others to get him, and will be a valuable source of intel."

Relieved, Will agreed. "Okay." He tugged on the rope. "Sure we can't climb down? Or up?" His ankle began to throb. Maybe climbing wasn't a great idea either.

"Nope. Turn around." She reached for the ripcord on his BASE parachute. "Hurry. We'll need to tie this off on the big rocks over here."

"Static line? Not enough time to pull ourselves?"

"Exactly. I also packed ram-air chutes in case we needed to leave in a rush. Hand me mine, too."

Will's knees started to tremble. He couldn't believe he was about to jump off a cliff. The first time his instructor had insisted, he'd lost his breakfast. And that was from a safe height, over six hundred meters. Only a stunt man, or someone desperate, would jump from sixty meters.

With incredible speed, Jags tied both ripcords to the tall sentinel rocks that had hidden Lex's approach. She tested the knots, as did Will, even though his hands were shaking now.

"Stop thinking," she said. "We'll be fine."

Jags grabbed his hand and they stepped back into the cave to get a running start. Will knew this was to prevent them from hitting the cliff face below, which made him even more nervous. "Let's each jump to the side. Away from each other. On my count."

Will closed his eyes. Was there a god? Would he see Maria soon?

"One, two, three," Jags yelled.

They both sprinted for the entrance of the cave and jumped headlong into space.

CHAPTER 75

Will hurled away from the cliff, floating for half a second in thin air before he felt the jerk of the parachute open behind him. The harness dug into his thighs, but he didn't have time to worry about that.

His heart pounded and he groped for the controls of the chute at his sides, wishing he had at least a little muscle memory to guide him. There was no time to waste. A clump of ancient structures loomed in the near distance and he could see the Nile a little further out.

The knob on the right slipped into his hand. But the left one. *Where is it?*

The sandy ground of the desert floor was approaching too fast. The wild wind buffeted his chute. Come on! Frantic, Will searched his left side.

Finally. His hand closed on the control.

Just in time, too, as Will adjusted the chute from both sides to keep from smacking into the side of a stone pillar. *Thunk*! His feet hit the ground, right ankle complaining, and he ran a few meters as the parachute dropped to the ground behind him. Will sank to his knees, and put his forehead on the dry sand. Shaking, he gulped a few breaths. His throat burned. *That ankle is going to be a problem.*

Jags kicked him, but not hard, rolling him onto his side.

"Hey!" Will said.

Jags smiled. "See, told you we'd be fine."

Will let out a deep breath. "Remind me to wear diapers next time."

Jags removed her parachute harness. "Get over yourself. We need to find our plane."

Will removed his harness too, and then patted his pockets. "Wait, have you seen my sat phone?"

"I looked before we leaped and it wasn't on the ground."

Will grimaced. "Then it did get kicked over the edge in the fight. I was afraid of that."

"Bummer." She pulled her own phone from a pocket and turned it on. "Running on fumes. Need power before I can make a call."

"Okay, let's go. We need to get those images to the rest of the team."

Burning off adrenaline, the two jogged around the hulking mountain in search of where they'd left their pilot and plane. Will's ankle ached. Night was falling and the area was deserted, the last tourist bus having departed hours ago. The wicked wind had died down and, while the heat of the day remained coiled in rocks, the air temperature was dropping fast, drying the sweat from his body as they ran.

Twenty minutes later, they arrived at the ribbon of sand they'd used as a makeshift runway only to be greeted by a smoking hulk of metal. As Jags unleashed a torrent of creative curse words, a few red cinders flared up from the charred frame of the plane.

"*Merda!*" Will swore, in Portuguese. He *had* heard an explosion back in the cave. How were they going to return to civilization?

CHAPTER 76

OREN, TURKEY

DECEMBER 24, 7:00 P.M. EASTERN EUROPEAN TIME

Out the window of the villa, Maddy watched dark clouds float across an endless sky. The sea looked choppy, as if a storm were coming. Somewhere, on the other side of the world, near a different sea, AJ and Elena were still dealing with an uprising.

She turned to Bear, who lay atop the bed. They'd had a long day, and tomorrow promised to be longer.

"It's Christmas Eve. Think AJ and Elena are safe?"

He didn't answer at first. "I sure hope so."

Sitting on the edge of the bed, she squeezed her hands together in frustration. "I miss him. She's not answering the phone."

"It's late there, but do you want to try one more time?"

"Sure."

She dialed Elena's number.

On the fourth ring, Elena said sleepily, "Hello?"

"It's me, Maddy. Are you guys okay? I've been so worried."

"Yes, sure. Sorry." She began to sound more awake. "We were attacked in the hotel room by some thugs and then the cell died."

Maddy put her hand to her mouth. "What happened?"

"They had no weapons, and were no match for our training.

The best part was AJ threw a dinosaur at them from across the room."

Maddy laughed with relief. "And no one was injured?"

"One of the thugs left with a broken nose, but otherwise we're fine."

"How'd you get your cell charged?"

"We shouldn't chat long. The power was on for an hour today and then died again."

"Okay. Don't wake AJ then. Just tell him Merry Christmas and I love him."

"Will do, Maddy. Take care of yourself, too."

"Thanks Elena. Later." Maddy ended the call and looked at Bear. "I want to fly over there and rescue them. Pull a commando raid and get them out."

He smiled. "Tempting as that might be, we're right where we need to be."

"I suppose. Is anyone working to stop that hack?"

"I'm sure they are. We have our mission, and it's important. Carries some risks, though."

She peeled back the sheets and slid in next to him before lightly touching his arm. "How's that arm holding up?" A good cuddle was in order before sleep. "Will it be ready if we see some action?"

He pulled away. "It's healin' up fine."

She sat up. "What?"

"I just want to discuss the operation before we call it a night."

She sighed. Would they ever be on the same page?

"Okay, anything in particular?"

He sat up, too, sitting cross-legged to face her. "Well, the director has a helo headed our way, but we won't get it until sunrise."

"I know. Because it's a big helicopter, right?"

"Yeah. I didn't want to talk it all through in front of Anu and Quinn."

"Ah, okay," Maddy said.

"She has no security clearance at all and could be collaborating with the enemy. And I'm not sure we should be collaborating with her cozy new pal Quinn."

Maddy frowned. "He's kind of like MI6."

Bear scratched at his stubble. "How do you figure?"

Should she even remind him about this? "OIF."

"Huh?"

"Order of the Invisible Flame. The master's European spy ring. Quinn belongs to it. Like me."

"That's right. Didn't recognize the acronym."

Maddy gave a mischievous grin. "I just made it up."

"Anyway, Bowman told me to work with him on this mission, but that he's not cleared for US government intel."

He doesn't need to be, Maddy thought. The master would have told him everything already. "When did the director tell you that?"

"While I was pushin' that radar unit halfway across Asia."

Ah, that was the call Bear had received. She'd have to ask the master later about the Order's relationship with other spy agencies. "Okay. Fair enough. As long as he can help out. What's on your mind?"

"Tactics."

She tucked a stray hair behind her left ear. "Because we've been followed every step of the way?"

"Yes. We need to get there first. Alive."

"God, I hope Will and Jags are okay. That dream about his neck still bugs me."

He reached out to grab her hand. "I'm sure they are. But they have the last piece of the puzzle. We don't know exactly where to be, or if it's at sunrise, high noon, or sunset."

"And we've missed the sunrise window."

"For tomorrow. Worst case, day after."

"Except Crookbottom said the solstice window only lasts for four days. We might be beyond the window."

"We might," he said, eyes serious. "But we've no choice. The director couldn't get us a helo tonight."

"Okay, what's the plan then?"

"If we don't hear from your brother, we're going to have to punt, and try to figure it out. Quinn handled himself well with a gun this morning, and we'll have him guard our backs while we scout."

She couldn't think of anything better. "Sounds good. At least we have a good lead on the Petra part. Hope it pans out."

His eyes still looked haunted. "Yeah, me too."

"Anything else bugging you?"

"Me? Nah."

She made her tone light. "You lying sack of shit. You're still bothered by the Vincent email, aren't you?"

Since the argument, she'd been thinking more about the last smoldering Vincent-related sparks. Although she'd miss some of the fun times they'd had together, she decided she could never trust a man who had cheated on her. Bear wanted her and loved her. She would tell Vincent to stop contacting her.

When Bear wouldn't meet her gaze, she tackled him, rolling on top of him to grab his chin, and made him look at her. "Repeat after me: 'Maddy is my girlfriend.'"

Half-heartedly, he tried to move his head from her grasp. "Aw, c'mon, Maddy."

"You heard me, handsome. Maddy is my girlfriend."

He made a sour face and said in a falsetto, "Maddy is my girlfriend."

"Oh. My. God. I am *not* going to go back to Vincent. Do you hear me?"

"That's what Amy said, two weeks before she left me."

A light bulb went off in Maddy's head. "Ouch. I didn't know." Her tone softened. "I'm not her."

"But—"

She put a finger to his lips. This called for show, not tell. They could talk about whoever Amy was later. Pushing herself up, Maddy ripped her shirt off and kissed him. It took him a few to warm up to the idea, but within less than a minute, he rolled her over onto her back and took control of the situation. Time fled.

Later, when she could talk, Maddy turned to him. "Can you feel it when I do this?"

"You're not touching me."

Lying next to him, she *listened*, and imagined him wrapped in a white bubble of love. "I am. Just a different way."

"Mmm. Maybe," he said, after a minute. "It's subtle. What are you doing?"

"I'm beaming at you."

"You're what?" His voice was husky.

"Sending you love."

"It feels . . . I dunno. Like I feel you. Like you're inside me."

She grinned. "That's what I was shooting for. Wanna try it?"

"Me?"

"Why not?"

"I'm not good at that shit. I blow things up."

She rolled over and put her hand on his chest. "Just try."

"What do I do?"

She giggled. "Imagine I'm surrounded by a bubble."

"A bubble? Really? Okay."

"Now use your imagination to fill that bubble with love and white light."

She reached out with her sixth sense. There he was. Barely noticeable, but the hair on her arms rose. He felt warm, and good, and she melted in to him.

After a few minutes, he started to snore.

Lying in the dark next to him, she thought about her feelings for Bear. They fit well together and made a great team. Being with him brought out the best in her. Made her stronger. For that matter, loving AJ made her stronger too.

She nudged Bear.

He woke up and rolled toward her. "Everything okay, baby?"

"Mostly. Can we talk for just a sec about AJ?"

"Sure. What's on your mind?"

"I've been vacillating about if I should adopt him or not,

306

wondering if he'd be better off with another family."

Bear made a noncommittal noise, tensing slightly.

"But he could be in danger with others, too. Like he is right now with Elena. His parents died in a random convenience store shooting. Also, he's too old for most people looking to start a family. And I love him."

"I see your points."

"I've decided I *do* want to adopt him."

He exhaled and stroked her back. "That's awesome. You'll be a great mom. Maybe the director could help cut through some of that paperwork."

"If AJ makes it home safe, I was hoping the director could do that."

"Okay, let's ask. I know AJ will be thrilled."

"Bear, if anything happens to me . . ."

"I'll look out for him."

"You're the best." She hugged him tight. "Thank you."

Content, she curled deeper into his chest, and fell fast asleep.

She dreamed. Pyotr was crawling up the whitewashed villa like a black spider on a white wall. He came to Anu's wrought-iron patio, slunk over the railing, and crawled into her room. Maddy tried to shout, to scream a warning, but the dream world held her prisoner and would not let go.

CHAPTER 77

For an instant, Will closed his eyes. The sounds and smells of the burning plane could almost be a campfire from his youth, when he was a Lake Tahoe Boy Scout and never dreamed he'd grow up to join a covert organization currently trying to stop Russia from invading the United States.

But when he brought himself back to the present, it was to stare at the glowing, smoldering wreck of their only transportation. There were definitely no hotdogs or marshmallows. It was sad.

Jags stood next to him, hands on her hips. "Looks like Lex outdid himself."

"Apparently so. Think our pilot is in there?"

Jags frowned. "Let's go look."

The plane wasn't large, just an eight-seater, and it didn't take them long to circumnavigate it. Will found a two-meter-long strut that had separated from the craft in the explosion, and used it to poke through the smoldering shell.

"Uh-oh," Will said.

"Find something?" Jags came over to his side.

Will focused his flashlight toward where the cockpit used to be. "Looks like dead pilot to me."

Jags lowered her eyes and dropped her voice. "Yeah. Hate to see that."

"Me too."

Will switched off his flashlight and turned his back on what he'd seen, chest heavy. The pilot who, just a few hours before, had enjoyed the challenge of landing in the desert, had people who loved him. Someone would mourn him as Will still mourned Maria.

Jags punched him in the shoulder. "No time for that, soldier. We've gotta get out of here."

Will shook his head to clear his mind. She was right. VanOps would take care of the pilot's family. He and Jags had a job to do. Had to find that lorandite.

Walking away from the wreckage helped clear his head but pained his ankle. He turned to Jags. "How did Lex get here?"

"I've been wondering the same thing."

"Crookbottom must've told all."

"Can't blame him."

"No. I'm sure Lex was, uh, persuasive."

"Right. And he got here in no time. We were in that cave for just a few hours."

Will shivered in the cooling night air. Darkness had descended upon the desert. "He must have arrived via helicopter or airplane himself."

"That's my thought."

Will recalled his mental image of the surrounding area. "Remember that airport over by Merowe? That little town?"

"Sure. We didn't land there because it looked like nothing but sand and the pilot insisted he could get us closer."

"I say we head over there."

"Roger that."

Jags took off at a jog into the night. Will groaned and picked up his pace. His esophagus was bruised from the garrote and every step hurt. Not to mention his light T-shirt was ill-suited to the cool night air.

Before long, they hit the deeper black of a paved road and headed for the lights of the town.

Surprising him, Will's belly growled. "Don't suppose we have time to eat."

"Maybe we can grab something."

He puffed hard while they ran. "Do you mean steal something?"

"Well, we don't have time to order camel steaks."

He shut up. At least the road was deserted.

After about twenty minutes, during which Will's legs joined his ankle in complaining, they reached a bridge over the Nile.

"Let's walk the rest of the way," Jags said. "We'll draw less attention."

"Great!" Will panted.

He peered over the edge as he limped across. The mighty Nile was narrow here. The rapids looked dark and deadly. "Want to go for a moonlight swim?"

"Not tonight."

"C'mon. There's at least ten different kinds of venomous snakes down there, including the black mamba."

"Don't forget the crocodiles, Mr. Dundee."

"Hard to forget them."

They cleared the bridge and continued walking until they reached the town about a mile later. On the left was a hospital, and the dome of a small mosque loomed in the distance. The foot and vehicle traffic picked up, all backlit by the sounds of a busy desert town after dark. Smells of barbequed meat hung in the air, as did laughter.

At the mile, they turned right on a street called Shirian El Shimal. The busier part of the town behind them, Jags picked up the pace again. Will kept up but wasn't happy about it. They passed green farmland, irrigated from the nearby Nile, and then finally a large open space. Will's ankle and calf were now burning with every step.

"Think that's it?" he asked. "Sure doesn't look like LAX."

"Ha," Jags chuckled.

The place was a ghost town. No lights, no moving planes, no people.

They drew nearer and strode down the middle of the open space. Will took out his flashlight and moved the beam across the ground. "Must be the runway. Looks like smaller tires."

"Yeah."

Will turned off his flashlight. "See any planes?"

"Not yet."

"I don't even see any hangars."

They kept walking. Will gritted his teeth against the pain.

After a time, they reached the end of the runway. They stopped and looked back.

"Hell's bells," Will remarked.

"Not a plane or hangar in site." Jags put her hands on her hips. "But it has to be around here somewhere."

"What would you do if you were Lex?"

"And there were no hangars?"

"Yeah."

"I'd throw a camo blanket over my plane."

"Yep, me too. Let's walk around the far edge here."

"Okay."

Within minutes, they spotted it: a small, unnatural mound about twenty meters back from the runway in an area of other minor hills. They ran over to it. They both grabbed a corner of the tarp and pulled it off, revealing an old twin-engine crop duster.

Will shined his flashlight around the frame. "Cessna Skymaster."

"Older than dirt."

"Looks like it's from the sixties or seventies."

Jags climbed into the cockpit. "Let's hope the farmer he stole it from maintained it."

Will's eyes grew wide as he realized what she intended. "Wait, what're you doing?"

"Getting us out of here. C'mon."

"I thought we'd go find his pilot. You know how to fly it?"

"Nope, but I'll figure it out."

Will peered inside. "But there's no key in the ignition."

Jags reached for wires under the control panel. "I told you I was a troubled youth."

"Oh, dear god," Will whispered.

She jerked her head at him, and he reluctantly climbed into the rotted-out seat beside her. She might be able to hotwire it and get it off the ground, but would they arrive alive?

CHAPTER 78

Seated at a low table under a vast tent, the Cessna Skymaster's pilot recognized the unmistakable sound of his plane taking off into the night.

He grumbled, debating finishing the food in front of him before acting—the bulti, a dish made of Nile perch, smelled delicious. But his high-paying client's eyes held the kind of fire that the pilot figured was better not to challenge. So, he called for the bill, asked to use a landline since the town held no cell tower, and prepared to finish his fish while tracking down the client. Based on where he'd dropped the man off, he had a pretty fair idea of where to begin the search.

CHAPTER 79

The sound of the villa's creaking patio door woke Anu from a light sleep.

In the dim glow of the moonlight, she lunged for the door of the bedroom. But the owner of the home had built everything at grand scale, and it was several steps away.

A quiet command echoed through the room. "Stop."

Oh no! He found me! Turning, she faced the man who'd been haunting her nightmares for days. Silhouetted against the night sky, Pyotr stood about two meters tall, and had wide shoulders, but a slim waist and narrow build, like a swimmer. He wore a black balaclava, and the only facial features she could make out were his eyes. She had imagined them to be dark as pitch or red as the devil. But one was white as the villa's walls. She put a hand to her mouth to keep from crying out. Between the disturbing white iris and the gun in his right hand, she felt like a rabbit caught in a snare.

In a flash, his face was next to hers and she felt the cold metal of the gun barrel pressed to her forehead.

His breath was hot, his voice a whisper. "Quick. Where are you going tomorrow?"

Anu slid to the floor, hands covering her head. She knew better than to resist; he would follow them anyway. "Petra."

"Where in Petra?"

"We don't know yet."

He pushed the barrel of the gun harder into her temple. Her body shook with fear.

"Where?" he demanded.

"We don't know yet. The others, Maddy's brother and the lady agent, have the information."

"But it's there? The meteorite?"

Tears dropped from her eyes to the floor. "We think so."

In the silence, a footstep squeaked in the hallway. Quinn had told her he was taking first watch and she could imagine him, pistol drawn, patrolling, seeking the trouble that had cut the power.

"Stay silent," Pyotr hissed.

Then he slipped away.

Anu broke into uncontrollable, wild sobbing. Having him track her was worse than death. Far worse!

A minute later, a soft knock came at the door. Then another, more insistent. Quinn's voice, muffled by the heavy door, asked if she was okay. Anu tried to stop the tears, to get up, to answer, but she was trapped in a surge of self-pity.

Keys jangled. The next thing she knew, Quinn was at her side, holding her, stroking her hair, soothing her with soft words. Her weeping found a new intensity from feeling safe in his arms. He encouraged her to cry and asked, but didn't push her, to tell him what happened. She liked him all the more for his kindness.

Later, as her tears wound down, she made two decisions.

One, she reached up and kissed Quinn, asking him to stay with her tonight. Life was short.

And two, tomorrow she would tell all. VanOps would protect her family and Pyotr could go screw himself. She would tear the GPS out of her arm, even if it meant gouging it out with a rusty pocket knife.

CHAPTER 80

The first thing Maddy did after waking from a troubled sleep was stretch her hand out to see if Bear was still there. He wasn't, and the sheets were cold. She rolled onto her back, closed her eyes, and pulled the covers up tight under her neck. What had she dreamed? It had felt like a real dream. Sometimes she could bring them back if she dozed.

"Hey, sugar. You're awake!" Bear burst into the room, bearing coffee. "The helo will be here in ten minutes."

She opened her eyes. "Well, I am now."

His short blond hair was damp, his stubble gone, and his black T-shirt and blue jeans looked freshly laundered—compliments of their kind host, no doubt.

She shook her head. There was a lot of light in the room. "What time is it?"

He moved toward the bed. "It's almost ten. Merry Christmas!"

She was glad to see the haunted look from last night was gone from his eyes. Sitting up, she kissed him, enjoying his clean-shaven face. "Wow, I slept in! Merry Christmas to you, too. Wasn't the helicopter supposed to be here at dawn?"

Bear handed her the coffee. "There was a mechanical issue with the first and they had to send another. We'll still make it there a few hours before sunset."

"That's only good if Will found a sunset clue. If it's noon or sunrise, we're in trouble."

"Yes, but I have worse news."

"What?"

"The power was cut last night."

That woke her up. "Here at the house?"

"Yeah."

"How long was it out?"

"Just three minutes. The backup system was messed with, too, and it took Mahmoud's guard that long to get the generator going. I'm guessing it wasn't Santa."

"Anything missing?"

"No, but Anu wants to talk to us."

"Finally!"

"Yeah, you may have been right about her all along. She and Quinn look pretty cozy, but I swear, if she's a spy for the enemy, I'll push her out of the helo. Quinn too if he's in on it. Get dressed and we can talk with her on board."

After a quick shower, Maddy entered the dining area to find the others already around the kitchen table. A simple meal of olives, black bread, goat cheese, thick yoghurt, and fresh fruit was laid out, and based on the dirty plates she spotted, she was the last to eat. As Maddy grabbed some food to go, she noted Anu and Quinn were holding hands. But Maddy was sure romance wasn't what Anu wanted to tell them.

In the distance, the sound of a helicopter became audible.

Outside the day was gray and windy. Thick layers of clouds covered the sky above a choppy sea. As they all gathered for its arrival, Maddy grabbed her cap to keep it from flying away. Quinn put his arm around Anu as they huddled against the wind.

Maddy trusted Quinn, but had Anu somehow turned him? Was it a good idea to be in a helo's close quarters if she was a spy?

Bear pointed to the right. "It'll land in that empty lot two houses down."

Once it had, and the pilot waved them aboard, they all ran under the moving rotors and climbed in. Maddy had wanted to see a comfortable cabin with four white seats trimmed in chrome. Instead, they had to sit in the military jump seats lining the sparse, functional cargo space. The sole decoration was a small plastic reindeer that hung from a knob in the cabin.

The pilot gave them all earmuff-style headphones with boom mics to enable communication over the rotor noise. She and Bear sat across from Anu and Quinn.

"Did anything happen while the power went out last night?" Maddy asked. "I slept through it."

Anu looked to Quinn and he nodded, as if urging her to speak. She cleared her throat. "Well, actually . . ."

She trailed off and her eyes began to well with tears. Quinn reached out and grabbed her hand.

"Pyotr snuck into my room," she said firmly.

As the helicopter climbed into the leaden sky, Anu told them how Pyotr had attacked her at the Sacred Cenote in Chichén Itzá and implanted a GPS chip in her shoulder. Her voice wobbling, she shared details of the note he left for her in Belize City, and how he interrogated her at gunpoint the previous evening.

Throughout it all, Maddy was proud of limiting herself to only one "I told you so" look at Bear. Mostly, she was angry—that bastard had been on their heels the whole time! And Anu had withheld information that could have gotten them killed.

Maddy curled her hands into fists. "Why did you decide to tell us now?"

A fierce light entered Anu's eyes as she met Maddy's gaze. "I decided that living with the fear of him following me everywhere is worse even than death. Even if he strangles me like he did Uncle Ravi, it would be better."

"Maybe we should strangle you." Bear growled. "You've put

this entire mission at risk."

Quinn tensed. He and Bear stared at each other, sizing one another up. The air in the helicopter grew thick.

"I'm sorry, Bear," Anu said, crying again. "I didn't want him to hurt my family and was petrified. I didn't know what to do."

Maddy tried to put herself in Anu's shoes. Would she have had the guts to do anything differently? "Thank you for telling us now." She put a hand on Bear's arm. "It was a brave thing to do."

Anu looked at Bear. "You can lock me up when we get there if you need to. I've helped you with the star chart as best I could. Perhaps I can still be of some use."

Bear nodded and relaxed a notch. Quinn leaned back in his seat. Maddy let a breath out.

"Back to Ravi. We don't know it was Pyotr that killed your uncle," Quinn said, clearly trying to further defuse the situation.

"True," Maddy agreed. "It could have been Lex."

"Quinn, could you protect my family in Bengaluru from Pyotr?" Anu asked.

Before Quinn could answer, Bear jumped in. "If we survive the ambush Pyotr has laid for us, I'll talk to the director about it." He rolled his shoulders once. "I wonder why the wand didn't work in Istanbul?"

Although she wouldn't trust Anu for a long time, Maddy was glad to see Bear's generous side resurfacing. "First things first, we need to get that GPS out of your arm," Maddy said.

Quinn felt the top of Anu's shoulder. "It's in there pretty deep. It'll need surgery."

"We'll want to give it to HQS to study," Bear said. "Maybe it's got some advanced tech that we can reverse engineer."

Maddy furrowed her brow. "I guess Pyotr knows where we're going no matter what."

Anu rubbed her shoulder. Quinn pulled a small walkie-talkie-looking device out of his pocket and held it up.

"What's that?" Maddy asked.

Quinn gave her a proud smile. "It's a battery-operated GPS jammer. Mahmoud gave it to me. I asked him about it this morning."

It was a little late in the game but, she supposed, better late than never.

Anu and Quinn engaged in a private conversation. It was a good time to share her other concern on a different headset channel. She had Bear switch frequencies and did the same.

Maddy turned to Bear. "Why did the director get us a helicopter instead of a plane?"

"He thought it would be easier to load the lorandite."

"You mean using a winch or something if it's heavy?"

"That's right."

"I've been thinking."

"Uh-oh."

She poked him in the ribs. "Stop. I'm thinking we should destroy the lorandite."

His blue eyes clouded over. "It's not our call."

"Bowman hasn't seen what this stuff can do." She glanced at the new lovebirds. "You saw what I was able to do last year."

"And a good thing."

"That's not the point. This stuff is dangerous! And in the wrong hands—"

"We're the good guys, remember?" he said.

"For now. Governments change like the tide, and good isn't always in season."

Bear crossed his arms. "We have orders."

"Screw the orders, Bear! If it's large, we may not even be able to move it. Touching it may prove fatal."

"We have to try," he said. "And don't you want to try to channel through it like you did the obelisks?"

"Sure, part of me is curious. But most of me is scared as hell. More likely than not, Pyotr is there waiting for us."

There was a long pause as Bear seemed to contemplate that. "I've been thinkin', too."

"About?"

"We're gonna need a distraction. Just . . . director's not gonna like it."

"Why not?"

"Expensive. But it's the only thing I can think of."

"Best give him a call then. Remember to ask about protection for Anu's family."

Bear grumbled and asked the pilot to connect him to HQS on the comms system.

Maddy took a small bite of the black bread she'd brought with her. It tasted dry. She was worried that Lex had harmed Will and Jags, who were still incommunicado. Had they been able to beat him in the overheard fight? Maddy hoped that, somehow, they were flying to Petra right now.

She sat back and watched the miles pass underneath them, knowing in her bones that a showdown was looming.

CHAPTER 81

RED SEA AIRSPACE

DECEMBER 25, 11:55 A.M. ARABIA STANDARD TIME

"We're running low on gas."

Will glanced over at Jags and the cockpit. Sure enough, the needle on the small airplane's fuel gauge was buried in the red. It was the second time they'd run low. The first time had cost them precious hours as they'd talked and bribed their way out of trouble at the airport just outside Aswan, Egypt.

"How far do you think we are from Petra?" he yelled over the roar of the crop duster's engines.

"Far enough that we can't coast. Too bad, though. See how the Red Sea is coming to a point?"

They were flying low along the eastern edge of the sea, hoping to stay off of any Israeli military radar. Below them, the Red Sea shone a dull gray in the afternoon's light. Far ahead, the sea terminated. "I see it."

"By plane, Petra is just half an hour." Jags shook her messy black hair out of her eyes. "But given this fuel situation, we're going to have to land and drive."

"About two hours then?"

"Depends on the Christmas traffic."

Will imagined a camel traffic jam. They both laughed.

"Don't suppose there's an airport up there."

"Doubt it."

"Think you can land this bag of bolts without killing us?"

"Relax, Argones. I did well in the VanOps training."

"Practiced much since then?"

"Nope." Her grin widened. "But it sure beats sitting at a desk in the NSA cube farm."

Just then, two fighter jets screamed toward them. They were painted in a camouflage pattern and had a small blue Star of David emblazoned beneath the cockpit.

The sleek planes were too close for Will's comfort. The noise was deafening.

He tried to keep his voice from trembling. "Are we about to get shot down?"

"I think that's the Israeli welcoming committee."

"Some welcome."

"They'd prefer we land in Jordan, I think."

The fighter jets took up a position on their left flank.

A voice crackled over the radio. "Do not transgress into Israeli airspace. Repeat. Stay out of Israel."

"I'm fine with that," Will said. "Maybe we can finally charge your phone."

Beep. Beep. Beep. A red light began flashing above the fuel gauge.

"Okay, we're heading down."

Jags banked to the right and began her descent toward the rocky Jordanian desert.

CHAPTER 82

"**T**en minutes until we land near Petra," the helicopter pilot announced over the headsets in a clipped New England accent. "Will put us down in Ma'an."

Maddy turned to Bear. "Think we'll land all right in this wind?"

"I think we'll be fine."

She wasn't so sure. Wind had been buffeting the tiny craft since they'd left Turkey. She looked out a side window. After the sea crossing, there had been nothing below but a lot of tan sand, although now they were entering a narrow foothill canyon. After Anu's confession, the group seemed nervous, and silent.

Anu and Quinn stirred from their naps, roused by the pilot's announcement. The veil in Anu's eyes had vanished, and Maddy was glad Quinn had helped the woman confess. Not only was it good to know Pyotr was waiting for them, but if you were headed to your possible demise, it was good to go with integrity.

Even if he strangles me like Uncle Ravi, it would be better.

Anu's words from before rang in Maddy's ears.

"Hey Anu, did your uncle Ravi ever mention a computer project to you that they were working on?" Maddy asked.

Anu looked out the window at the red stone city appearing

below, and then met Maddy's eyes. "No, not that I recall."

Bear sat up straighter. "Are you sure?"

"We talked about once a week, usually on a weekend to stay in touch. He worked on many projects and traveled often throughout India and Russia."

Hope fell like a stone. There went the chance of an easy answer to finding out where the computer hacking the Philippines was located. She wondered if it was already too late for AJ and Elena. But even if Anu had remembered something, the Russians and East Indians would still have the plans to build a new computer. If they got their hands on the lorandite. The team still needed to find that meteorite.

Bear pointed out the window. "Hey, Anu, isn't that tall peak over there the Mountain of Aaron? Tomb of the brother of Moses?"

Anu looked out her window. "That's only in the Islamic view."

"Oh, right," Bear said. "Jewish tradition has his restin' place a mystery. But still interesting."

"A mystery?" Maddy asked.

Bear's satellite phone rang, interrupting their discussion. He looked at Maddy after checking the screen. "It's Jags!"

Maddy's heart began to race as they all took off their headphones.

"Bear here." He listened for a moment, before putting the phone on speaker and turning up the volume. At least the helicopter was cruising now. "Y'all okay?"

Jags's throaty voice was a little hard to hear through the background noise. "Yes, yes, we're fine. A little banged up."

"That's easy for her to say. I can't walk and am about to starve to death," Will said.

Maddy smiled. That was her brother. He lived life uphill both ways.

"How close are you to Petra?" Bear asked.

"Less than two hours," Jags replied. "Finally got power for the phone battery."

"Okay. Divert over to Ma'an. Petra is not friendly. Repeat not friendly."

"Roger that," Jags acknowledged. "We'll regroup in Ma'an."

"Enemy status?"

"Bound and ready for the cleanup crew."

Lex was neutralized. He'd been such a thorn. Bear and Maddy exchanged broad smiles.

"Go ahead and order that up." Bear said. "Do you have disguises?"

"Negative. Lost in transit."

"Okay, we'll get some for you, too. Meet us at the university entrance as soon as possible."

"Okay. Sending final imagery from Jebel Barkal, too."

Maddy couldn't wait to see what they'd found.

"Excellent. See you soon." Bear rang off.

Bear gave Maddy's arm a squeeze. The timing would be tight, but the pieces were coming together. They all put their headgear back on to drown out the noise.

The modernized town was spread out before them, a small airport to their left.

"Buckle up, we're heading in for a landing," the pilot said.

The helo banked and headed for the paved runway in Ma'an. But before the pilot could land, a brutal wind shear caught the rotors and sent the helicopter shuddering toward earth.

CHAPTER 83

MA'AN, JORDAN

DECEMBER 25, 1:10 P.M. ARABIA STANDARD TIME

As the helicopter plunged toward the striped runway below, Anu said her final prayers. If she died, at least Pyotr would not have the satisfaction of wringing her neck.

The rotors groaned, and the pilot unleashed a litany of curse words.

Anu's stomach lurched into her throat, reminding her of a frightening ride at the fair when she was a child. She grabbed onto the armrests as Quinn put a hand on her thigh. Maddy and Bear were being thrown from side to side in their chairs. Outside the window, the ground rapidly approached. It seemed they plummeted for an eternity.

Anu braced for impact. Abruptly, the violent noise from above turned into a familiar whirring, and the pilot let out a whoop as the helicopter pulled up. Anu exchanged a dazed glance with Maddy.

"Let's try that again," the pilot said, tension still in his tone.

This time, however, the big bird descended without incident. When it touched down, everyone in their group exhaled at the same time.

Bear jumped up. "I'm heading to get disguises."

"Let me come with you." Quinn said.

For a minute, Anu thought they might come to blows, but Bear looked at her and Maddy and told the pilot to keep the rotors whirling in case they needed to take off. Then, he nodded at Quinn and tossed Maddy a phone, and they disappeared.

After the men left to go grab disguises, Anu looked out to the desert sky. Surya, the sun god, was picking up speed as he drove his seven-horsed chariot toward the western hills. They didn't have much time left.

Orange beads in her fingers, she turned to Maddy. "Is your heart still beating fast?"

The other woman gave a shaky smile. "Oh my god, I thought we were doomed." She fixed Anu with a long look, and then handed her a sick bag from next to her seat. "Here. You still look a little green."

"I'm fine," she said, although she took it, just in case. "How long do you think it will be before Bear and Quinn will be back?"

"Depends on the shops they find."

"Will they all dress as women, except Will?"

"Why not? You can hide a lot with a burqa."

"This is true." Anu took a last breath, wrapping her beads around her wrist. "Perhaps we should get a head start on looking at the pictures."

After a moment of deliberation, Maddy handed over Bear's phone. Anu considered apologizing again, feeling she deserved the hesitation after having lied to Maddy.

Deciding to get down to business, Anu swiped through the images. *They took quite a few.* She wanted an overview first. A lion's profile was painted on a cave wall in red paint. There was a set of hieroglyphs, a painting of a tunnel lit by the sun, and a drawing of a stream spilling out of a rock bank, an arrow above it.

"Definitely directional images," Maddy remarked.

"I agree. Let me look at the hieroglyphs. Hope these aren't coded like the other ones."

"Me too."

Anu swiped back to the Egyptian words and squinted. This was not her area of expertise.

But there it was. Simple and straightforward.

She knew exactly where they needed to go. And there might be enough time, but they'd be cutting it close.

However, from what she recalled of Petra, the Siq was the main entrance, and it was only a dim, narrw gorge. Which meant they'd be heading right into Pyotr's waiting arms.

She opened the sick bag and vomited.

CHAPTER 84

MA'AN, JORDAN

2:55 P.M.

The entrance to the Al-Hussein Bin Talal University was off Maan Shobak Road, about ten minutes outside of Ma'an. Will and Jags cruised the roundabout before settling in a small space across from one of the school buildings. They'd landed the thirsty plane on a tiny runway in the town of Aquba, where, luckily, they'd found a place to charge the phone and a local willing to sell a beat-up old car for American dollars. At least the car had gotten them to Ma'an.

They didn't have to wait long. Within ten minutes, a gun-metal-gray rental car pulled into the lot, slunk down the line of empty spaces, and parked next to them. It was full of women, dressed in black, each in full face veil. Only their eyes glinted as they exited the rental.

Even expecting them, Will did a double-take. They looked exactly like many of the conservative Muslim women he'd seen in this part of the world. "Guess it's time for the holiday family reunion."

Jags ignored him and got out of the car. "Bear, hand us our disguises."

One of the tall "women," whose eyes he didn't recognize, handed him an outfit that appeared similar to what he'd worn in Morocco. When in Rome. As Jags donned her burqa, Will winked at Maddy before he pulled on the tunic and expertly assembled his head gear,

330

glad that his dark beard would help with the disguise and that he got to dress as the sole male.

"Merry Christmas to y'all, too. Here's the plan," Bear said, gesturing to the shortest woman. "Anu here has studied the pictures and says we're headed to Ad Deir, toward the top of Petra. We'll take two cars, break into small tourist groups, and head up the gazillion steps to the top. Expect a distraction. But we need to all be in the open area in front of the Monastery before the sun sets." He glanced to the west. "It's a long climb, doesn't give us much time."

Jags patted Bear on the back. "Sounds good. Thorenson, did you bring us some weapons?"

Bear opened the trunk. "Compliments of the director."

Will's stomach dropped. He still didn't feel comfortable with all that steel. But he fished around until he found a semi-automatic pistol to hide under his tunic, and then double-checked his knives in their scabbards.

Everyone except Anu loaded up, even Maddy. Will raised an eyebrow at her.

"Defensive use only."

"Okay, sis. Just watch yourself." He pointed at the baby carriage. "Who gets that?"

"You do. You and Jags are the male-female couple," Bear answered.

Jags made a face, as the one woman Will still didn't recognize slid a weapon into a holster under his left arm.

Will held out his hand. "I'm Argones."

"I'm Quinn, from Jerusalem."

Curious. The man had a strong Irish accent. It also seemed he was from the Order. Did the Order and VanOps have some sort of working agreement? A good question for another day. The men shook hands.

"Nice to meet you. Let's hope we don't die together," Will said.

"Amen to that."

Bear shut the trunk with a thud that echoed in Will's gut. "Let's go."

CHAPTER 85

PETRA, JORDAN

DECEMBER 25, 4:04 P.M. ARABIA STANDARD TIME

Maddy huddled into her burqa, glad for both the warmth the wool garment provided and its protection against prying eyes. She hoped Allah would forgive her if He was at all offended by their borrowing of the Islamic dress. They meant no disrespect; they were simply trying to survive until tomorrow.

Quinn walked next to her, while a hundred yards ahead, Anu and Bear made for another set of Muslim women. Jags and Will and their knobby-tired baby carriage brought up the rear, fifty yards back. It was all Maddy could do not to look around. She knew they were being watched, knew Pyotr had probably been here for hours. Would their disguises hold?

They walked along a broad path of sand and gravel. Even though it was Christmas day, tourists were everywhere. Thus far, the climb was negligible, perhaps a two-percent slope. It reminded Maddy of the Arizona deserts near Sedona, all reds and browns and big round boulders.

Soon the Obelisk Tomb appeared on their left. It was a sandy, two-story crypt carved into the rock face with four squat obelisks gracing the top façade. Three open windows stared at them, along with a crooked doorway. *A man could be hiding in any of those spaces*. It was an obvious spot. She shivered, wishing she still had even her small sliver of lorandite.

They continued on, up the hill, along the path. The cliffs on either side of the path began to get taller, now about fifteen feet high. She and Quinn passed a small wooden structure, selling drinks, T-shirts, and magnets. Soon they entered the gorge that led to the rest of Petra, a narrow passage known as the Siq.

She turned to Quinn and spoke under her breath. "This is the perfect spot for an ambush."

His Irish voice was barely more than a whisper. "It is, if they know it's us."

"Good thing there's tons of tourists."

"And lots of other Muslim women."

They walked along the curving sandstone tunnel. Ahead, she lost sight of Bear and Anu. She dared not look back to see how Will and Jags were doing. To minimize risk, they wanted space and tourists between the groups.

"Quinn, did the master provide any instruction about whether to keep or destroy this thing when we find it?"

He pointed. "Look at that cool rock outcropping up there."

"Nice sightseer comment."

"I overheard part of your disagreement with Bear. No, the master didn't provide any direction, except to say he trusts your judgment." He paused. "But for what it's worth, I agree with you. Too much power."

The Siq became a little wider, enough that fifteen men could pass abreast if they so wanted. Maddy looked up. "Can you imagine armies trying to charge through here? The defenders could drop things from above."

"Rocks and flaming bundles of oil-soaked rags?"

"Yes, that type of thing."

"Would've been effective."

They trudged along in silence until the path underfoot became stone pavers.

Maddy looked around. "We must be getting close."

"Yes. Look at all the black on the rock walls."

"Think that's soot?"

"Could be. Those flaming bundles would have found easy targets."

Ahead the gorge narrowed. The red-rock walls here were easily seventy-five feet high. The unadorned rock walls gave way to an area filled with niches. Maddy kept her eyes peeled for anyone who looked like an assassin posing as a tourist. It was a cool day. Men wore hats, turbans, hoodies, and jackets. Pyotr's team could be easily hiding in plain sight.

They exited the Siq and walked into an open area. To one side was one of the ubiquitous T-shirt vending areas. On the other was the impressive two-story Al-Kazneh. Six smooth Corinthian columns graced the first-story façade, and above them were three tall display walls, bordered by additional columns. She had to crane her neck to see the top of the temple. But instead of feeling awe, she was alert for threats.

Quinn whispered, "Guy in the blue jacket. One o'clock. Don't stare."

Maddy glanced in that direction and then turned back, gritting her teeth as she did so. The guy was way more focused on the crowd than the amazing red-rock architecture.

"Let's keep moving," Maddy said. "We have to be on the other side of the valley, past the Great Temple, and up the trail before the distraction arrives."

CHAPTER 86

5:14 P.M.

Pyotr scanned the area with his military-grade Swarovski binoculars, seeking the adversary. *Where are they?*

Five of his team members were scattered throughout the ancient city dressed as tourists. Each wore a high-tech microphone that molded around their back teeth and also acted as a form of speaker. So did he, although the "molar mic" had taken some time to get used to.

He'd chosen to station himself along with one other man near the area's high point—above Ad Deir, the Monastery—to better see when the Americans arrived. It was a barren, windswept mountaintop, but held an arresting view of the valley below.

His team was loaded with standard Spetsnaz SR-1M sidearms, which he also carried under his jacket, beneath the wounded shoulder that still ached like a bitch. He was looking forward to revenge. The wound from Ephesus never would have happened if the baron had given him more help when he'd first asked for it. But at least he had a squad now.

Pyotr let the binocs fall to his chest and wiped the sand and tiredness from his eyes. Since he discovered that this was their destination, he'd not slept. A fast car had taken him to the nearest

Turkish airport, followed by a predawn flight here to Petra, where he met his new expedited team. Lack of sleep was typical when on a mission, but in this case any adrenaline he'd felt from breaking into the seaside villa had dissipated and he needed some Red Bull to keep him alert for the next stage.

Although he was still annoyed at the baron for pushing him to visit Anu, the gamble had paid off. She and her friends had been foolish, sitting outside like that as they talked through their discovery with the maps, and had celebrated like they'd just struck a winning goal. Satellites were way too powerful these days. A shiver went up Pyotr's spine, knowing he was being watched at this very moment by Soviet spacecraft. The invasive things were capable of reading license plates off cars.

He had thought the enemy would be here at dawn, but the day had dragged on with no sign of them. Surely, she wouldn't have lied—she had been so scared as to nearly wet herself. It was well into the afternoon. The sun hung low in the foreboding sky and the wild wind blew sand everywhere. Lots of static electricity.

He pulled the phone from his pocket and checked the GPS tracking monitor app. Nothing. Maybe the weather was interfering in the signal. Shouldn't, but it was new technology, and had never given a great signal anyway. Or maybe the tiny battery in the thing had died.

With nothing else to do, he decided to check in with the team below.

"One, how's it look?" he said in Russian.

Dimitri, called "One," was his second in command and the lone man he respected.

"I'm down here by where the gorge lets out. So far, zero," Dimitri replied.

If the VanOps group came in like tourists, they'd be coming through the long, narrow Siq.

"Two?"

"I'm south, near the Royal Tombs. Lots of visitors. No sign of the enemy."

"Three? Where are you now?" He had been assigned as a "rover."

"I'm inside what they call the Treasury. It's good cover."

Impressive piece of architecture, too.

"Four?"

"Great Temple. This place is huge."

"Five?"

"Hadrian Gate."

"Six? See anything I've missed from up here?"

"Nothing."

No sign of them anywhere. Pyotr was itching for a fight, but the baron had him on a leash. He'd insisted that Pyotr wait for the Americans to lead him to where the meteorite was located, and then take them all out after hours to avoid an international incident. Fool man. Too many rules. He felt like complaining.

"Dimitri, go to PC."

On his belt-mounted control unit, Pyotr switched to their private channel. No sense letting the grunts hear their talk.

"I'm here."

"This plan sucks," he said.

"He's the boss."

"I know that, but we could get the Americans to tell us anything with a gun shoved up their ass."

Pyotr scanned the tourist crowd below. A young family with a baby in a push carriage, an older couple holding hands, and a set of college frat boys passed through his line of sight. For some reason, the sight of the young family pissed him off.

"True, but he's got the rank," Dimitri said.

"Yes, but if we ambushed them when they arrive, we could have them lead us to the prize, nice and easy."

"Thought you said they didn't have all the pieces of the puzzle yet."

"So they said," Pyotr said darkly.

"The baron wants them to have room to figure it out. Sounds like a sound strategy to me."

"I suppose."

"Cool off, Pyotr—we'll have eyes on them as soon as they hit the valley."

The family with the kid in the carriage moved away from the group. He followed them with his binocs. "Did you hear the baron has my mother in the cells?"

Silence.

"Dimitri?"

"I heard."

The tone of the voice said there was more. "What?" Pyotr pressed.

"You don't know?"

"Don't know what, you ass? Tell me."

"He shipped her off to the place where he gets his girls."

Pyotr bit his tongue, drawing blood. But before he could turn his rage on Dimitri, a beeping warned him to switch off the private channel. It was a team member stationed twenty minutes away.

"Helo approaching from the north."

They were almost here.

CHAPTER 87

Bear turned to stare at the Lion Triclinium. "Let's pick up the pace—we need to be up at Ad Deir when that distraction arrives."

Anu complained, "My legs are burning already."

"You can do it. C'mon, you climb those pyramids all day long."

She wheezed, smelling of sweat and fear. "Yes, but we choose when to rest!"

"Fine. Go take a quick look inside."

Her eyes, the only thing visible on her face, gave him a grateful glance and she wandered over to the classical shrine flanked by worn lions. Bear held his ground on the stairs. The hair on the back of his neck had been warning him since the Siq that they were being watched, and he surreptitiously scanned the crowd. No one stood out as a threat. For once he was grateful that he was five feet eight, as he was sure his low stature was helping him to pass as a woman.

He took the opportunity to take a quick look out of the corner of his eye back down the stairs. Maddy and Quinn were a hundred yards behind, climbing the stairs, and Will and Anu brought up the rear all the way back in the valley with the stroller.

With his back to the scarf and jewelry sale table, he studied the three wall openings, one of which had eroded to form a strange keyhole shape. Part of him wished he were an innocent tourist, as this place fascinated him, but he was more concerned with the mission. It was game time.

Anu walked back to him, her chest no longer heaving. "Thanks."

He took off as fast as he dared up the chiseled stone stairs. "Sure, but let's hoof it."

With night coming on, most tourists were headed downhill, which made them look like salmon swimming upstream. He didn't like that they stood out.

"Why didn't we ride up on the donkeys?"

"They wouldn't rent them this late in the day."

"Ah."

The steep stone stairs, around eight hundred in total, twisted and wound up the narrow gorge. Bear knew the donkeys' hooves were doing serious damage to the stairs, but he'd have taken them anyway if it would have helped.

About two thirds up the hill, the steps took a sharp left. A path led off the main track into a narrow wadi. Anu looked around. They were alone on the stairs. She pointed.

"The year-round spring that was painted on the wall at Jebel Barkal is down there," she exclaimed. "The hieroglyphs from Will and Jags weren't coded. They basically said to head above this spring and watch for the lion's silhouette at sunset."

"That's great, but keep moving."

The distinctive sound of an approaching helo caught his ears. At last.

The steps dragged on, but soon the view began to open up. The vast area of Wadi Araba reminded Bear of the Grand Canyon.

The sound was coming closer. Adrenaline pounded through his veins.

A few minutes later they squeezed between two boulders and emerged onto a wide plateau. Clouds began to scatter and the sun appeared, low on the horizon. Ad Deir was just a bit farther.

The helo flew above their heads, headed toward the valley.

A minute later, there was a loud kaboom. The sound of the explosion, even expected, caused Bear to jump. Heart pounding, he looked down the hill but couldn't see a thing. At his suggestion, the director had ordered a DARPA remote-controllable helicopter and programmed it to crash into the valley floor below. Dust and smoke would be billowing into the air, and a good-sized fireball should be burning in the middle of the wreck. Tourists would be scrambling away from the scene. Bear was betting at least a few members of Pyotr's team would try to get close to the helo. Maybe they'd get lucky and one or more of them would get caught in the secondary fuel tank explosion.

Bear focused. "Okay, let's move."

They walked into the wide plaza in front of the Monastery. Searching for threats, Bear took in the café to the right and the immense carved temple to his left. Ad Deir was huge, the doorway alone taller than most houses. It looked like the famous Treasury building in the valley below, but was less ornate. As he walked toward the temple, Bear scanned the rocks above the café. The air smelled of cooked meat.

"We're looking for a lion of some sort?" Bear asked.

Anu also studied the area above the café. "A silhouette."

The sun dipped lower in the sky. She pointed and squeaked, "That's it!"

Bear breathed a sigh of relief. "We're in time."

"With none to spare. See the lion's head in profile over there to the left?"

Bear squinted. "I do."

"Okay, turn around."

Feeling the hairs on the back of his neck tingle even more, Bear moved his hand to his weapon as he turned. Even so, he couldn't stop his jaw from dropping at the ingenuity of the ancient Nabatean people.

The entire doorway was in darkness except for a podium carved only from shadow.

"The sun is creating the illusion of that podium," Anu whispered.

"Like in that article you mentioned. Now where do we look?"

"The hieroglyphs said to look at the top of the podium's shadow, but we have to hurry."

"Let's go."

Weapon in one hand, Bear hoisted Anu up the chest-high wall and onto the threshold before scrambling up himself.

CHAPTER 88

5:34 P.M.

Through his high-end binoculars, Pyotr watched the helicopter attempt to land in the valley. A gust of wind caught it and sent it spiraling toward the valley floor. Out of control, it spun like a top and slammed into the desert. It exploded on impact.

Was the VanOps team on board?

Most of the tourists scattered like ants, but a few ran to the helo to see if anyone required a rescue. He radioed the man closest to the scene. "Four. What do you see?"

"It's a fireball!"

"Can you get close? Confirm deaths?"

In the valley, Four ran toward the conflagration only to stop ten meters away.

"No bodies!"

Boom! Another explosion rocked the basin. Four was thrown backward like a child's doll.

Pyotr swore under his breath. No bodies? A decoy then?

He scanned the crowds. Most tourists were staring at the fire. A few were walking, most away from the crash scene, and a few at a slow pace. If he had staged that as a distraction, he'd be headed to his target quickly.

343

He took in the entire panorama below him, starting farthest away, near where the Siq dumped into the valley, and then moved his spyglasses to the Monastery below, where a tall man dressed in local attire was striding toward the entrance to Ad Deir, followed by a Muslim woman cradling a baby in her arms. He'd noticed them before. They'd left their carriage at the bottom of the stairs. They both walked faster than the rest of the tourists.

Pyotr adjusted his lenses to get a look at the man's face.

He smiled as he recognized the chiseled features of Will Argones.

CHAPTER 89

Maddy entered the plaza in front of Ad Deir, and spied Bear hoisting Anu onto the threshold of the massive doorway. When he disappeared into the vast interior, she risked a glance back toward Will and Jags and motioned with her head for them to hurry up.

She rushed across the square, all the time marveling at the vast building that was carved out of the red rock more than two millennia before. They arrived at the chest-high doorstep and Quinn offered her a knee. She looked around, decided she needed to take a calculated risk, and used his knee as a step, pushing herself onto the stone entrance. Turning, she reached down and grabbed Quinn's hand, helping him to scramble up.

Bear and Anu were up on a dais in front of a niche at the top of the right-hand set of stairs, where the lion-head rock nearby was casting a shadow. They groped the stone near the top of the illusory podium. Other than the platform, Will, and Jags, the large room was bare.

"Where is it?" Bear mumbled.

Anu's voice held the tone of an experienced archeologist in her element. "Move your hand, Bear."

Bear complied.

Anu put her face inches from the surface and traced her fingers along the stone. The last rays of the sun disappeared, throwing the room into shadow.

"There's a tiny lion's head," Anu said. "Never would have seen it without the shadowed clue. Press here!"

Maddy couldn't see the lion's head, but the result was astounding. A crack echoed through the empty chamber, followed by the grinding of what sounded like ancient gears.

"Step back!" Bear commanded, sweeping Anu back away from the quickly shifting floor of their dais. The two of them shuffled toward the edge while Maddy ran up the stairs on the left to see what was happening.

The floor of the niche was giving way an inch at a time, folding down into a ramp.

A skittering noise came from below.

Maddy called to Will. "Flashlight."

He tossed her his light and she caught it, turned it on, and illuminated the ramp. The stone slope hit the floor and the sound of the gears stopped. As soon as it did, dozens of camel spiders rushed up the ramp, each the size of a dinner plate.

"Look out!" Maddy cried.

Anu jumped off the ledge. Bear kicked the spiders onto the floor, where the rest of their party stomped the arthropods while Anu struck out at the beasts with her feet, soccer style. The spiders that survived scurried toward the doorway, and out into the darkening plaza.

When the last one had fled, Maddy heaved a sigh of relief. Jags ran up the stairs, pulled a flashlight, and looked down the tenebrous ramp. Maddy couldn't see much else from this angle.

"Okay. I'm going to head back to the plaza and guard your backs," Jags said, and then looked at Quinn. "I'd like you to stay just inside the doorway as another line of defense."

Quinn nodded.

Jags turned to Bear. "Thorenson, are you okay with taking the twins and Anu down there?"

"Yes."

"Be careful."

She trotted to the doorway, jumped down, and disappeared from sight.

"We need to watch for traps. Pits were big back then," Anu said.

"Okay," Bear replied.

He descended the ramp first, testing each step with his forward foot. Anu followed Bear and Maddy got in line behind her. Gun drawn, Will walked backward toward the opening to keep an eye on their rear.

Near the bottom of the ramp, Bear yanked the burqa over his head and dropped it on the ground. Maddy followed suit, while Anu and Will kept their disguises. Ahead, a narrow hallway made a right turn in about fifteen feet. At the corner, a colorful mural covered the entire wall. Bear's flashlight beam held steady on the painting.

"Is that illustrating the Exodus?" he asked.

"It does look like an army marching between walls of water toward a dark column, chased by another group," Anu said, her face lit with excitement. "This could be the find of the century!"

"That's great but not why we're here," Maddy said.

Bear sighed. "True enough."

He swung his leg as if to take another step, but immediately pulled up short. Wary, he patted the dirt below the ramp with his foot. In seconds, he yanked it back up.

"Pit."

Crouching down, Bear pulled a knife from his boot, clearing away dirt and sand until he was able to shine a flashlight into the depths.

"What's in there?" Maddy asked.

"Sharpened stakes."

Maddy took a deep breath. "They don't want us to find this, do they?"

"No, although this is not uncommon," Anu replied.

Bear plunged the weapon into the sand next to the hole he'd dug. It sank to the hilt. He repeated this until he found solid ground a foot on either side of the wall. After nimbly crossing, he turned and held his hand out to Anu, who stepped around the trap with care. Maddy followed suit, as did Will.

Bear was already moving, one cautious foot at a time.

Suddenly, Maddy felt a rush of air behind her as something solid *thunked* into the wall to her left. A vibrating arrow stuck out of the wall; when she whirled around, Will was standing stock still with his hands at his throat.

He let his hands fall and looked at them. No blood. "Bought a throat guard in Marrakech after your dream. Second time it's come in handy."

There was a gash in his headscarf and a line of black underneath.

"Good." She turned to Bear, who was on his knees again. "Any idea what happened?"

His flashlight illuminated a broken line of white at shin level. "Trigger wire made of sinew."

Maddy shook her head, hand on her heart. They were lucky it had just been one arrow.

"Sorry I missed it," Bear added.

"No harm done, but maybe you could look for others from now on?" Will asked.

"Will do."

Maddy's heart pounded, all her senses on high alert. Their group moved off again, stepping over the trigger wire. In another five feet, they found another, but it turned out to be the last before they made it to the corner with the mural.

Anu halted, drawn to the art. "This is amazing." She knelt and put her face to the painting. "Do you mind if I stay and study it?"

Bear and Maddy exchanged a glance. They didn't need Anu's expertise any longer.

"I suppose you can stay," Bear said.

"Thanks."

"All right. If you decide to follow us or go back out to Quinn, just be careful."

Anu mumbled her agreement, already lost in academic contemplation.

Maddy, Bear, and Will continued down the hall, watching every step. In another five feet the passage turned to the left. In ten more paces, Bear stopped.

"Now what?" Maddy asked.

"Moat."

"What's that shiny color?" Will asked.

Bear knelt. "In China, where all those terracotta soldiers are buried, there were numerous moats of mercury."

"Creative," Maddy said.

Bear stuck his knife into the dark liquid. Round silver balls fell off the blade and back into the dangerous moat. "It's not that wide, though. About five feet across."

"Yeah, but what's on the other side?"

CHAPTER 90

Will stared at the moat of mercury, which gleamed an ominous silver in the pale light. How to get safely across seemed to stymie the others.

"I have an idea," he announced softly.

"What?" Bear asked.

"First, I can straddle this." He stepped up to the danger and put his hand out to Bear. "You ground me."

After putting one leg in front to better plant his feet, Bear grabbed Will's hand. Then Will held onto Bear's wrist and stretched his left foot toward the other side.

"Wait." He didn't feel solid. Bloody ankle hurt like hell. He switched feet and tried again. That was better. He groped the far bank with his outstretched foot, seeking another pit. "Feels soft in the middle, but there's solid ground on the edges." He pulled on Bear's weight and swung his right leg back toward the group. "Jump to the sides. There's a little more room than the last pit."

"All right. I'll go first," Bear said, and took a step backward before bounding across and to the right edge.

He grunted and hugged the wall, arms outstretched, then turned around, crouched, and set to probing the pit with his knife, outlining the edges. At first Will wondered how the thin wood had lasted so long, but he supposed it was dry and dark down here, protected from the elements.

Soon, Bear stood and stepped to the back of the pit. "Argones, you next."

As Bear had done, Will took a step back to get a running start. His long legs easily spanned the moat. Maddy, always nimble, vaulted across after.

They progressed down the dark hallway, turned a corner to the right, and stopped. They'd come to a broad chamber, about thirteen by thirteen meters, with an opening in the back. The walls sloped to a point in the ceiling's center, like a tipi, or pyramid. The air here felt dry and thick with static electricity.

Will shined his light over Bear's head and to the right and left. Each slanted wall bore its own detailed mural.

On the wall to their right was an image of an ornate four-sided golden chest supported by two long wooden poles. Bright rays emanated from the box. Maddy moved her light to the mural, highlighting the winged angels on the chest's top. "That looks like the Ark of the Covenant."

"Aha!" Bear said. "Moses was behind the star chart!"

"Could that one show the fall of the meteorite?" Will pointed. "Looks like a ball of light moving through the sky, and a bunch of shepherds on their knees in front of a burning bush."

Maddy turned around. "And that one shows a swath of earth with a red globe at the end. Maybe the landing of the meteorite?"

"And then this one is the building of the pyramid over the meteorite, with all the dirt piled on top of it," Will said. Clever bastards. "Looks like the same style we saw in Jebel Barkal."

Maddy pointed her light toward the middle of the large room. In the center, directly under the point of the ceiling, lay a red hulk of stone with a flat, altar-like top. It was at least seven feet wide.

"Is that what I think it is?" Maddy asked.

Bear gave Maddy a hug and Will a high five. "Mission

accomplished."

Everyone grinned.

Maddy put her hand to her chest. "Wow. I can feel it pulsing from here."

"Don't get too excited yet. There are a half-dozen Egyptian cobras nesting around it."

As Will directed his light at the meteorite, three of the snakes reared up and displayed their menacing hoods. The hissing sound that came next made the hair on Will's arms stand on end.

CHAPTER 91

Again, the rearing Egyptian cobras hissed with anger.

"What are you doing?" Maddy asked.

Will held his flashlight beam on the snakes and pounded his foot on the floor. "They sense vibrations. Trying to scare them off."

"Good idea." Maddy took another look at the monstrous meteorite, sensing its latent energy. It was hard to believe that it existed and that they'd found it. "Think that's a crust?"

Will played his light on the front side. "Most meteorites have one."

"From the reentry?"

"Yeah."

She noticed something else in the glimmering light. "Look at that. The side of it is split open, and there are . . . spurs of some sort. Didn't see it before."

"How 'bout that? You're right," Bear said. "Shoot, maybe they just broke the obelisks off."

"I'll try to break a piece or two off, if I can get these cobras to leave." Will waved his arms and stomped his feet. "I have my climbing hammer in my pack still."

"That'd be cool," she said, her fingers twitching. She'd love to have another obelisk. She craved the sensation of holding this stone again.

"There they go!" Will said.

Moving together, the cobras departed, slithering back into the darkness.

Bear was almost to the meteorite. "Let's test the rest of the room for traps."

"Don't touch it," Maddy reminded him.

"Are you kiddin' me?" Bear turned to look at her. "That's why we brought you along."

Maddy grimaced. "Ha-ha. Throw some sand at it. Make sure it doesn't react."

Bear set down an LED lamp and threw a handful of dirt at the meteorite. Nothing happened.

"How're we going to get it out of here?" Will said.

"I still think we should just blow it up," Maddy interjected. "As much as I'd hate to lose it. Can't you guys feel the energy coming off it?"

The two men exchanged a glance before shaking their heads.

They walked around it, close now, but not touching it. Another vein of tiny obelisks sprouted from the rock.

"It might be too heavy for the helicopter," Bear said.

Will scratched the side of his face. "Might be? This rock is two meters square. It must weigh fifteen tons."

"I looked into that before we came. A Chinook CH-53E Super Stallion can do about fourteen and a half tons. That's what we brought."

"Might not be enough."

"Maybe we could get a Russian Mi-26," Bear said. "Cut a hole in the roof of the cavern, true tipi style."

The thing was a huge block of untamed energy. Maddy shook her head. "Don't you guys get it? This thing is likely more powerful than a nuke."

Bear shook his head. "Sorry, Maddy. We have a directive."

CHAPTER 92

5:58 P.M.

Anu hurried back up the stone ramp, anxious to tell Quinn about the amazing mural that pointed to this location as Mount Sinai. The recognition she'd get from this find would skyrocket her career into the archeological stratosphere. It was her big break. She knew Quinn would be more than thrilled for her and she wanted to tell him about it.

Knowing Pyotr could be watching, she paused and peered over the top of the ramp. The tall-ceilinged space had grown dark since she'd been underground. She could see Quinn's form, still in his burqa disguise, to the left of the tall doorframe.

Before she could say a word, shots rang out in the square. She gasped, riddled with fear. Pyotr must be shooting at Jags.

Quinn pulled a pistol from underneath his burqa, looked around the corner, and fired. Shots pinged off the stone doorway, and Anu ducked back below the surface to avoid flying rock chips.

A moment of silence.

She dared another glance. More shots, both from and toward Quinn.

With a grunt of pain, Quinn fell backward into the chamber. Anu jumped away from the ramp and ran to him, approaching from the left to stay out of the line of fire.

Anu turned his body toward her by pulling his shoulder around. His eyes. *Dear god, his eyes.* They stared, unblinking, at the ceiling.

A spike of pain cleaved her heart in two. She put a hand to her mouth as she realized that four men were running toward her from the courtyard. One fell, but the second, Pyotr, ran on, followed by the others. As Pyotr neared the entrance, the right side of his chest jerked backward, as if he'd been shot, but he shook it off and vaulted up the stone entrance.

Pyotr closed the distance between them, his white iris gleaming in the dim light as his weapon swung toward her. Another man in black stepped up behind him.

"Wait!" she yelled.

Pyotr pressed the cold metal to her bindi and placed his left hand on the back of her neck.

She stared him in the eye. "Did you kill my uncle Ravi?"

"No."

All went black.

CHAPTER 93

Maddy heard a scream come from the dark hallway behind them. Had one of the pits felled an unlucky intruder? Or perhaps an arrow had been triggered from another near-ly invisible sinew. But did this mean there were more assailants on the way? Was Anu okay?

Bear reached for his weapon, fumbling, as it wasn't under his left arm, but his right ever since his forearm had gotten hurt. Maddy stepped behind the meteorite, hoping this wouldn't turn into a fire-fight. Will kneeled down next to her, reached into his backpack, and grabbed a rock hammer.

"Wait! Give me that," she whispered.

When he did, she touched the hammer to the meteorite in several places. No pulse. No balls of lightning. It must be human touch that activated the strikes. She handed it back. "Just don't touch it with your hands."

"Okay." He started chipping away at the seam, and two obelisk-like chunks of meteorite fell to the floor. They were bloodred, about three inches long, a half-inch thick, and with sharp points at one end.

She reached down, grabbed them, and scooted back toward the room beyond that they had yet to explore. The room with the snakes.

A dark-haired man with mismatched eyes peered around the corner of the entrance to the chamber, weapon raised. Pyotr. She swore to herself. He must've hurt Quinn and Anu, and what about Jags? Where was she?

Maddy moved further back and ducked around the corner, concerned about the cobras. Will scuttled backward, too.

"Drop your weapon!" Bear shouted.

Pyotr laughed and shot at him, the retorts loud and echoing in the dark cavern. Bear dove backward as gunfire pinged off the meteorite.

Pyotr advanced toward the meteorite like a cat stalking a mouse, another man in black behind him. From their cover behind the doorway, Bear tried to shoot left-handed, but his shots went wild. Will pulled a knife from a wrist sheath and threw, missing Pyotr's torso, but hitting him in the thigh.

Pyotr and his black-clad accomplice ducked behind the meteorite, and she heard a grunt.

Maddy held powerful weapons of her own, but she hesitated, recalling the file she'd seen in Belize. "Pyotr, stop this. We can help you find your mother."

The firing stopped for a breath, and the knife clattered away on the stone. Then gunshots resumed.

Grateful for the LED lamp ahead, Maddy spared a brief glance around the back room to see if there was another exit, and to make sure she wasn't about to step on a snake. No obvious departure, and the snakes were coiled in a back corner. The space was a quarter the size of the front room, had normal vertical walls, a flat ceiling, and was completely bare. Maybe it used to be a storeroom.

Movement appeared on the far side of the meteorite, near the entrance. Jags, sans disguise, wrestled her way into the room, entangled with a man. Maddy caught a glimpse of the attacker's face. No tattoo, but she recognized the swollen nose from their fight near her loft.

Lex had caught up with them.

The two fought to the left of the doorway, arms entwined. Lex kicked, and Jags moved to the side, taking them closer to the pit.

Beside her, Bear's mouth was tight. He had his gun aimed at the duo, but held fire. No clear shot.

Jags freed up one hand and jammed a punch into Lex's nose. He teetered on the edge, suspended in midair, arms flailing.

Catching a hold of Jags's shirt, he fell into the pit, pulling her with him. Their mutual howl gave Maddy goosebumps. She gasped, recalling the pit held long, sharp, lethal stakes. Maddy put a hand to her mouth, horrified.

Bullets struck the doorway near her face, breaking her out of grief. She ducked low and peered out. Ball lightning exploded from the meteorite, bouncing around the room like a malevolent pinball.

Pyotr flew backward from the meteorite and landed on his backside, arms and legs high in the air. He dropped his gun, a wide-eyed look of shock on his face. The Russian must have touched the dangerous rock.

Several globes of fire rebounded throughout the space. Bear switched hands with his weapon and tried again to shoot Pyotr while Will threw another knife at the accomplice, who still fired from behind the meteorite. All went wide.

Frustrated at the situation, Maddy ground her teeth and frowned. Her finger began to twitch violently. She needed an edge. True to her practice, she quieted her mind and *listened*. Sounds became more intense, the smell of gunpowder stung her nose, but most of all she could feel the thrumming of the obelisks in her hands. She opened her heart, thinking of her love for AJ and those adorable freckles, and poured white light into the lorandite. Inside her, darkness fled, replaced by a golden brilliance.

In a flash of insight, she saw the worldwide implications if she failed to act. Pandemonium. Bloodshed. Death. A jumble of blood-soaked bodies, her loved ones included, marched across her vision. She wasn't responsible for the actions of others, but she could use her gifts to put a stop to their wicked behavior. *Mom's death wasn't my fault*, she thought. Her iceberg of guilt, which had begun to thaw in Ephesus, melted away into an ocean of certainty. Her skills wouldn't be used with the intent to kill, but to protect. And if someone died while she defended herself and her loved ones, so be it.

Peering around the corner of the doorway, Maddy saw that Pyotr had regained his gun. She raised her hands above her head and brought the two small pieces together so they would act as one.

Aiming both obelisks at him, she let her energy flow from her heart to her hands. A ball of lightning exploded from her grip. Pyotr ducked away just in time. Her finger twitched and another golden ball hit the meteorite.

A dazzling amber light illuminated the center of the stone. There was a boom as lightning streamed up from the huge rock, sparking and sizzling like a million Fourth of July sparklers. Small globes of ball lightning flew off the rock, and one hit Pyotr's accomplice. It took his right arm off at the shoulder and knocked him to the ground.

The earth began to shake under her feet. A tremor. Another. There was a new crack, this time from overhead. The roof, at the apex of the pyramid, split open, releasing a stream of light that sprayed into the dark sky overhead.

She returned her gaze to the meteorite. With the next strike, she meant to destroy the lethal rock, even if it meant she'd never channel the energy again.

But the effort exposed her form in the doorway. Pyotr took advantage and shot through the fireworks. She cried out in pain as a bullet hit the mini-obelisks, ripping the skin from her palms. As she pulled her hands to her chest, she dropped both slivers. The shards shattered, and the fractured sound was lost in the tumult. The streaming fireworks stopped.

Will knocked her to her knees, protecting her from further assault, and grabbed at what was left of the shards with his head scarf. Even though the ball lightning had died out, larger cracks were forming in the ceiling.

She peered around the corner.

The accomplice lay unmoving in the dirt. Perhaps recognizing the sloped chamber was doomed, Pyotr shot his pistol over his shoulder as he retreated, limping toward the door. She had to finish this.

Maddy rushed to the stone and touched it with her unharmed right hand. A feeling like golden sunlight shot up her arm and into the length of her spine. In a blink, the light spread throughout her body until she was aflame from fingers to toes.

Next, she brought her injured left hand up and forced the bloody palm open. The finger twitched once as she placed it next to her right index finger, hands pointing like an arrow.

Light flooded her.

I will shatter like that windshield on the road to Chichén Itzá, she thought.

No sound escaped her lips as she aimed lightning at the ground behind Pyotr, the massive energy flashing through her making her head spin. The earth between them exploded! Chunks of stone and dirt flew high into the air. Pyotr fell, clutching his calf, but the blast pushed her backward, away from the meteorite.

Colossal balls of blue lightning spun around the room, slicing through the flying debris, and obscuring everything with a thick dust until it looked like a sapphire spotlight spinning through fog. She felt weightless. Time stood still. The smell of a summer thunderstorm filled her nostrils.

Just as one of the deadly globes zeroed in on her, she allowed her knees to crumple. There it was, bright, bright, and coming toward her.

It struck the stone floor next to her, and she blacked out.

CHAPTER 94

Swearing at his injured arm, Bear let off one more shot at Pyotr as the man fled, limping into the dust. The last of the fire-globes faded. Maddy lay in a heap to his left, and the other Russian attacker was dead in front of him. The place reeked of gunpowder and fear.

He made a move to go check on her, and as he did, the earth shook. The massive walls swayed, looking like they were going to tumble down at any second. Nabbing the meteorite would have to wait.

He tapped Argones on the shoulder. "We have to leave. Now!"

Will nodded and reached down to help lift Maddy. Her left hand was bloodied, her breathing ragged. Bear waved Will off and pulled her on top of his shoulders in a fireman's carry. He was amped up, and she felt light as a kitten.

He took five long strides over to the chamber's entry door and looked down in the pit, fearing what he'd see. Ever since they had tumbled into the pit, images had been flashing through his mind of Jags and Lex impaled. And they were. Jags, however, had landed atop Lex, managing to only get a stake in one calf. Only. He grimaced at the sight.

Chunks of rock, falling from the ceiling, thudded around them. Argones looked at Jags. "You're okay!"

A crack in the floor widened, headed their way.

She reached her hand up. "Easy for you to say, cowboy. Get me outta here."

Argones knelt down and gently broke the stake still stuck in her leg so that he could pull her up and out of the pit. Lex's form remained atop the spikes, not breathing, eyes vacant. Argones put his arm under Jags's shoulder and they rushed out of the chamber ahead of the widening floor crack.

With Maddy on his shoulders, Bear kept his flashlight trained ahead of him on the hallway floor as he pushed ahead. The Russians had broken the remaining trigger wires. Arrows littered the floor and walls to his right.

He got a running start and jumped the moat, noticing as he ran past that the pit next to it had claimed an attacker. The man's body was impaled through the gut. Bear focused on the far side of the mercury. He landed safely.

Bear turned around. Argones and Jags peered down into the pit and made identical scrunched-up faces. Then they looked at the mercury moat.

Argones's eyes were wide as he looked from Jags's calf to the thing they had to cross. "That's a problem."

"Stop stating the obvious, Sherlock." She looked down and pointed. "Use what we have."

Argones reached into the pit, extracted the dead body, and flung it over the silver poison. He tested the pseudo-bridge and it worked, as the channel wasn't very deep. Crossing quickly, he reached back and helped Jags hobble across. Her face held pain and determination.

They moved on, but with caution. Pyotr was ahead. Would he ambush them? The earth rolled under Bear's feet, requiring him to use the cool hallway walls to keep his balance. Booming sounds of destruction pushed them up the hallway, adding insult to ears that still rang from the shootout. Jags grunted a few times in pain. A pungent smell like chlorine stung his nose.

Bear cleared every corner with his weapon. There was no sign of Pyotr.

Where they'd left Anu at the first corner mural, a slumped black-clad body clogged the hallway, an arrow through the throat. Must've been their first guy through. Bear guessed Pyotr had used his final accomplice to disarm the rest of the triggers on their way through the maze.

Bear paused near the top of the ramp, taking a moment to peer over the edge. Quinn and Anu both lay near the oversized doorway.

With Maddy still on his shoulders, Bear rushed to the door. Quinn's eyes stared into nothingness, but Anu's chest rose and fell. Will would have to help her.

Night had fallen. The unmistakable sound of helo blades whirred in the courtyard—the Russian version of a fast getaway car. Pyotr limped for the chopper and jumped in.

The temple's self-destruction accelerated. Rocks and debris fell from the ceiling. Dust choked the air. The earth split under Bear's feet, and soon there would be no ground left. The only way off the mountain whirred in front of him, with Pyotr Argones inside.

With nothing to lose, Bear dropped his flashlight and adjusted Maddy's weight, sprinting toward near certain death.

CHAPTER 95

6:15 P.M.

Will followed as closely behind Bear as he could, Jags leaning heavily on his side. His ankle screamed with the effort, but Jags's calf had to hurt worse. When they finally made it to the front of Ad Deir, Will realized Bear was sprinting toward a Russian helicopter that was spinning up dust in the darkened square.

Will stopped, his breath jagged in his throat. What was the man thinking? The helo must hold one or more of the enemy. But as a large sheet of the interior Monastery wall crashed behind him, causing him to jump, Will understood—there wasn't much choice.

Two meters away, Anu lay in a crumpled heap, next to Quinn's form. Will stepped over to the two of them and knelt. He felt for a beat at Quinn's neck, but wasn't optimistic due to the amount of blood.

No pulse.

Anu, though . . . He felt her neck. There was movement. Faint. But it was there.

Jags yelled at him, motioning him on toward Bear's retreating back, Maddy over his shoulders. She was still passed out. Silly woman, trying to channel all that energy. And now the entire mountainside was falling apart. Worse—was she going to be okay?

"Help me," Will insisted. They pulled Anu off the threshold and into Will's arms, and then Jags used him as a crutch as they limped toward the helo. Will was high on adrenaline and felt like he was flying across the plaza.

When they arrived, Bear motioned for Will and Jags to be silent and move around the other side of the helicopter. After setting Anu down, Will pulled his weapon and moved with stealth, calm as the eye of a hurricane. Jags also pulled a pistol and stepped closer to the helo.

Inside, it looked like it was just Pyotr and the pilot, struggling to bandage Pyotr's bloody calf wound. In a flash, Will understood Bear's plan.

Bear pounded on the glass door of the helicopter. As Pyotr turned to train his weapon on Bear, Jags opened the door and put her gun to the back of Pyotr's neck, where the dark hair met olive skin.

"Drop your weapon," she demanded.

"No."

Bear and Pyotr stared at each other like two angry, snarling wolves, their ruffs stiff.

Will glanced down. The makeshift bandage had fallen off of Pyotr's calf, and it was pumping blood. No wonder they'd delayed taking off. The man would bleed out soon.

Will's heart raced. He held a weapon on the wide-eyed pilot, who had his hands in the air.

"Yes," Jags insisted.

Will recalled what Maddy had yelled earlier. "Pyotr. Why don't we cut a deal?"

Without turning around, the man growled in his thin Slavic accent, "What kind of deal?"

"We'll help you find your mother. You tell us what you know and get us out of here."

The ground shook and small cracks appeared beneath Will's feet as Pyotr and Bear continued to stand off. He hoped this gamble would pay off. Quickly.

With her gun barrel, Jags nudged Pyotr's neck.

Pyotr tilted his head twice toward his chest.

Bear reached out and yanked a thin, black tactical neck-loop from around Pyotr's neck, and found a comms relay and a radio box that looked like a sat phone inside his jacket. Bear stomped on it all with his boot.

"All right. If I defect, will you grant me immunity?"

This was more than Will had hoped.

"If you agree to be an agent for at least five years, yes. Where is the computer that's causing havoc in the Philippines?" Jags asked.

Pyotr took a deep breath and relinquished his weapon, shifting to put pressure on his calf to staunch the bleeding. Blood also dripped from the Russian's thigh where Will's knife had found its mark.

"Chennai. I overheard my mother talking with Ravi Singh. It's in Chennai at the consulate general."

Bear threw Maddy into the back, jumped into the helo, and pulled Pyotr's hands behind his back. "No need for that," the man muttered. "The baron is an ass. I hate him."

"You'll need to earn some trust," Jags said.

"Chennai," Pyotr repeated.

A loud boom sounded through the night. The earth quaked, shaking and rolling. The columns on the façade of the Monastery crashed forward, and boulders from the surrounding area moved like jumping beans. It was a massive earthquake. Will had lived through a few small ones in California, but nothing like this.

With no time to lose, Will and Jags grabbed Anu's limp body and jumped into the back of the helicopter.

"Go!" Will yelled.

As the pilot swung the bird up above the plaza, Bear shuffled through some items on the floor. He pulled up a small length of rope and tied Pyotr's wrists together.

"How many men did you leave down there?" Bear asked.

"Two. They were too far to make it up here."

One of the small cracks in the plaza began to widen, and as Will watched, it rapidly spread, moving up the center of the doorway. The earthquake would very likely kill the remaining Russian men.

Bear tapped the pilot's shoulder. "Hover up here. We need to see what happens."

The pilot complied and tilted the machine, providing them with a good view of the destruction below from a few hundred feet above.

The gorgeous stone Monastery quaked and shook, and then the red façade split in half, tumbling into the chasm that used to be the plaza. The split worked its way into the mountain beyond, and soon the entire hillside broke apart. As the crack deepened, red-hot magma appeared from the belly of the earth.

"Wow," Bear said.

Pyotr motioned below with his head. "This will halt the US invasion. It was planned for New Year's Eve. They needed that material."

"Speaking of—anyone see the meteorite?" Will asked.

Jags pointed. "There."

The monstrous hunk of space rock stood on a small pillar of stone, outlined against the crimson fire.

As they all watched, the pillar shook, tilted, and crumbled. The lorandite fell into the earth toward the boiling lava.

"Pull up, pull up!" Will shouted.

The pilot yanked on the throttle and pushed the helicopter up toward the stars. They climbed fast, but would it be fast enough?

A minute later, a single explosion roared, churning up a cascade of molten rock before a violent tidal wave of energy whooshed up into them. Will was slammed into Jags. Lights on the control panel flickered and went out. Tossed like a toy boat in the ocean, the helicopter lost power and dove for the roiling mass of lava.

"My god," Jags whispered.

Stomach in this throat, Will held his breath and closed his eyes, which were stinging from the volcanic fumes. He held tight to his seat as it bucked under him. The pilot swore and flipped switches.

Finally, the rotors caught. The helicopter jerked upward as the pilot pulled them out of the volcanic vortex, but the sound of the explosion echoed in Will's ears for what seemed like forever.

CHAPTER 96

DECEMBER 26, 4:45 A.M. PHILIPPINE TIME

AJ lay on the couch in the hotel room. Elena had woken him up ten minutes earlier and told him to get out of the bed. When he'd asked why, she'd just told him it was a surprise. He dozed.

Thump. Thump. Thump.

AJ woke, wondering what the sound was. It sounded like . . .

He rushed to the patio door and looked out into the dark night. No city lights burned in any of the surrounding buildings.

The end of a black ladder dangled just above the patio railing.

Pushing open the sliding patio door, he jumped onto the patio. The ladder led to a hovering helicopter, and a man descended the rungs.

Elena put her hand on AJ's shoulder. He looked up at her for reassurance and she smiled at him. She and Garrod wore their backpacks. It could all mean only one thing: they were being rescued!

The man landed on the patio. He was dressed in midnight black from his boots to his helmet and wore goggles over his eyes. "Hey, AJ."

The drawl was unmistakable. AJ gave Bear a huge hug.

Bear bent over and put his hands on his knees. "Jump on my back."

AJ scrambled up and Garrod strapped him to Bear's sturdy shoulders.

In a flash, they were heading up the ladder. AJ hung on tight as wind buffeted him. Bear climbed hand over hand up the rungs. AJ's heart thudded with excitement.

All too soon they reached the door. Will pulled them inside, away from the ladder. Elena and Garrod climbed in, too, while Will removed the straps that held him to Bear.

Bear buckled him into a jump seat and grinned. "Merry Christmas."

"Where's Maddy?"

"In Dubai. We're heading back to her now."

AJ bounced up and down in his seat. This was the best Christmas present ever.

CHAPTER 97

NEW YORK, NEW YORK

DECEMBER 31, 11:45 P.M. EST

The lights of the city illuminated the rowdy Times Square crowd below, all huddled in down parkas and fleece jackets to watch the silver ball drop and celebrate another rotation of the wheel of time. The night smelled wet, but there were hints of barbequed meat wafting up from street vendors and taco trucks.

Bear stood on the rooftop of a swank hotel in downtown New York City, wishing he could enjoy the celebration happening below in the swirling snow, but Maddy was still unconscious.

AJ stood next to him and pulled at his hand, sensing his thoughts. "Do you think she'll be okay?"

Bear almost faked a smile for the boy, but didn't. The boy deserved the truth. "The doctors say she's a fighter and has a good chance of pullin' through."

AJ's freckled face wore a deep frown. A blue knit hat covered his red hair and big ears. "What's wrong with her?"

"She saved all of us."

He'd mentally gone over the fight many times since that night, and knew that the tide of battle had turned when she took out Pyotr's accomplice. And her parting shot, the calf wound she'd given Pyotr, had slowed him long enough for them to catch him.

Not only that, but destroying the lorandite was a checkmate move.

Part of him hated not being able to follow orders to the letter, but another knew that Maddy had been right. Such a powerful weapon did *not* belong in the hands of the Russians, East Indians, Chinese, terrorists, or any other set of bad actors.

He put a hand on AJ's head. "The docs aren't certain what's wrong with her."

Bear had an idea, though. One of the balls of lightning had exploded right next to her, and that was after she'd moved too much energy through the massive rock. Argones's theory was that anyone could touch the stone, but not control it, and suspected the static electricity in the dry desert air had magnified the ball lightning. Bear clenched his fists. Sometimes saving the world came at a cost. Tonight, that cost felt too high.

Argones walked up beside them. "Why don't you guys at least get out of the wet snow? The ball won't drop for another ten minutes."

Bear hadn't realized they were getting soaked. He shook his head and tiny droplets of water flew in every direction, catching the light with a beauty that made his heart ache because he wanted to share it with Maddy. The three of them moved under a large umbrella erected on the rooftop patio.

AJ looked up at Bear. "I'm getting cold. Can we go down to the room?"

"Sure. Get a head start. Will and I will be right behind you."

AJ scampered toward the gray door that guarded the rooftop from the party below.

Argones's eyes narrowed. "Do you think she'll be all right?"

Bear kicked at a snow-covered pebble. "It's been almost a week, Argones. That's a long time to be out."

Argones put a hand on Bear's shoulder. "It is. I'm concerned."

Bear walked toward the door, the freezing wind cutting at his cheeks. He made his tone light. "You're always concerned about somethin'."

Argones followed, smiling like a wolf, his white teeth catching the ambient light. "True. But that means I'm ready for a fight."

Bear was glad to see the man's confidence growing. "You handled yourself well at Petra."

"Thanks. You, too."

Bear opened and held the door for Argones. "It's too bad it all got destroyed during the mission."

"You mean the wall murals?"

"Yeah. The lorandite provides an interesting explanation for a lot of the biblical stories about Moses."

"How so?" Will asked.

Shaking snow off their boots, they walked down one flight of stairs and into a brightly lit hotel hallway.

"You saw the murals. Think about it. The burning bush? Fire from a meteorite. The spring that came from Moses's staff? The meteorite opening up a water source. And the dangerous power inside the Ark of the Covenant? The lorandite causing ball lightning."

Argones raised a hand, in a "slow down" gesture. "Religious folk wouldn't like that theory."

"Could be God sent the meteorite. It's all in how you look at it."

Argones opened the double doors at the end of the hall and glanced at Bear. "Perception is all."

Bear walked through the doors. "That's right. As above, so below."

Inside the suite, the party was in full swing with music thumping and liquor flowing. Christmas lights had been strung across the windows and along the walls, and a goateed waiter in a black tuxedo served champagne flutes on raised platters. AJ stood next to Elena, near the large bank of plate glass windows, while Jags and her redheaded girlfriend, Deana, foraged at the buffet. In the corner, Anu talked with Quinn's lookalike brother, Doyle, who was dressed in a black suit and had sad eyes mirroring Anu's. She had a double reason to grieve: Quinn and the loss of her big find.

Except for Anu, the women all wore skimpy cocktail dresses—red and sequined, low-cut and black, striking and silver—and most of the men wore suits. Bear looked down at his jeans but didn't care that he was underdressed.

Bear turned to Argones. "Do you want to attend Quinn's funeral next week?"

"I do. Bella said she'd stay and hang out with Maddy and AJ."

"Any word from her?" he asked. Bella was at the hospital now, having preferred the vigil to the party. Bear did as well, but the director had insisted he take a break. He'd been by Maddy's side for days, not even showering until a few hours ago.

"Nope. All is quiet at the hospital. That reminds me. Did we get that GPS out of Anu's arm?"

Argones had missed that particular Anu update during a rare moment when he slept. Turned out that Pyotr had knocked her out instead of killing her. Maybe the Russian did have some redeeming qualities. "Yeah. Outpatient surgery. Engineering found the GPS had a built-in failsafe. It turned off when scanned."

"Clever. Hope we can use that tech next time." Will pointed at Bear's arm. "Speaking of wounds, how's your arm?"

Bear grabbed the back of his forearm. "It's healing fine." The bullet's trail had added a central trunk to the lightning scar, making it look even more like a tree.

"Did you figure out how you were found in Ankara?"

"We think Pyotr led the Spaniards to me."

Will pulled at his beard. "How so?"

"Lex attacked him in Belize, knocked him out, and put a GPS in his shoe."

"His shoe?"

Bear nodded.

"Taste of his own medicine, eh?" Will asked.

"Yep. Got the story and found the tracker when we brought him in. The Spaniards knew when Pyotr went to Istanbul, and from there we suspect traffic cams."

"Gotta love technology, huh?"

Bear's phone rang. He pulled it out of his pocket and looked at the screen. "It's a video call from the director." He swiped the screen to answer the call. "Bear here."

"Officer Thorenson, who do you have there?"

"Hello, sir. Analyst Argones is next to me, and Jags is across the room."

Bowman wore a suit, but the background was not the office. "Wave her over, son." A bookshelf and purple residential wall gave the location away as his home. *Purple?*

Bear got Jags's attention and she limped over to join the conversation. Her calf had required surgery in Dubai to remove the stake, and the edges of a bandage peeked out from beneath her dress. They all moved to a quieter alcove.

"I'm proud of you guys," the director said.

"Thank you, sir," Jags replied.

"If it wasn't for your efforts, the traumatic events that played out in the Philippines would have happened here. Computer Armageddon. Followed by an invasion. Tonight would have turned out very differently."

Bear nodded, thinking about all the folks in the square below who had no clue how close they'd come to seeing major military action on American soil. "Thanks for getting us the equipment we needed."

"Of course, that's my job. We were also able to take care of that issue in Chennai."

It had taken a day for a team to disarm the computer in India, and more time for order to be restored in the Philippines.

Bear watched AJ head to the buffet. "Thanks for letting me play commando to get AJ. I don't think waiting for a commercial flight would have been good for him."

"He was a key witness. And I'm sure they were hungry."

Bear almost chuckled. "Still are."

"Jags and Will, I applaud your quick thinking to recruit our new overseas friend. He proved quite cooperative before we sent him home."

Ah. So Pyotr had become a US agent. It would take time before Bear trusted the man, though. Argones patted Jags on the back.

"And nice work solving the murder of Ravi Singh," the director continued.

"Thank you," Jags said. "It was obviously Lex. He still had that garrote when he attacked me in Petra."

The director wagged his finger at her. "Yes, but his identity is a good lead to figure out how Ravi's covert alliance with us was leaked to the Spaniards. And taking Lex out was no easy feat."

Bear recalled her dramatic tale of shooting Lex in the leg as he attacked, and wrestling with him as they fell. She managed to twist her body in midair, which forced him to land on the spikes first. Still, her leg wound would take time to heal.

"We found out he trained with a former commander in the Hungarian secret police, which is where he learned a fondness for the garrote," the director said.

"Easy to travel with," Bear said. "And those facial tats were a clever mask."

"Not clever enough. He deserved his end." The director frowned. "It is too bad we lost the prize, though. But at least you kept it out of enemy hands."

"Couldn't be helped, sir," Jags said.

"That's what you all said in your debriefs." He gave them a mock salute. "Enjoy tonight, take two weeks off, and take care of Maddy. I'm sure she'll be fine."

The three of them exchanged a worried glance.

Jags answered for them. "Thank you, sir. Happy New Year."

"And Happy New Year to all of you. But stop this 'sir' business." Bowman looked at Bear. "And Thorenson. As a special thank you, I reached out to some contacts who've been able to expedite AJ's situation. When Maddy wakes up, tell her the boy can live with her while the rest of the adoption paperwork gets finished. It should all wrap up in a few weeks."

"Great news! Thank you, sir."

Bear hung up his phone, wondering how he'd be able to take care of AJ if Maddy never woke up. He steered away from that morbid thought.

Jags headed back to her girlfriend and gave her a kiss on the cheek.

"Looks like Jags bats for the other team," Bear whispered to Will. "I'm sure you figured that out, though, eh?"

Argones's face turned a bright crimson as he gave a little cough.

Bear wondered what had happened between them, but didn't want to embarrass his friend further. "I didn't know either," he said. "Let's grab a snack."

They walked over to the buffet table with its spread of delicacies. Oysters on the half shell on a bed of ice. Caviar in a crystal bowl. Buttons of filet mignon. Green mint ice cream. Carrots cut into floret shapes. It all smelled delicious. Feeling the stirrings of appetite for the first time in a while, he grabbed a few goodies while Argones did the same.

AJ touched him on the leg and Bear bent down and gave him a hug. "Happy New Year, buddy. Looks like you get to live with Maddy."

AJ pulled back, his eyes bright. "Really? She still wants to adopt me?"

"Yes. The adoption paperwork may take some time yet, but yes."

AJ whooped and jumped up and down, spinning around in a circle. He danced off toward Elena as Bear and Argones walked to the window. The garish light of the neon billboards splashed over the crowd below as everyone looked up to the silver ball and the large digital display beneath it. It was almost time for the countdown to midnight.

Bear closed his eyes and focused on Maddy. Feeling a little silly, he imagined all the love in his heart, and all the joy in the room, headed her way. He saw her, as he'd seen her a few hours ago, lying in the plain hospital room on white sheets, her short dark hair a mess above her pale face. His heart yearned for her. He missed her. In his mind's eye, he filled her room with a white healing bubble of light.

Interrupting him, Argones elbowed him, and handed Bear a matchbox-sized silver case.

"What's this?" Bear asked.

"Happy New Year. I thought you might want to give these to Maddy."

Bear opened the case. Inside, two dime-sized chunks of ruby-red lorandite caught the flashing Christmas lights and sparkled. "Nabbed these when everything went down, did ya?"

"I did. They might make good earrings. Won't be good for much else. But since we didn't have time to shop for Christmas presents . . ."

Before Bear had a chance to respond, Argones reached into his pocket, looked at his vibrating phone, and cocked his head to the side. His green eyes grew wide.

"What is it?" Bear asked.

"It's Bella. Maddy's awake." Will's eyes twinkled. He pulled his harmonica out of its tooled leather pouch and began to play a celebratory jig.

Bear's heart soared to the top of the sparkling ball. Taking the deepest breath of his life, he turned and watched the ball drop. The crowd chanted the countdown, "Ten, nine, eight . . ."

He thought ahead to their life together. He hoped she'd decide to join the team, and they could live together. With AJ. He looked over to where the boy was bouncing around the room as if he had pogo sticks for legs. Warmth filled Bear's chest.

The room roared in time with the crowd, "One! Happy New Year!"

The column across Times Square erupted with fireworks. Tickertape and snow merged, and for the first time this evening, Bear's internal celebration fit right in with the hugging and kissing happening around the room. AJ flew into Bear's arms. The faithful partygoers below lit off rounds of sparklers, and sounds of honking cars and blaring horns filled the space between wishes for a fine new year.

EPILOGUE

Maddy let out a contented sigh. She stood on the vineyard's sunny back patio next to Bear. The party to celebrate AJ's adoption was in full swing.

The guest of honor laughed as he chased Damien around the yard with his new cousins. Izzy's pigtails bounced as she joined in the fun.

Adults sipped wine and nabbed appetizers from the table. Bella poured drinks. Will played the harmonica between flipping spare ribs and chicken on the barbeque. Elena and Garrod talked in the living room with Jags and her girlfriend. Bear's mom and stepdad had come down from Lake Tahoe for the day and were touring the old barn. Anu had even flown in for the festivities, although she still wore black.

Maddy and Bear had a moment to themselves.

"I called the director this morning," she said softly, reaching out to hold his hand. "I've decided to join VanOps."

She couldn't see his eyes behind his sunglasses. But she felt the sharp intake of breath that betrayed his surprise.

"You have? Wow. Well. That's great. Are you sure?"

"Yes. I've been thinking about it awhile, but I wanted to be certain."

"And you're sure now?"

"I am."

"What made up your mind?"

"A lot of things, like getting to be near you. Protecting AJ and my family before they ever know there's a threat."

"Something else, too?"

"Yeah. I don't know if spying is in my blood or not, but I realized when everything went down that I have some unique talents that I'd like to use to make the world a better place."

He squeezed her hand. "Moved through the guilt, eh?"

"Yeah. It feels like I have a responsibility to help."

"I could see that. It's why you always liked teaching, huh?"

She smiled, knowing she would miss the kids. "I'll need to give up teaching at the dojo for a while, but I don't think this kind of work could be done forever. Ten or twenty years, if we live that long."

"Some old spies linger in the field."

"We'll see." She paused. "I negotiated a bonus with the director, too."

"VanOps pays well."

"They should. We're putting our lives on the line."

"True."

She was silent for a moment. "If things ever escalate, I'll still want to use as little violence as possible."

"That's all part of the training. Are you feeling okay to start that?"

"I am. Other than a little twitch in my finger, which the docs say is nothing to worry about, I've been cleared for duty."

"That's awesome." He gave her a quick kiss. "You and Will decided to buy Bella out of the vineyard?"

"We settled on a way to work that out while you were chatting with your mom. With my signing bonus, new salary, and cash from the forthcoming IPO, I'll be set. Once I'm done with training, I also negotiated the ability to use this place as a 'VanOps Headquarters

West.'" She chuckled. "Or at least get to work from here between assignments."

He raised an eyebrow. "I like it."

"Will wants to build a guest cottage for vacation use and will help design the remodel. He wants to make the place more secure than Fort Knox."

"Not a bad idea in our line of work."

"Exactly. I'll feel safer about leaving AJ here if there's a high-tech surveillance system in place and a safe-room or bunker set up for him."

Bear took off his glasses and turned her to face him. "What about us?"

She grinned. "What about us?"

He cleared his throat.

How cute that he was nervous.

"Do you, um, want to live with me in DC while you're in training? With AJ?"

She gave him a lingering kiss. "Of course."

His chest puffed out. "We can get a bigger place. Rent a house with a yard for the dog."

"Excellent idea, Mr. Thorenson. But let's not get too comfortable there. The director said he's going to accelerate my training." She glanced at AJ and the partygoers she was going to do her best to protect. "The scent of trouble is in the wind and he wants me to be ready."

AUTHOR'S NOTES

Thanks for joining me on this VanOps mission. Now, I'll parse fact from fiction.

Bear's tree-like forearm lightning scars can happen to survivors of lightning strikes and are sometimes called "Lichtenberg figures." Usually, they disappear after a few days.

Will's sudden talent for the harmonica is based on a report from University of Miami neuroscientist Berit Brogaard. He wrote about an orthopedic surgeon who was struck by lightning and later developed a desire to play the piano. After the strike, the surgeon started to hear music in his head, which he began to transcribe. Months later, he became a classical musician, leaving his career as a surgeon.

The Internet of Things is real, and is all around us. It's true that many experts have called for tighter security, as the vulnerabilities of the everyday technology we use do pose the type of potential security risks described in the story. I hope I've exaggerated the ramifications.

Quantum computing is an up-and-coming technology, and has the capacity to break current encryption capabilities. In particular, it's believed that the RSA, Diffie-Hellman, and elliptic-curve Diffie-Hellman algorithms—all processes that are used today to encrypt web sites, email, and other types of data—could be broken. Breaking these algorithms would have large consequences for electronic security and privacy. However, at the same time, quantum-based cryptographic systems could potentially be more secure in the long run than traditional systems against quantum hacking.

It's also true that researchers are looking at superconductors to help produce the quantum machines of the future. Lorandite from a meteorite, however, is my invention.

In Moscow, Bunker 42 is real, and now a museum. The labs underneath are fictional.

The concept of female warriors, or Amazons, is based on archeological findings from burials indicating that about twenty percent of Scythian-Sarmatian women dressed for battle in ways similar to male fighters. Evidence comes from southern Ukraine and Russia.

According to a May 2014 article in *WIRED*, DARPA is experimenting with virtual-reality headsets to provide 3D simulations as a way of improving cyberwarrior capabilities. The details are fictional.

Regarding the lowest-ever BASE jump, experts are torn between a jump of 33.5 meters (110 feet) and a chillingly low 32-meter (105-feet) jump from inside the iconic St Paul's Cathedral in London. Either way, Will and Jags's jump at Jebel Barkal was far too low and rests in my imagination alone.

The meteorite in Danebury, England, is real. Discovered in the 1970s during an archeological dig at the local Iron Age hillfort, it was found placed inside a pit (c. 1200 BC), and is one of the first finds of a European meteorite.

Jebel Barkal exists and looks as described, with the exception of the hidden tunnel and chamber, which are part of the VanOps world.

The Valley of the Kings and the tomb of Thutmose III exist, and are a sight to behold.

Petra, now the driest of desert ruins, was once a lush town full of gardens and a complex irrigation system. Twenty thousand people lived there at its height. It does have a year-round spring.

Petra and the other cities such as Chichén Itzá and Beijing are aligned with the stars as described. The December 2013 article in the *Nexus Network Journal* is real and discusses the celestial orientation of Petra and other monuments in the ancient Nabataean kingdom. Ad Deir does have a nearby boulder with a lion's silhouette at the winter solstice, and the sun lights up the podium. The hidden room, and all it contained, is fiction.

From what I can tell, scholars do not agree on where Mount Sinai is located, and archeologists have found no evidence for its existence.

There was a comet during the window of time biblical scholars believe could have been the time of Moses. In 1486 BC, a comet with an amazing number of tails—ten—was recorded and illustrated in the Mawangdui Silk Almanac, which is now housed in the Hunan Provincial Museum in Changsh. Carl Sagan, in 1985, identified that comet as Comet 12P/Pons-Brooks, postulating that a piece of the comet impacted the earth with an explosion so large that the resulting debris clouded the sun for years, even causing a global temperature drop.

There is also an earthquake fault in the eastern Mediterranean. Called the Dead Sea Fault, it's a 1,100-kilometer (680-mile) line that has caused many earthquakes in the region. Flavius Josephus, an ancient Jewish historian, told about a massive earthquake in 33 BC, in which he described the deaths of fifty thousand people. There were earthquakes in the region in AD 363, 749, and 1033. In 1927, an earthquake hit the region, and measured 6.2 on the newly implemented Richter scale. That tremor killed hundreds in Jerusalem, Nablus, and Tiberias. Another 6.2 quake hit south of Aqaba in 1995. I hope you enjoyed the dramatic, fictional conclusion.

ACKNOWLEDGMENTS

This book wouldn't have been possible without Michelle Ocken's encouragement and support. She helped shape the earliest outline, found a plot hole during final editing, and helped brainstorm along the way. She deserves the dedication and a huge thank-you. While holding me on her lap, Mom taught me the love of reading about the same time I learned to tie my shoes. She's always been there for me and has an eagle eye for grammar. Besides fine-tuning the prose, line editor Andrea Robinson has a gift for making the characters and their conflicts come to life. AJ and Maddy owe the tension about the adoption to her. Marianne Fox provided world-class copyediting, and polished the manuscript to a fine luster. David Ter-Avanesyan, the cover artist for the VanOps series, found a beautiful way to illustrate the story in one image. I'm grateful that Thunder Creek Press is responsive, organized, efficient, and professional.

I wish I had space to name all my other friends, family, and beta readers who helped polish the book or get the word out. Special shout-outs to: Olivia Bernard, who saw the big picture from the outline, made numerous suggestions at the plot level, and was one of my best beta readers. Susan Greenawald and Joanne Evers brought back inspiration from Egypt. Many thanks to: Sandy DeMarco, Kate Schaefer, Julie Collins, Betty Ocken, Anita Males, Karyn Ross, Kim Oaken, Kathy Bridges, Charlie Thomas, Lori Stitt, Trish Davey and Toby the Red Panther, Vicki Day, Dawn Garcia, Michelle Meyers, Richard Davis, Margaret Cambridge, John Bernstein, Mari LaRoche, Eileen Rubart, Earlene Schanze, and Ruth Thompson. I'm grateful for each of their contributions.

The generosity of my fellow authors amazes me, and I'm deeply grateful for their kindness and support.

Although they were all a huge help, any errors in the book fall on my shoulders alone.

ABOUT THE AUTHOR

International award–winning author who blends intrigue, history, science, and mystery into nonstop action thrillers

Avanti Centrae is the author of the international award-winning VanOps thriller series. An instant Barnes and Noble Nook best-seller, *The Lost Power* took home a genre grand-prize ribbon at the Chanticleer International Book Awards, a shiny bronze medal at the Wishing Shelf Awards, and an honorable mention at the Hollywood Book Festival.

Her father served as a US marine corporal in Okinawa, gathering military intelligence during the first decade after the Korean War. Her work has been compared to that of James Rollins, Steve Berry, Dan Brown, and Clive Cussler. She resides in northern California with her family and German shepherds.

If you'd like to hear about specials for her fans, such as give-aways and deleted scenes, you can find her on her webpage (http://www.avanticentrae.com). Drop her a line, or sign up for her quar-terly-ish newsletter. She'd love to hear about your mysterious idea to incorporate into a future tale.

For more frequent updates, follow her on Facebook (www.facebook.com/avanticentrae), Twitter (@avanticentrae), or Instagram (www.instagram.com/avanti.centrae.author). Either way, let her know what you loved about Solstice Shadows and what you want more of in the series to come.

M.OCKEN

CPSIA information can be obtained
at www.ICGtesting.com
Printed in the USA
LVHW021317301020
670160LV00002B/100

9 781734 966220